SECRET

THE NARAVAN CHRONICLES 3

ISABO KELLY

T&D PUBLISHING

SECRET

Published 2018 by T&D Publishing
Cover design: © 2017 EJR Digital Art
Interior book design © 2018 T&D Publishing
ISBN-13: 978-1-944600-12-9 (Trade Paperback Edition)

This is a work of fiction. All of the characters, places, organizations, and events portrayed are either products of the author's imagination or are used fictitiously. Any resemblance to actual persons, living or dead, business establishments, events, or locales is entirely coincidental.

First printing T&D Publishing edition: May 2018
For information, contact T&D Publishing www.tanddpublishing.com

To Brian because he's patient with me.
And to my sons because they're not.

CHAPTER ONE

———————————

"WHAT THE HELL IS THAT?" DR. TI'ANN JONES SQUINTED AT the new image materializing on the molecular echo imaging readout screen. Ambient heat filtered in through the tent canvas, despite the temp regulators to keep the equipment cool, and she absently swiped at the sweat dripping down her temples. She poked a finger at the screen, indicating the scroll of elements that made up the unexpected object. "That can't be right."

Her colleague, Dr. Krin Freemont, glanced between the finalized view of the odd shape and the molecular readout table, a frown marring his nearly perfect dark caramel complexion. He pushed a shock of red hair out of his eyes and shook his head. "I have no idea what that is." He leaned back, the movement making his canvas chair groan.

"You're the genius. No miraculous leaps of insight here?"

Krin chuckled. "Hey, whatever that is, it's not a plant and it's not geological, therefore, it's not in my realm of expertise."

Ti'ann spared him a quick glance then grunted. She considered the heat trying to defeat the cooling system and wondered

1

if it was affecting the readout. They hadn't had any trouble so far, but that didn't mean the MEI hadn't decided to malfunction. She swung around to a secondary unit and started a diagnostic run, just to make sure everything was working properly.

"You're the paleo-zoologist." Krin gestured at the list of molecules that comprised the object. "It's got genetic material. It's organic, whatever it is, and it's sure as hell not plant life. That makes it your field, Dr. Jones."

"That," she turned back and poked the screen again, ",is not like any fossilized animal I've ever seen, heard of, read about or seen in any historical data. On or off this planet."

But she had to reluctantly agree with him. It was organic. The genetic material was native to Narava, but it was also composed of elements she'd never encountered in an animal, living or dead. Ever.

A beeping sound alerted her to the end of the diagnostic run. "Damn. The equipment is working fine," she muttered. "So, whatever it is, we're getting an accurate reading." She frowned at the image again, the mystery of it was as frustrating as it was fascinating. "You know, if it weren't for the genetic components, I'd swear that was a structure. Pyri-Stone and Quinn's Beryl Crystal is in the ground all around this area. Perfect building material."

"But even the earliest human settlers didn't build here. Especially that deep underground."

"What if…?" Ti'ann bit her bottom lip as an image of Narava's controversial native species, the Shifters, flashed through her mind—their long golden bodies and the multi-colored swirling eyes of their natural forms. She met her partner's jade gaze. "We could always ask—"

"No." He cut her off with a sharp gesture and straightened in his seat.

"You don't even know what I'm going to say."

"I know you better than you know yourself, Ti'ann. You think this has something to do with …*them*."

"Well, what if it does?" She lowered her voice and leaned in close to him. "Someone from a Shifter support group might know what we're looking at."

"No. You do not want to bring that kind of attention to our site. There are fanatics on both sides of the extermination argument. Especially with the current Senate debates. You don't know who might land here."

"There's a friend of a friend of a friend I can contact."

"No," he repeated. "Even if you can trust this person, their presence will attract attention. We'll end up with fanatics, protesters, politicians, news reporters…" He shuddered at the mention of the last group. "All of them trampling our site. Not to mention the possible violence. No."

"Do you have any other ideas?"

"Yes. We ignore this thing." He flicked his hand toward the screen. "And we get back to the rest of the dig."

"Can you really do that? This could be the biggest thing we've ever found. It could make our careers."

"Or it could be nothing at all."

"And we won't know which until we dig."

"So we dig. Without calling in outsiders."

"What if it's dangerous? Neither one of us has even a guess what it is. I don't want to unleash some as of yet undiscovered Naravan disease or hibernating monster because I didn't check all possible sources for information." Their jobs had always been complicated by a lack of good data about this planet's ancient history, so they had to be extraordinarily careful in their searches.

"What makes you think supporters will know any more than we do?" Krin challenged.

"The only way we'll know is by asking."

He groaned and turned to stare at the closed tent-door flap. "You're determined to contact these people?"

"I can't ignore this. *We* can't. You know we can't. Look at it. It's amazing, impossible. But I don't want to start digging if it turns out this is something potentially dangerous. We'll keep the arrival of this outside help quiet. Only you and I need to know the truth about their affiliations." She grinned and ducked her head to catch Krin's gaze. "Come on. You know you want to."

His reluctant smile made her chuckle. But when he faced her fully, his expression was serious. "Okay, we'll do things your way. But I want one concession. If you do this, we bring in security for the site."

"We don't have the funds. The grant barely covers our expenses as is."

"A friend of Devin's has some connections," Krin suggested. "It won't cost much."

"That doesn't sound entirely legal."

"You want to contact a secret support group and you're worried about legal?"

"Krin…"

"This is about keeping us all from getting killed." He launched up out of his chair and started pacing around the tent. His circuit was short with all the equipment in the way. He paused when he heard voices from just outside the tent then continued to pace when the sound faded away.

Ti'ann had never seen her best friend this agitated. Not even when he'd been contemplating the serious step of proposing to his partner Devin, or when he'd faced possible expulsion for punching his supervisor while pursuing his third Ph.D.

"You're really serious about this?" she asked. "You really think we need security?"

"Yes." He stilled and faced her. "I think if that anomaly has anything to do with *them*, we're gonna need all the help we can get."

"And what makes you think this man will be neutral on the issue? What if he sympathizes with one side or the other?"

"He's paid to be neutral. It's what he does. That's the whole reason I'd rather hire someone like him than go to a public security firm or to the Guards."

She rolled the end of her long braid around her fingers and pursed her lips. After a silent moment, she nodded. "Okay, Krin, if you honestly think we need security, go ahead." She turned back to the readout screen and focused on the anomalous shape causing all the trouble. "But you're responsible for coming up with a way to pay him. I'm not stealing artifacts or coughing up hard won grant money."

She heard Krin's sigh of relief and almost smiled.

"I'll take care of everything." He left the tent without another word.

"DR. JONES." One of the volunteers, Micca, stopped beside Ti'ann, drawing her attention. "There's a man here to see you."

Ti'ann stretched her back until her spine popped, sighed, then wiped the purple dust on her hands over her green khaki pants. She glanced up at the sky. The sun had arched past its zenith, starting its afternoon dip toward the horizon, but the valley was still awash in bright, hot light.

"Who is it?" she asked Micca, blinking at the young woman.

"I don't know. Dr. Freemont just told me to come and get you."

"Thanks."

When Micca turned and walked away, Ti'ann looked back at her dig site and the small animal bones she was unearthing. Their white coloring glowed in the dark purple grit covering the valley floor.

She activated the scanners surrounding the area she was working on, covering it with a magnetic blanket shield to protect it from being reburied by the sporadic winds that blew through the valley. Collecting her memo tablet from the large rock she'd set it on that morning, she nodded to the nearest person still carefully dusting specks of purple from an unclassified thigh bone and crossed to the lift platforms that carried the crew up from the valley floor to the campsite.

As the lift rose, she wondered if the members of the Shifter support group had arrived already. James Monroe, her contact in the group, had insisted on bringing several people with him, something that made her a little more nervous about her plan. She was glad Krin had insisted on security now. Keeping the reason for the presence of a small group secret was a lot more difficult than doing so for a single person. And that was just among her own team. Bringing in a group might well attract the attention of just the type of people Krin was afraid of.

But she wasn't expecting Monroe and his people for another three hours or so. It could be the security guy. She had no idea when he was expected. Though, she'd be surprised if Krin called her up for that. The security was officially Krin's responsibility. She was in charge of the Shifter support group. That suited her just fine. She was anxious to find out what their anomaly was, excited about the potential. The mystery of it had occupied her mind all morning, and she could barely wait for Monroe and his people to arrive.

As she walked down the rocky path leading from the lifts to the campsite, she pulled out her memo tablet and called up the list of elements making up the anomaly. Puzzling through the strange mixture of molecules, she only looked up and noticed her surroundings when she heard a hesitant cough. Blinking, she realized she'd reached the very edge of the camp and had nearly walked right past Krin. She started to smile.

Until she spotted the man next to Krin.

Her breath locked in her throat. She froze, unable to move or think or speak. Even when Krin stepped forward and made the introductions, several heartbeats passed before what he said worked its way into her brain.

"He's the man I was telling you about," Krin said, a note of hesitance in his voice.

She pressed her lips together to keep her mouth from dropping open and focused on Krin.

"Dr. Jones," he continued, despite the creases marring his smooth forehead, "this is Nathan Longfeather. He's agreed to assist us with our security issues."

Ti'ann nodded and was about to say they'd met before when a deep and, unfortunately, well-remembered voice said, "It's a pleasure to meet you, Dr. Jones."

Her gaze snapped around, locking with his dusky, green-amber eyes.

He didn't remember her.

She saw it in his expression, as plainly as if he'd pulled a knife out and shown it to her before plunging it into her gut. Oh god, he didn't have any idea who she was.

She suppressed the sudden tremors sneaking up her body and sucked in her top lip, pressing it hard with her teeth.

When he extended a hand at the introduction, she took it but pulled away from the warmth of his big palm with a jerk. She couldn't look him in the eyes, but letting her gaze wander over the rest of his face didn't help either.

He looked exactly how she remembered him—strong, high cheekbones; sharp, broad nose; sensuously firm lips on a wide mouth; smooth brown-red skin.

His straight black hair hung nearly to his waist, almost as long as her own. The top was held back from his face by a small braid.

His broad shoulders and narrow hips hinted at a temptingly masculine physique. Though, through his loose trousers and flight jacket, a person would have to guess at the degree of muscle and strength.

Unless that person had seen him out of his clothes.

Ti'ann's mouth dried at the memory.

She turned her attention back to Krin, so she wouldn't have to confront the man who appeared too often in her dreams. She clenched her teeth together and tried hard not to let the hurt show. But a quiet voice, deep inside, whispered, *Of course he doesn't remember you. Why would he, Ti'ann? Look at him. He's gorgeous. The kind of man most women would die to have. Why would a man like that remember someone like you?*

"I wasn't expecting him so soon," she muttered flicking a glance at Nathan before settling back more comfortably on Krin. Actually, she'd had no idea when he was expected. But she had to say something, anything to fill the void. Krin would start to worry if she didn't. And speaking to Nathan right now, when her chest felt tight and her stomach hollow, was impossible.

"I was told the situation required my immediate attention,"

Nathan answered. "And as I was between jobs, I had time to make myself available at the request of a friend."

There wasn't even a hint of the discomfort or embarrassment she was feeling in his voice. Just a relaxed confidence, edged for business.

Ti'ann took a deep breath and stiffened her spine, turning back to Nathan. "I'm not sure how dire our situation is, Mr. Longfeather. But Dr. Freemont thought it best we have some security. You came highly recommended from his friend."

She tried raising her voice above a mumble. But meeting his indifferent gaze was almost more than she could take, so she turned her attention to the tablet in her hand, pretending to focus on the row of anomaly data still on her screen. If she didn't have to look at him, she could pretend he was just an ordinary person, that she wasn't affected by his presence any more than he was hers. She could pretend he wasn't the man who had turned her world upside down three years ago and ruined her for all other men. She might even be able to convince herself her heart wasn't being crushed by the loss of an impossible fantasy. Lying though, even to herself, had never been one of her strengths.

Attempting a distracted tone, she said, "I assume Dr. Freemont's told you we won't be able to pay you out of our regular source of funding."

"We've already discussed a price and method of payment, Dr. Jones," Krin said, the tone of his voice hinting to stay away from the topic.

In her present state, she was happy to, as long as she could get away from Nathan Longfeather as quickly as possible. "Fine. In that case, I'll leave the particulars to you two. I'd appreciate it if you didn't interfere with the dig sites themselves, Mr. Longfeather. Otherwise, do what you think is necessary."

She kept her focus on her memo tablet, running a finger over the screen to call up more data as she walked past the men toward camp.

Nathan stopped her with a statement directed to Krin. "Would you mind if I spoke with Dr. Jones alone for a few minutes, Dr. Freemont?"

Her stomach tightened in panic. She couldn't be alone with him! Not yet.

Krin must have seen panic on her face when she snapped her gaze to him because he hesitated.

"I'm sure whatever you have to discuss with Dr. Jones can be discussed with me as well, Longfeather. We're partners."

"I understand. I just have a few questions for the doctor before I begin my survey of the area."

Krin held her gaze in silent question, waiting for her to make the call.

After a moment, she nodded. "They could use a hand at the secondary site," she said to Krin. When he continued hesitating, she added, "I'll meet you in the imaging tent in half an hour."

The appointment seemed enough to settle him. He extended his hand to Nathan. "Thanks again for coming on such short notice. Find me after you've done your initial survey." To Ti'ann, he added, "I'll see you in thirty minutes."

When they were alone, Ti'ann took a deep breath and faced Nathan. She kept her gaze on a spot just beyond his right ear. But the avoidance made her feel like a ninny, so firmed her shoulders and met his gaze. "What did you need to ask me, Mr. Longfeather?"

"First, call me Nathan. *Mister* Longfeather doesn't quite work on a man in my profession."

She nodded but didn't comment.

"Second, I'd like to know what you think I should expect here."

"I know it isn't entirely normal for a paleontology dig to require security, but it's always better to be safe." She studied her tablet again, so she could drop eye contact. She was not a good liar. Or so Krin always told her. "We're awfully close to Gremblewreath and we've had a few joy riders buzz by. Since the town is known for having a less-than-law-abiding element, we don't want to risk any of the equipment getting stolen or vandalized."

"I wasn't called all this way because of Gremblewreath thugs, Dr. Jones. I don't come cheap. There's a reason you and your partner have decided to hire my particular brand of services. But to do my job effectively, I have to know what I'm facing. What I'm really trying to secure."

She tried for a casual shrug, which felt stiff and insincere, and said, "You're here to secure this dig site. Some of our finds can be quite valuable in academic circles." Her gut tightened when she glanced over her tablet at him. He wasn't buying her story. She hated, *hated*, feeling so off-balance and uncertain in front of him. She was a professional damn it. Just because he didn't remember her, didn't mean she had to let him know he upset her.

He shook his head and settled his hands on his hips. "Keeping something from me is going to make it impossible for me to do my job, Dr. Jones. Enough of the bullshit, if you don't mind."

She narrowed her gaze and, for an instant, indignation overwhelmed her hurt and self-consciousness. "I was under the impression you were both neutral and discrete, Mr. Longfeather."

"That's what I'm being paid for."

"Then all you need to know is that you're guarding my dig site. All of it. You're here to make sure no one from the outside hurts my people."

"And just exactly who would want to hurt your people? Given this is just a paleontology dig."

She cursed silently and focused on the memo tablet again. Not only did he make her feel like an idiot, now he was making her act like one. "Mr. Longfeather—"

"Nathan."

She ignored his interruption. "The details aren't important. We scientists keep our discoveries close to the chest. Suffice it to say, we may—or may not—have found something of great interest. The find has the potential to cause some…complications. To avoid possible difficulties, Dr. Freemont felt we needed your brand of help. And if you're prepared for any kind of trouble, then that's really all the information you need right now." She held up a hand to stop him when he started to speak. "I am not prepared to go into any more details at the present. You're just going to have to deal with the information I've shared." She forced herself to look up and meet his gaze. She might feel like an ass right now, but she was a professional. And her work was too damned important to her to let him intimidate her. Or at least to let her intimidation show. "Am I clear?"

To her surprise, her outburst earned her a crooked, devastating grin. Ti'ann felt all the horrible hurt and mortification wash back over her, burying the strength she was desperately clinging to.

"Clear," he said.

His deep voice sent a skittering of desire down her spine, causing an unwanted rush of memory. The dark, cool hotel room, tangled sheets, sweat and lust, the hard strength of his body above hers, the brush of his long hair across her breasts.

She blinked and took an involuntary step away from him, her throat tight from a combination of pain and longing.

"Good," she said, but even to her, her voice sounded strained. She swallowed and forced out, "Any further questions can be directed to Dr. Freemont."

"I'll do that, Dr. Jones."

She jerked out a nod and turned to leave, but his husky voice stopped her.

"By the way, do you have a first name?"

Pain lanced through her. She kept her back to him so he wouldn't see how devastated she was by his simple question. "Of course."

"Would you mind telling me?"

The last time he'd asked for her first name had been under very different circumstances. Standing here now, with him politely curious, she felt like that other time must have happened to someone else. The sexy, blond woman she'd tried to be all those years ago was someone from a dream, with no connection to her real self. Why would Nathan see that woman in the person she was now? Straightening her shoulders, she kept her attention on the trees in front of her as she said, "Ti'ann."

Nathan said something under his breath, but she was too busy hurrying toward the safety of camp to hear him.

"I THOUGHT IT WAS YOU," Nathan murmured to Ti'ann's retreating back.

He could hardly believe it was her. And of all places to meet her again, in the backwaters of Narava. He almost hadn't recognized her. She'd had blond hair when they met three years ago. And her clothes, then lack of clothing, had kept her lush body on display. With her now brown hair pulled tightly into a long, thick braid, her curves hidden in loose pants and t-shirt, and her sexy gray eyes focused on everything but him most of the time…it was hard to see the woman he'd spent those spectacular, erotic nights with. He'd had to hear her name to be sure he wasn't imagining things.

He watched the natural swing of her hips as she walked away and his gut tightened as detailed fantasies began mixing with memory. She'd pretended not to know him just now. She was a crappy liar. He'd seen the spark of recognition before she'd attempted to mask it. She hadn't forgotten their time together any more than he had. Why she pretended they didn't have a past was a mystery he'd get to soon enough. When they had some privacy.

For three years, he hadn't been able to stop thinking about this woman and their two brief nights together. Despite his best efforts. For a few months after, he'd even considered trying to track her down.

He hadn't.

He kept telling himself it was best he'd left when he had. She was the type of woman a guy could fall hard for, and at that point in his life, he couldn't afford the distraction.

If only his ex-partner, Alex, had followed the same advice. Falling for Gina had nearly gotten them all killed. And Alex had always been the one telling Nathan not to seduce clients! Dumb bastard had gone and broken his own rule. Then married the woman! To be fair, Nathan liked Gina. She was good for his friend. And what had happened hadn't been her fault. He put the blame solidly on Alex's shoulders. But as far as Nathan was concerned, the fact that his friend was ridiculously happy with his wife did not make him any less of an asshole.

Breaking up their partnership after all the years they'd

worked together hadn't helped endear Alex to him either. Even if it had been the right decision. When Nathan saw Alex these days, he took great pleasure in rubbing the ex-mercenary's face in his idiocy. Since Gina thought their banter was funny, Nathan didn't even feel guilty about the abuse he heaped on Alex.

Thoughts of his ex-partner made Nathan frown. Until that moment, he'd had every intention of seducing the lovely Dr. Jones again. Though the first time, he hadn't known she was Dr. Jones. In fact, he hadn't been able to get her name out of her until the first time he'd made her come. Knowing her name didn't make any difference, though. Then or now. Then, he'd been too busy driving them both to exhaustion.

Now?

Now, he wanted… No, he *needed* to see if the passion they'd experienced in those two nights could possibly happen again. He had never experienced anything like it, before or after. Lust so intense, so drugging, he could barely keep his hands off her. He'd had to leave the suite a couple of times just to avoid exhausting her unconscious.

He smiled thinking about it. She'd actually kept up with him quite well, if memory served.

And that was one of the problems. Was he remembering those two nights for what they were or had he blown them all out of proportion in the last three years? After watching her gray eyes flash when she attempted to put him in his place, he was pretty sure his memories were accurate. He was looking forward to confirming that, as much as he was looking forward to making her admit she remembered him.

Unfortunately, she was now his client. That was the other problem. He never got involved with someone he was working for. He actually *followed* the rule Alex had always drilled into him. When working, Nathan kept his dick in his pants.

With a resigned sigh, he accepted he was going to have to do that now, too. For a little while anyway. He'd let Ti'ann pretend she didn't know him, and he'd resist dragging her off to his ship to prove how well she did. But as soon as this job was finished, he had plans for the good doctor.

Energetic plans.

CHAPTER TWO

The incessant beeping of his private comm-board made Senator Johnson roll his eyes. He sat behind his desk, ordered the music level lower and flicked on the vid-screen. "What is it, Barbury? You know I don't like to be disturbed at home."

"Yes, Senator. I understand. However, I felt this was rather urgent."

"It's always urgent," the senator mumbled, taking in his aide's flushed complexion and wide eyes. "Okay, what is it that couldn't wait until a respectable hour?"

"We've intercepted a transmission from James Monroe to a Dr. Ti'ann Jones, a paleontologist on a dig just south of Gremblewreath."

When his aide paused, the senator sighed. "And?"

"Well, the conversation concerned a discovery which Monroe showed great interest in."

"I don't see the importance of this yet, Barbury. Perhaps you'd like to clarify."

"Of course, Senator." The man shifted, pulling at his tie.

"It's that Monroe is, well, who he is, and we thought it suspicious that he had a sudden interest in the findings of a paleontologist, sir."

"Isn't Monroe a historian?"

"Yes, sir."

"And wouldn't it be entirely conceivable that he'd find something in the findings of a paleontologist interesting?"

"Yes, sir."

"So then…"

"Sir, he was seen leaving the city just under an hour ago with four other individuals. His flight plan logs their destination as coordinates just south of Gremblewreath. And two of the four people accompanying him were individuals known to be associated with Monroe's…other interests."

The mention of people associated with Monroe's "other interests" made the senator pause and consider. "Were any of *them* in the group?"

"I'm afraid our informants were outside detector range, sir. They couldn't say for sure."

The senator stood and paced behind his chair, his hands clasped behind him. He saw Barbury watching him from the vid-screen with wary eyes.

After a moment's consideration, the senator said, "Since the disappearance of Kira Farseaker, Monroe has become the big fish in what was a little pond. But the pond she left behind has been getting bigger. It wouldn't be prudent to allow Monroe's movements to go unmonitored. Is there any reason to suspect this paleontologist's findings are related to Monroe's other interests?"

"Nothing concrete, Senator. She logged a call to a Dr. Joan Craynmar who in turn put her in touch with Monroe. But Craynmar is a physicist with no known affiliations to any terrorist groups outside of her acquaintance with Monroe. An acquaintance that started in academic circles some years ago. It's entirely possible Monroe's interest is genuinely to do with history."

"But you don't think so. Do you, Barbury?"

"No, sir. I don't."

"Very well. Send a small group to the site. Have them go in as a special government inspection team conducting a routine survey and inspection of all scientific research sites on Narava. If this Dr. Jones questions it, threaten her funding. That should keep her quiet and amenable."

"Yes, sir. Any specific instructions for the team?"

"Make sure at least one of them knows something about science," the senator drawled. "And tell them not to make any moves without consulting me first, through you. Is that understood?"

"Absolutely, sir." Barbury's face was now composed, business-like, the flush of panic and excitement contained. "I'll see to it immediately."

After his aide broke the transmission, the senator stared at his vid-screen for a long time. This entire issue was going to give him ulcers. It should never have come to this. Public debates in the Senate. Questions pertaining to the ethical nature of government policy. Things should never have gotten this far. If not for that ass Ennoren and his fuck up with his ex-wife, Kira Farseaker, this whole situation never would have come to the fore. Though, he had to admit, some of the blame had to go to Senator Rodriguez and that blasted David Cario.

Ennoren had done one good thing before his death—getting rid of Rodriquez. That act was the only thing he'd managed to get right, though. Cario and Farseaker should have joined Rodriguez in death.

The senator snarled. If either Cario or Farseaker were still on the planet, he had every intention of finding them and personally blasting them out of their skins.

Unfortunately, he was nearly positive they were no longer on planet. And Ennoren was beyond his revenge. Unpleasant, the feeling of frustration and helplessness. But if he could stop Monroe from making things worse, that was something. The Senate was divided. He still had time to swing the vote in the right direction.

He narrowed his eyes at the vid-screen as a perfect, and ironic, idea occurred to him. He smiled, just a little, and ordered a coded, private line. He'd cleared away his smile by the time the small, bug-eyed man answered the call.

"Dr. Ripley. How are you this evening?"

"Busy."

The senator almost smiled again. These scientists weren't big on social skills. Instead, he glowered at the screen until Dr. Ripley's gaze shifted away.

"How is the experiment proceeding, doctor?"

"Fine. On schedule."

"Is it capable of following specific instructions yet?"

"Of course. Very detailed instructions, as a matter of fact. This one's far exceeded our expectations. It surpasses all of our previous experiments in both viability and longevity."

"Is it ready for testing then?"

"What sort of test?" The man's already huge eyes widened.

"A recognizance mission of sorts. To investigate a paleontology dig just south of Gremblewreath for any…controversial activity."

"'Controversial activity,' huh? I'm sure it would be capable of such an exercise."

The senator did smile this time. "Good. The instructions are this: search, gather information, report back to you. It is to do nothing without my explicit authorization. Understood? I don't want to give away the nature of this work before the timing is appropriate."

"Understandable. Nothing without your authorization." Dr. Ripley's narrowed his eyes and compressed his thin lips. "Nothing at all, Senator?"

"Well, killing Shifters is permissible, obviously."

"Obviously. Though we could use a few new specimens."

"Maybe at a later date. For now, make sure my orders are followed."

"I'm sure it'll live up to your expectations, senator."

"I hope so, Ripley. It will make my job much simpler if it works."

Senator Johnson broke transmission with a frown that quickly turned to a smile.

"HERE YOU ARE."

Ti'ann looked up from where she sat hunched over a reader as Krin stalked into her tent. She was surprised by the scowl on his face until she remembered she was supposed to have met him in the imaging tent more than half an hour ago.

Before he could say another word, she launched into her apology. "I'm sorry. I got caught up in this search." She waved the palm-sized pad at him. "Look at this. I think I found something that ties in with our mysterious new discovery. There was a paper published about fifteen years ago on the physiological degradation of Shifter cells after death. There're some similarities to the anomaly."

His eyes widened at her news, and she hid her smile, knowing she'd avoided a scolding by the skin of her teeth.

He dropped onto her cot beside her and took the proffered reader. She pointed at the name of the journal. "It went out of publication about a year after this paper. Arguments about the journal's acceptance of papers using 'unethical' methods of data collection and research."

He raised an eyebrow, his half-grin sardonic.

She smiled back. "Yeah, well, there's no direct reference to Shifter Research Center. The authors of this paper claimed the specimens they studied were collected under 'natural conditions'."

Krin's mouth dropped open. "Oh, I'd just love to know how they got 'natural conditions' past the referees without so much as an explanation. Considering how hard it is to find *living* Shifters in 'natural conditions' without a detector."

"That exact point was raised in a rebuttal paper three months after this one came out. Without a detector—"

"Which was only just perfected and impossible to come by in the private sector fifteen years ago."

She nodded. "The authors of the rebuttal paper claimed that Ripley and Hesh couldn't have possibly encountered so many 'dead' Shifters. At any rate, the issue died after a while, and so did this paper. I had to really dig to find it. Skim through it. Some of their results look incredible."

She sat quietly as she waited for him to finish the article. He could speed read when the mood hit him, a talent she envied. After only a few minutes, he looked up and stared at her, mouth agape.

"Holy shit, Ti'ann. They're talking about some really innovative genetic studies."

"I know. But the part that really caught my eye was the

section on the degradation of Shifter tissue after death. I mean, have you ever heard of an animal petrifying *instantaneously* at death without the aid of some natural disaster?"

"I always assumed they disintegrated."

"Me, too."

Krin grinned. "Do you think we've found the first Shifter graveyard?" He waggled his eyebrows.

Ti'ann chuckled. "Won't know until we've excavated. I don't want to jump to any conclusion. With all the non-organic material, this could still be something else entirely. But the single shift in base-pairs that Ripley and Hesh reported sure does look like the DNA we're seeing in that thing."

Her stomach danced. This could turn out to be bigger than she'd expected. Evidence of an actual Shifter graveyard would have all kinds of implications. It would also give them numerous fossils to study. She was about to show Krin the other papers she'd dug up when the tent flap opened.

"One of the diggers told me where I'd find the two of you."

They looked up simultaneously as Nathan Longfeather stepped inside.

Ti'ann sucked in a sharp breath as the weight of his gaze pinned her to the cot. The excitement of a moment ago quickly turned to dread. She wasn't ready to see Nathan yet. She'd thrown herself into her research to forget about him. It had worked. Too well. Now, he was taking up too much of her tent, the air around her growing thick. She swallowed and dropped her gaze to the reader pad, pulling it away from Krin. Saving the papers she'd found was a good excuse to avoid looking at Nathan until she could control her thumping heartbeat. Why did the man have to be so damned handsome?

"What do you need?" Krin asked.

The wary look on his face at her abrupt change of mood

didn't go unnoticed by her. His voice wasn't exactly hostile. In fact, if she hadn't known him, she'd say he sounded perfectly professional and courteous. But she did know him.

As she worked on the reader, she considered how much trouble Krin might cause if she kept reacting strangely to Nathan. Krin knew she was awkward around men she didn't know. Particularly very handsome men. He'd known her long enough to see her at her worse. But did he sense there was more to her behavior around Nathan than just her usual discomfort and insecurity? The last thing she needed was Krin acting righteously indignant on her behalf. Especially when he didn't know the history between her and Nathan.

"I need to go over all the personnel on site," Nathan said, "their jobs, their backgrounds, their personal lives. Any information you have about them. I'll also need to know more about this group you have arriving this evening."

Ti'ann's head snapped around. Krin's hand dropped to her arm before she could react.

"I told him Monroe and his people were coming, that they were expected. I thought he'd better know we'd called in other scientists to help with our newest discovery."

She relaxed but only a little. Nathan's scent—a strange mixture of spices she'd never smelled anywhere else—eased through the tent, filling her nostrils and fogging her mind. Her stomach tightened. The last time that smell had surrounded her, she'd been naked, sweating, and desperate to take everything Nathan was giving her. She bit the inside of her cheek to keep from groaning aloud—a reaction neither Nathan nor Krin would understand.

"Mind if I sit?" Nathan nodded at a field seat to one side of the tent.

She shook her head. Watching him from under her lashes as

he eased his long body onto the little seat, she worried the canvas and Stravex piping wouldn't hold his weight. The chair creaked but held, and she let out the breath she'd been holding. When she glanced back at his face, he was smiling at her. She looked away.

"From my estimates, you have around twenty people on site," Nathan began.

"Twenty-two," Krin confirmed.

Ti'ann tried to follow the conversation but discomfort kept her on edge. Not all of that discomfort came from the fact that Nathan didn't remember her. Her awareness of the raw, powerful maleness surrounding him had her nerves jumping. That energy had drawn her in three years ago without protest. She'd craved being near it and had run to him like a moepea bug flying into an exposed heating coil. The power radiating from Nathan still drew her. And that bone-deep lust embarrassed her more than the fact that he'd forgotten her. Especially because he'd forgotten her.

"I'll need a list of names for your people and their jobs," Nathan said, directing the comment to her.

"I'll arrange it," Krin answered.

"How about background information…family relationships, education, that sort of information?"

"We wouldn't have anything like that." Ti'ann spoke up before she could stop herself. "We don't delve into the personal lives of the people working for us."

Nathan gave her a look she couldn't read. She saw Krin glance at her from the corner of her eye but he didn't respond to her outburst.

"I presume you at least have past employment information," Nathan said, his voice level. "Surely, you require credentials for the people you employed."

"Of course. But that's confidential."

"Are we going to have this argument again?"

"What argument?" Her voice jumped up a notch.

"The one about how I need all the information you can give me or I won't be able to do my job."

"As I recall, I won that argument. Besides, breaking the confidentiality agreement with our workers isn't information we can give you, Mr. Longfeather."

He raised an impatient hand when she would have gone on. "Never mind. I just need their names. I can find out all I need to know without you having to violate your ethical difficulties."

"Is that legal?" she squeaked.

"Ti'ann," Krin murmured, touching her hand. "Let the man do his job." To Nathan, Krin said, "We'll try to give you as much information as we can, but as Dr. Jones pointed out, it does go against our agreement with our personnel to release information of a personal nature. Whatever you can find on your own, however, is your business. I'm assuming the background checks have to do with the way you'll secure the site, knowing who you're dealing with, that kind of thing?"

Nathan nodded but his gaze remained fixed on Ti'ann. She shifted on the cot and plucked at the edge of her t-shirt, anything to avoid looking directly at him.

They talked for another few minutes before Nathan excused himself to finish his survey of the site. She let out a loud breath the instant the tent flap closed, blocking her view of his retreating back. The sigh settled Krin's questioning gaze on her.

She raised her eyebrows. "What?"

"You know 'what'. What's going on with you and Longfeather? Have you met him before?"

"Sort of. I… It was nothing. He doesn't even remember me so…" She shrugged.

Krin's frown deepened. "What does 'sort of' mean, Ti'ann? Did he hurt you or…?"

"No. No, Krin, it was nothing like that." She tried a shaky smile. "Just… Well, you know how I am around handsome men."

"Handsome, heterosexual men? Yeah, I know."

His wry smile steadied her own grin.

He shook his head, turning serious again. "But I haven't seen you this edgy in a long time. You've always been uncomfortable but since grad school you've managed to at least look most handsome men in the face for the length of a conversation. What gives?"

"It's nothing. I swear. You don't need to worry."

He gave her an assessing look that made her squirm. She forced herself to sit still.

"I'm not so sure about that," he said as he studied her.

She finally shifted so her body angled away from his, a vain attempt to hide her expression.

"You're attracted to him," Krin said, his expression widening. "That's why you avoid looking at him. You want to look too much."

She shook her head and opened her mouth, but Krin silenced her with a raised hand. "Don't try denying it. We've been through this sort of thing before. But this Longfeather isn't some staid professor or a young hotshot digger. This man is dangerous. He has a dangerous job, he lives with the real possibility of death every day, and he won't settle into a quiet comfortable life with a paleontologist."

"Krin, you're jumping to conclusions. I'll admit I find Mr. Longfeather attractive. What woman wouldn't? But I have no illusions about him. Besides, he's hardly attracted to me anyway."

"Ti'Ann." Krin sighed, slouching back against the tent wall. "How often am I gonna have to tell you you're a beautiful woman and men *are* attracted to you?"

She gave him a level look. "You're biased. And we both know you're full of shit. Besides, you're gay. How would you know if a heterosexual man found me attractive or not?"

She flinched when he cocked an eyebrow at her. They'd had this conversation before. But all of Krin's assurances didn't matter. She knew she wasn't attractive to the opposite sex. Oh, she was smart—she was an excellent paleontologist. However, being a top scientific mind wasn't the kind of thing that drew men like Nathan Longfeather. Her two very brief relationships and her even briefer fling with Nathan had proven that well enough. Men got bored with her quickly. They wanted beauty and seduction and she just didn't fulfill that desire, even when she tried. She squirmed at the remembered humiliation from the time she had tried with the "staid" professor. That had been so embarrassing. Or her attempt to keep the "hotshot digger" interested by dying her hair blond. Not that it had helped.

She'd known from a very young age she'd have to use her intellect to get through life. Her parents had drilled that lesson into her. "Use your mind, Ann," her father had said, again and again. "Don't try relying on your looks. You'll only be disappointed. You're not like your mother." Since her mother was gorgeous and had turned her looks into a hugely successful modeling career, Ti'ann knew her father was right. Her romantic history had only reinforced his prediction. So she accepted her fate—smart but alone—even if Krin couldn't.

"Can we drop this?" She met Krin's brooding expression. "We have work to do. I'll eventually get used to Longfeather."

One corner of his mouth crooked up and he rolled he eyes. "Okay. I'll drop it. For now. But if he does anything, I mean anything at all to make you any more uncomfortable than you already are, let me know. I'll take care of it for you."

She grinned and nodded. They both knew full well she'd never tell him anything of the sort. But she felt better knowing Krin was there for her if she needed him.

Just as they left her tent and were on their way to the imaging tent, they heard the sounds of a ship landing.

CHAPTER THREE

JAMES MONROE WASN'T WHAT NATHAN HAD BEEN EXPECTING. For some reason, Nathan had expected the historian to be a bit more…academic looking. And older. Not a well-tanned, classically handsome athlete with a squared jaw and blue eyes.

Something more than his looks bothered Nathan. Monroe wasn't just a historian. Nathan couldn't say for sure how he knew—instinct probably—but he'd been a hired gun long enough to trust his gut. He was sure there was more to Monroe than this academic guise. Distrust and suspicion were immediate and intense.

Hanging back while Ti'ann and Krin spoke with the man, Nathan observed the group with Monroe. One extra person than had been expected. He studied each, trying to guess which one was the addition. Three women and one other man.

The man had short, brown hair, a thick mustache and beard, and dark eyes behind thin glasses. Nathan's lip twitched at the affectation. Glasses for vision correction hadn't been required in a century and a half, but recently academic types had taken to wearing them again as an accessory. Just another in a series of fashion trends Nathan didn't understand. But it told him something about the man's character that he bothered with fashion. Nathan listened as he was introduced to Ti'ann and Krin as Mike Warez, the geophysicist. One expected person down.

The next to be introduced was Juanita Baker. She shook hands firmly with Ti'ann and Krin but didn't smile. She had a thick mane of black, curly hair, and an expression just a touch too hard make her attractive. Whatever sensitivity or vulnerability she had was well-hidden. She was the molecular scientist. Also expected.

The natural historian was introduced as Val Hyde, a petit, green-eyed blond who could have been Monroe's sister. Their features were somewhat alike, square and broad, their coloring similar if not identical. And Val was just as lovely as Monroe was handsome. She greeted Ti'ann and Krin with an infectious grin and an enthusiastic handshake that nearly pulled Ti'ann off her feet.

The little laugh that jumped out of Ti'ann captured Nathan's full attention. Her face was flushed, her gray eyes sparkled, and her full lips were wet from a quick flick of her tongue.

The sight nearly pulled a groan from him. Her expression conjured remembered images of another time, of throaty laughter and flushed skin. He tried to force himself to look away, but she turned before he could and caught him staring. He held her gaze a moment too long before he made himself face Monroe's group again. Under different circumstances, he might have smiled at the sudden flush of her cheeks.

The last person to be introduced was a woman named Clare O'Malley. Unlike the other two women, Clare threw her sensuality out for all to see. Her tight clothing hugged generous curves. Her wavy red hair was pulled up in a wildly exploded bun with sexy tendrils hanging free to frame a pale, stunning face dusted with faint freckles over her nose. The freckles were the only thing marring her otherwise porcelain skin and the one thing that made Clare attractive as far as Nathan was concerned.

The woman swiveled up to shake Krin and Ti'ann's hands then draped a slim arm across Mike Warez's shoulders. Monroe didn't mention what Clare did, and no one seemed comfortable enough to ask. But Nathan had a pretty good idea from her body language why Clare had been invited on this little expedition. He had a feeling Mike wouldn't have come along otherwise.

She wasn't what she seemed either though. Like Monroe, Clare was hiding behind her charm. Her chocolate-colored eyes were carefully hooded, alert to everything going on around her. Nathan made a mental note to watch Ms. O'Malley. Closely.

He glanced back at Ti'ann in time to catch her watching him. Her expression went through a series of contortions too fast for him to interpret before she looked away. He frowned, but Monroe spoke, drawing back his attention.

"I don't mean to seem abrupt," James said, "but we've come a long way to see this anomaly of yours. May we take a look at your findings now?"

Nathan was looking forward to this part, too. Ti'ann's reluctance to tell him anything about the "anomaly" had been irritating, not because she was resistant to sharing information with him but because he was going to find out what they were hiding anyway. She'd been evasive for the sake of it and it did make his job more difficult.

Ti'ann shook off whatever had upset her a moment ago and answered with a courteous, "Of course. The imaging tent is this way."

Monroe's group trailed Ti'ann and Krin to the tent. Nathan took up the rear, watching the body language of the historian and his group. Monroe's excitement seemed to radiate from him, infecting even the unsmiling Juanita. Whatever Ti'ann had found, Monroe obviously thought it was important.

When they entered the imaging tent, Ti'ann went to the largest viewing screen, sat in front of a small console, and called up a series of files. As this was his first opportunity to see the mysterious discovery, Nathan found himself crowding close to the screen with the others. On the slate gray background, a multi-colored image emerged. He stared for several minutes before it resolved into a group of boxes and spheres stacked in layers on top of and around each other, the various colors a visual indication of different elements making up the thing. Whatever the hell it was.

He was no expert, but that image didn't look like any fossil he'd ever seen before. In fact, it looked a bit like the structure of one of the safe houses he and Alex had once had in the Sapphire Mountain Range—before they'd blown it up. This was a lot bigger though. He glanced at the scale reading at the bottom left corner of the screen. The object was twenty kilometers long at its thickest point and nearly three kilometers deep.

"Holy shit," Monroe breathed. "It has DNA and non-organic components?"

Nathan's gaze flicked to the list of elements to the right of the image. He couldn't make sense of most of it any more than he'd been able to interpret the color code on the image itself, but the genetic material was obvious.

Val pushed forward, studying the structure over Ti'ann's shoulder, her entire body vibrating with intensity. "Can we see it now? This is a file right? Can we see what it looks like at this moment?"

"Sure." Ti'ann hit a series of keys on a pad next to the viewer, then swiveled around, the movement forcing Val to take a step back, and flick a button on a large rectangular box festooned with colored lights and toggle switches. Three of the lights flickered from yellow to green and a green light went red. She knocked two toggle switches up and flipped three down with a quick swipe of her hand. Another two lights turned green.

"Give it a sec," she said, smiling up at Val. "The scan sensor node is still dropped to the same depth as this image so it shouldn't take too long."

They all waited with varying degrees of impatience, Val practically bouncing in place.

"Do you know what it is?" Ti'ann asked the anxious woman.

"Maybe. No. Well, maybe." She bit her lip and paced back to Monroe.

They didn't speak, but she stared at him intently for a moment, and Nathan had the distinct impression information was passed in that look. Juanita put a hand on Val's shoulder, a gentling gesture that seemed at odds with his first impression of the molecular scientist.

"I've never seen this mix of elements before," Mike murmured. When Ti'ann moved the filed data on the structure to a second, smaller view screen, Mike moved close to study the list. "The Quinn's Beryl Crystal and Pyri-Stone is unique to this area." He moved his hand down the list of inorganic material. "But coramite is extremely rare in this region, isn't it? When was the most recent geological survey done?"

"Less than two months ago," Krin said. "I checked the data myself. No natural reserves of coramite were detected."

"Strange," Mike murmured.

"Is there any data on human habitation of this area, James?" Ti'ann turned in her seat to address the historian. "Just after the first colonists arrived maybe? Something we wouldn't have come across in our searches."

"No. Humans didn't move into this part of the planet until about fifty years ago. There was a pioneer settlement just north of where Gremblewreath is now. They surveyed and mined for lanimium in the northern valleys, but most records indicate they couldn't find anything of sufficient value this far south so didn't bother coming down this way."

"Is it possible some of them might? Could this be a human construction that wasn't on record?"

He frowned at the filed image. "I can't discount the possibility with absolute certainty, Dr. Jones. But I doubt it. All the records indicate the settlers didn't move farther than about five kilometers south of Gremblewreath's current location. Obviously, people have come down this far on surveys and such—your own dig being a good example. But there's no evidence to suggest humans settled here."

"You think that's a building?" Juanita asked, turning away from the still bouncing Val to face Ti'ann.

Ti'ann shrugged, a gesture that made her long braid shift over her shoulder to fall down her back. Nathan watched for a moment, distracted from the conversation, struck by an overwhelming need to undo the braid and run her thick hair through his fingers. He snapped back from his fantasy at the sound of her voice.

"I hesitate to call it architecture when the genetic material is so prominent. At the same time, it doesn't look like any fossil I've ever seen before." She glanced at Krin, a frown creasing her brow.

Krin nodded and turned to Monroe. "Dr. Jones found a paper that was published about fifteen years ago. In it, there was some information about the change in Shifter cellular structure at death. Specifically, the way Shifter cells instantaneously petrify."

Nathan's attention zeroed in on Val's shocked gasp. Krin's reference to Narava's much debated native species had Nathan's instincts jumping and suspicions rising. Val's reaction, though, wasn't surprise at the mention of the Shifters. Her shock followed the news about Shifters petrifying at death.

"How would they know something like that?" Val said. "Who were they? Where did they get their data? Was it Shifter Research Center?"

Val's questions came so fast, Krin had to raise a hand to slow her down. "The researchers were doctors Ripley and Hesh. I haven't heard of Dr. Hesh, but Dr. Ripley is one of the more prominent researchers—" Krin sneered the word, "—at SRC."

Monroe stepped closer to Val when she started trembling, another response from the small woman that was more extreme than Nathan would have expected. His eyes narrowed. Something there…

"There was debate about how they'd obtained the samples," Ti'ann said, also staring hard at the natural historian, "as there's no evidence of Shifter fossils. At least, not that we know of."

Her back straightened just enough Nathan could tell she was intensely interested in their reactions.

The way Monroe's group dealt with the mention of Shifters and the sudden nervous energy filling the imaging tent confirmed Nathan's suspicions. There was more to this group than their academic credentials. He kept his insight to himself while he watched.

The only person in the room who hadn't tensed at the mention of Shifters was Clare O'Malley. She stood to one side, observing in a controlled, neutral way. A lot like the way he was watching the group, he thought, surprised. Could she be their security? He'd seen more outrageous mercenaries. It was possible. Especially given how cool she was in the midst of the tension.

Her only outward sign of emotion came when Val started pacing the tent. She crossed to the young woman and took her hand, stilling her restless movements at the same time as giving assurance. "You okay, Val?"

The small woman almost smiled. "I'm either very good or not very good at all."

The molecular echo imaging scanner announced it had finished its run and was ready to display the collected pattern. They all turned to the screen, watching quietly as the image solidified.

A list of elements present in the object scrolled beside the image, matching the saved file. Monroe and Warez leaned in close to scan the data. Val stared at the image as if her life depended on the final picture.

"What do you really think this is, Dr. Jones?" Juanita asked. "In light of the Ripley and Hesh paper."

Ti'ann answered without taking her gaze from the image forming on the view screen. "I can't help but wonder if maybe it's some sort of Shifter graveyard."

The tent fell silent, leaving Ti'ann's words to hover in the air.

AS THE IMAGE TOOK SHAPE, Ti'ann studied it, frowning. When it came to full resolution, she sucked in a sharp breath.

"Krin," she whispered, without looking over her shoulder. She glanced at the saved image, then back to the newly formed picture. "Do you see it?"

"Uh-huh."

She looked up to see him standing at her shoulder, his gaze also darting between the new and old images.

"I don't believe it."

"What is it?" Nathan asked from behind them.

"The two readouts aren't identical," Monroe answered for her. "The new one is slightly different. There." He pointed at one of the box shapes. "There seems to be something…more there now."

"It's changed? That sort of blows the graveyard theory, doesn't it?" Clare said. "Unless another's just died in the last day without anyone noticing."

Ti'ann glanced at Clare. Her mildly sardonic response drew a scathing look from Juanita but the rest of the group ignored her.

Ti'ann turned back to the readout, too caught up in her own paradigm shift to worry about the others. If the image really had changed, then it definitely couldn't be a fossil. Unless Clare was right. But how could a Shifter have gotten that far underground?

"Ti'ann, do you have a flask nearby?"

Busy debating possibilities, she didn't immediately notice the commotion going on behind her until Nathan said her name.

She spun around to see Mike Warez holding a trembling Val, who'd dropped to her knees. Her green eyes were huge in her small face as she stared at the imaging screen.

"I think she might need an anazepam," Nathan said.

He stood near her chair, his gaze on the natural historian. But his body heat radiated out to sizzle over Ti'ann's skin. She swallowed back her reaction to Nathan and rose from her seat.

"I'll be right back."

Monroe held up a hand, stopping Ti'ann in her tracks. "Val will be fine. Drugs won't be necessary."

The small woman nodded, taking deep, slow breathes. "I'm

allergic to most meds anyway." She managed a weak smile and, with Mike's help, got back to her feet.

The minute Val looked under control again, Ti'ann's curiosity got the best of her.

Turning back to Krin, Ti'ann asked, "What do you think this is?" She tried to remain calm but excitement leaked through, despite her best efforts. Her stomach tightened as a myriad of theories ran through her mind. When Krin's only response was a shrug, Ti'ann faced Val, intent on questioning her. She stopped, however, when she saw the way Val and James stared at each other, saying nothing. The expressions on their faces were serious and disturbed.

After a few silent minutes, as the tension in the room mounted, James finally shook his head. "It's up to you, Val. If you feel you can trust them…"

Ti'ann frowned, wondering why trust was required, but before she could ask, Val straightened her shoulders and spoke.

"What I'm going to tell you can't leave this tent," she said, focusing first on Krin and Nathan before finally settling her startling green gaze on Ti'ann. "Dr. Jones, this is highly delicate information. If this were to be made public…" She paused, leaving the repercussion of exposure unsaid, the weight of the consequences heavier because of Val's silence. "Can I have your word that you won't reveal anything said here?"

Ti'ann took the request as seriously as it was given. She thought hard about whether or not they'd be able to keep an obviously important secret.

Finally, she said, "I'll give you my word, Val. But—" She held up a hand when the woman would have spoken again. "But there are twenty other people in this camp and I won't be able to vouch for them. Is this secret of yours something that's likely to get out when we dig?"

Val shrugged. "Depends on what we find. I'm not positive what that is." She pointed at the view screen. "I've got my suspicions. My hopes. But until we know whether my suspicions are true or not, I can't allow this information to be made public."

"And if your suspicions are proven true?"

"Then I doubt we'd be able to keep the secret."

"Okay, then." Ti'ann nodded. "For the moment, I think Krin and I will be able to keep your information quiet. And Mr. Longfeather was hired for his discretion." She tried to ignore the way he shifted next to her. She didn't dare look up to see his expression.

Monroe flashed them a look, his gaze turning reflective, but he didn't comment. The rest of the group waited quietly, leaving the final decision with Val.

"Okay. I'll trust you with this, Dr. Jones. I think I can." She paused, her head tilted to one side. "In the Senate debates over the cognizance of Shifters, one of the arguments against Shifter intelligence is that there's never been any evidence of habitations—actual buildings or structures built by Shifters. There's a very good reason for that."

Ti'ann's heart started pounding. She locked gazes with Val and hung on her every word.

"What buildings and structures there were," Val went on, "those that were obvious enough to be discovered by humans, were destroyed. Not all buildings were discovered. Shifter architecture, like Shifter nature, is designed to blend into the environment. They took advantage of their surroundings and developed whole cities that merged flawlessly with those surroundings. But the two biggest cities were destroyed within twenty years of each other."

Shifters built cities.

Ti'ann felt like she'd taken a punch to the stomach at the revelation. She'd never heard rumors of such a thing outside the wild ravings of the tabloids. And no one took those seriously. Even the Shifter support groups didn't back those stories. The realization struck her like a blaster shot—she'd never really believed their anomaly was evidence of Shifter architecture. Now to discover they built *cities*. Whole cities.

"How was this kept secret? How is it possible?" Ti'ann asked.

"When the right people, with enough power and influence, make sure evidence and records are erased, they stay erased," Monroe said. His voice was hard with disgust.

"But after all this time? Surely someone would have uncovered the information by now. All the work the Shifter support groups have put into protecting the species, I can't believe they wouldn't know about this."

Monroe looked decidedly uncomfortable and Ti'ann narrowed her eyes. "Do they know?"

Val ignored her question and continued with the story. "Humans had only settled Narava a few decades earlier. The span of one generation. The presence of Shifters went unnoticed for a long time. When a few curious Shifters inadvertently revealed themselves to humans, the colonists were terrified. Almost immediately, the killing of Shifters was approved, though it wasn't made law for another thirty years. Unfortunately for the human hunters, Shifters were used to being prey and were perfectly capable of evading detection.

"The first city was discovered by accident. The group that stumbled across it was horrified by the reality facing them. If Shifters could build cities then they could also think and reason. If they could think and reason, and because they could hide so well, what was to stop them from wiping out the human population? With that fear motivating them, the hunters moved in with weaponry unlike anything the Shifters had ever seen. They destroyed the city and killed thousands of Shifters."

It was so quiet in the tent, the only sound Ti'ann heard was the quiet whir of the temp regulators.

Val continued. "I'd like to think those humans were ashamed of the carnage and that's why all records of the incident were destroyed. But it's more likely they wanted to prevent the public from becoming aware of Shifter intelligence. Some would say to prevent hysteria." Val shrugged, her opinion of that theory clear.

Ti'ann found herself sitting again but didn't remember dropping back into the chair. She looked around and noticed most of Monroe's people stared at the ground. They probably knew this story as well as Val. Clare was the only one who seemed interested. Her attention was subtle, but intensity underlay her casual curiosity.

"A group was formed to look for more cities," Val continued. "It was made up of those who destroyed the first city as well as others who shared their opinion. The public knew nothing of this…organization. As far as we know, they don't even have a name."

"What happened then?" Ti'ann asked, unable to curb a morbid need to know everything.

"Detector technology didn't exist at the time. Nothing had been found that consistently identified a shape-changed Shifter. The group spent years combing the planet for other cities. Some Shifters were able to disguise their homes further or moved altogether. Some still believed a truce could be negotiated with humans."

"Jesus, Val," Krin said, his voice sharp with shock. "How the hell do you know all this? How could you know what was going on within Shifter communities back then? Hell, Shifters having communities period is a surprise to me."

Nathan leaned close to Ti'ann's ear and whispered, "I'd like to know why you didn't tell me these people were part of a Shifter support group."

The heat from his breath sent chills over her neck and spine. It took a great deal of will power to keep from jumping away from him, or melting into him, despite the underlying threat in his comment.

Ignoring him, she focused on Val but suspected Nathan would demand an explanation from her later.

Val glanced at Nathan and frowned as if considering something.

"As a security person, do you maintain confidentiality of clients after you've finished your job?" she finally asked.

Nathan straightened. "I wouldn't get much future work if I didn't."

"So anything you see and hear while you're working for Dr. Jones and Dr. Freemont will remain confidential?"

"Yes, but I've already guessed you're part of a Shifter support group."

Val actually smiled. "I'd have been very disappointed in your powers of observation if you hadn't figured that out by now, Mr. Longfeather." The woman laughed. "I've revealed much that may or may not come to public attention over the next few months. There's little to no concrete proof of what I say so not many people would believe it. Yet. But there's more to be told, more that may come to light as we investigate this." She gestured at the imaging screen and the current representation of the anomaly. "I need to be sure I can rely on your future discretion."

Ti'ann's excitement over what Val told them, the sheer joy

of possibly discovering a Shifter city was dampened by a slight tingling of unease. What else could Val tell them? What could possibly be more confidential than the information she'd already imparted?

Without meaning to, Ti'ann looked up at Nathan. Strong and solid, his presence was a lot more reassuring than it should have been. All her hurt feelings and discomfort over their past paled compared to the thought of having someone close who could actually protect them all from trouble. She was glad Krin had insisted on calling Nathan in. She was relieved to have him in camp.

Nathan glanced down then, meeting her gaze. She couldn't read anything in his expression. But even without touching her, his stare sent shockwaves of sensation across her skin, raising the memory of his fingertips gliding down her throat, over her collar bone, circling her breast. She swallowed hard, hoping he didn't notice her response, yet unable to look away this time. Her already thumping heartbeat kicked up an extra few beats.

After what felt like an excruciatingly long moment, he turned his attention back to Val, and Ti'ann could breathe again. She hadn't realized she'd been holding her breath.

So much for reassured feelings.

Blinking back a haze of lust and confusion, she forced herself to pay attention to the moment at hand. Now was most definitely not the time to get distracted by Nathan Longfeather.

CHAPTER FOUR

Ti'ann stared at the place where Val had stood a heartbeat earlier, but her mind flinched away from accepting what she saw.

Where a pretty, petit, young woman had once been, now stood an amazing, golden-skinned Shifter.

The Shifter's body was long and smooth, its limbs slender. It didn't have a mouth or any visible ears, but its eyes were large swirls of green and yellow. It tilted its head to one side in a gesture that reminded Ti'ann of the woman Val. A moment passed before her brain recognized the woman and the Shifter were the same being.

Beside her Nathan cursed under his breath. The rest of the tent fell into another heavy silence. She glanced at Krin to see him supporting himself against a table, his eyes wide with shock.

Val's voice disrupted the silence and snapped Ti'ann's attention back to the golden creature. The Shifter still stared at them, but a mouth had formed in its otherwise featureless face.

"This is the real reason we require your secrecy. I can't be sure how the rest of your team will react to a Shifter in their midst. I'll keep up the guise of Val Hyde while I'm here." It moved its gaze to focus on Krin. "To answer your question, I felt it was important to let you know, to establish a level of trust between us."

The Shifter moved its unblinking gaze between Ti'ann, Nathan, and Krin. "I'm what's called a Keeper of the History. We're one of the oldest surviving lines. Our history goes back long before humans settled on this planet and named it Narava. I'm one of the few Keepers to hold information from so long ago."

"That's why it's so important Val's identity remain secret," James said. "If certain parties in the Senate were to discover the existence and identity of Keepers of the History, the Keepers would be immediately targeted for extermination. We're placing a great deal of trust in you at the moment. I hope it's trust well-placed."

"Why?" Ti'ann spoke before she realized she would. Shock still thudded through her. She looked directly at Val when she asked, "Why are you trusting us? We could be anybody. We could be a danger to your entire species."

The mouth in Val's golden face lifted in a grin. "Your nature…emanates from you. I can be fairly certain you're not a danger. At least, you wouldn't aim for our destruction."

"My nature emanates from me?" Curiosity got the better of her again. The conversation fascinated her. With a creature whose intelligence was still being debated! How could anyone who'd met one of these amazing beings think them predatory beasts?

She stopped in mid-thought and paused to consider. She

couldn't doubt Shifter cognizance now, not when Val was standing there destroying any preconceived notions she might have had. But were they predators or prey? Val claimed they were prey. But the ability to shift would be useful to both. Which was more likely? With their intelligence, they'd make deadly predators. That was very reason those original humans were terrified enough to destroy an entire Shifter city. Was there something to their fear? Should she be afraid of Val?

Before she realized what she was doing, she found herself leaning toward Nathan and the security he represented. She gave herself a mental slap and straightened, annoyed that she kept turning to him every time she got nervous. She was not *that* big a ninny, damn it. She'd been standing on her own her entire adult life. She did not need a man who didn't even remember her to keep her safe.

Val interrupted Ti'ann's thoughts. "I'm sure you've heard the reports of our telepathic abilities? That's our primary form of communication. In fact, it took us years, nearly a generation, to learn how to communicate with a mouth and a word-based vocabulary."

"You mean your vocabulary isn't word-based?" Krin moved away from the table and stepped closer to Val.

"Telepathically, words are quite limiting. Our language is… beyond words. It's difficult to explain without showing you. Unfortunately, except for Mr. Longfeather—" everyone followed Val's swirling gaze to look at Nathan, "—none of you have the necessary telepathic trait for me to give you an example. And his talent is limited. Perhaps with training…" Val trailed off, head tilted in consideration.

"Fascinating," Krin said. "So when you say our nature emanates from us, do you mean you're able to read our minds?"

Krin didn't sound nearly as disturbed by the possibility as Ti'ann felt. She'd heard Shifters could communicate telepathically, but it hadn't occurred to her they might be able to read human thoughts. Outside of her own discomfort at the idea, that information further complicated the predator versus prey debate. Being able to hear ones prey would be a huge advantage to a predator. But it would also be useful to a hunted species.

She thought back to the way Monroe and Val had stared quietly at each other and realized he must be able to talk with Val telepathically. It made sense, given his position as the head of the group. Could any of the others talk with her…it…mind to mind?

"We don't read your minds," Val assured Krin. "Not without permission. But as a species, you don't have much control over your thoughts so sometimes they leak out. In any case, we can generally feel your intentions and natures without having to read your minds. I think you would say we 'sense' things."

"It's a bit like empathy," Juanita supplied. "Though not nearly as precise. Shifters can be fooled."

Krin smiled, ignoring Juanita's underlying warning, his eyes wide. "Val, would you mind?" He held out his hand. "I've always wondered what Shifter skin feels like."

Val grinned and stretched out a long hand to him. They linked fingers and Krin laughed. "So smooth."

Ti'ann found herself rising and moving closer to Val, her curiosity getting the best of her. She would have attempted to touch the Shifter, too, if Nathan hadn't held her back with a hand on her arm. His touch shocked her more than the impersonal contact should. She gasped as electricity zinged over her skin, raising the small hairs on the back of her neck. He dropped his hand quickly, breaking contact, but not before she felt her world tremble.

"How do your cells maintain cohesion?" Krin asked, his attention riveted on the Shifter. His comment pulled Ti'ann back to the conversation. "Does it take a great deal of energy to maintain this form? Does changing shape require a lot of energy? How do you eat? What do you eat?"

"Dr. Freemont, I'm sure Val will be happy to answer all your questions about Shifter biology later," James interrupted. "For the moment, we have other issues to deal with."

Val grinned at Krin and shifted back to the petit blond woman while still holding his hand. He gasped but his grin widened.

"I'll be happy to talk with you, Dr. Freemont—"

"Please, call me Krin."

"Krin. But James is right. This thing you and Dr. Jones have discovered is…it may well be a truly significant find to your people and mine."

"You've told us about your cities for a reason," Ti'ann said. "Do you think this is an abandoned Shifter complex? Maybe one sunk during an earthquake?" She felt excitement bubbling up at the prospect. Worry over the predator-prey debate got buried under the possibility of discovery. Then she remembered the new scan. "But how could it have changed? There haven't been any tremors or activity of any kind that might have altered the shape."

"I've a suspicion it's an old Shifter city. But like you, I know that wouldn't explain the change in the structure. Unless it's a living city."

"A living city?" Ti'ann breathed. The possibility was more overwhelming, more awe-inspiring than anything she could have anticipated. She'd hoped their anomaly would be a significant discovery, but this… A city, a living city full of Shifters? If she'd thought discovering a Shifter graveyard was going to draw attention, this news could change…everything. "That deep underground?" she continued. "Is it common for Shifters to build underground?"

"No. An underground city has never been recorded in our history. We typically don't dwell in caves or beneath the soil."

"Typically?" Ti'ann asked.

Something in the way Val said the word made Ti'ann look closer at her…it…

Ti'ann groaned inwardly at having to make the correction again. Shifters were asexual so Val wasn't a he or a she, but she'd met Val Hyde the human woman and, right now, looking at that human woman, Ti'ann found it hard to think of Val as an 'it.'

"I wouldn't want to jump to any conclusions yet, Dr. Jones. I think we'd need to excavate first."

So Val wasn't prepared to claim the anomaly was a living city yet? Ti'ann found the Shifter's hesitance reassuring. She didn't want to leap to false conclusions either. The fact that it might be a city period was overwhelming and exciting enough.

"Would there be a natural entrance, one we could access without having to dig?" Krin asked.

"I don't know. As I said, we don't normally bury our cities," Val answered.

Ti'ann tapped her fingers against her thigh as she considered their options.

A city.

A Shifter city.

Even if it wasn't living, this was an amazing find. Who knew what they might discover inside? Her mind strained against the sheer magnitude.

They'd dig, she decided. How could they not? She briefly

considered calling in an archeologist friend from her undergraduate days but dismissed the idea with an unconscious shake of her head. Until they knew what they had, the less people here the better.

"What is it?"

Nathan's voice made her jump.

"Sorry?"

"You shook your head. What's wrong?" Nathan asked.

"Oh. Nothing. I was deciding whether or not to call in an archeologist friend for the dig but decided against it. We're not sure what we have yet."

"And I'd prefer if no one outside this tent knew what we expected," Val reminded them. "For the moment."

"I'll need to tell my people something. They'll want to know what to look for. And the diggers will need to know what not to cut into."

"Tell them it's a graveyard," Mike said. "That theory should satisfy their curiosity. We can say our natural historian here—" he nodded to Val with a smile, "—was able to pinpoint a rare reference to such things from early colonial times."

"You think they'll buy it, Krin?" Ti'ann turned to face him, watching his expression as he thought.

"I think so. We can put the graveyard forward as the most workable theory." He pushed his hair off his forehead and nodded.

"Okay then," she said. "We'll use that story. Although, Val, if it *is* a city, why is there DNA mixed in with the other elements?"

Val's brow creased. "We'll know more when we've excavate."

Ti'ann frowned at Val's evasive answer. There was something Val wasn't telling them… Something was left unsaid. Ti'ann didn't think it was anything dangerous, or she was sure Val would mention it rather than put Monroe and the others at risk. Ti'ann was determined to excavate the anomaly. But anxiety mixed with her excitement and curiosity. What was Val hiding? What the hell would they find?

CHAPTER FIVE

Tɪ'ᴀɴɴ sᴀᴛ ᴀᴛ ᴛʜᴇ ᴇᴅɢᴇ ᴏғ ᴛʜᴇ ᴄʟɪғғ, sᴛᴀʀɪɴɢ ᴏᴜᴛ ᴏᴠᴇʀ ᴛʜᴇ valley. Lonrach's crescent shape hung just above the horizon and Rupach hadn't risen yet. Darkness enveloped her, leaving the valley floor below invisible. She'd had to get away from the camp and Krin's excitement over Val. Ti'ann found the Shifter fascinating, too. But there were still a lot of unanswered questions. Things had gotten very complicated in the last few hours.

She was truly excited about their discovery and the dig. But she recognized the potential laser cannon they were courting. This discovery could change everything. The problem was, would it force an end to Shifter exterminations or would it cause a resurgence in human fear, re-energizing the anti-Shifter faction?

After that stuff with David Cario, Kira Farseaker, and Commander Ennoren thirteen months ago, she had no idea which way the Naravan people would lean. Thanks to Cario bringing down Ennoren, the leader of the exterminations, more people were sympathetic to the Shifters' plight. Would knowing they built cities increase that sympathy or destroy it?

The sound of crunching sand and rocks caught her attention. She turned and saw Nathan Longfeather step from the shadows of the woods at her back and into the clearing at the cliff's edge.

Ti'ann's heart pounded as he stared at her. She'd avoided him all evening after they'd finished with Val and Monroe. She didn't trust herself around him, not the way she'd reacted in the imaging tent, leaning into him like he was someone she could trust. Worse, she couldn't look at him without visceral images of their nights together overwhelming her good sense. She had to keep reminding herself that he'd forgotten her, that he'd thought so little of their time together he hadn't bothered to remember her. If she didn't keep that in mind, she was going to lose herself in her memories and do something completely humiliating. Like try to remind him who she was.

Fortunately, avoiding him that evening had actually been pretty easy. She even thought she'd be able to survive having him in camp because there was really no reason for them to interact much. And if she didn't have to see him, she didn't have to face her own embarrassment. Or risk making a bigger fool of herself than she had three years ago.

She hadn't counted on him finding her alone at the edge of the valley, star gazing, though.

"Should you be out here alone?" He spoke quietly, an echo of their surroundings. He sauntered closer. Though saunter wasn't enough of a word to describe his fluid, sexy-as-hell movements as he walked to her side.

"There aren't any large predators here to worry about," she assured him, amazed when her voice came out steady and calm. Her heart hammered so fast, she was surprised she could breathe enough to speak at all. Swallowing the rising desire threatening to overwhelm her, she made herself look him in the eyes, or as best she could in the darkness.

"Where's Dr. Freemont? I thought he was with you."

"He went to bed an hour ago." She paused, studying the tense lines of his shoulders in the weak moonlight. "Do you need me for something?"

"Yes. You've hired me to secure this site. I need to be able to account for everyone."

"How can one man account for twenty seven different people spread out over the entire campsite?"

White teeth flashed against his dark skin and her body reminded her how nice those teeth felt scraping across her skin.

"That's all part of the job, Dr. Jones."

He drawled her name, robbing the title of its usual security, making the words Doctor Jones sound sexy, not safe. Combined with thoughts of his mouth on her naked flesh, Ti'ann felt a little trickle of panic creep through her lust. Panic that she wouldn't be able to sit here and have a conversation with him without doing something irrevocably stupid. Like kiss him.

"And one person can keep track of twenty seven people quite easily with the right sensor array," he continued.

"Sensors?"

"They're around the entire perimeter of your camp and dig site. They alert me to movement in or out of the site."

She frowned. "So you knew I was still within the perimeter?"

"I did."

"Then I don't understand why you were looking for me."

Before she could protest, or really think coherently, Nathan sat down on the ground next to her. A spill of pebbles tinkled over the edge of the cliff into the valley.

This close, his scent wrapped around her, drawing her

toward him. The air seemed to thicken, and the semblance of control she'd clung to slipped. She glanced at his mouth then forced herself to turn away and look out over the valley. He was too close now. Holding eye contact was no longer possible if she wanted to think. She was just grateful the dark night hid her expression.

"What do you think of the Shifter group?" he asked.

"What do you mean?" She heard the hoarseness in her tone now, but if she didn't look at him, maybe she could manage the rest of this conversation. Not looking at him didn't disguise how deep and seductive his voice was in the dark, though. More memories played with reality, adding meaning to the timber of his words, putting her back into that suite three years ago. The only light in the dark bedroom filtered in through the open curtains from the university town below. She could still feel the warmth of his breath as he whispered against her shoulder, his chest a solid wall of heat at her back.

"Do you trust them?"

She blinked as his question jerked her back to the conversation. Digging the hand he couldn't see into the rocky ground next to her, feeling it bite into her palm, helped her concentrate on what he said so she could answer. "Not entirely. But I don't distrust them either."

"Meaning?"

"Meaning they have their own reasons for doing what they're doing and those reasons may not always be to my teams' benefit. I know Val is holding something back. But she…it has still given us more information than I expected. Val didn't have to show us its Shifter form or give us the secret of the Keepers of the History. So they're relying on our good intentions as much as we're relying on theirs."

"They divulged a lot of sensitive information for a first meeting. That kind of honesty worries me."

The comment startled a chuckle out of her. "That's your job though, isn't it? You're not supposed to trust people." The brief moment of lightness drained some of her rising tension. She eased her grip on the rocks and flattened her palm against the soil.

"True."

The humor in his voice made her a little giddy again, but she was better able to focus on the moment now. "What do you think they're still hiding?"

"Hard to say. I imagine they have a lot of secrets. But I think they revealed so much to gain your support. If you're on their side, they'll be able to use whatever you find to their benefit in the debates."

"Depends on what we find. This discovery could backfire on them—cause more fear among humans rather than less."

"It might. That's why they need you and Freemont. Your credentials and the way this discovery is presented to the public will go a long way toward how people receive the news."

He shifted, a slight movement, but Ti'ann found herself holding her breath until he settled again. She couldn't take actual physical contact with him, not right now. She was too edgy from the memories assaulting her. She'd never survive the rest of this conversation if he actually touched her.

"I suspect Dr. Freemont is already sympathetic to their cause," he said.

Ti'ann sighed. She suspected so, too. "Even without knowing Shifters were cognizant, Krin's always supported an end to the exterminations."

Silence settled between them for just a moment. An oddly comfortable silence, she noted.

Then she turned to look at Nathan. A mistake—she almost forgot what she wanted to ask—but she needed to see his expression.

"Did you know Shifters were capable of what we saw today? Did you know they were an intelligent species?" He hadn't seemed nearly as overwhelmed by the news as she and Krin.

He shrugged, his gaze fixed over the valley. "I've had my suspicions." He picked up a stone and tossed it out into the darkness.

She heard the chink chink sound as it struck the ground below.

"It was shocking coming face to face with it. I didn't know for sure until today."

"But you weren't completely surprised. Not like me and Krin," she said.

"No."

"Why?"

He stayed silent, not answering her question, not turning his gaze from the valley.

"Sorry. You'd probably have to compromise a former client to answer that question."

His smile flashed in the darkness, her only answer.

She'd forgotten how frustratingly evasive he could be when he didn't want to tell her something.

She looked back out over the valley, appalled by the familiarity of that thought. It implied she knew him. But she didn't know him. Not really. And he didn't even remember her.

"How long have you been interested in paleontology?"

"Why do you ask?" The personal question surprised her.

He shrugged. "Curious. Takes a lot of hard work and study

to do what you do. I just wondered what brought you to this field."

"My dad was a scientist. He got me interested. Paleontology followed my natural curiosity about animals and what life was like on Narava in the millennia before humans settled here." She shifted her position, unfolding her legs so they hung out over the lip of the cliff.

Her heart was still thudding too hard, too loud. His curiosity threw off what little composure she'd gained in the last few minutes. Why would he be interested in what had brought her to her career? She reminded herself he wasn't curious about her in a personal, she's-a-female-he's-a-male sort of a way. He'd no doubt ask Krin these same questions.

Dammit, this was stupid. She was thirty-two years old, for Pete's sake. She hated the way he made her feel—the mixture of need and embarrassment toppling her self-assurance. She resented Nathan opening up her carefully packed box of insecurities again. She knew men didn't generally find her very attractive, and the few who had hadn't stayed interested for long. Her history with men was abysmal; even Krin would admit that. But she'd spent the last three years learning to deal with her reality, and she'd gotten good at it. She'd found a semblance of security and strength in that acceptance. Now Nathan appeared in her life again and blew her surety into tiny bits, making her doubt herself all over again. At least if he remembered her—

Oh no. She stopped mid-thought, almost gasping out loud. If he remembered her, that would be so much worse. Then they'd both have to feel awkward and uncomfortable. He might make excuses and disappearing on her again. Or worse, he might not comment at all. How humiliating.

As she really considered the situation, she realized it was for the best he didn't remember her. To him, she was just the asexual Dr. Jones. So long as one of them kept that in mind, everything would be fine.

The tension through her shoulders eased as she recognized the blessing his lack of memory actually was. She didn't have to be embarrassed in front of him. As far as he was concerned, there was no reason for her to be. Dr. Jones was just another client. She almost smiled in relief.

Now, what would Dr. Jones the scientist do next when talking to someone she wasn't supposed to know?

"HOW LONG HAVE you worked in security?" Her voice was quiet, distant. She pulled her legs up to her chest, wrapped her arms around them and rested her chin on her knees.

He couldn't tell if it was a defensive move, but the pose made her profile appear both innocent and erotic. Sitting here with a contemplative expression, her hair silvery blond in the weak moonlight, it was so easy to see the woman he'd been preoccupied with all these years. And she was even more fascinating than the first time he'd met her, so much more to her than he'd guessed.

He turned to face her, wondering what she was really thinking. She wouldn't look at him.

In a way, he was grateful. Every time she did, his dick reacted. Those big, soulful eyes of hers tugged at him, urging him to touch her. And his willpower wasn't nearly as strong as his sanity required. He swallowed and concentrated on answering her question.

"About thirteen years now."

"Why security?"

"It seemed like a good idea at the time."

He grinned when she frowned and rolled her eyes. Her look

of frustration captivated him. He could sit here and frustrate her all night just to see that expression on her face.

Okay, so he'd rather spend the night satisfying her instead of frustrating her, but this was a close second. And since he couldn't spend the night satisfying her, as long as she was his client, frustrating her would have to do.

"What did you do before going into security work?" Her natural curiosity once again overcame any other emotion.

He'd watched her curiosity dictate her actions all evening. Even when he thought she was shocked speechless, when most people would have concentrated on the political ramifications or dangers they were facing, Dr. Ti'ann Jones had focused on the riddle and the discovery. That kind of natural curiosity told him a lot about her. And promised some very interesting sex.

"This and that," he answered. That look again. He almost chuckled.

"Not much for sharing details, are you Mr. Longfeather?"

"*Mr.* Longfeather?"

"Nathan, then." She shrugged as if it made no difference to her.

He remembered her groaning and panting his name in the dark. Just hearing her say it brought back a rush of sensory memories. He sucked in a breath. He knew he was torturing himself. It wasn't like him, but he couldn't seem to help it.

Any more than he could help easing a little closer to her, near enough that her heat permeated his jacket and warmed his arm. Her scent was elusive, caught and carried on random breezes, drifting around him in tempting eddies. He'd know her scent anywhere.

He let his gaze roam her face and settle on the curve of her neck. What would she do if he leaned in and kissed her, just there? The last time he'd done something like that to her, her reaction had led them into yet another delicious round of sex. For a long moment, he considered the spot just below her ear, the soft skin and her warm smell. Without conscious thought, he leaned a little bit closer.

Warning claxons went off in his head and he straightened away just enough to regain some semblance of control. One touch. All it would take was one touch and he'd be lost.

He couldn't decide if that was bad or not.

When the silence between them stretched too long, he decided to give her curiosity some ease and his errant thoughts something else to focus on. "I started out studying archeology."

Her head snapped around, her eyes wide. "Really? You were an archeologist?"

The impact of her direct gaze was almost as bad for his self control as a touch would have been. And now that she faced him, leaning in to capture that curious mouth of hers would be oh so easy.

He forced himself to answer evenly. "Never made it quite that far," he admitted. "I never finished my degree."

"Why not?"

"I was kicked out."

He didn't think it was possible, but her eyes got wider. "For what?"

"Tomb raiding."

She sat back from him a little, her gaze intense. Then to his utter surprise, she started laughing. The sound went straight to his cock, and it was all he could do not to drag her over his lap and kiss her until she moaned.

He stuffed his hands into his jacket pockets to keep from reaching for her. "What's so funny?"

"Sorry. Sorry. It's just… Krin and I were arguing about hiring you, and I told him we were not going to give you any artifacts from the dig to pay you off. I didn't realize you'd made a career out of just that."

"Ex-career, thank you very much." He scowled which only made her chuckle more. This was the most relaxed she'd been with him since he'd arrived at the camp. He liked her this way. Even if he was having a harder time controlling himself than he'd expected. There was hope for his Dr. Jones yet.

He watched her expression change the instant she realized how at ease she was, watched her face close up and her shoulders hunch a little. To his relief, her eyes still sparkled with that wicked sense of humor. Oh yeah, there was hope.

"So, then, you went from tomb raiding to security work?"

"Something like that."

She nodded and turned back to face the dark valley. From this height, the bottom was fathomless and black. A gentle breeze rustled through the trees, cooling the night until it was almost cold. He didn't notice the chill, and he was dressed for it in a light jacket and long pants, but he did notice when Ti'ann shivered. Her loose fitting t-shirt wasn't nearly thick enough to protect her from the night air. Without hesitation, he slipped out of his jacket and draped it over her shoulders.

Her gasp was quiet, but he caught the telling noise. Because he couldn't resist, any more than he could refuse to take another breath, he slid his fingers across the side of her neck, hooked her braid, and gently pulled it out from beneath his coat. The feel of her silky hair against his palm sent ripples of need through his gut, tightening his stomach muscles. For an instant, he tightened his hold on her braid, considered tugging her closer, losing himself in her lush mouth. She blinked up at him, and his battle with control slipped further beyond his grasp.

It had taken less than a day for her to destroy all his years of self-discipline. And he could tell by the look in her eyes that she wasn't even doing this on purpose. There was no soft smile, no heavy-lidded looks, no teasing touches. Just a solid, steady gaze that did more to seduce him than anything else she could have done in that moment.

"Why did you do that?" she asked, her voice husky.

"What?" Thinking coherently wasn't high on his list of priorities at that moment, not with her so close he could feel the brush of her breath against his mouth.

"Your jacket?"

"You shivered. You're cold."

She shook her head but didn't try to move away from him or take off the jacket. The pulse in her neck pounded visibly. If he pulled her braid just a little, he could move her head back enough to gain access to the skin over her throat, a place he wanted to nibble and kiss more than he wanted his next meal, his next job. Hell, his next breath.

She broke the spell by leaning back. He reluctantly released his hold on her hair.

"We'd better get back to camp," she murmured. "We've got a long day tomorrow."

He didn't want to leave. He wanted to stay in the dark, talking with her, letting her seduce him. But he didn't want to push his luck either. Too much more of this and he would forget the sex had to wait. He was halfway to dragging her back to his ship as it was—after less than a day in her company! Any longer out here on the cliff-side and he'd have to kiss his professional good intentions goodbye.

She started slipping the jacket off her shoulders, but he shook his head. "Keep it. I'll get it back from you tomorrow."

He could see the argument in her expression, in the way she pressed her lips together and narrowed her gaze. To force her hand, he stood up and flicked on the small torch he carried, gesturing with the beam of light back to the woods.

"After you, Dr. Jones."

She scrambled to her feet, holding the jacket around her shoulders with one hand, and followed him into the trees, the light angling along the narrow path. He wasn't going to get much sleep tonight, thinking of her wearing nothing but his jacket. Frustrating. But knowing she had something of his sparked a deep level of primitive satisfaction. He smiled. He was looking forward to the time when they made these fantasies reality.

CHAPTER SIX

HE STUDIED HER FROM THE COVER OF THE TREES. HER GROUP was digging in a new section of the woods. She was the one— the leader. If he followed her, he'd learn everything he needed to, everything Dr. Ripley wanted him to report. She didn't know he was here; she'd never guess.

He silently pursued her as she moved through the trees, then watched her take an airlift to the valley floor. Remaining at the cliff top, he studied her for a while. She was focused on her work, absorbed in her task, staying to herself and not talking with anyone around her. From this height, he couldn't hear her anyway.

He left her for a short time and went to investigate the others. He recognized Monroe. His instructions were to watch him, too. He took note of the people with the historian, their names when he heard them, what they looked like, and their conversation.

He memorized and recorded what he could. Some of the words didn't make sense. He knew he was supposed to understand language, recognize the words being used. But he couldn't fully comprehend some of them. Part of him insisted words limited speech. The pictures and feelings in his mind seemed a more thorough way to communicate. And yet another part of him knew words.

It didn't matter that he couldn't understand everything. He was to record and inform. They'd tell him what to do next.

He scanned the area for any of the ones he was allowed to kill. They wanted him to kill Shifters, to practice. But he couldn't find any in camp.

He paused over one human. She was small and fair. She seemed familiar. Had he seen her before? At the lab? No, that wasn't right. He watched her for an hour. Something… He'd have to keep an eye on her. He could almost hear her even when she wasn't speaking. That was important for some reason. He couldn't understand why, but it was.

When Monroe and the small one did nothing more than stare at the digging, he decided to go back to the first one. The one he needed to learn more about. She was in charge. She was the one he needed to study. He hesitated over leaving the small one, but his instructions urged him to his task.

He stopped at the top of the cliff again to watch her, still bent to her work. Closer, he thought. He needed to be closer.

TI'ANN LOOKED up when she heard footsteps. She squinted into the bright sunlight beyond the shade of the canvas tarp covering her dig area, vaguely wondering what she'd done with her eye-shades. She'd been deep in thought, her concentration turned to things other than chipping away the bits of hard earth encasing a handful of little mammal-like bones. The new excavation occupied some of her thoughts. But mostly, she'd been thinking about the man walking toward her.

"Is something wrong?" She scuttled to her feet and wiped dirt-covered hands along her thighs, leaving purple streaks on her tan pants.

Her heart started thumping hard, like she'd been running. Their time on the cliff last night had left her reeling and more off balance than ever. So much so, she wasn't even sure how to talk with him right now. What should she say? Should she ask him about last night? Bring up the fact that, for just a moment, she could swear he was going to kiss her? Or would that only reveal her own desires? Would he tell her she'd imagined things and leave her more embarrassed than she already was?

At the least, she should offer to return his jacket.

She was humiliated by the fact that she'd slept in it, surrounding herself with his scent. Dreamed restless, sweaty dreams of having him in her bed again. In her. She woke that morning aching with need, angry that she couldn't control her desire for Nathan. Yet she'd still pulled the jacket up to her face and breathed in deeply before getting out of bed.

If she brought up the garment, she was terrified he'd see her guilt and guess what she'd done. Though why she thought he'd care, she didn't know.

Over the course of the morning, as she chiseled carefully at the dirt, she convinced herself she'd imagined the way he'd leaned into her last night, the way his gaze kept dropping to her mouth and neck. And when he'd pulled her braid out from under the jacket, he was just him being polite. He hadn't meant anything by it.

The idea that maybe he had been coming on to her left her both shamefully excited and heart-wrenchingly devastated. Devastated because he didn't remember her. Which meant he probably slept with the women he worked for all the time. She wasn't significant to him now and definitely hadn't been three years ago. She was just another in a long line of conquests.

"Nothing's wrong. I'm just checking the site," Nathan said, nodding at her work. "That takes more patience than I think I have left."

Ti'ann forced herself to sound steady and professional. "Would you like to give it a try? We could always use another volunteer." Her voice came out a little breathy, but she hadn't squeaked or wobbled, so she counted that as a mark in her favor. She might be crumbling and weak inside, but Nathan didn't need to know. She tried not to think about how hard it would be to concentrate if he took her up on her offer.

She gazed past him. The sun beat down onto the valley floor, waves of heat shimmering in the distance. The tarp offered protection from the sun but not from the heat. Looking back at Nathan, she noticed sweat already beading on his neck and forehead. If he helped on the dig, he'd only get sweatier, and that made her start thinking sweaty thoughts.

He chuckled. "I think I'll stick to what I do best, Dr. Jones."

Given the direction of her thoughts, she had to bite back a groan at his potential double meaning.

To pull her mind out of Nathan's pants, she switched to the other topic that had preoccupied her all morning. "How's the excavation going?" She stepped away from him and sat on a boulder still mostly in the shade.

"Fine, as far as I can tell. The diggers are doing a lot of sporadic cursing when the Excavation Digger Unit encounters a blip. But I think they're on schedule."

She restlessly bounced her foot. "I almost can't stand to be down here. I know it doesn't make sense, but I want to hover over the diggers' shoulders until they break through." She stared up at the valley wall opposite and smiled. "The thrill of discovery I suppose. I'd like to be the first to see what there is to see."

"Every scientist does. Why don't you go up to the site?"

"Because I'm of more use down here. They'll call when it's time." She felt a little dancing in her belly at the thought. The anomaly was almost enough of a distraction to keep her mind off Nathan. Her foot bounced faster.

"You're really excited about this discovery, aren't you? No matter what it means."

She glanced up at him, her foot going still. "Of course. Now that you know as much as you do, aren't you curious?"

"Yeah," he admitted with a shrug. "I'm curious. But not excited."

"Curious but not excited?" She stared at him. How could he not be excited? They might be teetering on the edge of making history.

A tumble of rocks skittered down the valley wall at her back. She glanced over her shoulder to see a blackbird landing on a ledge about a meter up the wall. It squawked at them then started grooming its feathers. When she turned back, Nathan had moved to her side and sat down on the sunbaked ground next to her. He was too close now, making her nerves jump. Her foot started bouncing again. Remembering the feel of his hand on her braid last night made her thighs clench, and it took all her willpower just to stay seated. Though she wasn't sure what she wanted more, to run away or climb onto his lap. Either would be bad.

"I'm not excited," he said, cutting into her thoughts, "because one way or another, this is going to bring attention, probably a lot of unwanted attention, to your dig. Dr. Freemont was right to call me in. You'll need the security. As soon as the news breaks, I'll have to call in more people. This may turn into a long term job."

She sucked in her bottom lip. "Sounds expensive." She felt a little ridiculous for keeping the information about their dig from him yesterday. He knew as much as she and Krin did now. And he'd been right. Knowing everything meant he could plan and strategize better. Her only excuse was that she'd been hurt and surprised by seeing him again after all this time. She hadn't been thinking logically. Her emotions had gotten the better of her, and she'd allowed pride to speak for her. She was just grateful he wasn't holding that over her now. She wasn't sure she could take an "I told you so" from Nathan at this point.

"We'll worry about the money later," he said. "The important thing now is to make sure you and your team don't get caught in the middle of a planet-wide civil war."

"Civil war? You're exaggerating a bit, don't you think?" She knew this could change everything in the debates, one way or another. But war?

"Maybe. Maybe not. The Shifters are a volatile subject."

That was true enough. She braced her foot against the bolder to still her restless movements. To her surprise, Nathan lurched forward and caught her ankle. She barely had time to gasp before he jerked away from her, holding something in his hand. He tossed it across the valley, cursing under his breath.

"What was it?" Her nerves zinged from the brief contact with him.

She watched as the little black shape he'd thrown out into the sunlight unfolded and scurried away. The stinging horns on its small head twitched then flattened back against its scaled body. "Oh, a Scurian bug. They're not poisonous."

"I know. But their sting is painful and annoying. I didn't think you'd want it slowing you down."

She glanced at him then looked back across the valley floor at the bug. "Thanks." Good thing she already had a red face from the heat, because she was sure he'd consider her blush excessive given the simple gesture. Her pounding pulse from such quick skin to skin contact would probably be viewed as excessive, too. How did he do this to her without any effort at all? It wasn't fair that he could control her body with a simple touch, when he didn't even know who she was!

As she watched, the blackbird swooped down over the Scurian bug, claws extended. It overshot its target and the bug darted off in the opposite direction, taking refuge under a boulder. With a screech of defeat, the blackbird took to the air, spiraling up to the top of the valley.

"He doesn't sound happy about missing his dinner." Nathan chuckled.

Her skin tingled at the sound. "I'm sure the bug doesn't mind not being dinner."

"True." Leaning back on his hands, he tilted his face up to the sun.

She tried ignoring the beauty of his profile, tried not to notice the silky lengths of black hair falling into the purple dust, or the way his position exposed the strong column of his neck. A bead of sweat ran down into the hollow of his throat. That should not be sexy, she told herself. Sweating male flesh should not make you forget who you are. But it did. All she could think about was tracing her tongue over his neck, kissing the hollow of his throat. Climbing over the top of him and rubbing her aching breasts against his solid, hard chest, grinding herself against his erection until he groaned. She imagined his big hands gripping her waist, his mouth capturing hers… She practically tasted him as their tongues tangled.

Three year old memories got overwhelmed by current

fantasies. New things she wanted to do to him, places she wanted to touch and kiss and explore.

She told herself to look away. There were other people in the valley. She couldn't afford to embarrass herself in front of the students and volunteers. But she continued to stare.

The muscles in his forearms flexed as he balanced on his palms, drawing her attention to their strength, and then to his very capable hands and perfectly shaped fingers. He had great hands, and he knew exactly how and where to touch her body to make her scream. Tension gathered low in her abdomen as she imagined his fingers trailing down her stomach. Followed by his lips.

Stop! She had to quit fantasizing about him this way. She'd only end up hurting more. Did he realize she reacted to him every time he was near her? Would he care if he knew?

She cleared her throat. It didn't matter, either way. She had more important things to worry about right now. "I should get back to work." *Work, Dr. Jones. That's what you need. More work.*

He rolled his head to look at her, sending more of his long hair spilling back over one shoulder. "Are you working to a deadline on this dig?"

She'd have been suspicious of the comment—was he making fun of her discomfort?—if he hadn't spoken with such genuine curiosity. "Not exactly. The early winter floods will force us out of the valley in another two months, but the fossils will still be here six months after that when the water recedes. The problem is we've only got enough money to fund us until the floods. When that's up, we'll have to have something to show for our time here if we want to get more money to come back."

"I'm sure you'll have more than enough." He nodded toward the top of the valley.

"Hmm. But whether the museum will thank us or curse us for this discovery depends on what we find." She felt the nervous energy working its way back down to her foot so she stood and returned to her abandoned bones.

"Do you think it's some sort of city like Val described?"

She shrugged as she knelt, picked up her brush, and began the careful removal of chiseled debris from around the bones. A little more work and she'd be able to extract the fossils, secure them in a magnetically cushioned jacket, then label and pack them in an environmentally sealed container for storage and transport back to the museum lab. The focus her work required would hopefully keep her mind off other things.

"If I think about it too much," she said, "I get carried away with what it could be. We'll know soon enough."

He grunted as he got to his feet. A moment later, she felt the press of cool metal against her shoulder.

"You look like you could use a drink," he said as he motioned her to take the temperature-controlled flask.

With a grateful sigh she gulped down a few mouthfuls of water. "Thanks. I didn't realize how thirsty I was." She handed the flask back, careful not to touch his hand when he took it from her fingers.

"Don't you keep water down here with you?"

"There're a couple of flasks around here somewhere. I think they're with Glen." She nodded toward another area shaded by a canvas tarp and surrounded by marker pins where two of the graduate students were hunched over their respective work.

The blackbird picked that moment to return, landing on its ledge again. This time it started picking at the rocks and sparse plants sticking out from cracks in the valley wall.

"Why don't you have a flask of your own?"

"Hmm?" Nathan's voice broke into her distracted observations of the bird. "Oh. If I get thirsty I just go get one of theirs."

"You'll give yourself heatstroke if you don't drink enough."

He sounded like Krin. "I'm fine. Thanks for the water."

"Here." He handed the flask back to her. "Keep it. I'll get another."

"I'm all right. Really. You don't have to do that."

"Yes, I do." He walked away without taking the flask from her outstretched hand.

"Okay. Maybe he's worse than Krin." The bird answered her with a screech.

She looked at the flask. It was the jacket all over again. Now she'd have two things to return to him. Excuses to see him that she didn't need. The fact that she'd conveniently forgotten to mention returning his jacket wasn't lost on her. A silly part of her wanted to keep that small piece of him. But forcing him to ask for it back would only embarrass her more. She'd return flask and jacket this evening. How to do that without the entire camp knowing about it was another worry.

With a grunt of irritation, she threw herself back into her work in an effort to forget Nathan, the damned flask, and pretty much everything else going on around her.

She'd just finished labeling and transferring the newly freed fossils when Krin came trotting down the valley toward her.

"We may have a problem," he said without preamble.

"The excavation? Is the EDU malfunctioning?"

"No. At least not any more than usual. But I've called a stop for the evening. They're seven meters down. They can finish the last three tomorrow."

Ti'ann looked around and for the first time realized the entire afternoon had slipped away without her noticing. The sun was low, filling the valley with shadows. She shivered as sweat cooled on her back. She'd been so absorbed she forgot to eat lunch. Something she had no intention of telling Krin. He'd immediately start trying to force food down her throat before he explained their possible problem.

"So what's happening?"

"We've just got word from Gremblewreath. There's a group of government officials there making inquiries into our dig. They claim to be part of an inspection group checking all scientific study sites throughout Narava. Have you heard of them? Did the museum message you about this?"

"No. And no one else I've talked to in the last month has mentioned a planet-wide inspection. That's the kind of thing *someone* would talk about. Just coincidence we're the first site they're checking?"

"Right. Coincidence."

"Who sent word?"

"Friend of Devin's who's working as a façade designer in Gremblewreath. I think Devin asked her to watch out for me."

"Devin is going to be a very good husband." She smiled but couldn't hold the expression as concern trickled into her bloodstream. "Is this group on their way down here?"

"As far as Willa could tell, they're planning the site inspection tomorrow after they've finished collecting information."

"The new excavation?"

Krin shook his head. "I think we should keep it quiet if we can."

"But if they're really government inspectors, we should cooperate."

"And if they're not? Can we risk exposing the new site before we know what we've found?"

She blew out a breath. "No. No, we can't. But someone in the group is bound to talk."

"We'll spread the word tonight. Mention we're afraid they'll leak the information before we get a chance to analyze and publish the data. Most of the group is used to keeping new discoveries quiet. Competitive field, Naravan paleontology." He grinned a little, but his gaze was serious.

She pursed her lips and stared at the dirt between her feet. The sun was low enough that there wasn't much shade left under the tarp. Little specks of sand winked purple in the waning light.

"Something's likely to slip," she said. "I doubt we'll be able to keep it a complete secret. But a Shifter graveyard shouldn't spark off too many warning signals with the government." Krin's look said different. She sighed. "Have you told Nathan yet?"

"No. I thought you might want to tell him."

"Me? Why me?" Her voice actually squeaked. Damn.

Krin raised an eyebrow. "I thought you were talking with him."

"Not if I can avoid it," she mumbled. But when his eyes narrowed, she quickly said, "He's come to talk to me a couple of times so of course I've talked back. But aren't you supposed to be dealing with him?"

"Ti'ann, what's with the panic? You've talked to him once you can talk to him again. You don't have this much trouble talking to Monroe or Warez."

Because I've never slept with Monroe or Warez, she wanted to scream.

Krin must have read something in her expression, damn him, because he suddenly grinned.

"Stop smiling," she snapped.

"Has he hit on you?"

"No! Of course not. Why would he?" That episode on the cliff last night had been perfectly innocent. She was sure of it. He was just being a nice guy. Like with the flask today. She'd imagined the heat in his eyes and the way his gaze dropped to her mouth. Nothing personal. Also, nothing Krin needed to know about.

"Maybe he's got a soft spot for brainy women in baggy clothes," Krin said with a shrug. "How do I know? I don't see why he wouldn't. Unless he's gay."

"He's not gay."

"So sure?"

"Aren't you?"

"Yeah, I know he's not gay. More's the pity." Krin sighed.

"Krin!" She was almost as shocked as she sounded. "What would Devin say?"

"To keep my eyes in my head." He laughed. "Hey, just because I'm in love doesn't mean I can't appreciate another handsome man. Devin would probably drool over him, too."

She laughed even as she felt her cheeks heating. Talking to Krin about Nathan was not helping her. If only the man was gay! She thought about that a moment and changed her mind. If he were, she'd have never had those soul-rending few days with him. Even now, even faced with the reality of knowing that time hadn't been important enough to him to remember, she didn't have a single regret.

"So, you'll talk with him?" Krin nudged her with his elbow, forcing her to look at him.

"All right. Fine. Though I don't know why you care so much."

"I just want you to get it through your thick head that you

don't have to be scared of him or intimidated by him. You are not a mouse!"

"Damn straight," she said, straightening her shoulders. "I'm probably more like a wombok, since they're bigger than mice."

He groaned. "Ti'ann. What am I going to do with you?"

"Love me?"

He smiled and put his arm around her shoulders. "Besides that?"

"You can ask me to stand up for you at your wedding."

"I already thought you knew that was your job. You don't expect me to make it through the ceremony without you?" His eyes widened in panic only partly feigned.

She chuckled. "Wouldn't dream of it."

CHAPTER SEVEN

Ti'ann finished the last few details of storing her newest animal skeleton and sealed over her grid. She had to get something to eat before she talked with Nathan. She was starving now that she realized she'd missed lunch. Of course she should eat first.

She wasn't stalling.

She was being practical.

Ti'ann kept telling herself that all the way up to the campsite, while she stored the little skeleton and then headed toward the canteen. She kept telling herself she wasn't trying to avoid him right up to the point she bumped into him while trying to avoid him.

"Oh. Hi. Nathan. I was just looking for you." She thought the lie would be well-lost in her stuttering. She was wrong.

"Really?"

His sarcasm didn't help her nerves. She glowered at him, but he didn't seem the least fazed.

"Krin got word earlier today from Gremblewreath," she

said. So there. She really was looking for him. She flinched inwardly at the childishness of her thoughts. Bad enough to be intimidated by the man. Now she was reverting to infantile behavior.

"What sort of news?" His gaze narrowed as he studied her.

"There's a government inspection group making inquiries into our dig. They're supposed to be inspecting all scientific research sites on Narava. But no one we know has heard of them."

"Your site has the dubious honor of being first? That's very coincidental."

"That's what we thought. They'll be here sometime tomorrow. We're going to keep the basis for the new dig quiet."

"Will the rest of your group go along with that?"

"They should. We're used to keeping new findings close to our chest before publication."

"And Monroe's group?"

"Given who they really are, I'd say they'll keep the secret out of habit."

He nodded, his gaze turning inward as he thought. She glanced away, knowing to stare too long at his face was a hazard worse than Scurian bugs. Her gaze settled on the canteen and she caught a whiff of something that smelled marvelous. Her mouth started to water. She really needed to eat. Soon.

"Will this government group know about Monroe being here?"

She whipped her head back to face him and dizziness washed over her. She blinked back spots of color and grabbed the nearest solid thing to keep steady. When her vision cleared, she realized the nearest solid thing was Nathan.

"Sorry," she mumbled. She jerked her hand away, but not before her skin started to sizzle.

"You all right?" He clenched her shoulder, shocking her into looking up at him. He was scowling. "You didn't drink enough today did you?"

"It's not that. I'm fine. Just a little dizzy spell. I need to eat is all." She tried pulling out of his grasp without being too obvious. She couldn't stand having him touch her because once he did she didn't want him to stop. Unfortunately, he was intent on keeping hold of her shoulder. She'd only end up hurting herself if she tried twisting away. But the contact was driving her nuts.

"When was the last time you ate?"

She tried tugging away again, but his fingers clenched tighter.

"Breakfast, okay! Will you let me go?"

He released her shoulder only to grab her hand. He turned and pulled her toward the canteen tent. "You need to eat."

"Yes. That's what I just said. In fact, I was on my way to the canteen when you stopped me."

"I thought you said you were looking for me."

Ti'ann cringed. Shit. Now he remembered things. "I was going to eat first then come find you. So you can let go now. I promise to eat."

"I'll believe that when I see you swallow."

"Nathan, I'm perfectly capable of feeding myself."

"Then why didn't you?"

"I was concentrating. I forgot. I don't usually forget. I usually eat like a goat." She felt like she was explaining her actions to an angry parent. Nathan was definitely worse than Krin.

He pushed her through the open tent flaps into the canteen. At this time of night, the place was nearly full. All faces looked up when they entered. Her cheeks got so hot, she was sure they were glowing. She tried freeing herself from Nathan again but the effort was wasted.

He tugged her to the nearest empty bench and pushed her down. "Sit. I'll be right back."

She sat without comment and swallowed around the lump in her throat.

First, he doesn't remember her, then he thinks she's an invalid that needs tending. Next, he'd assign her her own personal watchdog. With her luck, he would be that watchdog.

Ti'ann tried not to notice the sly looks of the people in the tent, but she felt like crawling under the table to hide.

Krin sidled up to the bench and scooted her over so he could sit.

"What was all that about?" he asked quietly, watching as Nathan filled a tray of food from the auto-cooker units.

"I was telling him about the inspectors and I got a little dizzy."

Krin looked at her sharply. "You forgot to eat lunch again, didn't you?"

"Hey, you make it sound like I do that all the time!"

"You do."

Nathan returned to the table with a tray overflowing with so much food there was no way she'd be able to eat a third of it.

"I didn't really mean I eat as much as a goat," she said, staring as he plopped the tray down in front of her.

"Some of it's for me. Eat."

The order made her spine straighten.

Before she could object, Krin echoed Nathan. "Eat."

She raised her brows at her friend. "How old do I look to you?"

"Old enough to feed yourself. Eat."

She scowled, but since she was starving, she dug into the food. If that's what it took to get them to shut up, she'd eat.

Nathan took a seat across from her and pulled a plate off the tray. It was piled almost as high as hers with slices of spiced meat, vegetables, and two thick chunks of brown bread.

Krin picked a piece of spiced meat off her plate and said, "Did she tell you the news?"

They spoke quietly so the people sitting at the opposite end of the bench wouldn't hear. The rest of camp would know soon enough but there was no reason to start the questions rolling before everyone was informed.

Nathan grunted. "Have you talked to anyone else yet?"

"Not yet. After dinner." Krin stole another piece of meat off Ti'ann's plate. She smacked at his hand, and he grinned at her, unrepentant.

"I'll want to be there, hear what you advise them to say," Nathan said.

"Any extra security precautions?" Krin asked.

"I'll set up more monitors so we can keep track of anyone getting near the new excavation site. You may want to secure your molecular imaging files. I'll set up a monitor on that tent as well."

"Do you think they'll single out Monroe's group for questioning?" Ti'ann murmured after swallowing a lump of food.

"Probably. If they do, it'll confirm your suspicions. How long will they stay?" Nathan asked Krin, but he kept a close eye on her.

She had trouble swallowing under his scrutiny.

"Don't know. My friend in Gremblewreath didn't hear. She did say the techs tending their lift-car mentioned they were carrying some crates of equipment and luggage, so they may be planning to stay awhile."

"Damn," she cursed around a mouth full of food. Swallowing hard, she continued. "That's gonna put a major time delay on the new excavation. I don't want to work on it while we've got strangers here, but we're so close to breaking through."

"I know," Krin said with a sigh. "What can we do? If we continue digging, they'll want to see what we find."

"What reason will you give for holding off on the site? They're going to notice the new dig even if someone in the group doesn't mention it."

She and Krin looked at each other and shrugged. "Equipment problems?" she said. "EDU malfunctioning, maybe."

"And we're waiting on a part delivery from Gremblewreath," Krin finished, grinning. "An ingenious idea, Dr. Jones."

"They didn't give me that Ph.D. for nothing." She chuckled and shoveled in another forkful of food.

"They'll be able to check on any order you've sent to Gremblewreath for parts."

Nathan sounded annoyed. Ti'ann faced him but his head was bent over his food so she couldn't see his expression.

"They can check all they want," she told the top of his head. "We did call in an order for a spare part for the EDU last week. We're still waiting on it. Glen Thompson, our grad student, and Krin rigged the unit so it'd continue working."

"How'd you rig it?" Nathan looked up.

None of the annoyance she'd heard in his voice showed in his face.

Krin chuckled. "I've done some tinkering with machines, and Glen was repairing industrial equipment for years before starting his Ph.D. We've managed quite a few repairs on the EDU. It does need the new part to regulate the output rate, but in the meantime, we can still use the unit. Anyone who knows anything about EDU's will recognize the importance of the part we've ordered. Anyone who doesn't wouldn't know the difference anyway."

"And your diggers won't mind?"

"Not having to deal with the unit for a few days? No, they won't mind. They need to de-stress anyway." Krin laughed and snatched a piece of sponge cake off her tray.

Because she was watching, she saw Nathan scowl. Now what was that about? Didn't he believe Krin?

"You'll see when we tell them tonight," she said. "They'll be happy to take a few days away from the EDU."

"I'm sure they will," he said, his tone neutral.

Weird. She hazarded a closer look at him. If he proved to be this moody all the time, maybe she wouldn't have to be intimidated by him. Maybe he was too weird to worry about.

He turned suddenly and caught her gaze, his look so intense it nearly stole her breath. Okay, so weird or not, he was still intimidated. At that moment, she felt like a cornered marri-mite staring down the steely gaze of a snake. A very sexy snake. She lowered her eyes first and concentrated on her food, but eating wasn't easy.

She finished her dinner while Nathan and Krin talked about the types of video and audio monitoring equipment to be used and where the micro-monitors would be placed.

When she couldn't manage any more food, she took a deep breath and patted her stomach. "Much better," she sighed, grinning at Krin.

"Good. You need to stop forgetting about lunch. You'll make yourself sick."

"You said you don't usually forget to eat," Nathan said, his voice quiet.

"I don't." She put her hands up before either one could say another word. This was ridiculous. "And even if I did, I'm a grown woman and I can take care of myself, thank you both very much. I don't need two more fathers. The one I already have is more than enough. Now, if you'll excuse me, I have some reading to finish."

As she stood to go, she said to Krin, "Can you arrange to get everyone together in about an hour? We'll go over all this stuff then."

"Yeah, no problem. The Meeting tent or around the fire?" He grinned, cutting through her annoyance with his waggling eyebrows.

"'Round the fire. You bring the beer."

NATHAN WATCHED her leave the canteen with a mixture of frustration and possessiveness. Frustration he was getting used to around Dr. Ti'ann Jones. He couldn't be near her without wanting to touch her, and when he touched her it screwed him up for hours afterward. His blood still hummed from holding her arm on the way to the canteen. Those brief moments on the cliff last night kept rising up to torture him—what might have happened if not for his damned rule about clients. Even her baggy clothes were becoming a turn on, because all he could think about was the delicious curves hiding under all that material. And how much fun it was going to be to strip her out of her clothes.

Wanting her was one thing. The possessiveness he'd been feeling, however, bothered him. He didn't have any claim on her. She wasn't even acknowledging their past—a fact he was almost grateful for because if she started walking through those memories with him, client or no, he'd be inside her within minutes. But none of that gave him an exclusive claim on her. She wasn't his. Hell, until Ti'ann, he'd never want any woman enough to be possessive. But Ti'ann was different.

He was actually jealous of Freemont. Which was ridiculous. The man was engaged to an artist—a male artist. So there was no logical reason for him to be jealous of their relationship. Just because she relaxed with Freemont in a way she didn't with him. Just because she smiled freely with Krin. None of that should have bothered Nathan.

Except she'd relaxed with Nathan once before, three years ago. And the result had been volcanoes and fireworks.

Maybe she had someone in her life and that's why she was acting so differently with him now. He hadn't thought of that. He hadn't checked on any other current relationships beyond the people in the camp.

Fuck. After the way he'd been fantasizing about her, his sanity would not do well knowing she was seeing another man. He wasn't sure he'd be able to allow that as an obstacle. Not only was he going to break his rule about fucking a client soon if he wasn't careful, he was very tempted to break his general guide of not sleeping with other men's women. That was usually more trouble than it was worth. He'd never knowingly done it before. With Ti'ann, he'd take the risk. If she'd be willing.

Even worse than all this, though, was he found himself worrying about her. He hated that she wasn't taking care of herself. He hated that these government inspectors might mean trouble for her.

"Fuck," he muttered under his breath.

He stood, snatching up Ti'ann's tray and his plate. "Where's this meeting?" he asked Krin, moving toward the recycling unit.

The young man stared at him with piercing eyes that saw too much.

"Just beyond the camp boundaries to the southwest in that huge clearing. You know the one?"

"Yeah." Nathan needed to get out from under Freemont's scrutiny before he gave himself away. He was afraid he already had. But how much trouble would the young scientist cause him? Would he try to keep Ti'ann away from him? Nathan ground his teeth together. He could try. But it wouldn't be a healthy thing to do.

To calm his irritation, he took a long walk around the camp-site, checking on his perimeter sensors. After the meeting, he'd set up the micro-monitors around the new dig site and the imaging tent. Then maybe he'd hike up to the other side of the valley, just to make sure there was nothing unusual over there. The exercise would do him good. Maybe he'd even be able to sleep tonight.

He knelt down by one of the perimeter sensors hidden in the base of a tree. It had registered a very minor blip earlier in the day just after they'd started the new excavation. Opening the well-disguised console panel, he keyed in his personal code and checked the current efficiency level of the sensor. Working fine. According to the sensor readout, both the one in the console and the one sent to his pocket-comm, the thing passing had only weighed about fifteen kilos. Too light to be a human. Magori-fox probably.

Angling his torch to the ground, he hunted around the area until he found the tell-tale paw prints not far from the tree, barely visible in the dry dirt. Magori-foxes weren't dangerous to humans but they were territorial. If one of the team stumbled across the animal's den and it happened to have young, the hapless person could be in some trouble.

He glanced at his watch. Still plenty of time before the meeting. He tracked the fox through the trees, following its furtive path as it angled closer to the main camp. Strange. They usually avoided humans, and Ti'ann's team had been here long enough to alert any fox in the area. He tracked the prints to within a few hundred meters of the new excavation site.

And then the tracks stopped.

Vanished. He searched for a hole or the opening of its den. No evidence of the animal turning around. Magori-foxes didn't climb trees, but he checked that, too. He hunted for anything he might have missed, anything that indicated where it had gone. Even in the dark, he could usually track animal movements. But he found nothing.

The fox had just disappeared.

He glanced at his watch. He'd have to leave now if he wanted to make the meeting. Frowning, he looked around the area one last time. Overhead a blackbird landed and cawed at him. He stared at the bird, his eyes narrowed. Why was a blackbird flying around in the dark? Could it be...? That would explain the fox's disappearance.

Very quietly, he said, "If that's you Val, you'd better speak up now."

The bird squawked at him, fluffed its feathers, and settled down on the tree branch.

You're letting this assignment get to you, Nate old boy, he thought with a groan.

He touched the metal tags hanging on a leather thong around his neck, fingering them through the material of his shirt where they rested coolly against his chest. He'd been avoiding the Shifter issue for most of his adult life, ever since his mother's cousin, Thomas Farseaker, had tried to talk him into joining the fight at eighteen. He hadn't wanted anything to do with it. There was no money in it. And he'd been eager for adventure. He wasn't going to give that up just to fight a battle he didn't necessarily believe in, one that wouldn't help him take care of his mother. Now, here he was caught up in the middle of the Shifter fight anyway. And this time he knew, really knew the truth about Shifter intelligence.

He glanced at the fox prints then back up at the bird. Its black eyes were closed. A gentle breeze blowing through the upper branches ruffled its feathers in the growing evening gloom. With a grunt, he headed back toward the main camp and the clearing where the meeting would take place. There was a logical explanation. He'd find it soon enough.

NATHAN LONGFEATHER HAD SPOKEN to the bird as if the bird was the small woman. That wasn't within normal parameters for human behavior. Either the man was insane, a word he was still having trouble translating, or Nathan Longfeather thought the bird was really Val. That would mean Val was not a human woman.

Shifter.

He was supposed to recognize Shifters. How could he not have known before? He'd have to question Dr. Ripley when he returned from this assignment.

Despite his confusion, he was sure of one thing. He was supposed to kill Shifters. That's what he did. That's what they wanted him to do.

He needed the practice.

CHAPTER EIGHT

Terrance Samuels, in his guise as Chief Scientific Inspector, studied the two scientists facing him. Dr. Ti'ann Jones and Dr. Krin Freemont. Typical. Ordinary enough. He scanned the site, looking at the people walking around until he spotted Monroe. He made sure not to focus on anyone in particular, while tracking Monroe's movements from the corner of his eye.

"I appreciate your cooperation, doctors," he said. Both doctors leaned toward him. He spoke quietly under normal circumstances. But when he wanted to intimidate, he spoke softly on purpose. It forced people to listen very closely to everything he said.

"We'll be happy to show you around. Is there anything in particular you'd like to see or will a general tour do?" Dr. Freemont asked.

"A general tour of the site will be sufficient for now. We'll have more specific questions and concerns to broach later."

As they began walking, Dr. Freemont attempted conversation. "What would your particular specialty be, Dr. Samuels?"

Terrance smiled. "Physics." He knew from the reports that neither of them had studied much in the field of physics and would only have superficial knowledge, so it was a safe enough specialty for him to claim. Senator Johnson's obsequious aide, Barbury, had insisted he claim a scientific background, as if Samuels wouldn't have thought of that himself. He hated dealing with idiots. But so was the job. There had to be buffers between himself and the senator.

"Are there many physics researchers on your tour of the planet?" Dr. Freemont questioned.

"Several. There's a team in the Sapphire Range that will be our next stop. They're studying the nuclear fission processes in a lava-well beneath the permafrost."

"Sounds like it will make a good paper."

"A few I'd say."

He kept a serious but pleasant expression on his face as they toured the facilities. He left the detailed recording of the site to the other two members of his team. He was here to take in a general overview and assess the attitudes of doctors Freemont and Jones.

He noticed Jones spoke very little, leaving the small talk to Freemont. But when they came to any of the groups working on bones or casts of plant species, Jones commented or added direction where needed.

Neither discussed the new excavation they'd begun, though he knew about it. Neither discussed the presence of Monroe and his team. The subjects weren't avoided in an obvious manner, but they weren't brought forward into the conversation either.

After they'd covered most of the valley, he decided to push a little.

"I understand you've a historian and a few other scientists newly arrived on site. Will this added expense eat into your budget?"

"We've made allowances." Dr. Freemont again.

"We'll need to review your books."

"You'll have to discuss that with the museum, I'm afraid. We're not at liberty to open the accounting records without written authorization. I'm sure you understand. As soon as the museum has forwarded the correct documentation, we'll be more than happy to provide you with a full accounting."

"Do you anticipate any reluctance on the part of the museum?"

"I wouldn't think so," Dr. Freemont said.

"Dr. Jones?" Terrance watched her profile carefully.

"I can't imagine why they might object." She answered in a pleasant, professional voice. But did he imagine the bite?

"Good. I see you're using some of the more mundane methods for excavating."

"We find these methods both efficient and cost effective if we have the hands to implement them. Fortunately, we've three volunteers on this dig who're more than willing to get their hands dirty." She smiled as she mentioned the volunteers. Then she turned away, letting her gaze run over the valley.

He saw the pride in her expression. But there was something else there. A watchfulness. He'd have to study her more before he could decide the cause.

"I'd like to meet these new researchers you've called in. Would you mind explaining their presence?" He looked at a small electronic notepad, though he knew the cover careers of Monroe's team by memory. "Monroe, a historian, Warez, a geophysicist, Baker, a molecular scientist, and Hyde, a natural historian." He looked up. "And Clare O'Malley, affiliation unknown."

"Clare is a friend of Mike Warez," Dr. Jones supplied.

"Ah. And the others?" His questions were delivered in a tone of voice gauged to be interested but not obvious, insistent yet pleasant.

"We may have discovered something quite interesting," Dr. Freemont said. "We'll know more when we've been able to excavate further. The malfunctioning of our only EDU has set us back a few days, but as you can see, we've got plenty of work to keep us busy."

"What do you think you've found?" He focused the weight of his gaze on Freemont.

"We just don't know yet. We were hoping the combined expertise of the others would help us figure it out before we began excavating. Unfortunately, we're all confounded, so we have to dig."

"Have you forwarded the files onto your lab for analysis?"

"Not yet."

He watched Freemont closely, impressed when he didn't flinch or look away. He suspected Jones wouldn't stand up to the scrutiny as well and so switched his focus to her. "Why not?"

"Logistics and jealousy," she said with a chuckle. "Logistically, by the time the lab has fully analyzed our data, we can have the site partially excavated, even with the EDU repairs required. We were too jealous of our potential discovery to share the glory with the lab."

Her grin was genuine. That part of the story had to be true. As far as it went. She was a competitive scientist; there was no doubt about that. She wanted her place in the history annals. He could use that. But she was hiding something. She wasn't as good at lying as Freemont. The younger man had a poker face that would take a lot of work to crack.

Jones, on the other hand, could be manipulated. He was sure of it. He smiled at her, his most charming smile. The first he'd allowed. Her slight blush confirmed his guess. Good. Two things he'd be able to use to get information.

"Worried the lab would steal your glory, Dr. Jones? I doubt they could."

Her blush deepened, but she met his eyes squarely when she said, "Paleontology is a competitive field on Narava. I wouldn't want to take any chances."

"Of course not. What made you decide to bring in Monroe in particular? You haven't worked with him before." The quick change of tone and subject made her blink. He thought he'd caught her out when Freemont stepped closer and opened his mouth.

To his surprise, she answered. "No, we haven't worked with any of Monroe's team before. He was recommended by a colleague whose opinion I trusted."

"Dr. Craynmar."

Her eyes narrowed. "Yes. You know her?"

"Her laboratory in Aveon is one of our future stops." He thought of mentioning Dr. Craynmar's friendship with one of Jones' few ex-lovers but decided against it. While it might fluster her, it would also reveal his specific interest in this site and these people. How and why would a scientific inspector know about their personal relationships? No, better to let her think his knowledge was purely professional.

"We contacted her," Dr. Jones said, "when we knew we needed fresh eyes but didn't want to risk bringing in anyone that might try to beat us to publication. Dr. Craynmar was kind enough to direct us to Monroe because she could vouch for his scientific integrity."

"And you trust the integrity of his entire team? Even Ms. O'Malley?"

"Clare isn't a scientist. She's just Warez's friend. Monroe wouldn't have allowed her along if she was a risk. I trust Dr. Craynmar's recommendation of Monroe so I trust his judgment on this issue."

"Would it surprise you to know Ms. O'Malley is a currently unemployed striper from the Docks?"

"Yes. But it's not really my business as long as it doesn't affect my work." She didn't try to hide her surprise, but she didn't flinch from the news either.

Hmm. He started doubting his first impression of Dr. Jones. That didn't often happen. His gaze narrowed. He shouldn't underestimate the good doctor. She had a sharp mind. That was more than obvious from her records. Trying to trip her up verbally would only spark her suspicions. No. He'd have to charm her.

He sighed inwardly. She wasn't his type. Not in the least. She was too plain and earthy. He preferred women who looked after themselves and attempted to flatter whatever assets they had. Dr. Jones didn't bother much with her own femininity. Maybe with better clothing and a little make-up, she could be attractive. If she let her hair down, he imagined it would look quite sexy. He did love long hair. But as she was… Ah well. He'd done worse things than flatter a lonely woman to get information.

He smoothed a hand down the front of his linen suit. "Perhaps we could see the data for the new excavation now."

"Of course." Freemont extended a hand for the three of them to precede him and Jones back to the lifts.

Terrance took in the valley one last time as they rose to the cliff above. Everything looked perfectly ordinary. The only nervousness seemed the typical unease of people being inspected. Nothing to indicate collusion with the Shifter terrorists. At least not from most of the team. He didn't discount either Freemont or Jones however. They were careful in what they revealed. Even more careful than would be expected of scientists jealously guarding their finds. The way they revealed information was almost rehearsed. But he was confident he'd flush out their loyalties and get the information he needed. He always did.

TI'ANN WAS SWEATING by the time they reached the imaging tent. The day was hot and there was no breeze under the trees so their campsite was muggy and uncomfortable. But she wasn't sweating because of the weather.

So far, they'd revealed just enough truth that she hadn't had to out-and-out lie. She was fine so long as she kept to mostly truths. Unfortunately, they were really going to have to lie now, and she only hoped she could pull it off.

Terrance Samuels was very smooth and incredibly handsome. Even in the middle of this wilderness, his tailored clothing spoke of wealth and meticulous style. His manners were impeccable, his intelligence unquestionable. He wasn't exceptionally tall, only a little taller than her five foot ten, but his charm gave him a kind of stature that went beyond size. And when he smiled, a flash of white teeth against chocolate skin, he was the kind of man that normally sent her scurrying into a hole of insecurity.

But she wasn't reacting that way to Dr. Samuels. There was something in his dark eyes, something hard and merciless that made her nervous for reasons that had nothing to do with his looks.

The other two men with him had been introduced only as Mr. Griffith and Mr. Temore. If she'd thought it biologically possible, she'd have laid money on Mr. Temore being part Binnean. He was huge, wide and covered in dark hair. He even had green eyes, so characteristic of Binneans. The only thing he was missing was the long nose and brown skin. He was white beneath his thick layer of dark hair, and his nose was snubbed. Mr. Griffith was also huge, but his body hair was normal and his beard was neatly trimmed. They both looked like well-dressed thugs to her. But maybe that was the point.

Nathan appeared as they reached the imaging tent. To Ti'ann, he looked cool, collected, professional, and distant. The perfect hired gun. He nodded to the group in the same professional manner and waited to be introduced. She left the introductions to Krin, afraid her voice would give away how much seeing Nathan affected her. Weirdly, despite the fact that he made her heart pound a little faster, she also felt safer with him here.

"You were so jealous of your discovery you felt the need to hire security, Dr. Jones?" Dr. Samuels asked, pulling her away from thoughts of Nathan. "I'm surprised. That isn't usually part of a paleontology dig."

The inspector turned his charming smile on her, but for reasons she couldn't fathom, she felt nothing when she looked at him. Not even insecurity.

"No," she said, "but under the circumstances, we both felt it a wise idea."

"And what circumstances would those be?"

"Our vicinity to Gremblewreath. The vandalism problems we had a week ago. I assumed you knew." She couldn't believe the lie came out so easily. She was so surprised by her own skill, she nearly gave herself away by showing her pleasure at having pulled it off.

"We weren't aware of any complaints being filed with the Gremblewreath authorities." Samuels' voice had hardened just a little, a better matched to his eyes.

"We didn't report the incidents," Krin put in.

He was definitely a better liar so Ti'ann let him finish this concoction.

"Not officially. Unofficially, the local Guards told us there was nothing they could do. Rather than have valuable samples destroyed by free-riders, we choose our own security option. The museum was happy to cooperate with the decision. As I'm sure they'll tell you."

Ti'ann tried not to react to the last two statements. The museum's cooperation was a new element to the lie, and she had no idea if it would stand up to a check. She must have reacted in some way because Samuels turned his full attention back on her. He didn't ask her anything, but he studied her face so closely she was sure he saw her every thought. To her surprise, Nathan came to her rescue.

"I was recommended to Dr. Freemont by a mutual friend on the museum's Board of Directors. Mr. Johan Alexander. He'll be happy to answer any questions you have about my job here."

Mr. Johan Alexander? Who the hell was Johan Alexander? Granted, she didn't know all the members of the board because it was a huge group of mainly silent members. But for them not to have told her this…

She glanced at Krin to see him wiping surprise from his own expression. So. This was one of Nathan's inventions. Well, if the fabrication stood up, she didn't care whose idea it was, so long as it got Samuels and his team off her site.

They stepped into the imaging tent and Krin gave Samuels and his men an overview of the equipment and its functions. He showed them one of the last scans they'd done in the valley and how the images as well as the molecular content of the samples allowed them to pinpoint dig sites which would be productive.

"And the scan for this most recent dig?"

To Ti'ann, Samuels sounded efficient and impersonal, no more interested in this particular aspect of the inspection than any other. But she felt the hairs on the back of her neck raise, and her heart started thumping. God, she hoped Krin could pull this off because they'd never believe her.

Krin groaned and shook his head. "I'm afraid we're having trouble with those files." He pulled up the scan they'd done just before they'd detected the anomaly. "See here, this line, and those distortions. The ground up here is more difficult for the imaging equipment to accurately scan. You can see there's a lot of uncertainty about the elements. This was taken just before we scanned the new excavation site. We got one good reading of the new site, and the rest have been like this, full of questions and distortions due to the terrain."

"And the one good scan?"

"Was accidentally erased by one of the grad students."

The anguish and frustration in Krin's voice sounded so authentic Ti'ann had to remind herself they hadn't really lost the files.

"Glen was trying to adjust the imager to compensate for the difficulties—he worked on industrial machines before he started his doctorate thesis. He tweaked something and it erased the one good file. We'd already decided to dig so it's only a temporary glitch. We'll try to get a better scan from a different angle when we've broken through more of the overburden."

"I see."

She'd been impressed with Krin's story, so well told and believable. But Samuels' reaction wasn't reassuring. She couldn't tell if he believed them or not. She wanted to say something, add something that would help, but thanks to a lot of practice over the years, she managed to keep her mouth shut. The only thing she'd do if she tried to talk now was to screw up a perfectly good piece of fiction.

"That must have been disappointing, Dr. Jones."

Damn, Samuels was going to make her talk anyway. She could do this, she could. "It was. It'll leave a minor hole in the methods of the final write up. But these things happen in the field. My own fault for not having a backup." Shit! She wasn't supposed to mention back-ups unless he did.

"Do you have back-ups of other files?"

"Most," Krin answered smoothly. "In that cabinet." He nodded to the locked safe where they kept their files. "We tend to back-up once every two days. Unfortunately, we didn't before Glen got started. Bad choice, but it's easy to say that in hindsight."

"Of course." Samuels was studying the safe, his eyes narrowed.

She didn't trust that look. An ordinary inspector wouldn't be so interested in their file safe.

She darted a nervous glance at Nathan, but he didn't seem the least bit flustered. Well, why should he? This was his job not his life. Her career, her passion, her purpose for being were on the line here.

He caught her gaze, suddenly, without moving his head. She wondered if he saw her fear. She swallowed and tried to smile. He winked then focused on Samuels again.

She blinked and her nerves tingling for reasons that had nothing to do with the inspectors.

"I wonder if I could speak with some of your people now," Samuels said with another of those patented charming smiles.

"Of course. Will we start with the graduate students?"

He paused, considered, then said, "That would be fine."

Samuels, his men and Krin walked out of the tent. She was a step behind Krin when Nathan stopped her with a brief touch on her shoulder. "The monitors in here overlook the safe. We'll know if they try to access it."

She glanced back at him. "Thanks. Do you think they'll search anywhere else?"

He smiled, but it wasn't a pleasant expression. "They might try."

She swallowed hard. She'd never seen that look in his eyes before—hard, determined, and ready for battle. She walked out of the tent with a shiver tingling down her back. She hadn't really grasped until that moment that Nathan Longfeather was a very dangerous man.

CHAPTER NINE

<hr>

TI'ANN FELT LIKE THE DAY DRAGGED ON FOREVER. BY EVENING, she was covered in purple dust and sweating like she'd walked into a sauna. And yet somehow Samuels had managed to get through the entire day immaculate and without breaking a sweat. That just wasn't fair.

When she finally reached the privacy of her tent, she stood in the center of the small space feeling like gravity had suddenly increased. She needed food, and she needed a shower. After a few mind numbing minutes, she finally decided on a cool shower so she could relax and enjoy her dinner. She changed from her dusty boots into a pair of plastic sandals and grabbed a clean t-shirt and pants.

At the tent flap, she glanced back at her bed. Nathan's jacket was still there, hiding under her blanket so Krin wouldn't notice if he came into her tent. She really needed to return that to Nathan. The fact that she'd "forgotten" last night and had slept with the garment again was not good. And having his scent next to her all night had *not* helped her sleep. With a sigh, she headed toward the shower huts. Shower then food. After that, she could deal with…everything else.

Most of the camp was in the canteen for dinner so she didn't even have to wait in a line. She slipped her change of clothes into the dry cupboard of one of the two shower huts then stepped inside, clothes and all, keyed in her personal code on the protected panel and waited for the door to seal shut. The water flow started thirty seconds after the door sealed, soaking her. She stripped when the timed burst shut off and tossed her now wet clothes into the small washer unit at one side of the hut to finish cleaning. Then she worked her wet hair out of the braid and soaped every part of her she could reach before the water blasted her again.

When the shower water shut off and the dryers clicked on, she ran her fingers through her hair and started to braid it back up while the dryer did its work. With a great deal of effort, she kept her mind off the tense afternoon, having Samuels inspect the new dig, then question Monroe. She'd wanted to scream just to break the tension during that conversation. Now she was too tired to think about it. Instead, she wallowed in the feeling of being clean.

The warm air clicked off and Ti'ann slipped her clean clothes out of the cupboard and dressed, then pulled her freshly washed clothes from the unit and unsealed the door. She'd barely stepped out of the hut when Terrance Samuels blocked her path. She let out an involuntary yelp and almost dropped her clothes.

"Sorry to startle you, Dr. Jones. Ti'ann."

That bloody smile was back. Too charming by half, and it got on her nerves. "It's quite all right, Dr. Samuels." She made a point of remaining formal with him. "I wasn't expecting anyone to be around. Have you finished dinner already?"

"Actually, I was hoping you'd join me."

"Oh." She could feel the sweat starting to trickle down her back again. She'd felt so clean just a minute ago. "Of course. If you'll just give me a few minutes to drop these back to my tent."

"I'll walk with you." He extended an arm gesturing for her to lead the way.

Her mind froze as they walked. Any small talk she might have been capable of vanished into the ether. She'd never been great at small talk and social situations anyway. Since Samuels wasn't supposed to be there on a social visit, she felt even more awkward.

She went into her tent and let the flap dropped behind her, leaving Samuels outside. Taking the moment of solitude to collect her courage, she set her clothes on her bed, patted the place where Nathan's jacket hid, took a deep breath, and prepared to face the smile again. Terrance was waiting patiently, his hands clasped in front of him. He would have looked perfectly at ease, and incredibly sexy, if it weren't for his eyes. The hardness and focus there belied his casual, charming air.

She tried on a smile and said, "Shall we? I'm starving."

He chuckled and allowed her to lead the way again. It took a great deal of effort not to show how antsy she was as they walked to the canteen. She kept her hands away from her braid and even managed to avoid fidgeting, but it was a close thing.

She forced out a polite, "How did you find the day?"

"Very informative. Thank you. You and Dr. Freemont have been very cooperative."

"Will you need to stay on site for long?" Did that sound too desperate?

"Another day or two and our inspection should be complete. Don't worry, Ti'ann, we've come prepared. We won't inconvenience you."

"No inconvenience at all, doctor." She really wished he'd stop using her first name.

"You've been studying paleontology since your second year of college. How do you find the subject?"

"Fascinating. Otherwise, I'd do something else."

He chuckled again. "Not many people would consider changing occupations after establishing themselves in one."

She shrugged. "I wouldn't have gone into paleontology to begin with if I hadn't liked it."

"Would you still have chosen a science?"

"Yes." Hell. She did not want to have this conversation. She squirmed inside. The subject was too personal, and she didn't even like Terrance Samuels, nonetheless want to get personal with him. This would be easier if he did all the talking. She didn't care how much personal information he revealed. "How about you, doctor? How long have you been a physicist?"

"Nearly fifteen years." He raised a hand and smiled. "I know. I don't look old enough, but I started young."

She tried to smile but her face felt stiff. "And what's your specialty?"

"Chemical physics. I ran a lab until about four years ago when I was recruited for this job."

Then silence. "Do you enjoy your work now?" Jesus, why couldn't he just ramble? Krin always told her men loved to talk about themselves, but Samuels didn't expand more than a sentence or two before falling quite again. How was she going to eat dinner like this?

When they entered the canteen, the tent fell momentarily silent. Conversations started again, but they were muted.

Terrance gestured her to a seat and walked to the auto-cookers. Instead of sitting and letting him bring her food, she followed to get her own plate. It barely ruffled his composure.

She sighed. This was both embarrassing and awkward. She looked around, hoping Krin was somewhere nearby, ready to rescue her, but he wasn't. In fact, as she watched, the tent started to quietly clear out. Anyone with enough of his or her meal eaten made an excuse to leave. By the time they sat down, only about seven people were left in the tent. She couldn't blame them. She didn't want to be there either.

"So tell me," Terrance said as he settled a napkin in his lap, "what brought you to this part of Narava?"

She raised an eyebrow at his table manners. They didn't tend to go in for formality out here. "We conducted surveys of a few likely sites. The geologics of this area indicated two layers of rock ideal for preserving bones, one at just over 50,000 years ago and another at 5 million years ago. A preliminary MEI scan indicated the presence of enough fossil material to make this site exciting." She shoveled food into her mouth so she could stop talking.

She glanced up, noticed the precision with which he ate, and almost choked. Every piece of food was cut smoothly to a perfect, mouth-sized bite. His knife and fork were set precisely on the plate when he wasn't eating, and he wiped the corners of his mouth every time he set his utensils down. There was a time in her life when even if his looks hadn't intimidated her, his table manners would. She'd been taught well by her parents and had eaten at enough formal dinners to be comfortable with that sort of polite behavior now. But it seemed so out of place in their little canteen in the middle of nowhere Narava.

"Are you bothered that Monroe and a few of his people have

to leave before you've broken ground on the new site?" Samuels asked.

She blinked at the change of subject and it took her mind a minute to catch up. Swallowing a tingle of panic, she said, "There's no point in them hanging around while the EDU is down. And they have business to attend to. They'll be back soon enough." There, that sounded about right. Exactly the thing she'd say if all this was true.

Monroe had concocted a story to get Val away from the site because, while none of the three inspectors carried visible detectors, they were government officials—legitimately or otherwise. Monroe didn't want to risk Val being discovered. Ti'ann couldn't blame him. She'd be happy to have the Shifter out of camp, too.

"The fact that Clare O'Malley is staying isn't...concerning?" Samuels asked, studying her closely.

"Why would it be?" Ti'ann forced a half-laugh. "Besides, Mike is also staying. Why would Clare leave?"

"Of course."

With smooth confidence, he returned to small talk about her career path. He kept the conversation going through the meal, suave and never awkward, never seeming aware of her discomfort. He called her Ti'ann instead of Dr. Jones despite her insistent use of his title. And he never corrected her or requested that she call him Terrance. She managed to swallow her dinner, but it settled like a hard lump in her stomach. The sooner she could get away from him, without appearing rude, the better. From the corner of her eye, she could see the remaining people quietly clearing the canteen. She kept wondering where Krin was. Why wasn't he here to take his share of this discomfort?

After she'd eaten as much as she could stomach and he'd finished his meal, she decided enough was enough.

"Thank you for a lovely dinner, doctor," she said with what she hoped passed as a smile. "If you'll excuse me, I have a few things to do before I get to sleep. We have an early start in the morning."

He stood when she did and walked with her to the recycling unit then out of the canteen. "It was a pleasure talking with you, Ti'ann. I hope we'll get the chance to talk more before my work here is finished." He took hold of her hand, squeezing it affectionately, refusing to release her until she'd agreed to speak with him again soon.

Her legs felt like jelly as she walked away, knowing he was still watching her. She wanted to rub her hand over her shirt to wipe away his touch but managed to contain the impulse until she'd rounded the imaging tent out of his line of sight. She rubbed her hand down her thigh then ducked inside to make sure all was as it should be. Nothing looked disturbed. The safe appeared secure.

The safe was safe. She wanted to laugh at that thought and wondered if maybe she wasn't going just a little hysterical. She'd never been hysterical before. Getting hysterical was the sort of thing pretty, delicate women did. But she felt a definite need to squirm and wash her hands and laugh all at the same time.

She thought she should go find Nathan. He'd calm her worries. Her next thought was just how insane that would be. Nathan most definitely didn't have a *calming* effect on her. If anything, being around him would send her completely over the edge. She didn't trust herself with him. And in her present state, she was very likely to embarrass herself if she tried talking to him.

Though, she had a good excuse. She could return his jacket.

But then she wouldn't have it in bed with her tonight, surrounding her with his scent.

She groaned out loud and sat down in one of the seats by the imaging console. She was acting like a moron. Nathan wasn't any safer to her peace of mind than Samuels.

Though, having Nathan around today had been very reassuring.

Damn but she wanted the man again. Still. He was the sexiest man she'd ever known and too many memories had assaulted her since his arrival, too many remembered sensations and longings.

Was it really so bad that he didn't remember her? Did she care at this stage?

So their previous meeting hadn't been as spectacular to him as it had been for her. It's not like she was in love with him. Yes, it was humiliating to be forgotten. But Nathan had managed to give her the best sex of her life. She'd never felt so free and uninhibited before. And right now, on the verge of emotional breakdown from the stress of Samuels and the new find, the thought of throwing herself back into that blissful release appealed a lot.

She *had* thought maybe, just maybe he'd been hitting on her that night on the cliff. Though she'd convinced herself she'd imagined the heat between them, it was possible he was interested in her, even if he didn't realize they'd met before.

Was she brave enough to try seducing him? Would he laugh at her?

She flexed and fisted her hands against her thighs. Her two previous lovers had both laughed at her for attempting to act sexy. And as Krin had so accurately pointed out, Nathan was no staid professor or hotshot digger. True, Nathan hadn't laughed at her three years ago. But two nights of freedom couldn't overcome a lifetime of uncertainty. Odds were in favor of him dismissing her attempts at seduction because she'd experienced that more often than anything else with men.

With everything else going on, she wasn't sure she'd be able to stand having Nathan turn her down. There was only so much mortification her pride could take.

She stood up and squared her shoulders. Tonight, pride would win out over bravery. She was just too tired to be courageous.

But as she stepped out of the imaging tent, she stepped into Nathan.

"Oh." She came up short and the abrupt move made her stumble back a step. He caught her shoulders and held her until she'd righted herself. "Sorry about that. I wasn't expecting to see you." She forced herself to look at him. Heat warmed her cheeks and her stomach flipped a giddy little summersault. Thoughts of pride and bravery vanished under awareness of the feel of his hands on her shoulders.

He kept his hands on her long enough to thrill her, fill her with a hope that she hated as much as savored. Then he released her and took a step back.

"I didn't mean to startle you," he said, his voice quiet. "I wanted to make sure you were okay."

She narrowed her gaze. "What do you mean?"

"Dinner with Samuels." His brows lowered and his mouth turned down in the barest of frowns. "His idea?"

"Ah." So he wasn't talking about her rapid heartbeat and breathless state. He hadn't noticed she was on the verge of throwing herself at him. "Yes, dinner was his idea. And it was the most uncomfortable meal I've ever been forced to eat." Even trying to eat under Nathan's scrutiny last night had been easier to take. "But I'm fine."

"What did he want?"

"To chat, I guess. I don't know. I was too anxious to be away from him to care what he wanted."

Nathan stared at her for a very long moment, but she couldn't decipher his mood at all. What was he thinking? Did he have any idea what she'd been thinking just moments ago?

Would he laugh at her if she kissed him?

"Be careful around him," Nathan finally said. "I've check into him a little more. There's not much there. But he's definitely not here for the reasons he claims."

She glanced around and lowered her voice. "He's…?"

"Back at his ship. And being watched."

She wanted to ask more questions but also didn't want to be overheard. She asked the one thing she really wanted to know. "He's not a legitimate inspector then? You're sure. He's here because of the dig."

Nathan nodded.

They'd known from the beginning the coincidence was too much. Having Nathan confirm their suspicions made her stomach sore. She glanced back at the imaging tent.

"Everything is going to be fine, Ti'ann," Nathan murmured.

She faced him again and realized he was standing closer, so near she wouldn't have to lean very far to fall against him. She flicked her tongue out to wet her dry lips and watched his gaze drop to her mouth. Oh god. That look. So hot, so erotic. So well remembered.

No longer able to resist, she did lean toward him, watching his mouth as intently as he'd stared at hers. That mouth had done the most wonderful things to her body three years ago. And she wanted…*needed* to have him again. Even if she was making a fool of herself, even though he didn't remember her, even if this would hurt her even more when it ended. She didn't care. He was heat, strength, comfort and freedom all combined into the sexiest, most handsome man she'd ever known. Walking away from this chance would be worse than taking it.

She met his gaze, so dark in the moonlight, and started going to him.

"Goodnight, Dr. Jones." Ti'ann jolted out of the moment, straightening just in time to see two of the volunteers passing on their way to their tent. One of the girls, Micca, waved as they walked by.

She nodded to them, unable to speak around the thumping of her heartbeat. When the young women were out of sight, she faced Nathan again. He was farther away now. And his expression was unreadable again.

"Get some sleep," he murmured. "I'll make sure Samuels doesn't do any harm tonight."

She wanted to say something, anything. But her mind was a blank. He walked away well before it started working again.

Standing in the chilly night air, she realized once again she'd forgotten to mention his jacket. Which meant the garment was waiting for her in her tent, filling her bed with the smell of him.

She'd return the jacket tomorrow.

VAL WAS NEVER ALONE. He'd been watching all day. The others were always with it—watching, protecting. He found the situation frustrating, but he had patience. He could bide his time.

He overheard their plans for three of them, including the Shifter, to return to Capital. He couldn't take the chance the

Shifter would escape him and not return. He was supposed to kill Shifters. It was part of his purpose.

Though he wasn't supposed to take action without permission, he felt sure Dr. Ripley would approve his efforts to keep the Shifter here so he could kill it. Their ship was easy enough to disable. It would take time for them to repair. And when they did, he would disable it again.

He felt secure enough in his efforts to keep Val from leaving that he broke from the hunt to check on the others who'd arrived. He'd been warned about them just yesterday. He wasn't to interfere. They weren't even to know he was here. That suited him. He didn't like the look of them.

They made her nervous. Ti'ann Jones. The leader. He saw it in her when she thought no one was looking. He sensed it, almost smell it, like she gave off an odor of fear. It was hard to believe they didn't notice too. But they weren't as skilled as he was.

He considered her fear. Of course they would make her nervous. They were a danger to her. She'd be afraid of him, too, if he let her see him. But that wasn't his job. He was here to collect information. Information the inspectors wouldn't be able to get. They weren't good enough.

He'd seen the big male—Nathan Longfeather—setting up the monitors and surveillance equipment. Nathan Longfeather would make sure Terrance Samuels and the other two didn't find anything important. He kept a close watch on them and ensured they were never where they might discover something. Nathan Longfeather's human form handicapped him, but he was thorough and efficient at his task. E appreciated efficiency and thoroughness.

He paused.

E. That's what Dr. Ripley called him. Project E. He was the fifth one, the successful one. He was the best.

He hadn't considered a name for himself before. E. They all had names. Even the Shifter was called by a name. He was better than they were. He should have a name. E.

E was a good name.

CHAPTER TEN

NATHAN WATCHED SAMUELS AND HIS TWO MEN AS THEY CREPT through the quiet campsite to the imaging tent. Samuels had waited until several hours after midnight to begin this search, well past the time ordinary "inspectors" would be up and around. Their furtive approached confirmed this wasn't a part of the "inspection" they wanted Ti'ann and Krin to know about.

There was nothing there for them to find. He, Krin and Ti'ann had made sure of that. But Nathan kept an eye on Samuels anyway. He wasn't about to lose track of the man's movements.

Not now. Not after the trouble Monroe was having with his ship. Nathan's suspicions had been peaked when Warez explained the type of malfunction. It sounded a lot like the ship had been sabotaged. A very sophisticated job, too. He didn't tell Warez or the others because without looking for himself, he couldn't be sure—that was the beauty of the work he suspected done. To anyone who didn't know better, it looked like an ordinary glitch. But Monroe and his people didn't need to know about Nathan's concerns yet. They were already too tense and having difficulty disguising that nervousness.

The only people who might want to sabotage Monroe's ship were currently digging around the imaging tent. So Nathan kept to the shadows and monitored them. He couldn't afford to rely on the sensors he'd set up, and while a shield secured his own ship, the other vehicles were vulnerable to tampering.

When the three had split up earlier that evening, Krin was a willing recruit to follow the other two men while Nathan stayed with Samuels—the dangerous one. Unfortunately for his peace of mind, Samuels' next move had made it tough for Nathan to stick to the shadows.

Seeing the man chatting up Ti'ann had pissed Nathan off, and not just because he knew Samuels was picking on the more vulnerable doctor to interrogate.

He hadn't been able to get close enough to overhear most of their conversation. When he had, it only confirmed what Samuels' body language had indicated. He wasn't escorting Ti'ann to dinner to discuss the inspection.

Samuels was just lucky Ti'ann had been so uncomfortable with him or he'd be dead already. It gave Nathan a little twinge thinking Ti'ann hadn't exactly been comfortable with *him* at first either. But he liked to think that was for other reasons. At least, he hoped it was.

When he'd tracked Ti'ann to the imaging tent after dinner, he hadn't been thinking clearly. What he should have been doing at that moment was following Samuels. Instead, he hunted down Ti'ann to check on her. To confirm she hadn't actually enjoyed dinner with Samuels.

And then he'd nearly thrown everything to the wind and kissed her. She'd looked up at him with those big gray eyes, her desire plain, and he hadn't been strong enough to leave her alone. If not for the disruption of passing people, he'd have swept her back inside the imaging tent and started on all those things he'd been fantasizing about for days.

The distraction had been enough to save him, though. He couldn't afford to indulge his mad need for her tonight, this obsession with her he couldn't seem to shake. Not while Samuels and his men were in camp. Not while Nathan was the only one around who could keep Ti'ann safe. However, protecting her meant keeping his hands to himself for a little while longer.

But only until he could call in backup. As he watched the inspectors give up their fruitless search and leave the imaging tent, he considered the short list of people he could trust at his back.

He followed Samuels and his men as they made their way to the new excavation site, remaining silent and carefully out of sight. Alex used to top the short list of trusted associates, but he was no good to Nathan anymore since he was officially out of the mercenary game. Who else could he trust as much as he'd trusted his former partner? He smiled in the darkness when he realized he had the perfect candidate, someone who would definitely not have to worry about hormone distraction out here. Though he'd probably spend the whole time cursing the heat. Nathan almost laughed. Yeah, BinRal would be perfect for the job.

TI'ANN WOKE with a crick in her neck and an ache in her gut. Anxiety didn't usually hit her until she was fully awake and out of the warm cocoon of her bed. But then, she usually didn't lay awake most of the night worrying about landing in the middle of a political mess that could cost lives. Even when she did manage to sleep, she'd dreamt of Shifter deaths, standing before the High Court defending her actions, and watching Nathan get shot. Even the scent of Nathan's jacket next to her hadn't helped. In fact, in some ways, it had made her dreams worse, more vivid. She would have happily taken the more erotic dreams from previous nights.

Last night was not one of her best nights.

Rubbing her eyes, she crawled out from beneath the covers and checked to make sure the file disk from the new dig was still safely in its spot under her cot. Having that in her tent hadn't helped. She kept worrying Samuels would sneak in and find it. Fortunately, she got to pass the disk off to Krin tonight. His turn to lose sleep.

After splashing cold water on her face, she risked a glance in the little mirror hanging above the washbasin. She shouldn't have. The circles under her eyes looked like bruises. She sighed. Lovely. Maybe she could hide the circles behind sunshades. If she could remember where she'd left her shades.

The morning was crisp and already edging toward warm when she walked out of her tent and headed toward Krin's, overly conscious of the disk hidden in the pocket of her trousers.

Her partner was already awake, dressed and combing through a journal when she walked in. "How'd you sleep?"

"All right." He looked up. "You obviously didn't. You okay? Maybe you should try and sleep some more."

She raised a hand. "If I couldn't sleep last night, I won't be able to sleep this morning. Better to get to work anyway. Do you know where my sunshades are?"

He rolled his eyes, dropped his reader on his cot and went to his clothing trunk. "You really need to keep better track of these. I found them at the primary site yesterday," he commented as he pulled her shades from inside.

"Yeah, yeah. Thanks." She grinned and held them up in front of her face. "Are they dark enough to hide the circles?"

"No."

She scowled at his response then shrugged. He was probably right. Nodding to her hip, she said, "Think my pocket is safe?"

His frown was not reassuring. "You can't even remember your shades when you get focused on your work. You sure your pocket is a good idea? What if it falls out and you don't notice? Or worse, Samuels is right there when it happens and he does notice?"

"You have a better idea? Your clothes aren't baggy like mine, you can't hide it on you. People would notice if you suddenly wore looser fitting pants. And we don't dare leave it anywhere in case Samuels goes searching through the camp. You know he's suspicious of our story about the file being erased."

"Yeah." He sat on the edge of his cot and she joined him. "We could always put it back in the imaging tent, hide it in plain sight with the rest of the files. He's no doubt searched there already."

"They'll search that tent again." Nathan's voice made them both jump.

"Shit, Longfeather, how do you move around so quietly?" Krin put a hand over his heart.

She was too busy trying to catch her breath to speak. He was gorgeous. And she looked like someone had punched her in the nose.

"When this is done, I'll teach you." A hint of humor touched his sexy voice. "You're right. They searched the imaging tent last night. Obviously found nothing. But they'll go back. They searched the new site as well. They even fired up the EDU to see if it really was broken."

"Good thing we undid mine and Glen's tweaking. Did they search anywhere else?"

"Most of the empty tents and a few areas around your primary dig site. They didn't make it as far as the secondary site. They tried searching the ships too but got singed on mine. That and sunrise being only an hour away put an end to their activities."

"You were still following them?"

Nathan nodded.

"Did you get any sleep?"

"I'm calling in help today."

She didn't miss the way he avoided answering Krin's question. Her eyes narrowed. When she looked closer, she saw the strain around his mouth and eyes. It was subtle, but the signs of fatigue were there.

"How long until this help arrives?" she asked. He needed rest or he wouldn't be any good to any of them. She chose to ignore the fact that if she'd been able to follow through on kissing him last night, she'd have tried to keep him up all night herself.

"This afternoon," Nathan answered. "I'd better warn you, he's a Binnean mercenary from t'Clav clan. There shouldn't be a problem, though, since you don't have any other Binneans working here."

"Thanks for the warning," Krin said with a chuckle.

"Will you be okay until he arrives?" she asked.

Nathan raised his eyebrows, his look so sardonic she wanted to squirm.

"Of course," he said, his voice subtly laced with humor again. "Why wouldn't I be?"

"I just thought you must need to sleep sometime is all," she mumbled, staring at the floor of the tent. "You must have been up all night following the inspectors around."

"I got enough sleep to keep doing my job. No need to worry, Dr. Jones."

"Fine." She shrugged. She had an overwhelming need to leave the tent but wasn't sure how to make her escape without humiliating herself further. She couldn't believe she'd actually considered seducing him last night. What the hell had she been thinking? He'd spent the night protecting her dig site. He didn't have time for a romp in the sheets, even if he might want to indulge with her.

In the full light of day, she had to face facts. She looked like death after her sleepless night. He looked as gorgeous, as sexy and confident as ever. They were not in the same orbit. And she had to stop pretending they could be.

"Looks like your pants are the best hiding place today, then," Krin said, patting her thigh. "If the inspectors are likely to search the site more, we can't afford to leave the disk anywhere."

"Gee, aren't I lucky," she mumbled but spared Krin a half-smile.

"That's not a good idea." The hard edge to Nathan's voice surprised her.

"Why not?"

"You've had it all night."

"So?"

"So they may figure out one of you is carrying it after they've searched your tents."

The thought of Samuels going through her tent gave Ti'ann

the creeps. And she still had Nathan's jacket. Would Samuels notice it wasn't hers? Not that what he thought about her personally mattered, but he might say something out loud that she would have a hard time explaining. She really should give that jacket back to Nathan. Now would be good.

Except the conversation was too serious. Now didn't seem the right time to bring up something as trivial as Nathan's coat.

"You think they'll try and physically search us?" Krin asked. "That'd be a bit obvious, wouldn't it?"

Nathan looked right at her when he answered. "I don't think Samuels is above searching in a more subtle way."

"What?" Her voice squeaked, but it was more because he was staring at her so intensely than because of what he said.

"He may use…other methods to try and search you, Dr. Jones."

When she finally got his innuendo, she almost laughed. "Yeah, right."

"I don't know, Ti'ann. Samuels has been very attentive to you. He may be trying to seduce information from you."

"You're joking." She looked between the two men, shocked to see such matching expressions of conviction. "Oh come on! You two are way off here. And anyway, Samuels gives me the creeps. There's no way he's getting close enough to search me."

Krin didn't look convinced, and she didn't dare look at Nathan to see what he thought.

"Krin, he's not gonna make a move on me to see if I'm hiding a file disk he doesn't even know about. Both of you are overreacting."

"Maybe." Krin shrugged and sighed. "I don't like this, though."

"I'll be fine." When he pursed his lips, she gave him a light slug in the arm.

His brief scowl moved quickly into a grin. "You're not supposed to win these arguments you know? Disrupts the balance."

She chuckled, relieved by the break in tension.

"I still don't think you should carry the disk," Nathan said.

"Yeah, well, we don't have a lot of options. Unless there's someplace you don't think they'll search, the best place is on one of us."

"We could give it to Monroe, to take back with him," Krin said suddenly, his eyes widening.

"I am not letting these files fly off with someone else," she said immediately.

Before Krin could argue, Nathan added, "They're not leaving this morning anyway. Another malfunction in their ship."

"Another?" Krin asked.

"That sounds awfully suspicious," she said at the same time.

"Exactly. So they're staying."

"Do you think Samuels is sabotaging their ship?" she asked.

Nathan shrugged but didn't answer her question. She really hated when he did that.

"I can put the files in my ship," he said instead. "It's shield protected. They'd have to have some serious firepower to get through. And that'd be very obvious. They left everything as they found it last night. They don't want us to know they're not inspectors. At least, they don't want us to have proof they're not what they claim."

"Your ship is a great idea. Why didn't you suggest it sooner?" Krin's initial enthusiasm turned to suspicion in a nanosecond.

"After the singeing they got last night, they may try to break into it today just to see what I'm hiding. I didn't want to risk it.

But if it'll keep Dr. Jones from doing something stupid, I'll take the chance."

"Hey!"

"Great. Give him the disk, Ti'ann."

"What the hell do you mean by something stupid?" She jumped to her feet and rounded on Nathan. "I resent that comment. When was the last time you noticed me doing something stupid?"

As soon as she said the words, she nearly choked on them. Of course he'd noticed her doing something stupid. Three years ago she'd done something most people would consider extremely stupid, even if she didn't regret it. Then she remembered. He didn't know she was that woman. Her moment of shocked panic disappeared, and suddenly she was righteous and angry again. She was actually relieved he didn't remember her. Ha!

"Not feeding yourself or staying properly hydrated is stupid. The last thing we need is for you to get so caught up in your work you forget you've got the disk and drop it."

"Listen, Longfeather." She actually poked at him, not quite brave enough to touch him, not when she had a witness, but the gesture made her point. "I'm the one whose career is on the line here. If I fuck up, it's my life. It's my best friend's life. I take that seriously." She lowered her voice. "There is no way in hell Samuels and his men are going to get this disk from me. You got that? I'm keeping it, I'll take care of it, and that's all there is to it."

For thirty seconds, the only sound in the tent was her breathing. She couldn't even hear Krin behind her. Nathan looked like a storm ready to break. But she didn't back down. She couldn't now even if she wanted to. She wouldn't be able to look herself in the mirror. She might hate confrontation, but she was not going to be belittled or written off as a scatterbrain. Not by him. Not by anyone.

Even if she was a scatterbrain sometimes.

To keep her hands from shaking, she fisted them and set them against her hips. There. That had to look defiant. She waited, nearly panting from the earlier anger and now the strain. Adrenaline ran riot in her bloodstream. If he didn't say something soon, she was going to crack.

"Fine." His voice was devoid of emotion when he finally spoke. "You carry the files."

Her hands dropped like weights to her sides, leaving her shaky. She'd won. Wow. That made two arguments in a row. Krin was right. This could go to her head. She smiled because she couldn't help it and nodded.

"Great. All settled. Now, I need to eat. Are you two coming?"

Krin was instantly at her side and ready to leave. "I'm starving. Let's hurry. I want to get down to the dig site before Anya starts on that big block hammered out yesterday."

Outside, just before Nathan joined them, Krin leaned close to her and murmured under his breath, "All hail the mighty wombok."

Ti'ann snorted and clapped her hand over her mouth to keep from laughing out loud.

As they walked to the canteen, Nathan slightly out of step and behind them, Ti'ann could feel the hard edge of his glare between her shoulder blades. Mighty wombok or not, she had a funny feeling they weren't through with their argument.

CHAPTER ELEVEN

———————

VAL SLIPPED IN BESIDE KRIN ON THE BENCH LOOKING COMPOSED but strained. Nathan studied the Shifter. He wanted to ask how long it could hold its shape. Was it wearing to stay shifted? But he didn't dare talk about it out loud. Not while Samuels was in the same tent.

"You all right?" Krin murmured.

"Fine. Tired." Val attempted a smile, head tilted to one side.

"Your ship?" Nathan asked.

"Almost fixed. I don't know what's wrong with it. Glen's been out there all morning with Mike and Juanita trying to fix it. Juanita's a whiz with electronics, but even she can't figure out how so many things could go wrong."

"Do you think they'd mind if I had a look?" He tried to make the comment casually. "I've repaired a ship or two in my time."

"I imagine they'd be happy for the help. Can you two spare him for a few hours?"

Krin nodded. "Yeah, if it helps get your ship fixed."

Val smiled and played with the food on the plate in front of it.

"Are you eating?" Krin asked so quietly, Nathan could barely hear him from across the table.

"All the time," Val said with a genuine grin.

Shifters took their food from the air around them, directly into their cells. Apparently, they could do that while shifted too. The humor in Val's comment surprised him. He'd learned a little about Shifters from Krin who'd learned from Val. A lot of it he'd heard before from his mom and her cousin back when he wasn't going to get involved with the Shifters and hadn't believed half of what Thomas told him anyway. But he'd never stopped to wonder if Shifters had a sense of humor. He almost smiled back at Val.

"The inspectors as much as told us they'd only be staying for another day and a half." Ti'ann spoke quietly, keeping the conversation as private as possible in the communal canteen. "Might be easier just to stay now."

He sat next to her on the bench, out of some morbid masochistic streak he was sure. Every time she moved, he had to clench his jaw to keep from grabbing her and doing something he was sure she'd prefer was kept private. When she talked it was worse. Her husky voice shot sparks of heat down his spine. But at least sitting next to her, he didn't have to look at her. Looking at her now left his control in tatters. Last night he'd come very close to tossing aside his good intentions. This morning had only made matters worse.

He was almost relieved for the excuse of working on the ship so he could be away from her for a few hours. Maybe then he'd be able to look at her without losing it.

He couldn't believe he was turned on by the fact that she'd yelled at him. He wasn't into verbal conflict as an aphrodisiac.

Never had been. He didn't get hard when women argued with him. Except, obviously, when it came to Ti'ann Jones. If Krin hadn't been there, he'd have had Ti'ann on her back in a nanosecond.

The question was why did he get slammed by lust when she stood up to him?

It wasn't until they'd sat down in the canteen that the answer hit him. That morning, in Krin's tent, he'd seen the woman he'd known three years ago. All the passion and fire she kept tightly braided and in baggy clothes had exploded out with her temper. The time they'd spent together so far, the moments when he was certain she still wanted him, had been restrained by circumstances. For his part, he was resisting a client. He wasn't sure why she held back, but she did. Until this morning.

He had no doubt now his memories of those nights with her weren't exaggerated. The lust and insatiable need had been real.

By the afternoon, BinRal would be here to cover Nathan's ass. The Binnean was going to have a field day with this. First Alex. Now him. He'd never hear the end of it.

"We may have to stay," Val said, answering Ti'ann's question.

It took him a few blinks to pull himself back to the conversation and away from the way Ti'ann's skin would feel once he disposed of those damned baggy clothes of hers.

"But as we've made excuses to leave," Val finished, "won't it seem worse if we don't?"

"Not if the ship can't be fixed," Krin said. "Then you have a perfect reason for not leaving."

Nathan kept quiet about his own suspicions. He'd know more after he looked at their ship.

"Where's James and Clare?" Ti'ann asked.

"James had to make a call but he's on his way here after. Clare said she needed a shower."

Ti'ann shifted next to him, her thigh briefly brushed against his, and Nathan felt like his head was going to explode. He stood abruptly, knowing he needed to get away from her. Now.

"I'll go see what I can do for your ship."

He dumped his plate and hurried outside without looking back. He took a deep breath once he was beyond the camp. He rounded a tree, stopped, and squeezed his eyes shut for a minute. This had gone way too far. He couldn't even sit next to her without his cock reacting. He opened his eyes and headed for the landing pad. Maybe he should just leave. He didn't need this in his life. She had him so screwed up he could barely think straight. And the worst part was she wasn't *doing* anything. She wasn't walking around in tight clothing, she wasn't flirting. She hadn't brought up their past, not even alluding to it. She wasn't going out of her way to get near him. In fact, if anything, she avoided him. He'd been the one hunting her down all over camp, making excuses just to be in her presence.

Was that it? The hunt? She wasn't interested anymore so he had to have her?

He considered that as he cleared the woods and headed toward Monroe's ship. When she'd looked up at him last night, there was no doubt she wanted him. He didn't know why she was ignoring their past or why she tried avoiding him, but one thing he was certain of, the attraction between them went both ways.

So much for his theory that it was just the hunt.

He marched up the side-ramp leading into Monroe's ship and found Juanita and Mike hunched over a panel in the rear of the vessel. Glen called up from a repair access tube in the hull. "That should do it. Try it now."

Mike hit a switch, his fingers danced over the flat screen, and he and Juanita sat back. A low hum started ticking over, choked and died. "Fucking hell," Juanita hissed.

"Not yet, Glen," Mike called back. He looked up then and noticed Nathan. "Hey, Longfeather. What're you doing here?"

"Came to see if I could lend a hand. Mind filling me in?"

"Our auxiliary drive is jumping and shorting primary power. We're trying to bypass the break in power flow so we can reactivate the primary couplings. It'd only be a temp fix but at least we'd be able to get out of here and have the drive overhauled once we get back to Capital. But every time we think we've isolated the break and bypassed, the primaries short out again."

"Can I have a look?"

"I don't mind. Glen, come on out so Longfeather can take a look. Maybe fresh eyes will help."

Glen's blond head popped out of the shoot entrance half a meter from the panel where they were standing. "Be my guest," he said in disgust. "I've never seen anything like this. And I've been repairing machines for years."

"Some ships have their own quirks," Nathan said.

"Yeah, but those are usually high class, or really old, or fast hotshots. This is just an ordinary on-planet cruiser same as half the planet owns. This thing should not have quirks."

Nathan shrugged noncommittally as Glen pulled himself up to the main deck. With a hand gesture he offered the task off to Nathan. "All yours, Longfeather. If you can fix this, I'll shout your genius to the entire camp."

Nathan chuckled. "No need to go quite that far."

He dropped easily into the repair shoot and hunched down to crawl into the access tube. The panel covering the area Glen was working on lay on the floor next to a handful of tools. A network of wires, power links, colored alinar tubes and control terminals half removed from the hole in the wall gave Nathan a good idea of the work Glen had been trying to do. He studied the arrays and ran a few numbers into the auxiliary drive control terminal. He frowned. Another series of codes. Ah. As he thought. A very sophisticated piece of work.

He checked over the alinar tubes until he found the one he was looking for, designed and color-coded to blend so well with the others you'd have to really know the workings of the ship to know it was an add-in. Even an ordinary repair crew wouldn't be likely to spot this.

He hunted through the tools on the floor but couldn't find what he needed. "You have a Borman's rig up there?"

"I'll get it," Mike called down.

He crawled back into the main shoot and poked his head up over the edge of the floor. Mike came trotting back from the front of the ship with a small oblong gray device used to handle, remove and insert the alinar tubes. "Is one of the tubes shot? We don't have any spares."

"Don't worry." Nathan took the Borman's rig and ducked back into the access tube. Removing the add-in without actually frying the whole drive system was tricky work. If someone who knew what they were doing rigged this, and Nathan was certain it had been done by a pro, then one false move could turn the ship into an inactive lump of metal only good for donating parts.

It took him well over an hour, but when he finally got the tube removed safely and the links all realigned, he took a deep breath. "Try it now."

He backed away from the panel, into the repair shoot, far enough to get out quickly if the whole thing popped. He waited as the low hum of the drive turning over started through the ship. He counted to twenty, the hum increasing in speed and got higher in pitch. He held his breath until it whirred to full life and the sound dropped into the low rumble of a warming drive system.

Shouts and cheers erupted above him. Grinning, he jumped up from the shoot, Borman's rig in hand. He'd have to dispose of the tube safely but he had the facilities in his own ship.

"What did you do?" Juanita demanded. Her stern face relaxed into a grin.

He held up the rig. "I hate to tell you this, but your ship was sabotaged. And someone very slick did it. If you'd stumbled across this—an add-in alinar tube—and tried to remove it, at the very least you would have blown the ship's systems out."

"At the least?"

"Sabotage?"

"What the hell?"

All three spoke at once. "Why would someone do that?" Glen asked, confusion creasing his sun-tanned face.

Juanita and Mike exchanged a look behind him. Nathan kept his expression neutral. "Maybe Gremblewreath thugs?" Mike suggested in a tone that wasn't very convincing.

"Maybe." Nathan didn't think Glen was fooled. In hindsight, he should have waited to tell Mike and Juanita when Glen wasn't around. But given how much Glen had already seen and done on the ship's repairs, he wasn't sure the grad student would've been happy without the real explanation.

"This to do with the new dig? You think maybe someone doesn't want us to uncover a possible Shifter graveyard?"

"Could be," Juanita answered. "We've been trying to keep the theory quiet, but people talk."

"So why would they want to keep you guys here?"

"Maybe it wasn't supposed to keep us here, necessarily," Mike said. "Maybe it was just a warning to the group in general.

Or maybe just to inconvenience us. We might want to check all the ships." Mike tilted his head down to focus on Nathan over the top of his little glasses. His look said, "Go along with this."

Nathan didn't react to the look, but he was willing to go with whatever story they invented. He doubted Glen believed it. It wasn't a great story given the trouble they were going through to keep the graveyard theory a secret from the inspectors. Who else outside the camp would know? But he wasn't going to be the one to point out the illogic.

"I'll start checking over the other ships today," Nathan said. It wouldn't hurt. He might even check the inspectors' ship. Quietly, of course.

"That really sucks," Glen said to no one in particular. "What happens when we find out for sure what's down there? Someone gonna try to sabotage the whole dig?"

"Doubt it, Glen," Nathan assured him. "If we can't be intimidated, this will probably stop." More likely it would stop when the supposed inspectors left. Holding up the tube, he said, "I need to dispose of this properly. I'll start the checks on the other ships when I'm finished and I've made a tour of the site."

He studied Glen for a minute, debating. The man's record was perfectly normal. He had an ambition for science and a clever mind with mechanics, but he'd had to work his way into graduate school because he'd failed too many classes trying to get his primary degree. He was an eager worker and had received great reports from both Ti'ann and Krin during his time in the field. There was nothing in his past that screamed dodgy character. Nathan would check his impressions with BinRal before he did anything—considering how fucked up his mind was at the moment by Ti'ann—but Glen was proving useful with repairs. If he trained him to hunt for these types of traps, together they'd be able to check the ships over in no time. Leaving BinRal free to keep an eye on Samuels.

"Mike, I'll want to talk with Monroe when he's free. Could you tell him to find me?"

"Yeah, no problem."

Clare O'Malley picked that moment to come sauntering into the ship. Her dark red hair was wet, falling in thick curls around her face. "You find the problem?" she asked.

"Nathan fixed it," Mike told her. "We're gonna run a check on the other ships as well. Just to be safe."

She stared at Mike a minute, then hit Nathan with the most calculating look he'd ever seen.

"Someone rigged the ship so it wouldn't take off, didn't they?"

He stared back without responding. If she was their security, the fact someone got in was on her head and they both knew it.

When he didn't respond, her shoulders dropped and her mouth turned down in disgust. "Fuck." She stared at the floor for a minute then looked back up at him. "Can you show me what was done? How to spot it?"

He watched her closely as he considered her request. Unlike Glen, Clare's record was spotty. She'd worked a number of jobs, including as a stripper in the Docks—a city built on the Dreic Sea off the coast of Capital that housed the underbelly of Naravan society. There was even some ambiguity surrounding her job in the Docks. She'd only worked in the strip club for a few weeks, quit suddenly, and four days later the Mafia family running the Docks shut the club down. The story was splashed all over the vid-screen for weeks. O'Malley had remarkably good timing, getting out so conveniently before the raid, before she could be harassed by any of the anxious reporters swarming the story after it broke, before she had to talk to the Guards about her time in the club. And that wasn't the only occasion where she'd shown remarkably good timing.

After watching her, he was pretty sure she was working security for Monroe. Her reaction to the sabotage seemed to confirm this hunch. But there was something else to Clare O'Malley. He just couldn't put his finger on it. He needed to keep a closer eye on her.

"I'll need an extra hand to check out the other ships. You volunteering?"

She pursed her lips and nodded.

He agreed with the barest movement of his head. He hadn't agreed to show her anything worthwhile. But it would keep her close, and he'd be able to keep an eye on her. "Meet me at my ship in three hours. I have a few things to do first."

"Anything you need help with?" Glen asked. "You're gonna be pretty busy. You need me to do anything?"

So eager to help. Good or bad?

Nathan headed to his ship, puzzling over the situation. He didn't trust Clare. The act was too good, the past too sketchy, her knack for being in the right place at the right time too coincidental. At the same time, he hadn't found anything in her past to make him think she was dangerous to this group. No anti-Shifter or government connections. Anywhere. Even in the Docks she'd never affiliated with any one family or individual that would bother with the Shifter issue. Hell, her only connection with the Shifters started with this group and Mike Warez.

But that was the other thing bothering him. Her relationship with Mike. It seemed too contrived. There was no spark between them. According to his checks, the two had only been together for a month. Too soon to have lost the passion. So that was probably a set up. But why? If she was security, why not just be security?

Then there was Glen Thompson. With his squeaky-clean record and ordinary past, Nathan would have been inclined to trust him. Until he'd volunteered so quickly to help. Something about that eagerness had sounded alarm bells. Maybe he was over-reacting. Glen was always on hand to help. Maybe he was just a helpful person. He hadn't volunteered to assist with anything suspicious or even anything specific. Just whatever Nathan might need him for.

He cursed quietly as he pressed a spot on his comm-link to deactivate the shield around his ship. He'd survived for years on his instincts about people and situations. Now, he was doubting himself. There was no real reason to be suspicious of Glen. Yet he was. But was it his instincts sparking or was he reading the whole situation wrong because he could barely think straight for more than an hour at a time?

He reactivated the shields around his ship once he was inside and headed toward the aft storage hatch and the disposal unit. BinRal couldn't get here fast enough. He needed a clear head on this soon.

E WATCHED Nathan Longfeather leave the ship. He'd fixed it. He was the only one who could have. The others had been working at it for hours without finding the add-in. Nathan Longfeather had removed it without freezing the entire system. Nathan Longfeather needed to be watched.

E studied the ship. He needed to disable it again. He couldn't let the Shifter get away. It was in the eating tent now, still surrounded by others, with Ti'ann Jones. He couldn't allow Ti'ann Jones to see him. But he was patient. He'd catch it alone soon.

He allowed his body to relax, change, flow into something

new until he could move more freely. Within the blink of an eye, he was camouflaged and slithering toward the Shifter's ship. So many forms to take. It made his task so easy. Nathan Longfeather couldn't do what he did. He wouldn't be a threat to E.

He'd never even see E coming.

CHAPTER TWELVE

Ti'ann's first look at the big Binnean mercenary nearly stopped her heart. Not because he looked any bigger or hairier than any other Binnean she'd seen or dealt with before, but because the first thing he did when being introduced to her was smile. While Binneans were huge and strong and known for their aggressive behavior, they didn't tend to look terrifyingly scary. Until they smiled. Their smile flashed sharp white teeth and somehow seemed threatening even when it was supposed to be a friendly expression.

"Dr. Ti'ann Jones, Dr. Krin Freemont, this is my associate En-BinRal Ol Binda t'Clav."

The Binnean bowed his head slightly. "I'm pleased to meet you."

She must be getting paranoid because when he lifted his head, she could have sworn he winked at her.

They exchanged a Binnean handshake with BinRal, she and Krin with an open palm facing out and fingertips pointed up. BinRal greeted them by placing his fist against their palms.

"Thank you for coming to help us on such short notice," Ti'ann said to get past her shock. His fist had been gentle and smooth. There was probably nothing to worry about. Just because he smiled. And maybe winked.

"I'm happy to help, Dr. Jones. I understand this may prove a very interesting case."

"I'm afraid so."

"I look forward to it then."

She glanced at Nathan. His face betrayed no specific emotion, just the usual intensity always surrounding him. Though, his eyes were a bit narrower than usual, not quite a scowl but almost, if she looked close enough. And his mouth was harder, his shoulders a little tighter. Was there something wrong, something he didn't want to tell them? Or maybe it was just her imagination. Like BinRal's wink. "Samuels and his men will want to meet BinRal."

"I already told them I was expecting an associate this after-noon. I'll arrange a meeting now. Have they been in your way today?"

"No. Amazingly. They've just hovered around, watching and studying. Samuels occasionally talks with people but never long enough to interfere with their work. They're asking ques-tions about the new dig, Monroe's team, and the molecular echo imaging files. Glen's kept up the story of trying to adjust it and erasing some of the files on accident. No one else dealt with the MEI besides Krin and me so they can't say much. Samuels did ask about our funding today—sources, names of the private grants, that sort of thing."

"Anything to worry about?"

"Only if they try to get some of our grants canceled."

Ti'ann noticed a brief emotion of some kind flashed through Nathan's green-hazel eyes then it was gone. Trying to read his expression was harder than trying to read a rock. At least she had imaging equipment for the rock.

"I doubt they'll be able to affect your funding." His voice was quiet and neutral.

"Let's hope." Her gaze narrowed. "You were able to fix James' ship earlier?"

"Yes. But something else is wrong."

"What? How?" Krin's voice was low when he asked. They were alone, not far from the lifts down to the valley, in the middle of the woods. Despite the relative privacy, both she and Krin took a step closer to the two mercenaries.

"I haven't had enough time to find the problem yet. But we'll find it."

"I don't understand," she murmured. "I thought it was Samuels or one of his team tampering with their ship. But they were never out of sight of one of our people all day."

"I know."

"Well?"

Nathan exchanged a look with BinRal that told her absolutely nothing but must have spoken volumes to the Binnean because he shrugged.

"I have some suspicions," Nathan said finally.

His voice was so low and deep she barely heard it. She had to lean closer to catch that much. Unfortunately, being so close to Nathan meant his delicious male scent permeated her senses, and that only clouded her brain. Her heart thumped a little faster and she had to resist the urge to move even closer. Instead, she leaned back again. "And those are?"

"Better left unmentioned for the moment. I'll fill you both in when I know more."

She hated his evasiveness, but at least he'd promised information soon. The fact she and Krin, well Krin really, were paying for him to be here didn't seem to deter him from withholding information.

The two mercenaries excused themselves for their meeting with Samuels, leaving she and Krin wondering.

"What do you think?" he asked, staring after the two.

"I think I'm a little worried now. And not just about Samuels."

"I CAN'T FIND ANYTHING," Samuels said, keeping all emotion from his voice. "If there's some clue to what they've found, they're keeping it well-hidden."

"Have you tried persuasion? Threatened their funding?"

Samuels kept his expression as emotionless as his voice while he talked to Barbury on the vid-screen. He hated the man with a passion, but he'd never let it show. He knew Barbury was only the messenger boy.

"There's no reason to threaten their funding. They've been very cooperative and given us the run of the place."

"What about Monroe and his group? Have they been cooperative?"

"Very. Albeit in a guarded way. They don't allow me to speak to anyone alone, except for Monroe. But they're not obvious about it. Monroe and two others were supposed to leave yesterday. He had some problem to deal with in his department at the University. Two women had families they needed to return to. Two were planning on staying behind to update the team when the dig began again. I've checked it and the excuses pan out. However, there's been some trouble with their ship so they're still here."

"Trouble?" Barbury smiled in a knowing way.

The expression made Samuels want to snarl, but he'd never give in to the impulse in front of someone like the aide. "Not of my doing, as a matter of fact. It's of little consequence. They're saying all the right things out loud and giving me nothing to work with."

"Are you absolutely sure they're hiding something? If all the indications you're getting are of full cooperation, maybe we read this situation wrong."

We?

"I'm positive they're hiding something, and I'm certain it has to do with the new dig. They've hired two security specialists. Both of which have checked out. The museum board approved their presence on site. They claim it's because of some trouble from Gremblewreath. It's very coincidental, though, that they've hired in security just before they started this new dig and just after they placed the call to Monroe. They're hiding something. I just can't find the evidence. However..." He watched with some satisfaction as Barbury's face went from doubt to interest. The man was predictable and too easy to read for someone in his position.

"However?"

"One of the team has been willing to talk to us."

"Damn it, Samuels, why didn't you mention that earlier?"

He raised an eyebrow at the vehemence. "This individual has told us what the teams' theory is about the new dig. Without any hard evidence of their original imaging data, I can't afford to take this information as complete truth. It may be the ravings of a disgruntled worker."

"What's the theory? What do they think they've found?"

Samuels wanted to sigh. He almost didn't want to report this to Barbury. If he reported directly to the senator, he'd know the man would take the information in its proper perspective.

Having Barbury pass it on was a guarantee the data would be slanted and exaggerated. Of necessity, there had to be a buffer between himself and the senator. Barbury wasn't much of a buffer, but technically it was enough.

With some reluctance, he said, "They think they may have found a Shifter graveyard."

"What?" Barbury said, his voice whisper-quiet.

"Shifter graveyard. As in the remains of a lot of Shifters."

Barbury was silent for a long time, long enough that Samuels tweaked a button on the comm-link to make sure it hadn't locked up or disconnected.

"What does this mean?" Barbury finally muttered.

"It means they *may* have found a lot of bodies. Nothing more. Nothing less. I doubt it will affect the political climate. Not that we should simply ignore the situation. I still think the good doctors are hiding something."

"You'll continue investigating then?"

"No. Not like this. There's not much more I can do as a site inspector. We've seen everything, talked to everyone, and have no excuse to stay longer. As I said, they've been very cooperative. I may have a way to get more information from Dr. Jones, but that will take time. I suggest we put certain areas of the site under surveillance."

"Won't the security people find your equipment?"

His eyes narrowed. The look was enough to make Barbury blanch, his tan skin paling. Samuels didn't bother answering his question. "We'll pull out tomorrow mid-day. I'll contact you when we've learned anything new." He cut the transmission and glowered at the screen. After a moment, he turned his thoughts to the task ahead.

Despite his reaction to Barbury's question, he didn't want to underestimate Longfeather and the Binnean working with him.

They'd been in the business a long time. They were still alive so they were most likely very good. He suspected Longfeather had been keeping tabs on them since they arrived. He was sure the man knew they weren't what they claimed to be.

Longfeather would sweep the site for monitoring equipment after they left. Samuels considered the challenge. It would be interesting to see if he could outwit the two mercenaries.

He even had a perfect excuse to return to the site in a week or two, an excuse that no longer seemed so disagreeable. Dr. Ti'ann Jones.

CHAPTER THIRTEEN

"I was hoping you'd join me for dinner again this evening, Ti'ann. On our last night."

Ti'ann tried smiling at Samuels, hoping it didn't look like a grimace. It was an effort to keep from touching the disk hidden in her pocket just to make sure it was still there.

"I'm sure Dr. Freemont and I would be happy to join you." There, that should make it a more comfortable meal. She didn't want her dinner sitting like a lump in her stomach again tonight.

Samuels gave her a charming, almost boyish smile. "I was hoping we could be alone."

Her heart started to hammer. Fear and panic vied for attention. *Okay, you can do this Ti'ann. You can make it through another meal with him without giving anything away.* She was going to have to hand the disk off to Krin first though. Thoughts of his and Nathan's suggestion that Samuels might try to seduce information from her made her mouth go dry. She couldn't afford to be the one carrying the disk tonight.

"Well, Dr. Freemont and I usually share our evening meal so

we can talk about the day's work, but I'm sure we can make an exception tonight." Was that stammer in her voice obvious? She was sure her cheeks were bright red.

"Great. I'll meet you at your tent this evening. Around seven?"

"Fine." She nodded and walked away, her body shaking. First things first, find Krin! She searched the entire site before she found him at the landing pad talking with Monroe.

"Hi. How's your ship?"

Monroe nodded to her, his smile slight. "Still giving us trouble. Nathan's been over it twice and he's found three malfunctions which haven't solved our problem." He raised his hands in surrender. "We won't be leaving before the inspectors now. Which means we won't bother leaving. At this rate, we'll probably have to call in another ship when we are ready to go."

"We'll arrange something. Krin, can I talk to you a minute?"

"Sure." He nodded to James and followed her toward the woods. "What's up?"

"Samuels wants to have dinner with me again tonight. Alone." Okay, there was definite panic in her voice now. What if she gave something away? What if she slipped up? She was a bad liar. She knew it. She'd bet Samuels knew it too. That's why he'd targeted her.

Krin's look was hard. "What'd you tell him?"

"I kind of had to say yes, didn't I? What excuse did I have?"

"Maybe you can come down with a sudden bug of some kind. Something that forces you into bed for a few hours."

"Would that work?"

Krin looked doubtful. "Maybe. Our med-kit is pretty sketchy just now. Maybe we don't have the right herbs to heal you and our med-scan is malfunctioning?"

"That's an awful lot of malfunctions, Krin. Molecular scanning equipment does not malfunction that much."

"I know. I know. It was just an idea."

"Well, one thing's for sure. I can't carry these files tonight."

"I'll take them. I'm supposed to keep them tonight anyway."

"Where will you put them?"

Krin thought a moment then grinned. "I think we should take Longfeather up on his offer. They'll be safe in his ship."

She sucked in her lips and took a deep breath through her nose. "I'd rather not, if we can do anything else."

"Why?"

Why? That was the question. It wasn't that she distrusted Nathan exactly. She already trusted him with the information. No reason she couldn't trust him with the disk. Was there? "These are the only files we have of the original scans. I'd rather you or I kept an eye on them. It just feels safer that way. If we lose them, we won't have the comparison of the structure before and after the change. I don't want to risk losing that."

"You think Longfeather might take off with the disk?"

"No. No. Not anything like that. I don't know. I'd just feel safer if you or I had it."

Krin cocked his head to one side, considering her. The gesture reminded her strangely of Val. "Okay," he said. "I'll find somewhere to keep it. It's small. I can put on a pair of loose trousers with pockets for dinner. Not too obvious?"

"No. The evening's supposed to cool off a lot. That should work."

"We're going through an awful lot of effort to conceal something Samuels doesn't even know about." He sighed.

"Do you want to take the chance he'll find out?"

"No. I don't. So I know we can't be too careful. I'm glad

Longfeather called in backup. The inspectors are just the first wave. They won't be the only, or even the worst."

"Yeah. I guess your initial gut instinct to hire security was right. Devin will be so disappointed."

Krin grinned. "I can't wait to tell him. So does this mean you're glad I hired Longfeather?"

"Sure." She couldn't help smiling back when his grin turned sly. "I thought you didn't like him?"

"You've stopped acting scared of him. Or I guess intimidated is a better word. That was the only reason I didn't like him."

"I'm still intimidated by him, you know."

"I'd have never guessed the way you were yelling at him this morning. You were more intimidating than intimidated."

"Hmm. That was unusual. You know me. I wouldn't normally do something like that."

"Outside of the department meetings, you mean?"

"Those don't count. That's part of the job." She was grinning now, her panic under control. Krin had a way of doing that for her. Probably why they were such good friends—he kept her from hyperventilating and she kept him from jumping in without thinking. Most of the time.

"So you want to hand that disk off to me now? We can go to my tent. Probably not a good idea to do anything out in the open."

"Are you coming back to work on the ship?"

"Yeah. Glen and Nathan are combing the thing, but they can use all the extra eyes they can get. Nathan's even enlisted Clare to search some of the auxiliary systems. That's where he discovered the sabotage earlier."

"Clare? I didn't know she had any mechanical skill?"

Krin shrugged. "Nathan seems to think she's capable."

"Oh." When Krin's eyes narrowed, she knew she'd let something slip in that one seemingly innocent word. "What?"

"Nothing. Just wondering why that bothers you."

"It doesn't. Why would it? It's her transport too, right." And the fact that Nathan might have decided he wasn't interested in Ti'ann after all when there was the gorgeous Clare O'Malley on hand—even if she was in a relationship with Mike—wasn't a fear she was prepared to admit to Krin.

She had no basis for her jealousy anyway. Nathan wasn't hers. She was just his client. A few conversations here and there that felt like more to her didn't mean he was actually interested in her. Even if it had seemed like he wanted to kiss her last night. Maybe he had. But then again, maybe he acted that way with all women and would be as likely to hit on Clare if the opportunity arose.

"Right," Krin said, watching her too closely. "Except Clare wasn't going to leave."

"It doesn't bother me that she's working on the ship, Krin. That'd be stupid."

"Then it bothers you that she's working with Nathan."

She stepped back. "Why would it bother me?"

"Because I've seen the way you look at him when he doesn't know you're looking. You want him. You want him so bad you actually yelled at him. And Clare O'Malley is sexy and vivacious and you think she's competition."

"I don't think she's competition." You had to be able to compete to be in competition with someone, and she damned sure couldn't compete with Clare. "Besides, just because I may be a little interested in Nathan doesn't mean the feelings are returned so there's no reason for me to be jealous of Clare. He can do as he pleases. I'd be more worried about Mike's reaction than mine."

Krin stood there staring at her. He'd always been able to see past her defenses. It was comforting at times, but this wasn't one of them.

"You're not very observant for a scientist, Dr. Jones."

"What does that mean?"

"It means if you paid any attention at all, you wouldn't be the least bit worried about Clare."

"I'm not. So I must be paying attention to something. Listen, I don't want to talk about this. We have a lot bigger things to worry about at the moment. Like who's sabotaging Monroe's ship and why."

"We're not done with this discussion," he warned.

She rolled her eyes. "But for now, please? We do have bigger worries."

"I'm not letting you get away with avoidance for long." He blew out a breath and glanced toward the landing area. "But I do want to get back to helping with the ship."

She swallowed a sigh of relief. "Do you have any guesses on the saboteur?"

"No. I'm sure Nathan suspects someone, but he's not talking."

She thought about it a moment, weighing up the people in camp. "Do you think Samuels might know something, even if he and his men aren't directly involved?"

"He might. Why?" Krin's expression darkened. "You're not thinking of doing something stupid are you?"

"I thought I told you earlier, I don't do stupid things."

He didn't look convinced. "If you're thinking of asking Samuels questions, don't. You're a crappy liar, and we don't need Samuels any more suspicious than he is."

"I wasn't going to lie. I'll be perfectly honest with him. We're afraid someone's been tampering with James' ship and I was wondering if he'd heard anything during his questioning. I'm not supposed to suspect him, right? So why wouldn't I ask?"

"Ti'ann… That's not a good idea. Leave the investigating and digging to Nathan and BinRal. It's what they do for a living."

"It's what we do for a living too, Dr. Freemont. We investigate and dig." She grinned at his exasperation.

"Don't. Just don't."

She didn't answer. She wouldn't take chances, but if she had to eat with Samuels, there was no reason for her to pass up the opportunity to pick his brain. Maybe he had some insight the rest of them didn't. Or maybe he'd give himself away. Okay, that wasn't likely to happen, but you never knew. "I'll see you later. Meet in your tent about six."

"Ti'ann…"

She walked away before the lecture got rolling. She'd had enough lectures already. She suspected she'd hear a few more before the day was out.

NATHAN STUDIED the tiny pinhead sized chip in the micro-tongs. He and BinRal exchanged a look. They didn't have to say a word. The chip was so new, such an advanced piece of technology, neither of them had seen a real one before. In fact, it was only theory as far as most people were concerned. He'd heard rumors a few had been made, and he understood how the devices were supposed to work. But this level of technology had to be extremely expensive. Not something just anyone would carry around with them. Not when cheaper methods were available.

"What's it do?" Glen leaned in close to the tongs.

"It hazes electronics," BinRal said. "A bit like a miniature electro-magnetic pulse, but timed and focused. It doesn't burn out all electrical systems in one pulse, it actually hits specific areas at a specific time."

"It can be focused and controlled," Nathan said, "unlike a real EMP. This pulse can be set to a degree that limits the damage to temporary blowouts. Easy to fix. Set to a higher limit, it can fry a system. Set higher, it can vaporize the system."

"Holy shit. And it's that size? You could plant one of those anywhere."

"That's the real nasty part. They can be a bitch to find." Nathan leaned back on his haunches. "We found this on accident. Otherwise, we wouldn't even know what we were looking for."

"Even if we had, it'd have been difficult to find. It has a camouflage film covering. It can blend into any system it's planted in." BinRal rose to his feet.

They'd been crouched beneath a panel in one of the storage hatches, scanning for more add-ins. They'd found the little device when its film caused a minor blip in their readings, the sort of blip that usually went unnoticed. They only noticed this one because they hadn't been able to find anything else to explain the malfunctions.

Nathan climbed to his feet, careful not to loosen the micro-tongs. "I think we need to hang on to this."

"Be useful to study," BinRal agreed.

"Hey, can I help? I've never seen anything like it. I'd love to know how it works."

Nathan resisted the urge to look at BinRal and gage his reaction to Glen's request. He couldn't usually read the Binnean's expressions anyway. "We'll have to go over it first, to check for traps," Nathan said. "Once we're sure it's safe we might be able to arrange something."

He put the chip into the small safety container BinRal handed him and sealed it up. "Glen, could you get Monroe to run a test of all systems? We should be able to fix the problems now that this is removed."

"Shouldn't we check for more?"

"One of these can disable a village and they probably cost a fortune. I doubt more than one would have been wasted on the ship. But keep your eyes open for that tiny blip we noticed. If the electronics continue to give you problems, we'll search for another one."

He and BinRal returned to his ship to lock the small chip away. "That's a very sophisticated trick," BinRal commented as Nathan sealed the secured safe in his cabin. "Something less costly would have been sufficient to disable their ship for days. Seems overkill, doesn't it?"

"Yeah. It does. Someone must really want Monroe to stick around."

"Samuels is the only one with a motive. Probably the only one with access to this type of technology."

"I know. The add-in could have been a decoy. This chip could have been placed at the same time as the add-in, so the saboteur didn't need to make a second trip. That would explain a lot."

"You're not convinced."

Nathan shrugged. "I don't have any other ideas. I'm still suspicious of Clare and Glen, but I seriously doubt either of them could have rigged this. There's no indication in either of their records that they might have access to this type of equipment. Samuels is the only real choice."

"But…" BinRal grinned his toothy, disturbing grin and raised his brows.

"But something doesn't feel right. I can't place it. I just feel like there's something we're missing."

"Possibly. I'll check the perimeter sensors again."

"Yeah. And we'd better check the monitor records around the camp as well."

"I'll put more in place around the landing pad."

"Can you do that tonight?"

"You have something else to do?"

"I thought I might toss Samuels' ship before they leave tomorrow. See what I can find."

"That ship isn't going to be any easier to get into than yours."

Nathan grinned, waited for BinRal to glance at the safe then back again before he said, "Might as well test it, see how it works."

BinRal nodded. "That could backfire on you, you know. What if you short out their entire drive system and they can't leave? Alex would suggest you try something else."

"Alex isn't here, and I'll take my chances. He was always too cautious anyway."

"Almost always."

"Don't remind me." He didn't like to be reminded how similar Alex's fall was to his own situation with Ti'ann.

"You're in trouble, aren't you?"

He scowled at the Binnean. "I don't think it's fair you can read my expression, and I can't read yours."

BinRal chuckled. "I like her. She's smart."

"Yeah, she's smart." And irritating, and stubborn, and beautiful, and sexy. "Don't you get distracted too."

"She's not Binnean. Besides, I wouldn't want to get between the two of you."

"Don't start with me. Please. Nothing's happened between us." Not recently anyway. And not for lack of wanting. "I learned well from Alex's fuck-up." Not well enough to keep his hands off Ti'ann. But he sure as hell wasn't going to tell BinRal that.

"I doubt Alex considers his marriage a fuck-up. And if nothing's going on between you and the good doctor, why am I here?"

"I need your help." And he left it at that. He knew BinRal was going to give him a hard time. He'd known it before he called him in. But he didn't have to take the ribbing gracefully.

A proximity warning alarm sounded from the sub-console near Nathan's bunk. He punched in a code and brought up a holo-display of the exterior of the ship. "Dr. Freemont."

"Looking perplexed."

Nathan glanced at BinRal to see if that was humor or indifference in his voice. He shouldn't have bothered, since BinRal's face didn't give anything away. "Think we should let him in?"

"Probably."

He deactivated the external shield and lowered the ramp to let Krin in, then set it to reactivate as soon as the young man's weight was off the ramp. They found Krin standing just inside, frowning. "What can I do for you, Dr. Freemont?"

"I think I need your help with something."

CHAPTER FOURTEEN

Nathan raised a brow when Krin told him what Ti'ann was planning. "You *think* you need our help?" For a heartbeat, Nathan felt like the ship dropped away from under him and he was tumbling in zero Gs with no handhold in site. "Her plan is a very bad idea."

"That's what I told her."

"Maybe not," BinRal said quietly. "She might be able to get information we can't."

"No," Nathan said.

"What kind of information? She's a terrible liar," Krin said.

"BinRal, with what we know now, we can't let her do it."

"What? What do you know?"

"We found a devise on Monroe's ship," Nathan said, "something new and very high tech. Not the kind of thing just anyone can get their hands on. Whatever we may have thought before, Samuels is the only one likely to have access, and he still has the best motive."

Nathan studied Krin while he explained the situation, gauging the man's reaction. Between the two of them, they could still talk Ti'ann out of her mad plan. But if Krin changed his mind and decided her plan might work… Nathan wasn't sure his own sanity could take that.

"But Samuels and both his men were never out of sight. How'd they rig something else?"

"The device we found could easily have been set up at the same time as the add-in."

"So you think Samuels is responsible? Ti'ann could be walking herself into a very dangerous conversation."

"Exactly."

"Don't tell her."

BinRal's softly spoken suggestion sent a sudden rush of anger through Nathan so strong and so unlike him he had to bite the inside of his cheek for several breaths before he dared speak.

"Don't tell her?" His voice was quiet.

"Don't tell her. Dr. Freemont has said she can't lie well. If she doesn't think Samuels is responsible, if she doesn't know about this new evidence, she won't be able to give anything away. Her questions will be genuine and natural for such a curious personality. I doubt Samuels will suspect anything. If he's inviting her to dinner, he's looking for information himself. He probably considers her the easiest one to manipulate. I think you should play up to that. Who knows what he might tell her?"

Nathan hated the plan. Hated it in the depths of his soul. Hated it because Ti'ann would be alone with Terrance Samuels and even if Samuels wasn't out for information, the two of them alone together was unacceptable. Unfortunately, he also knew it was a good plan. One that may or may not work but it would cost them little. Samuels likely wouldn't hurt her, not physically, even if he realized what she was doing. He'd give himself away. Ti'ann would be safe enough questioning him.

And if she were any other woman, Nathan would have thought of this plan himself.

He still hated it. "It might not work," he warned BinRal, one last-ditch effort to stop this.

"Nothing lost if it doesn't. Samuels just won't answer her questions."

"Are you two nuts? Ti'ann can't do this. What if Samuels realizes we know something? What if he's dangerous to her?"

Nathan had to clench his teeth together to keep from agreeing with Krin. "He won't do anything to her. He can't afford the exposure. They're just supposed to be science inspectors not spies. Hurting Dr. Jones for asking questions would reveal his real purpose." Nathan paused a minute, considered. And realized what was bothering him about the chip.

It was too obvious.

If the chip was found, however unlikely that was, it would be evident none of Ti'ann and Krin's crew would have access to something like that, and Monroe's team wasn't likely to sabotage their own ship. So it gave Samuels away. But Samuels wasn't dumb. Even when he'd tossed the campsite the night before, he'd checked for monitoring equipment. He hadn't found any, but it was because Nathan was good at his job, not because Samuels was careless.

So where did that leave them? The identity of the saboteur was still a mystery.

"Nate?"

He looked up at BinRal. "It's too obvious to be Samuels."

"The chip?"

"He's too smart to do something so blatant when something

more mundane would have been enough. The chip was overkill. And it points at Samuels. He would never have left something like that in place."

BinRal stared at the wall for a brief moment. "So. We still don't know who we're dealing with."

"Does this mean Ti'ann is safe asking Samuels questions or not?" Krin looked from one of them to the other, his brows raised.

"It means we still let her ask the questions. Either she discovers something or she doesn't. But we can't afford to pass up the opportunity." Admitting it out loud was like pulling his fingernails out slowly.

"So we let her have dinner alone with Samuels and ask him any questions that come to her and hope for the best? Is that it?" Krin didn't look all that happy with the idea.

Nathan knew how he felt. "Yes. Don't worry. We'll keep a close eye on the situation. Nothing will happen to her."

"I have your word on that, Longfeather?"

Nathan didn't even hesitate. "Yes."

TI'ANN SAT across the table from Samuels, two plates piled with delicious smelling food in front of them, and she had no appetite. She felt the gazes of others in the canteen. Krin was there too, but he was sitting with the grad students. Both she and Krin would have preferred a different arrangement, but she'd promised Samuels they'd eat "alone".

So much for enjoying her dinner. She would have sighed, but Samuels might notice. She tried smiling instead, even as she wished Krin wasn't halfway across the tent.

"So what did you think of our dig? Anything Dr. Freemont and I need to fix to keep our funding intact?"

"Everything appears satisfactory. Some of your equipment is in need of updating."

She chuckled. "If you'll pass that on to the museum grants committee, I'd appreciate it." She tried a mouthful of vegetables. Okay, this was okay. They even tasted like vegetables. No problem.

"I will." He stopped eating and focused fully on her. "Given our schedule, we should be back in about two weeks to finish our report."

The vegetables hit her stomach like a rock. "Really? Why?"

"It isn't complete in its present state. We'll need to come back when you've returned to working on the new dig site."

"I see." But she didn't so she asked. "Why?"

Samuels smiled, but the charm didn't reach his eyes. "To finish our report. We're very thorough in our work, Ti'ann."

She mumbled something around a mouthful of tasteless food. He was already planning on coming back. Damn it to hell. How were they ever going to get this thing excavated?

He startled her by reaching across the table and touching her hand with his fingertips. "I had hoped you'd like the idea of me returning."

Her hand felt frozen in place. How did she move it without offending him? How could she not move it when her entire body was screaming to jerk her hand away?

"Well, obviously you're welcome." She slid her hand out from under his to take a drink from her cup. There, she'd seen that done by some of the women in college and it worked great. She'd have to remember the move.

"Ti'ann?"

"Yes." Her voice squeaked, but only a little.

"Do I make you nervous?"

She felt a hysterical giggle bubble up in her throat and nearly choked trying to hold it back. "No. No." She glanced at him and shrugged. "Well, okay. Maybe a little."

He smiled. She didn't like that smile at all. "That's all right. I'm a patient man."

Great. That's what she wanted to know. She shoveled another bite of food into her mouth so she didn't have to respond. She glanced at her plate. What the hell was she eating? Meat in thick sauce and potato mash. She usually liked potato mash. Now it tasted like dust. She was going to lose a lot of weight at this rate. Krin would never let her hear the end of it.

"I heard James has been able to repair most of his ship's malfunctions now." She swallowed, not quite believing she'd brought the subject up.

"Yes. I'd be afraid to travel in that thing. He should really turn it in when he returns."

She nodded in agreement. "There were an awful lot of glitches. Does that happen a lot, do you think? I don't know much about vehicles, but it seems unusual."

"I wouldn't really know. Mechanics isn't my field either."

Samuels shrugged elegantly as he took a sip from his cup. He was drinking a soft white wine from his own supplies. She'd stuck to water to keep her head clear. She was regretting that now. Wine would be good.

"Dr. Freemont tells me Monroe is a bit worried someone's been tampering with his ship."

"Gremblewreath thugs?" He didn't seem surprised by the idea, but then he didn't seem guilty either.

"Maybe." Now what? How did she ask if he suspected anyone in camp? He sure wasn't giving himself away. She was better with bones. She could get the bones to tell her their story.

"You don't think so?" he asked with mild interest.

"Well. It's just that none of the other ships have been affected. I can't imagine why someone from Gremblewreath would tamper just with James' ship."

She watched his eyes sharpen, the only part of him that tensed.

"Is there proof the ship was tampered with?"

"I haven't heard. You'd have to ask Nathan. He's been helping them with the repairs, but he hasn't told me much about what they found. Krin doesn't know either. But it still seems like an awful lot of malfunctions."

"Yes." His expression turned distracted, focused on something other than her words.

She watched him quietly for a few minutes, waiting for some response. When she couldn't stand the wait any longer, she said, "Do you have any ideas? You've been over the entire camp with a micro-scanner, I'm sure." She smiled to make light of her last statement. "Have you seen or heard anything unusual?"

His gaze shifted back to her, and for an instant, she glimpsed emotionless, dead eyes. Then he blinked and the charm was back. She felt a shiver creep up her spine.

"No. I'm afraid not. I wish I had."

"I suppose everything seems unusual to you anyway," she rushed out before she could stop and think. "Don't know what I was thinking? The whole site is new to you." Shit. She could hear the jitteriness in her own voice. Probably a good thing she'd already admitted to him that he made her nervous because she was acting like an idiot.

Her social skills needed some serious work.

He deftly turned the conversation to something innocuous,

and she paid enough attention to answer and mumbled comments when necessary.

When the meal was finished, she actually felt the tension in her gut coiled for release.

"Would you go for a walk with me tonight?"

Standing just outside the canteen in the dark cool evening, she was acutely aware of being virtually alone with Samuels. Only a few people remained inside, everyone else had moved off to the bonfire, a social event she normally enjoyed.

She did not want to be any more alone with him than she was already. Maybe she could think of him as one of the old department heads, someone that didn't intimidate her anymore? She glanced at him. His smooth chocolate complexion was dark in the low light, too fine to be an old man in her department, too handsome to be anything but intimidating. His gaze remained steady on her, watching her every gesture and expression. Nope. There was no way in hell she'd be able to think of him as harmless.

"I'm really tired," she started, but he took her arm, choking off any further objections.

"It's my last night," he murmured near her ear. "Just a short walk."

Her throat was too dry to answer, but she was pretty sure he wouldn't have accepted excuses anyway. He guided her into the woods, in the opposite direction from the bonfire. Her heart hammered, and she swore she saw spots before her.

"I've enjoyed getting to know you, Ti'ann." His voice was soft and seductive.

She had to fight back a wave of panic. What could she say? He'd know if she lied. She was too flustered. "Thank you," she muttered.

He wrapped his arm around her shoulders, drawing her close

to his side. She bumped into him causing them both to stumble. "Sorry."

Damn it, Ti'ann, you're a grown woman. Suck it up. You can handle this. You know he's not serious, that this is only about getting information from you.

But she was having trouble keeping her balance. Outside of Nathan, no other man this good-looking had ever made a pass at her before. She didn't have a clue what to do about the smooth and charming Terrance Samuels.

He stopped in the middle of a path leading to the valley lifts and faced her. "I'm looking forward to returning." He brushed a finger over her cheek, across her chin.

She clenched her teeth to keep from squirming away. "I'm sure you'll be busy when you come back." She tried stepping away from him, but he managed to get an arm around her waist, holding her in place.

"I'll make sure I have some free time."

She came close to screeching when he lowered his head to hers. Shit, he was going to kiss her! What the hell did she do? Was she supposed to kiss back? She really really didn't want to kiss back. But what if he caused them trouble because she didn't play along? She squeezed her eyes shut, felt his lips brush hers and then a voice broke the moment.

"Sorry to interrupt. I need to speak to Dr. Jones," Nathan said.

Her knees weakened. She watched Samuels' eyes narrow, darken, but his expression stayed passive. She couldn't move away from him fast enough. She glanced at Nathan. His face held no expression, no emotion.

"It must be important," Samuels murmured, the statement more a question.

A question Nathan didn't bother to answer. He stood on the camp side of the path, immovable, waiting.

Terrance smiled down at her. "Perhaps you and I can have breakfast together tomorrow, before I have to leave."

She mumbled something noncommittal, he stroked her cheek again, and then he was gone. She stared into the woods for a heartbeat then turned to watch him pass Nathan. They nodded to each other, neutral expressions on both men's faces. When Samuels was out of hearing range, she blew out a pent up breath and leaned against a tree.

"Are you okay?"

Nathan hadn't moved any closer, so she turned her head to look at him. Her smile shook a little. "Yeah, I'm fine. Grateful to see you. He scares the shit out of me. What did you have to talk to me about?"

He stalked toward her, his face suddenly full of emotion, and most of it looked like anger. She stumbled away from the tree, not so grateful to see him anymore. He came toward her like a beam from a laser cannon, all focus and power and deadly intent. She backed away, tripped over a root, her feet tangled and she came up hard against another tree. By the time she'd freed her feet, he was in front of her, pushing her back against the trunk.

She sucked in a breath. His hands were hard on her shoulders, his eyes hooded and impossible to read. "What?" Panic tickled through her again. Just when a woman thought she was safe.

"Never do anything like that again. He's dangerous."

"He's not the only one," she whispered.

"You're right. He's not."

And suddenly his mouth was on hers, her body flush against his. She was so surprised she stood immobile while her stomach exploded with giddy heat. *Oh my god!* Nathan Longfeather was kissing her. And he was kissing her like he wanted her, like he'd kissed her that first time three years ago.

His tongue touched hers and sent a shock of energy bolting from her stomach down her legs. He tasted like wine. That surprised her too. Then she kissed him back, struggling to taste more of him, feel more of his hard body against hers. Her senses came alive with the smell of him, the feel of him. She ran her hands up to his shoulders, kneading the strong muscles, then around his neck. She burrowed her fingers into his hair just above the leather strap holding it in a low tail. It was as thick and smooth as she remembered.

She moaned, delighted by the contrast of cool hair and hot skin beneath. Her fingers traveled back to his neck. Would he mind if she tasted the skin over his pulse? Would he stop her if she tried to loosen his hair? She tried to drag her mouth away from his. His hands came up to frame her face, holding her where she was. So she fell back into enjoying the feel of his tongue against hers. Each breath filled her with his scent until he was the only thing in her world.

When he started pulling away, when his tongue withdrew from her mouth, she fought the urge to cry. What was she doing?

She eased back before he could and tried to put some distance between them but there was still a tree behind her. She'd just made a complete fool of herself, responding so eagerly, so desperately.

She couldn't look him in the face as she stammered, "That was…"

"As amazing as I thought it would be. As amazing as I remembered."

Her gaze shot to his. He was smiling, and the look in his

eyes reminded her of a predator watching its prey. But it was his words that really hit her. "Remembered? You remember me?"

He raised a brow. "Of course." One of his hands moved to her neck, circled around her nape, his thumb rubbing gentle patterns in the skin beneath her ear. "I was wondering, though, why you never said anything."

"I… I thought you didn't know who I was. With my hair brown again, and…" She sucked in her lips in an attempt to keep from saying anything else mortifying.

"I wasn't sure when I first saw you again if you were the same person." He reached back and tugged on her braid. "You *did* look a bit different then. But it didn't take me long to figure it out."

Blonde hair and a tight red dress did make a difference. It had been part of her attempt to seduce her then boyfriend on their last night of the conference in Aveon. She'd even had a friend help her with makeup. She had barely recognized herself in the mirror. It was one of the few times in her life she felt feminine—not gorgeous or stunning or beautiful, but feminine, womanly. Then Brad had walked past her in the hotel bar with a stunning woman on his arm. He'd had the gall to wink at her before continuing on up the hotel lifts. He'd denied that part later, said he hadn't even seen her, but it didn't matter. She'd been devastated. Nathan Longfeather had sat down beside her at the bar when she was on her third shot of Binnean whiskey.

"I recognized you," she said.

The intensity of his gaze made her stomach dance. "You did a good job of keeping it to yourself."

"I was embarrassed you didn't remember me."

"I remembered you. I just had to hear your name to be certain." He ran a finger along her cheek, caressing the soft area beneath her bottom lip. "Do you remember how I had to force your name from you when we first met?"

Did she remember it? He'd been on top of her, inside her, his finger placed just right to keep her hovering, painfully just at the edge of a rare and precious abyss. She'd tried begging, pleading, but he kept repeating, "Your name," in that soft, seductive whisper. "Tell me your name." A kiss on her cheek. "I'll give you everything you need. Just tell me your name."

"Ti'ann," she'd panted, a tear slipping down her temple. "My name's Ti'ann." She'd felt his smile against her jaw then his finger shifted, his rhythm increased, and Ti'ann couldn't speak or remember much more for some time after. That knife-edge decent into pleasure had been anything but rare over the next two days, but each one had still been precious.

Now, he leaned in close again, kissing her temple, her cheek, moved across to her ear and the sensitive skin beneath. She started shaking. Memories melded with the present, swamping her senses. Three years of depriving herself of this had left her so sensitive his touch almost hurt. When his tongue flicked out, tasting her, she let out an involuntary sound some-where between a moan and a squeal.

"We need to get to your tent," he groaned against her neck. "Too many people could walk past us here. I don't want to get interrupted again."

"Again?"

"Last night."

"Oh." All the hurt and insecurity fled under the firm knowl-edge that he'd wanted her this entire time, that she hadn't been imagining things, that he really did remember her.

"Your tent," he reminded her, his voice strained.

"Yes." Though she wouldn't have noticed if the entire camp walked by at that moment. She was incapable of thinking, aware of only him. She felt drunk and dizzy and not the least bit worried about being drunk and dizzy. He could take her up against the tree and it wouldn't cross her mind to object. In fact, she'd relish it.

"I'm not sure I'll be able to walk that far," she murmured, as she stroked her fingers over the hard muscles of his chest. He felt wonderful.

"Don't tempt me." He kissed her again, deep and hard and she forgot what they were talking about.

CHAPTER FIFTEEN

AFTER SEVERAL LONG MINUTES, NATHAN PULLED BACK AND PUT some space between their bodies. He was breathing hard and so close to losing control he could barely see straight. Ti'ann looked up at him with heavy-lidded eyes, her mouth bruised from his kisses; so damned sexy. He needed to get them some privacy soon or he was going to fuck her against the tree. Not that she looked like she'd mind.

He glanced away, into the forest. He'd prefer taking her to his ship where he knew they'd have complete privacy. Anyone could walk into her tent. But they'd have to walk through the woods and avoid the bonfire to get to the landing pad without running into anyone. It was a long walk. He wasn't sure he'd make it to her tent, nonetheless all the way to his ship. So her tent it was. For now. To take the edge off. Then maybe he'd talk her into spending the night in his ship with him. BinRal would be able to keep an eye on things. Just this one night. If he could have this one night, he was sure he'd be able to think straight again.

"Come on." He took her hand and headed toward camp. He was walking too fast for her; she had to trot to keep up, but he couldn't slow down. Even holding her hand was making his blood race.

As they neared the edge of the clearing, he listened for voices. Everything sounded quiet. Most everyone would be at the bonfire, enjoying a few drinks and some story telling or songs. So they should have a clear path. The last thing he needed now was to get stopped on the way for some long conversation that brought Dr. Jones out of her sensual stupor.

"Almost there," he said more to himself than to her as they started across camp.

"Hurry."

Her voice, quiet and thick with longing, nearly undid him. God, yes, he'd hurry.

He pulled her through the tent flap and into his arms in one move. Better, but not good enough. He stripped her, tasting skin as he revealed it. Part of him wanted to slow down but he couldn't. He'd been thinking about this since he saw her again. He hadn't been this wound up since he was a teenager. His clothes hit the floor, and he kissed her again.

Her fingers tangled in his hair, tugging at the band holding it back. He helped her loosen it then unwound her braid. Thick, heavy waves of brown silk fell into his palms. Better than blonde, he decided. Perfect. Her. He stepped back to look at her, naked, her hair falling around her shoulders like a cloak, her skin flushed and warm. She was the sexiest woman he'd ever known. Like a mythical goddess.

For a beat, he just looked at her. She stared back, a brief flash of uncertainty crossing through her gaze. Oh no you don't, he thought, and pulled her into his arms. This was no time to shy away from him. He wanted Ti'ann, the lust-drugged goddess, and he intended to have her.

He pushed her onto the narrow cot and covered her with his body. The bed groaned under their weight. *Wonder if it'll hold?* Didn't matter. If it collapsed, they'd just have to finish on the floor.

She panted against his ear. Her hands were all over his body, petting and kneading him, driving him closer to insanity with every touch. Her tongue flicked against his neck, slid up his throat and he shuddered. "That feels good."

He shifted and moved until he had her sprawled on top of him. He'd last longer this way. He hoped.

Something bunched under his back and he wiggled to flatten it out. Because he was watching her, even in the dim light he saw a flush crawl across her cheeks. "What's wrong?"

"Nothing." She pursed her lips and wouldn't meet his eyes as she said, "That's your jacket, if you want to move it."

He raised his brows, so surprised, for a minute, he was silent. Then, "You have my jacket in your bed?"

"I meant to give it back the next day, after you loaned it to me that first night. But… I…"

"You've slept with it this entire time?" His already racing heart thumped harder. The thought of her sleeping with his jacket sent jolts of excitement though his blood.

She swallowed. "I like the way it smells."

He groaned and squeeze his eyes closed. "Were you naked?"

She wiggled, the wet heat of her brushing his abdomen. Stars danced behind his closed eyelids. Every nerve in his body, already tensed and eager for her, went into overdrive.

"Uhm. Yes," she admitted softly.

"Fuck." He breathed out between his clenched teeth. "If I'd know that, I'd have joined you in this cot a hell of a lot sooner."

His cock jerked in anticipation and he was about a nanosecond from thrusting into her.

"Really?" she asked, a touch of humor in her voice.

When he opened his eyes, she was smiling down at him without a hint of the embarrassment from just a moment ago.

"Why did you wait?"

"Job. You're a client. It was nothing. Stupid. Never mind." His vaunted rule was pointless now. Had been from the moment he saw her again. He never could have made it to the end of this job without getting her naked again. He'd been fooling himself to think he'd ever stood a chance of resisting her.

He cupped her face and pulled her down for a kiss, devouring her mouth, so beyond desperate now he couldn't pace himself.

She broke the kiss and asked, "Do you want your jacket back?"

"No. Keep it." The idea of her having a piece of his clothing with her was like a branding, like leaving his scent on her, and it appealed to such a primitive part of him he barely recognized the impulse. He didn't want to analyze it either. "You looked better in it anyway."

She smiled, the expression wicked and sultry, then dipped her head. He felt her breath hot against his skin and her mouth moved lower. He had a pretty good idea where she was headed and really liked the idea, but he didn't think he'd survive it. Not now. Not this time. He pulled her back up and kissed her, keeping her curious tongue well occupied.

Her hair fell across his shoulders, tickling his chest. She used some sort of flower-scented soap and it surrounded him now, filling his senses. He remembered she smelled of something similar the last time they were together. Would that scent have infused his jacket now? Maybe he did want the jacket back if it smelled like her, like the two of them mingled together. He reached up and cupped her cheek, watching shadows play across her face in the dark tent. She was so stunning, so sexy; she robbed him of all reason. And if he didn't get inside her soon, his heart might just burst from the strain.

Pulse hammering, he said, "I have to… I can't wait… I want to go slower, but…"

She put a finger over his mouth. "Now. Now is very very good."

He couldn't agree more. With a growl, he pushed into her wet heat. Her eyes closed as he entered her, her head falling back. Her long hair tickled his thighs, adding another sensual layer of sensation. He forced himself to breathe slowly as he gently worked himself into her. The feel of her clenched around his cock pushed him too close to the edge, but turning back now was impossible. Still, he didn't want to hurt her. "You're so tight," he whispered, groaning when she shifted to settle farther onto him.

"It's been awhile."

"Are you all right?"

"Almost." She rose up until he was nearly free of her then dropped her hips hard against his, taking him fully in the single motion.

"Fuck," he muttered again, squeezing her hips. Sensations bombarded him—the cool air on his cock when she lifted herself off him, only to be swallowed by her heat when she pushed back down. Her tight, slick channel squeezed him mercilessly. His control in tatters, he almost lost it completely.

"I'm better now." Her wicked grin made his cock pulse.

She rode him so slowly it was like tortured. He clenched his teeth, trying to think of something else. He caught her scent again and his brain sizzled. "You're killing me," he murmured, reaching up to caress her breasts. She shuddered when he toyed with her nipples and increased her rhythm. "Better. Now, faster."

"No." She slowed again.

"Yes." He pinched her nipples until she moaned.

"Not yet," she pleaded, but she moved faster.

"Yes. Now. I want to feel you come." He moved one hand between them, pressed his thumb against her clit and held the pressure.

She threw her head back. "Oh, god."

Her voice strained as she held back. She'd been more vocal in the hotel room. He'd loved all the noises she made, all her little sounds of pleasure, her groans of satisfaction. Once they'd taken the edge off, he was definitely taking Ti'ann to his ship for some privacy where she could make all the noise he wanted her to.

He watched her face flush, felt her body quiver; he was enthralled by her movements.

"Ti'ann. Come for me. Now." He increased the pressure of his thumb on her clit, stroking it in tandem with her movements as she rode him. Then her body jerked as a squeal she tried to hold in erupted from her.

Feeling her clench tightly around him robbed him of what little control he had left. He thrust up and finally let go. He gritted his teeth as he came, arching his back reflexively. His body shuddered with the intensity of his orgasm.

When they were spent, Nathan collapsed back onto the cot, pulling Ti'ann down onto his chest, both of them panting hard. He felt her hot breath on his skin and savored that tickle of sensation, a sensation he'd never been able to forget.

Still inside her, he held her hips, drawing small circles over her soft skin. She trembled and clenched around his still semi-hard cock. His groan turned into a chuckle when she sighed. "You sound pleased."

"Yes."

She also sounded sleepy and content. That was one of the many sounds he liked to hear her make. "Let's go to my ship." He kissed her temple through a mass of sweet smelling hair. "We'll have more privacy."

She sat up a little to look down at him. "We're going to need more privacy?"

"You didn't think I was finished with you yet, did you?"

Her eyes widened.

"I'm not. Come back to my ship. I'm going to need most of the night with you."

She stared at him for a long minute, not smiling or blinking. He waited, holding his breath, fully prepared to beg if he had to. If she refused, he'd stay here and seduce her again, and again if he needed to until she agreed. The longer she stared, the more he decided talking her into coming back to his ship might be fun.

Then she grinned, a secretive cat's grin, and his heart started thumping.

"I think I'd like more privacy," she said.

TI'ANN WOKE FEELING warm and safe, and sore. She hadn't felt this sore in...three years. She lay spooned up against Nathan, her back to his chest. His arm was heavy and secure around her waist, a brace she was grateful for considering how narrow his bunk was. She stared across the small cabin at a featureless metal wall wondering if he had anything to drink.

She slid out from under his arm, onto the floor, and almost

collapsed when her wobbly legs wouldn't hold her weight. Bracing a hand against the wall, she waited while her body stabilized. Damn, she was sore. She grimaced as she moved, only to grin a moment later with a memory of how she'd gotten like this. Not a night she'd ever forget or regret. She stumbled naked out into the companionway in search of an auto-cooker or a cooler. She kept one hand braced on the wall to stay upright then fell, almost literally, into a closet-sized bathroom only a few steps past Nathan's room.

Might as well stop here first.

She looked around the tiny cubicle, all very functional and utilitarian. Like the rest of the ship. There didn't seem to be any wasted space. The vehicle was sleek and small and fast, yet it was cleverly designed with enough room for a couple of people to live in it for a few weeks. It reminded her of those old Earth stories of mobile homes. Personally, she couldn't imagine living in such a confined space for very long. Her tent wasn't big, but she had an entire campsite to live in.

She used the small toilet then washed as best she could using the miniscule sink, hampered by the size of the room and the inability of her muscles to fully cooperate. When she felt mildly refreshed, she eased back out into the companionway to find something to drink. She stepped into the solid wall of Nathan's chest.

"Oh. Sorry."

He pulled her close and she rested her hands on his shoulders, liking the feel of muscles flexing under her touch. He was still naked too and his skin was warm against hers. He stared down at her, his hands smoothing up and down her back. The expression on his face was strange, impossible for her to read, but not blank, not that neutral working look he got sometimes. There was definitely something there.

"You okay?" She would have pulled back if he hadn't tightened his grip.

"Fine. You?"

She smiled, tentative but genuine. "I'm sore and thirsty. Got anything to drink around here?"

His expression cleared and he grinned. "Sorry. I should have thought of that earlier. Come on." He took her hand and pulled her a little farther up the companionway to a small auto-cooker, then punched in an order for two containers of water and a container of fruit juice. "You need the sustenance," he told her with a crooked smile that made her stomach dance. "Do you want something to eat?"

"No. I'm just thirsty."

His eyes narrowed. "And sore. How sore?"

"Very," she groaned. "I'll get over it."

"Did you shower? The hot water would do you good."

"I didn't want to make that much noise. I was trying not to wake you."

"Too late, I'm up." He handed her a container of water and waited until she'd finished it before taking a sip of his own. Then he handed her the fruit juice and nodded at her to drink.

She did, a little self-conscious under his scrutiny. Her gaze dropped. Oh. Bad idea. He hadn't been joking about being up. Her gaze jumped back up to his chest, but despite her best effort, she peaked again. He was an impressive man.

She gulped down some of the cold juice and handed the container to him. "Want some of this?"

"No. Drink it all. You need it."

Yes, she thought, peaking again because she couldn't not look at him. She was definitely going to need all her energy. She smiled into the container as she finished off the last of the juice. Not that she minded. She hadn't felt this free, this satiated in years. She might only get this one night from him, and she intended to take advantage of the situation before he got tired of her.

He pulled her close when she'd finished her juice and kissed her, gentle despite the pressure of his erection against her stomach. She could feel tension running through his arms and chest, but his kiss was relaxed and confident. When he eased back, she expected to be led back to his room. Instead, he took her into the tiny bathroom cubicle.

There was barely enough room for them both. They couldn't move without touching one another. He pressed a code into the palm-sized console next to the door. The toilet and sink retracted into the walls, and the room became a shower with two jets of hot water pummeling them.

She groaned in pleasure, hunching her shoulders forward so the water would work from her shoulders down her back. "This fells wonderful."

"That's just the beginning."

He pumped soap onto his hand from the dispenser positioned near where the sink had been, lathered the soap up, then began washing her. He massaged as he went, squatting down in front of her to start at her ankles and feet. There was so little room in the cubicle that she ended up standing between his spread legs while he balanced on his toes in front of her. The position put his face close to the most tender part of her body. She felt his breath hot against her curls, and held her own breath, hoping he'd lean just a little bit forward.

He continued cleaning and massaging her, working up her legs, across her butt, gently between her legs, so gently she thought she'd scream. He rubbed up her stomach, kissing her belly as he stood. The touch of his lips made her knees weaken. She wanted him on his knees in front of her again, but she was enjoying the torturous washing so much she stayed quiet, waiting. He washed her stomach, spent time in kneading and caressing her breasts. Her breathing quickened and she forgot about her sore muscles.

She tried pressing closer, but he eased her away and turned her so she was facing the wall. Water sloshed over her arms and shoulders, hitting her with warmth from both sides. He worked soap and strong hands down her back, pushing her hair over one shoulder to get it out of the way.

"How does that feel?"

"Wonderful," she murmured, leaning her forehead against the wall.

"There's more to come."

"I don't think I can take much more."

"Yes, you can." He moved his soapy hands into her hair and started massaging her scalp. She dropped her head back so he could rub her temples. The jets shot hot water over both her shoulders, and between their bodies, creating a buffer between them. When she let her head fall back, the water grabbed her hair and swung it down her back again. He eased his fingers through the length, gently untangling knots.

"That feels so good. I'll reciprocate when you finish. I promise."

"Not this time." He kissed the side of her neck, making her shiver. "But next time maybe."

She loved the sound of that, liked they might end up in the shower together again. She wasn't sure she'd be able to get enough of him. He was like a sensory glut, better than being turned loose in a bakery with all those delicious cakes and pies at her disposal. She knew it couldn't last. He'd get bored with her again. But right now, she needed this release, needed to indulge her sensual side without feeling embarrassed or ashamed.

Her other two lovers had made her feel shy about her love of touching and tasting and feeling and talking during sex. She'd tried once, with each of them, to indulge her senses, to please them as well as herself. But they'd both been turned off by the idea and her efforts. Brad had laughed at her and told her she wasn't that kind of woman so not to try. Jack had been appalled she wanted to talk during sex or try new things. He'd been insulted that she didn't think he was man enough to lead the way. So she'd let him. And been bored but content with his conversation and company. Until he'd dumped her for a girl half his age, even younger than Ti'ann had been. He told her he was bored with the sex when he left. She still didn't understand that part, but she knew it was her fault.

The only person she'd ever been able to truly indulge herself with was Nathan. She'd let loose and felt completely uninhibited with him. He never laughed at her or told her she wasn't "that kind of woman" while she indulged her every fantasy. Oh, he'd gotten bored a lot faster than the others, as evident by his hasty departure, but at least she wasn't bored while he was with her.

Nathan turned her into a spray of water to rinse her hair. Facing him again, she felt the need to lean into him, kiss his strong chin, lick the water off his neck. When she tried, though, he held her back with his hands still in her hair.

"My turn to indulge," he said, his voice deep and husky.

His words were so close to her thoughts she sucked in a sharp breath. Then his hands moved to her breasts again and she thought, *Okay, you can indulge all you want.*

"I love looking at you like this," he murmured. "Your skin flushed and wet, warm from the water."

"The water isn't the reason my skin is warm."

"I love that, too." He leaned down, taking her nipple in his mouth.

She dropped her head into the water and groaned. "You can do more of that if you like."

His chuckle was hot against her skin. "I intend to." And he kissed lower, moving down to her stomach, dropping to his haunches again in front of her.

"You can definitely do more of that," she said when his mouth moved lower.

"Are you still sore?"

"What?" She couldn't think anymore. She was practically on her toes, waiting and willing him to move his mouth between her legs.

"Are you still sore?" he asked again, his voice patient and quiet.

"I can't tell. No. I'm fine. If you don't stop teasing me, I'm going to scream."

"So scream."

Since she wasn't much of a screamer, she moaned loudly instead and clenched her fingers in his wet hair. She tilted his head so he was looking up at her, his eyes dark with desire and humor. "Stop teasing or I'll make you pay later."

He grinned and leaned forward to lick a circle around her navel. "I look forward to it."

And then he eased lower, his mouth moving to where she wanted him, and she forgot about everything else but the play of his lips and tongue. When she came, she screamed.

He wrapped her in his arms and held her until the last ripples of pleasure eased from her body. Then he stood, keyed the water off and the air dryer on. "I love the noises you make," he said, kissing her cheek.

She was too spent to stay upright without his support. "Your turn next. As soon as I can stand again."

His laugh was quiet and tickled her nerves. He dropped his hands to her butt and lifted her. She wrapped her legs around him to keep her balance. "You don't need to be able to stand," he murmured against her lips and then he slid into her.

TI'ANN WOKE WITH AT START, looked at the readout above Nathan's computer console and realized the sun was already up. Damn. She'd intended to leave before dawn, to get back to her tent without anyone noticing. She did not want to explain last night to Krin. He'd probably be happy for her, but she wasn't prepared to talk about it yet.

She rolled away from Nathan and was surprised when his arm tightened at her waist, pulling her back against his chest. "I have to get up," she said, wriggling around to face him.

He lay on his side, keeping his arm firmly around her. His eyes were nearly gold in the dim light, most of the green lost. "Not yet."

"I have to get back to my tent. I don't want to waste the day answering Krin's questions about this."

He didn't smile or grin or otherwise crack the hard line of his mouth, not even to frown. "Will he be upset?"

"Not if I'm not."

"Are you?"

"No. Of course not. I'm surprised you'd ask."

"You were going to leave without waking me."

"I would have said goodbye."

"Good. Now go back to sleep. You don't start work for another two hours."

"At which point everyone in the camp will be awake and moving around."

"You embarrassed to be with me?"

"No!" She dropped her gaze to his chin. "I didn't think you'd want this broadcast around the camp. They talk you know."

He shrugged. "Doesn't bother me. I'm too exhausted to be awake right now. Go back to sleep." He closed his eyes and pulled her tightly to him so her cheek rested against his chest and his chin on top of her head.

He felt so warm and being wrapped in his arms felt so good that she sighed and gave in. She was exhausted too. And he wasn't chasing her away so there was no point running.

Krin would never let her hear the end of this.

CHAPTER SIXTEEN

Ti'ann returned to the trench, frowning over the call from the museum. She nodded to BinRal in passing. The Binnean had stayed near the new site since they'd started digging again late that afternoon, after Nathan was positive Samuels was gone. Nathan, however, had disappeared almost immediately—off securing the rest of the site. She hadn't seen him since.

She joined Krin at the side of the trench, her gaze turned to the volunteers, grad students and excavators chiseling away the remaining muck and rock left after the EDU had taken out as much of the overburden as possible.

"What did they want?" Krin said under his breath.

"To tell us they're glad Nathan Longfeather is working out, they're happy about our new discovery, and could we have a report in with our hypothesis in two weeks."

He looked up at her sharply. "How did they know about the new dig?"

"Good question." She kept her eyes on the trench, as she

thought over the call. "Did you go to the committee for the funding to hire Nathan?"

"No. I made other arrangements. Does this mean they're paying now?"

"That's the impression I got. What other arrangements?"

"I was going to borrow the money from Devin."

"Krin…"

"Don't start." He held up a hand. "Doesn't matter now anyway."

She sighed out her irritation. "Okay. Fine. I still want to know how they knew about our find."

"Nathan mentioned a friend on the Board. Suppose he told him?"

"That's right. Mr. Alexander. I thought that was just a story."

"Well the museum is paying for security now. Bet Nathan's Mr. Alexander had a hand in that." Krin fell quiet and they both watched the work below.

After a few minutes, she called into the pit and motioned one of the volunteers out, taking up a chisel herself. If she just stood there, she had too much time to think about all the questions she had. While she was grateful Samuels was gone, they still had the mystery of who'd been tampering with Monroe's ship, Samuels' impending return, and the tenuous state of some of their equipment. She didn't even want to begin thinking about the situation between her and Nathan.

Ti'ann stepped onto the mini-lift as soon as Pat stepped off. The small platform did double duty hauling buckets of rock and soil up out of the trench and moving the team in and out of the more than ten meter deep pit. She had no idea how paleontologists worked before the advent of platform lifts and Excavation Digger Units—even if their particular EDU was constantly in need of repairs. Though she did enjoy getting down to the delicate work with the old fashioned brush and chisel. And work was always a good distraction from more…difficult thoughts.

Not that she regretted her night with Nathan. The entire experience had been too satisfying and freeing for regrets. But he'd been able to snap back into his work mode this morning with ease, an ease that left her reeling with uncertainty. He'd seemed to want her around right up until they left the ship, and then he'd sent her on her way without a backward glance. Without even a touch on the shoulder or a gentle look or something to say he'd enjoyed their night together. Doubt crept in during the day. Was that it then? One night and she'd have to look at him every day, want him every day, remember in exquisite detail what they'd shared, and not be able to have him again?

She'd told herself she was prepared for that. If all he wanted was the one night to work off his needs, then she was going to take what she could and not look back. Unfortunately, her logic failed her. She wanted more than one night.

She tried hard to concentrate on digging. She sat cross-legged in the dirt, knocking hammer against chisel to break apart the covering rock. The longer she focused, the easier it was to avoid thinking. So when a layer broke open to reveal something that wasn't just rock, she had no idea how long she'd been working.

Scrapping away the extra chips with her hands, she brushed an area until it was free of dirt and fingered the smooth surface. It was green with a hint of gold. The color stood out sharply against the blue/brown dirt and purple rock they were clearing away.

"I've found something," she said and all work in the trench stopped. Those nearest to her shuffled around to look and passed the word along to those farther away. Anya, the grad student nearest Ti'ann, shouted a description up to those standing around the top of the pit. The mini-lift activated and climbed upward.

Excitement rippled through the group, catching her up in the thrill. "Krin, do you have the hand scanner?" she shouted up as she brushed more dirt away from the green, trying to expose more of the new material. The hand scanner, at this range, was a hundred times better at reading the molecular content of an object.

Krin jumped off the mini-lift, already on his way down before her shouted request, and handed her the scanner. She ran the rectangular, inch thick box over the top of the green/gold object, keyed in the appropriate codes, and swept it across the object again, slowly, methodically as it scanned. While the devise ran its analysis, the area was sketched and recorded by a volunteer, and the coordinates were entered into a palm computer onto the 3-D site map. When the scanner beeped its completion, she keyed in another set of codes and waited. Krin sat on his haunches, a hand on her shoulder for balance, watching the readout screen as intently as she was. She couldn't feel his breath so murmured, "Breathe," to remind them both.

As the data started scrolling up the screen, her gaze darted through the contents. There was the genetic material again, concentrated in the green/gold object instead of being mixed in with the other local "ingredients" their anomaly was made of. The DNA had the same single base pair shift they'd found in the earlier scans. She gasped, paused the scrolling text, and pointed to one element they hadn't detected earlier. Aminophentine-carboxylase, an enzyme that was extremely rare in nature. "Isn't that...?"

"Exactly what Ripley and Hesh reported in decomposed Shifter remains," Krin finished for her.

They both looked back at the green/gold surface. Smooth, featureless, warmer to the touch than it should have been in the damp earth. She let the information finish scrolling and read the scanner's theory of what the object was based on known data. "Inconclusive. Organic. Most closely resembles animal specifications. No evidence of bone structure."

"Holy shit," Krin whispered. "You think it's…?"

"A Shifter skeleton?"

"Yeah."

"Yeah." She glanced up at the faces hovering around the edge of the trench, looking small from that distance. Those in the trench were working again, but they were quiet enough she knew they were listening to what she and Krin said. "Val?" she shouted. The mini-lift hummed to life and ascended.

The Shifter, still in its guise as a human woman, jumped off the lift before it settled back into the bottom of the trench. Val anxiously looked at the scanned data, read the scanner's hypothesis.

"Well?" Ti'ann asked, in a quiet voice.

In a murmur she could barely hear, Val said, "Part of a dead Shifter."

Monroe called down to Val and the Shifter looked up at him, quiet but concentrating. It only lasted a few seconds, but in those seconds, Ti'ann was sure Val had told him everything. Shame she didn't have that trait. Communication via telepathy had to be very handy.

For appearances, Val pulled a small flat comm-link from the pocket of a short-sleeved shirt and reported the findings to Monroe in a quiet voice. From so far away, it was impossible to gauge his reaction to the news.

Farther along the trench someone called, "There's more here. Looks like what you found, Dr. Jones. But there are streaks and chunks of other material in it. Almost like marble."

Ti'ann edged past the other people squatting and sitting in the rubble, continuing to dig. The newly uncovered area wasn't a smooth, featureless patch but a curved and dented area of about half a meter square.

"It's pretty," Micca, one of the volunteers, commented.

This was Micca's first dig, Ti'ann remembered as she scanned the new patch, and she wondered if the volunteer thought this kind of historic find was normal. Well, she'd learn better soon enough—if this dig didn't send her running from paleontology.

"Beautiful," Val murmured, echoing Micca's comment.

Ti'ann hadn't realized the Shifter had followed her. The scan revealed a similar composition to her part of the anomaly but with the addition of some precious and semi-precious stones streaked through it.

"This is really…?" Ti'ann heard the awe in her own voice.

"It is," Val confirmed.

"And more."

Ti'ann and Val spun to face the new voice. A man Ti'ann had never seen before stood in the trench, his back to Krin and the rest of the team, facing herself, Val and Micca. "Who the hell are you and what are you doing on my dig site?" There'd been no warning, no sound of the mini-lift moving.

The man smiled a little and looked at Val. Val's green eyes widened as it stared back. They stood silently for long minutes and tension rose with each passing second.

Ti'ann squinted up to the top of the trench. Just at the edge, BinRal stood with a blaster in hand aimed at the stranger. Next to BinRal, Ti'ann was surprised to see Nathan standing with his blaster trained on a second newcomer, a woman who looked down into the trench but didn't seem to take any notice of the weapon pointing at her head. It was impossible to see her expression clearly, but she looked to be frowning.

Ti'ann swallowed and turned back to the man staring at Val. He was tall and thin, with short-cropped dark hair and an amazing shade of silver eyes. They were like quicksilver or mercury and seemed to flow and melt and reform as she watched. It was so disturbing she found she couldn't look him in the face. His clothes were simple, similar to the shorts and t-shirts her team wore. But he had bare feet, and his toes looked strange. She stared at them but couldn't put her finger on what was wrong. She let her gaze travel to his hands, which were, to her relief, free of weapons. His fingers looked funny too. Kind of rounded off and smooth. She stared for several heartbeats before she realized he didn't have any fingernails. Or toe nails. And it wasn't as if they were torn off or removed, the skin was smooth and undamaged. The nails just weren't there.

She glanced up at the woman again. She couldn't see her feet at all and her hands were fisted. As she stared at the woman's clothing—a match to the man's and the only thing she could really distinguish clearly—she started to wonder if they were really human.

Val's voice caught her attention. "It doesn't seem possible," the Shifter murmured to the man. "There's been no contact at all. We were sure you were dead, but…"

The man was silent for a few breaths, then Val grinned, nodded and said, "Yes. That's why I came. Am I helping you or should I translate for them?"

Another silence, another nod from Val, and Val turned to Ti'ann, grin huge but eyes worried. "Dr. Jones, this is more exciting than I hoped. I don't know where to start." It glanced at

Micca hovering behind her shoulder then shrugged. "I think it's important now that I come clean." Val winked and shifted to natural form.

Around the trench her group let out a range of gasps and shouts and behind her Micca fainted. Ti'ann turned in time to catch the girl as she sank forward. After lowering her to the ground, Ti'ann spun back to Val to see the stranger also in Shifter form. Her gaze jumped to the woman standing at the top of the trench and there stood another Shifter. For several heart-beats, she stared, not quite believing what she saw.

They looked different from Val. Their bodies weren't nearly as smooth and featureless. The one who had taken a male human form was noticeably smaller than the one who had taken a female form, the difference obvious even with the one so far above them. And their bodies showed subtle differences in shape. The one in the trench had stockier limbs and a wide face. The one above had a thicker middle but gracefully slim limbs and a much narrower head.

"Holy shit," Krin said from behind the new Shifter. "Val, what the hell's going on?"

Val stood so both Ti'ann and Krin where in view. The new Shifter moved to one side so it was no longer blocking half the trench. Ti'ann glanced past Krin and saw one of the grad-students, Joanna, leaning against the wall with her head between her knees.

"Dr. Jones, Dr. Freemont," Val said. "These two are...well, let's call them Zim and Sar. Their identifications aren't part of your vocabulary." The mouth formed in Val's Shifter face lifted and dimpled its cheeks. "They are of a line that was long lost to us."

"Lost? How?" Krin said.

"When? What do you mean lost?" Ti'ann said at the

same time.

"It's a long story, one to be told in a more comfortable place. But I have the answer now to your question about what this anomaly is." Val paused and the other Shifter in the trench—Sar or Zim?—nodded. "You've uncovered the outer border of an underground city. An active Shifter city."

Ti'ann dropped back against the trench wall, sucking in deep breaths so she wouldn't fall down. Her head spun. She'd been afraid to really hope, afraid to consider the possibilities. In fact, she'd been convinced they'd actually found a Shifter graveyard after the data the hand scanner reported.

But it wasn't a graveyard. It was a city. Shifters really built cities!

She turned to see Krin leaning over, his hands braced on his knees. He sucked in deep breaths too. He looked up at her, a heavy lock of red-gold hair in his eyes, and grinned. And despite her moment of panic, she smiled back.

"Oh, my god," she whispered. And Krin broke into a full-blown laugh. She joined him, giddy with the realization that they'd stumbled onto something so huge. She stood away from the wall and hugged Val without thinking about it. The Shifter lifted its arms and hugged back. It felt solid and friendly and comforting all at once.

She turned to face the new Shifter. "Thank you," she said. "Thank you for allowing us to know about this."

Its silver eyes flicked to Val then back to her. A mouth formed in its face and the mouth smiled. After what looked like an effort, it said, "You are welcome."

She realized suddenly, by the effort it took to say those words, it probably didn't understand their language the way Val did. "Can you understand us at all?"

Val answered. "They can, in a way. They know you

protected knowledge of this place from the inspectors. They've been watching you since you arrived, knew when you'd discovered their city, and waited to see what you'd do. They had every intention of thwarting your attempts to excavate if it became necessary. When they realized you intended no harm, they thought to make contact before you found out anyway."

Ti'ann stared at the new Shifter, watched its silver eyes blend and flow, and thought, that one's Zim. She glanced up quickly to see the Shifter above them watching the proceedings. It hadn't formed a mouth or any features recognizable to a human beyond the large silver swirls of its eyes. The silver looked a nice contrast to the gold of its skin. Sar, she thought. That one just seemed to be Sar.

Her gaze caught Nathan's for a brief instant. He had the blaster lowered but still in hand. She wished she could read his expression from this distance. Though, even close up, she usually couldn't tell what he was thinking.

"There was debate," Val said, into the hush. "Over whether to contact your group or not. They've been isolated for a very long time. My presence helped. Their ability to understand your language and the use of words, they picked that up from me. Without me even knowing."

Ti'ann was sure she'd have been upset to learn they'd been in her head without her knowledge, but Val sounded fascinated. In awe. The awe part she could understand.

"Val, I've got so many questions I don't know where to start?" She paused. "Should we offer them hospitality or…? They probably eat from the environment like you though, don't they?"

Val grinned again. "They do." Val stared at Zim when saying, "There have been some unusual changes in their lines. But we'll learn more of that soon."

"So, now what?" Anya asked. She and Glen were hovering over Joanna, who still had her head between her knees, but her face was turned toward the two Shifters.

"Yeah," Glen said. "They're here and we know about them. Now what do we do? Continue to excavate?"

"Now," Val said in a voice that carried to the entire group, even those standing at the top of the trench, "we tour the city."

Silence filled the woods. Not even the birds made any noise. And then Krin started laughing again, the sound of it breaking the stunned group into a chorus of noise.

"Excellent!" Krin said, clapping Zim on the back. The Shifter looked at him and even without features managed to convey shock at the gesture. "Sorry," Krin said, still laughing. "I'm just excited. No harm meant." He glanced at Val who nodded that all was fine.

"Can we go now? Do we have to take any precautions? Decontamination procedures or anything?" Ti'ann could barely talk around her excitement. A Shifter city. She was about to walk into an actual Shifter city! Two weeks ago she hadn't even known such a thing existed and now she was going to see one!

Val talked silently to Zim for a moment, giving Ti'ann enough time to glance around her group. All of them looked excited, though some looked suspicious and wary. She wished she could see the expressions of the group at the top of the trench. BinRal looked relaxed and vigilant. The usual. If he was surprised, excited, offended, stunned, even worried, he didn't show it in his body language. Nathan, on the other hand, looked tense and ready to pounce on something. Even at this distance, she saw he was scowling.

"What?" she mouthed the question at him, lifting her hands in a gesture she hoped he could interpret from so far away. He shook his head and motioned her to join him.

She was torn between staying with Val, hearing Zim's conditions for their entry into the city, and going to Nathan. He looked so angry she was almost afraid to talk to him. With reluctance, she said, "I'll be right back," to Val and Krin.

Krin's eyebrows lowered, concern plain in his green eyes. She didn't try to calm his fears. She was worried too. She nodded politely to Zim then she crossed the trench to the mini-lift and rode it back to the top.

Nathan motioned her to one side, away from the others. He stopped so he could still see the crowd, but her back was to them. "What the fuck are you doing?" he hissed.

She took a step away from the venom in his voice. "I'm about to see something no one else has ever seen before, that's what. Even Val hasn't seen this city. What are you so upset about?"

"I'm upset because you could be running headlong and care-less into a massacre. You don't know what these Shifters are like? You can see how different they are from Val. The Shifters we know might not be violent, but we have no idea if these new Shifters are. How do you know this isn't a lure to get you under-ground and kill you all without leaving any evidence?"

She stared at him a moment with her mouth open. If she were being perfectly honest, it hadn't even occurred to her that the Shifters might mean them harm. After her own suspicions when Val had first arrived, her ready acceptance of the newcomers shocked her. She looked at the ground and tried to think beyond her excitement and curiosity.

Did it make sense that the Shifters were here to harm her group? They had to know by now her team had records, equip-ment, regular contact with people outside the camp. If nothing else, the Shifters would have picked up the information from Val. What would be the point of contacting them, then luring them away to kill them? And why tell them about the city at all?

She nibbled at her bottom lip and twisted the end of her braid around her finger as she thought. It didn't make sense that the Shifters would come forward like this if they intended harm when they could easily kill off her group in some shifted form, hide or destroy the bodies and get rid of the equipment before anyone realized there was something wrong. Depending on how many Shifters there were of course.

And maybe that was it. Maybe there weren't very many and they needed to get the group somewhere where their weapons were no good and a small group could ambush them. Or maybe they were afraid if the team disappeared without a trace more humans would be sent in to search the area.

She rubbed circles at her temples as her head spun. She looked up to see Nathan watching her, his look so intent she felt the need to fidget.

"You're right," she said in a quiet voice so it wouldn't carry. "I didn't even think about the possible dangers. Not very smart of me. I assumed these new Shifters were the same as Val, passive and non-threatening. But they're different. So we can't assume anything. But Nathan—" she stepped closer, her voice lowering with her intensity, "—I really want to take this opportunity. If this is authentic, if this is really a Shifter city that no one, not even the other Shifters, has ever seen before..." She sighed and spread her hands. "How can I resist?"

His frown didn't exactly relax, but the lines around his mouth didn't seem so deep and the furrows in his brow were less fixed. "I don't like it. But I can't stop you." He grunted something under his breath that sounded suspiciously like a string of curses. Straightening his shoulders, he said, "If you're doing this no matter what, then you're going to do it as safely as possible. Only a few of you will go down into the city at a time and either BinRal or I will accompany each group." He paused a minute then said, "Or Clare. No one is to wander off alone. Never more than five people will be down in the city at once. And if at any time either I or BinRal feel these Shifters pose a threat, you'll abandon the city without argument."

She opened her mouth to object, closed it again before he could so much as grunt at her, and considered his points. Finally, she nodded. "All right. That seems fair." She turned back to the trench, conscious of Nathan behind her. He didn't touch her, even though he stood close to her, but she felt him along the entire length of her spine.

"Krin," she shouted down into the trench. "Could you come up here?"

He jogged to the lowering mini-lift and joined her at the edge of the trench.

"Nathan's worried so we're going to take some precautions."

Krin frowned and looked between her and Nathan. With a shrug, he said, "He's the expert. What kind of precautions?"

His acceptance was so swift she went blank for a minute, forgetting what she was supposed tell him. Was Krin worried, too? How had she overlooked the dangers so easily? Nathan filled in the silence, outlining the steps he wanted to take to make sure everyone was safe. She listened and felt another touch of shock when Krin agreed without argument. He'd been as excited as she had about the city. He'd been more accepting of Val and the fact that the Shifters weren't dangerous. Had something happened while she was talking with Nathan?

"Did Val say anything while I was gone?" she asked Krin quietly when Nathan finished. "Do they have any more to tell us before we go into the city?"

"We shouldn't need to go through any decontamination process. Their city isn't sealed off from the outside environment and no human vectors have ever infected Shifters before. They said we might need to carry oxygen cylinders with us because, while they're used to the underground air composition, it might take humans a few days to adjust."

"Did they tell you what the change is? Why these Shifters are different from Val?"

Krin glanced back at the two strangers now standing on the edge of the trench as Val introduced them to Monroe and his group. A realization shocked through her. "James can talk to them directly," she murmured.

"What?" Nathan leaned in to hear her but didn't touch her.

She turned to face him and Krin again. "He's never come out and told me, but I'm sure Monroe can talk with Val telepathically. I've seen them do it. Did you know about that, Krin?"

"Val told me. He's the only one of their team who can. So?" He lifted his head and his eyes widened. "So he may be able to tell us if the new Shifters pose a threat since he can communicate the way they do."

She frowned a little. "Maybe. At least he might be able to get an idea of their mood. Hostile or otherwise." She glanced back at Val, still in Shifter form but for the mouth. The mouth was smiling a lot and Val seemed at ease. Would it turn against Monroe and the others if it had to choose between supporting humans and supporting this new group of Shifters? "You know Val better than I do, Krin. Can we rely on her…it to let us know if there's danger?"

"Yes," he said without hesitation. "Val feels indebted to us for trying to help them while the inspectors were here. Val's loyalty isn't a problem."

She nodded, trusting Krin, but not trusting the situation now that Nathan had brought it to her attention. "Okay then. We can assume Val will warn us if it detects something unusual. But we still go with Nathan's security measures."

A little tingling started in her stomach and worked its way through her limbs until even her fingertips felt suffused with nervous energy. Despite the possible danger, she felt her blood pumping with excitement, the thrill of discovery overwhelming her fear.

She was grinning again by the time they reached Monroe and Val. "We've decided it best if only a few of us go down at a time," she said, which was true so she was able to say it without worrying about lying. There was no reason to let the new Shifters know they were concerned about ambushes.

Monroe said, "We were just discussing that and came to the same conclusion. We don't want to overwhelm the city with too many curiosity seekers." His eyes were intent on her, despite his relaxed, amiable expression. Was he worried as well?

"I think we can take volunteers for the following groups, but I'd really like to be in the first group," she said. "If no one minds." She felt Nathan move behind her, but no one voiced any objections.

"I'd like to go with the first group, too," Krin said. "And obviously Val will have to go to translate. Monroe?"

"Yeah, I want to go."

"I'll be going with the first group." Nathan didn't ask and didn't leave any room for objections.

Monroe raised an eyebrow but didn't comment, which was probably for the best, Ti'ann thought with an internal sigh. "We can bring one more person with us," she said. "Shall we ask for volunteers?"

They put it to the others. In the end, Glen was picked to accompany them. Clare had been eager to be in the first group until Nathan pulled her aside and quietly spoke to her. Afterward, she seemed more willing to pass on the first look.

Ti'ann had to suppress a sharp bite of jealousy when Nathan pulled Clare aside by the arm and kept a hand on her shoulder as he talked to her. She glanced at Mike, who didn't seem to notice or mind, and felt small for her jealousy of something as simple as Nathan touching another woman, even in a casual way.

Ti'ann and Krin spent a few more minutes arranging the rest of the team into the smaller units that would be allowed to explore the city over the next two days. In the meantime, they were to continue working on the original excavation sites. For the moment, they called a halt to excavation of the city. That would have to be part of a future discussion, or negotiation as the case may be, with the Shifters.

"Will we need anything? Food and water? How long will we be allowed to stay?" she asked.

Val translated for her and said, "You should bring some food and water with you as they don't have any suitable sustenance for humans. Other than that, you should be fine as you are. They tell me the temperature is warm enough that you'll be comfortable."

They gathered flasks of water, sealed packages of food, and two oxygen cylinders. By the time the sun dipped low to the horizon, they were following Zim and Sar to the entrance to the city.

E WATCHED FROM A DISTANCE, surprised and confused by what he saw. These weren't like the Shifters in the files he'd been fed. They were different. They talked of cities. An entire city of Shifters. An unexpected hunting ground. Dr. Ripley would be pleased with all the practice he got killing Shifters now. He knew he had to follow, had to witness and record all the information he could. This was important. This was why he was here.

But he hesitated as Ti'ann Jones, Nathan Longfeather and the others followed the two new Shifters. There was something different about them. Val called them Zim and Sar but those weren't their real names. He could almost hear their names, almost understand. It disturbed him that he could understand when they weren't speaking. But he was getting used to that with Val. He could hear Val when the Shifter wasn't speaking out loud.

Dr. Ripley hadn't warned him, but he'd been collecting enough information to figure it out by himself. Val told the others that Shifters were telepathic. That had become common knowledge, though Ripley had never told him. Perhaps he was telepathic too. Another skill to augment his superiority. He would be able to hunt Shifters by following their thoughts. If he could only understand.

He still hesitated, knowing they were getting too far away and soon he'd have to run or risk missing something important. There was something else about Zim and Sar that disturbed him. What was it?

E finally moved to action. He shifted into the form of a small, fast animal and scurried after them, careful to conceal his presence from the Shifters. But even as he followed, he puzzled over the question. What was it that bothered him about Zim and Sar? In his pre-occupation with the mystery, he forgot he was hunting to kill.

CHAPTER SEVENTEEN

THE ENTRANCE TO THE SHIFTER CITY, A PLACE VAL CALLED Lost City, was cleverly disguised to blend in with the area. Ti'ann looked back at the forest from the tunnel that had been impossible to see until they'd walked between two very specific trees. She'd never seen such clever camouflage. They never would have found this entrance, even by chance, because they were never in this part of the woods. In fact, if they'd been able to continue excavating, they still wouldn't reach this part of the site for months because it was the part of the city buried deepest underground.

Awed, Ti'ann turned back to study the tunnel itself. It was dug out of the surrounding blue/brown soil and purple rocks and covered over by natural foliage.

With Val, Zim and Sar leading the way, they walked for half a mile, moving down at a steady and steep incline, before they came to any of the green/gold material that had made up their first view of the anomaly. As they approached what looked to be a solid surface, Ti'ann whispered to Val, "I thought you said this stuff was Shifter remains."

"It is." Val didn't bother whispering back. "The city walls, the basic structure of the city, is made up of those who've died."

"What? How?" Krin moved closer to Val.

"As their time approached for the final shift, they formed a necessary part of the structure. When they died, they remained that way, forever providing shelter to their lines."

As the group watched, the wall of solid green/gold moved, swinging backward without a sound. Ti'ann gasped as the corridor beyond was revealed. A path of green/gold shaped like flat-stones led away from the door, into a huge cavern, surrounded on both sides by strange, glowing blue plant life.

"Luminescent plants."

Nathan's whisper sent a shiver over Ti'ann's skin.

"Sar says they grow well here," Val said. "The luminescence comes from a symbiotic relationship with two different types of bacteria and a single fungus that work together."

Ti'ann looked around at the architectural structures, amazed to think they were Shifter remains. The chamber was lined in the green/gold material, smooth on the walls and ceiling, resembling stones underfoot. Within the smooth walls, the base material was decorated with streaks of color from various stones and gems. Brilliant sky blues and amethyst purples, deep red rubies next to crystalline diamonds painted the walls, giving both texture and depth. Twisting columns of green/gold lined the stone-shaped path and supported the roof of the cavern. The columns were also heavily lined with different colored stones, winking in a rainbow of red, orange, yellow, blue and purple. The blue luminescent plants gave the place a neutral lighting, like an ordinary light fixture humans might use, which meant all the decorations sparkled with their full range of color.

"What about the mixed elements from the surrounding area, the precious and semi-precious stones we found in Micca's part of the wall?" She gestured to one patch of colorful stone, the Quinn's beryl crystal that was so prominent in their early scans of the city.

"The dying ones pulled in what they thought was aesthetically pleasing to add to their part of the structure," Val said. "This is the first time I've seen Shifters using their final shapes for such an extensive structure, though." Val fell silent a moment and then said, "Sar tells me it's a consequence of having to build underground. Above ground, we have a few areas dedicated to those who die, but this… This entire complex has been built on the bodies of the dead."

"Jesus," Glen muttered from behind Ti'ann. "No disrespect, Val, but that's pretty disgusting."

"It's part of our culture to remain with our line even after death. Here it's been taken to the extreme."

"So many dead though. This is a large city. It must have taken thousands of Shifter bodies." Ti'ann flinched at the idea.

Zim motioned them forward and they moved down the tunnel, deeper into the city.

"It's been growing and developing for nearly a century," Val said as they walked. "In the beginning, only two Shifter lines moved here. And many died within the first few years." Val's voice dropped, tinged with sadness.

"I still think it's creepy," Glen muttered.

"Why did the two lines come here in the first place?" Krin asked, ignoring Glen.

Val fell silent, talking with the other two Ti'ann realized, then said, "They chose this place because it was as far from our normal inhabitance as possible."

"And why did they move?" Ti'ann repeated Krin's question.

"That's a long story doctors." Val shrugged Shifter shoulders in a curiously human looking gesture. "When humans landed on this planet, we were divided in our reaction to their presence. Some wanted to make contact and friendly overtures, others wanted to isolate ourselves and stay hidden. Almost immediately, we recognized our inability to communicate with humans. There was a lot of debate."

Val's rueful grin looked strange in the otherwise alien face.

"Our debates can go on for years before decisions are made," Val finished, gesturing them down another tunnel.

This tunnel was high and narrow, the arched ceilings lined with more ornately shaped and decorated Shifter bodies. Ti'ann found the idea of being surrounded by what was in essence a century worth of skeletons more than a little disturbing. She had to think of it as stone or she wasn't sure she'd be able to go much deeper into the city.

"What do they use for light besides the plants?" Glen asked. He walked ahead of the group, but behind Zim and Sar. His head turned constantly as he took in his surroundings.

Ti'ann wasn't sure she wanted the tunnels any better illuminated. Part of her was curious, as usual, but too much light and would she start seeing actual bodies?

After a brief pause, Val said, "They've refined the use of the two bacteria and the fungus that initiate the glow of the plants into a…well a bulb which is used for light. Some areas of the city will be more illuminated than others, depending on the number of plants and the use of these bulbs."

They walked at a slow pace, allowing the humans time to look at everything. They passed through a small chamber lined with glowing trees and turned down another tunnel—one of many branching off from the chamber. This tunnel was more brightly lit by overhead chandeliers with the "bulbs" and was lined with orange and red glowing trees. In between the trees, abstractly shaped stone statues, flowing and bending into shapes that looked like nothing in particular but were still somehow pretty, lined the walk. Where there were no statues there were stone benches, and here, for the first time since entering the city walls, they saw the first inhabitants.

Shifters in different shapes and sizes turned to watch them. The silence was eerie in the high ceiling tunnel. Ti'ann nodded as they passed, wondering what else to do since they didn't even use the same basis for language as humans.

"Some are sending greetings," Val said into the silence. The green and yellow of Val's eyes whirled fast.

"Only some?" Ti'ann asked, as she studied the different faces. These Shifters were more like Sar and Zim than Val. They were either small and stocky or long limbed but heavy around the middle. There were at least four different eye colors that Ti'ann could see. Most had silver eyes like Sar and Zim, two had copper colored eyes, another a vibrant shade of sky blue and another three or four had an orange florescent color that blended well with the orange leaves on the trees.

"Others are… Not all are pleased," Val said.

"Are we in trouble here, Val?" Nathan asked.

Ti'ann felt him tense even with half a meter of space between them. Until this moment, she'd been uncomfortable having him so close yet so far away. Suddenly, she wanted him closer.

"No. They don't mean harm," Val said. "They're just not happy about having humans introduced to the city."

Nathan sucked in a sharp breath that sounded like a gasp of pain. Ti'ann turned to see him holding a hand to his temple, his eyes closed. "Nathan? What's wrong?" She fell back a step and touched his arm.

He jerked away. "I'm fine. I think." He looked up at Val. "They're trying to talk with me, aren't they? Tell them I can't. They aren't being very gentle about it."

James grunted agreement. "I'm used to my telepathy now, but this is still…uncomfortable, Val. Could you get them to talk through you?"

Ti'ann was surprised to hear James talk about his telepathy so openly. Until she considered where they were. Monroe being a telepath was the least startling thing about the day.

Zim looked back at Val, head lowered. After an intense silence, Nathan straightened and took a deep breath.

James sighed and grinned. "Better. They don't have the touch of Val's kin."

Ti'ann nodded absently. Now that neither man was in pain, the way Nathan had jerked away from her touch hit her insecurities. She tried to ignore the gnawing hurt. She had more important things to concentrate on. But the fact that Nathan wouldn't touch her today left a hollow ache in her stomach even the magnificence of this experience couldn't quite overshadow.

"Val, I thought you said Nathan wasn't strong enough for you to talk to."

"He's not. That's why it hurt him. He isn't trained and they were shouting in their attempts to be heard. Since they were shouting in our language instead of yours, it was probably also very disorienting."

"It was." Nathan's voice was quiet and lethal. "Tell them not to do that again."

"They won't," Val assured him.

"That'd make a pretty good weapon, Val," Glen murmured, studying the Shifters nearest them.

"You'd have to have some sort of telepathic spark to be

affected," James said, clapping Glen on the shoulder. "So it wouldn't be very effective on most humans."

Glen nodded but didn't comment.

"We shall continue?" Zim's voice sounded more confident this time as the words were forced out. The mouth in Zim's face disappeared almost as soon as the question was finished.

As they started moving again, Ti'ann felt like an exhibit in a museum with all the many colored eyes watching them. "Val, could you tell them that we're grateful they've allowed us to see their city. We find it amazing and beautiful and are looking forward to seeing more."

Val grinned. "I'll convey your gratitude right away, Ti'ann."

James looked back over his shoulder with a grin that matched Val's. "Ever thought about going into diplomacy?"

"No, thank you," she said with feeling.

Krin laughed. "I can't see it either," he said, dropping an arm around her shoulder affectionately.

She smiled, then remembered. "Val, you never finished telling us why the two lines moved here. What happened with the debates over contacting humans?"

Krin dropped his arm and moved closer to Val to hear the story.

"The debates went on longer than any other we've ever had. Several decades. Too long really because by the time a decision was made, humans had settled and formed stable communities of their own. And in the end, the decision was not unanimous. It was the first time ever that a consensus could not be reached. The majority wanted to make contact with humans. They were prepared to send out delegations from each line to study them, learn how to use a word-based language again and, eventually, to make contact. But two lines refused to participate."

"They were still part of your community?" Ti'ann's voice

was quiet even though the Shifters now filling the corridors they walked through wouldn't be able to understand them.

"They were. For a little while longer."

Ti'ann nodded and looked around at the growing number of Shifters they passed. She noticed another eye color—purple so dark it was nearly black.

The chambers and tunnels they were led through were all decorated with statues and plant life, the walls thick with textures like sculpture and glittering with stone highlights. The deeper they moved into the city, the more elaborately textured, twisted and decorated the walls were. Curls and swirls of stone faded into the shadowy heights of the caverns, their twists and turns accented by the colored stones to give the appearance of movement. Some corridors gave the illusion of water flowing over the walls, others looked like the stone itself was moving. One chamber they passed through, what Ti'ann was coming to think of as an intersection, was covered with glowing vines that traveled up the walls and hung in decorative drapes from the ceiling. The walls behind the draping winked with color.

The deeper they got into the city, the wider the tunnels and chambers became. At an intersection, she looked down one of the side corridors and saw a series of arches leading into yet more tunnels or chambers. She realized she was so completely lost she'd never get back out again without help. A shiver traveled up her spine, and she wrapped her arms around her waist.

"You all right?" Nathan said near her ear.

The brush of his breath made her shiver more. "Fine." She was so drawn to the warmth of his body, she felt herself tilting back toward him. He straightened away and dropped a pace back, forcing her to catch herself before she fell on her ass.

"I'm assuming the two lines split off from the community

after contact with humans was made," Krin said, pulling Ti'ann's attention away from Nathan.

"Just before. When it was clear the other lines would go through with revealing ourselves, the two threatened to separate completely from the rest. Nothing like that had ever been done before. As a community, we'd argued, disagreed and debated, but we'd always remained united. No one believed they'd be able to follow through with their ultimatum."

"Until they did," James said.

"So they left and came here. But how could you have lost touch so completely if you're telepathic?" Krin said. "Didn't anyone ever try to find them?"

"At first. We searched the planet, willing to compromise to bring them back. It was a devastating blow to the community to have two whole lines leave. They blocked themselves from us telepathically so we couldn't find them. After a while, we gave up searching. By that time, we had bigger problems."

"The reaction of humans to Shifters," James finished for Val.

"The missing lines became legends," Val said. "Keepers of the History vowed to hold their names and histories as part of our own, to keep them alive with us. Some of the newer lines, the younger Keepers haven't been able to uphold this vow. The war with humans has occupied too much of their energy. But I still tell the story of the lost lines."

They passed into a massive cavern that had been squared off and was filled with structures that looked like buildings. On the ground, multiple layers of boxes with elaborately decorated facades filled in circles and squares of space that were separated by more of the flat-stone lined paths. Boxes, cones and spheres of a size with the ground buildings hung from the ceiling, dripping with plant life and colored lights. From the ground, there didn't look to be any way of reaching the structures suspended from the roof.

Ti'ann leaned close to Krin and pointed up to the squared corners of the ceiling. "This must have been part of what we saw in the MEI scan. It's hard to compare the scan to what we're seeing."

"The image it gave us seems to have been confined to the outer walls and the larger structures. I wonder why it didn't image us the interior."

"Maybe it couldn't scan through the Shifter bodies."

"I think what you were looking at in those images," Glen said, "was only the very top and outer parts of the city. What we're seeing is probably outside the drop sensor's range."

"The city goes much deeper," Val confirmed. "And is much more complicated than the image you showed me when we arrived."

"James, what Shifter support group are you part of?" Glen's question made James stop short.

"Hopefully, one you've never heard of before," he said wryly. "The ones with names are usually the ones involved in dodgier dealings, or outright terrorist groups. We aren't terrorists."

"Oh, I didn't think you were," Glen said. "It's just pretty obvious with Val and all that you're part of one of the groups. You can talk telepathically to Val, too? That must be amazing."

James smiled. "It is. It's one of the reasons I have to do what I do."

"No doubts then?" Glen's gaze flicked to Val as if he realized he'd said something that might offend.

"Never."

"Did you ever meet Kira Farseaker or her father, Thomas?" Nathan asked, surprising them all.

Ti'ann glanced back at him but, as usual, couldn't read his expression or gauge his mood. She really really hated that.

"You knew Thomas Farseaker?" James asked.

Nathan nodded.

When Nathan didn't elaborate, James said, "I knew them."

"Did you work with them? Were they part of your group?"

"I suppose since Thomas is dead and Kira is gone, I can tell you they were."

"You took over for Kira."

James' eyes narrowed. "What makes you say that?"

"Something my mother said."

The entire group stopped moving, except for Zim and Sar.

"Your mother?" James said. "I don't know your mother, do I?"

"You wouldn't, no." And even though they stood another minute waiting for him to say more, Nathan remained impassive.

"You're not going to explain are you?" James smiled when he asked.

"Not any more than you're going to tell Glen the name of your organization."

With a chuckle, James trotted off after their quickly retreating guides and the rest fell in behind him.

They edged through the now crowded paths to an open circular area ringed by Shifters. Inside the circle were a myriad of statues and sculptures all quite alien to anything Ti'ann had ever seen. She glanced around at the Shifters standing at the edge of the circle, many of them with their heads leaning in to each other as if talking.

"Why are they all looking at the sculptures from out here?" she asked Val.

"Wait," Val said with a hint of anticipation.

Ti'ann glanced at Krin who shrugged and they turned back to the sculptures. After waiting for a while with nothing happening, Ti'ann started to get restless. Then a rustling moved through the crowd. If they used external voices, she was sure they'd be murmuring. She looked closer at the objects scattered through the circle, but she couldn't see anything different.

Then Krin sucked in a breath and Nathan hissed a curse. Glen gasped out, "Jesus."

Ti'ann followed their gazes and watched in shock as one of the sculptures reformed, almost taking on the natural shape of a Shifter before changing and moving into another abstract form. Colors suffused its body in subtle variations of shade until a combination was reached and the colors stopped changing. After a breathless pause, the colors started changing again and the crowd of Shifters started applauding. The gesture startled Ti'ann. She hadn't thought about Shifters applauding.

"Performance art," Krin said, grinning. "Devin would love this."

Before she could process what she'd just seen, something else in the circle changed. This time, the new sculpture admitted a series of noises that sounded like wind blowing through pipes followed by the echo of thunder. Music, she thought in shock. Music and sculpture combined. The song rolled in and out of her hearing range and when the last notes faded away, the Shifters applauded again.

They watched for another few minutes before continuing down another path through the buildings. "That was amazing," Ti'ann said to Zim and Sar through Val.

"There are a number of those areas throughout the city," Val said. "They brought that with them from our older communities. The artists spend their lives moving through shapes and colors, utilizing forms and sounds to find the perfect piece. When their time comes, they form that shape for the last time and die a permanent piece of art."

"Wow." Krin shuddered. "I'm not sure Devin would want to do that. Even for his art."

Ti'ann knew he was more concerned with how he'd feel about a sculpture made of Devin's corpse than about how Devin would feel.

"Is there something different about the Shifters who form art pieces and the Shifters who make up the structures of the city?" she asked because she couldn't not.

"Nothing different but choice. At least, there's no genetic difference. The artists in our communities have chosen that path. Obviously, Lost City Shifters still respect their work and their desire to form a final piece of art on death." Val paused a moment, before saying more quietly. "So many others died, the artists were not required to add their bodies to the city's structure."

"And the… What happened to the Shifters killed in the exterminations?" Krin murmured.

Ti'ann bit the inside of her cheek, not sure this was the best time to bring that up, when they were surrounded by Shifters who weren't entirely pleased to have them here. At least no one but Val, and maybe Zim or Sar, could understand Krin's question. Still, bringing up all those killed in the exterminations while in this city felt wrong. Yet, her own curiosity had her waiting for Val's answer.

Val's shoulders drooped. "Their bodies were completely destroyed, ground down to dust. Or sent to Shifter Research Center for study. Not a way any of us wants to end."

A silence that hurt Ti'ann's ears hung over the group for several moments. Then Ti'ann changed the subject. "How do they keep track of time down here?" The conversation had gotten too sad. "Or do they bother?"

Val straightened visibly and her tone lightened. "There are a few windows to the outside. From those areas, the time of day is disseminated out through the city by a series of horns and bells which echo in the tunnels."

They passed an open arch in one of the buildings. Inside, Shifters were seated around a raised platform on which a single Shifter was playing some sort of wind instrument. The song was haunting in the relative quiet of the city.

"I'm not sure why, but I didn't consider what kind of musical taste Shifters would have," Ti'ann said. "Since they don't make external noise to communicate, I didn't consider they'd use sounds of other kinds."

Val smiled and made a hand gesture that Ti'ann had never seen it make before, a gesture she couldn't interpret. "We can't live our entire lives in our heads. And we do have external hearing. We appreciate sound as much as visual art."

"I'm surprised no one from Gremblewreath has heard the sounds," Glen commented.

"The walls are thick and keep most of the normal city noise contained from casual listeners," Val said after a pause. "Your team never heard anything, right?"

"True."

"It's not fully sound-proofed, but enough to avoid being easily overheard."

They continued on through the huge chamber and into another tunnel. This one was simple, lined with draping vines of light. It branched into a huge number of additional tunnels. "Where are we going now?" James asked Val.

"Oh," Val said after a silent exchange with the other two Shifters. "They're showing us to accommodation for the night.

They say we can explore as we like for the remainder of the night and we'll switch groups in the morning."

Val seemed surprised enough by the offer that Ti'ann said, "I thought we'd only be here for a few hours. I didn't realize they intended to let us stay."

"I didn't either," Val said. "Maybe our presence has been less of an upset than they anticipated."

"Thank them, but decline," Nathan said. "I don't think we should impose."

Val's green eyes whirled and focused on Zim. Ti'ann watched the silver swirl of Zim's eyes for a minute then had to look away from the disorienting sight.

Val broke the silence in a quiet voice. "They would like to offer us a great honor. They want to introduce us to their Supreme Councilors, their…government leaders. Tonight. They want to meet us all. But…"

Ti'ann felt a little trickle of fear skittered through her stomach, though she wasn't entirely sure why.

Val glanced back at Nathan. "Apparently, they're quite curious about you."

CHAPTER EIGHTEEN

Nathan followed the group, keeping an eye on the Shifters as they passed, trying not to think too closely about the reason the Supreme Councilors might want to see him. Absorbing the reality of a Shifter city and its inhabitants was more than enough for one day. There were thousands of them, for Christ's sake. This was beyond even his and BinRal's ability to secure against. It was going to take a bloody army if they proved hostile. And they had every reason to consider humans hostile given the extermination laws.

The impact of their attempts to communicate with him still had him shaken. They weren't even trying to hurt him, he was sure, but their efforts had nearly brought him to his knees.

If Val hadn't pointed out that he had a touch of telepathic ability, he'd have never known. Now he didn't want it. He felt vulnerable, something he hadn't experienced in years. He could fight and defend himself against most weapons and attacks, but he had no defense against this and it pissed him off.

They edged through a crowd of Shifters into a spherical

shaped cavern. Every time he passed a group of them now he got the chills. He'd thought Ti'ann was interfering with his thinking. This was worse.

Thinking of Ti'ann took his mind off the Shifters. But it didn't help his sanity much. He couldn't touch her, or let her touch him, without wanting her again. He was a fucking mess. Sleeping with her hadn't helped his state of mind at all, only made matters worse, sharpening the edge of his need instead of blunting it. He should have let BinRal come down here with this group. He should stay as far away from Ti'ann Jones as he could get. He wasn't going to survive this if he didn't.

Unfortunately, he'd never forgive himself if she didn't survive because he couldn't keep his dick under control. So he came into this cavernous pit full of Shifters and tried not to touch her so he could make sure she was safe. He was a little worried about himself. More than a little worried. He wasn't prone toward being a hero, not without getting paid. The fact that he wanted to be Ti'ann's hero was a disaster waiting to happen.

Zim and Sar led them through another set of convoluted corridors until they came to a tunnel lined with doors. They were led through one door into a chamber that branched into a hive-like rise of more arched doorways.

"This is one of their lines'…housing units," Val stumbled over the phrasing. "Kind of like a family home."

"Which line?" James asked, his head thrown back as he looked up to the higher levels.

"Ours," said Zim. All eyes turned in the direction of their guides as Zim spoke. Silence followed, waiting to see if the Shifter had more to say.

"Yours is one of the oldest lines, correct?" Krin finally asked. "I've seen more silver eyes than any other color."

"They're of one of the first two lines to come here." Val said then tilted its head to one side as if listening to something.

"What is it?" Krin's voice was quiet but still echoed around the hive.

Val looked at him and smiled. "They were telling me something of their history and pointing me toward their own Keeper of the History. I would very much like to talk to him."

"Him?" James spun around to face Val.

Nathan tried to focus on Val, but his gaze kept bouncing around the "house" to all those doors over their heads. Looking everywhere at once, watching for possible danger, he almost missed the significance of what Val had said.

"Him," Val confirmed. "Haven't you noticed the difference?"

"Are you telling us they aren't asexual anymore?" Ti'ann asked.

Her voice made Nathan take an involuntary step closer to her. He stopped, forcing himself not to move.

Val was quiet for a minute then said, "They're sexually reproductive now. That's why there are so many more lines. Our naturally high mutation rate means that lines split off to form new lines regularly during our asexual reproduction. But this splitting of lines has increased with cross-fertilization. Zim and Sar's line is very successful in this environment, so it's grown a lot compared to the others."

Nathan considered this change. Shifters like Val procreated by a process similar to budding, each individual developed another individual and "gave birth" to it without needing the help of a partner—which meant Val's kind weren't male or female; they didn't need to be. The new Shifters being different sexes meant they needed two of them—a male and a female—to make a baby. That was a huge evolutionary change for a species. But what did this mean to both Val's kind and humans in the extermination debates?

"Jesus, they're different sexes now?" Glen muttered, echoing Nathan's shock. "How could that happen?"

Val fell silent again, listening as Zim stared back. Sar wandered off in the direction of one of the doors. Nathan watched Sar go, frowning. This was a perfect place for an ambush. But so far, they could have been ambushed anywhere. He only knew where they were inside the city because he'd brought a tracking devise with him. He was certain the others were lost. Except maybe for Val, but only because Val had access to the thoughts of the other Shifters.

He backed against a wall near the entrance into the family home and kept his gaze circling the layers of doors. There was no way they'd be able to defend against an attack from here, but he'd at least have enough warning to try. He pulled out his comm-card, pressed a point along its surface and waited for BinRal's response. The coded reply came in "all clear". He sent a code to indicate he was still not certain of their safety then turned his attention back to the group.

"Parasites?" Glen said. "What do parasites have to do with anything?"

"When we evolved the ability to shift, we lost our vulnerability to parasites and the damage they can inflict on our offspring," Val said.

"The Red Queen." Ti'ann's voice was quiet, as if she was talking to herself. She glanced up as all eyes turned on her and said, "It was an evolutionary biology theory started on Earth during the late twentieth century. Among other things, it provided an explanation for the evolution of different sexes."

When everyone continued staring at her, she lifted a hand, palm up and said, "Basically, an asexual species will out-compete a sexually reproductive species in no time because every member of their population reproduces, whereas only half the population of a sexual species can reproduce. Because of this, scientists were baffled as to why sex was so prevalent.

"The Red Queen theory says, in essence, that the world is competitive to the death so species have to…constantly change just to stay in the same place. Species are in constant competition with all other species around them, so in order to give their offspring a fighting chance in an ever-changing environment, they have to continue to evolve new strategies against competing species, like parasites. The best way to change constantly is mixing DNA from different individuals—sex."

"Why was it called the Red Queen?" James asked.

"The Red Queen was a character from a couple of nineteenth century Earth novels by Lewis Carroll," Nathan answered, earning surprised looks from the entire group. "There's a scene in one of the books where Alice, the main character, finds herself running at top speed with the Red Queen and her court. She wonders why, even though they're running as fast as they can, they never seem to get anywhere. The Red Queen tells her that in the Queen's country, they have to run as fast as they can just to stay in the same place. If they want to get anywhere, they have to run twice as fast. I assume that's where they got the name?"

"It is." Ti'ann smiled at him with such pleasure he felt his heart start to hammer. He looked away before he lost himself in her eyes.

"So animals and plants have to keep running just to keep from falling prey to the parasites, is that it?" James asked. "And sexual reproduction continues."

"That's the theory anyway," Krin said.

"Apparently, this is a case to support the Red Queen," Val

said with a touch of humor. "Our scientists claim we were a sexually reproducing species until we evolved the ability to shift. With shifting came a very high mutation rate, changing our DNA frequently enough between generations that parasites could no longer keep up with us. The most accurate hypothesis our bio-historians have now is that we reverted to asexual reproduction within four generations."

"And no one objected?" Glen asked, incredulous.

Val laughed. "This was before we had more than very primitive cognitive abilities, Glen. Sex was for reproduction, not for fun, so there was no reason to object to losing it."

Zim formed a mouth and said, "We have not returned to that primitive state of existence. We do enjoy sex now."

The humor as well as Zim's rapidly increasing ability to use words stunned Nathan. "You're learning quickly."

Zim faced him. "It is easier with Val's help. We did not have a translator familiar with the use of words when humans first landed. We understood the concept of word-based communication but did not practice it."

"Are you male or female?"

Ti'ann would be the one to ask, Nathan thought, curbing his own questions.

"Male," Zim said. "Sar is my mate."

"This is so amazing," Krin breathed, practically bouncing in place.

Ti'ann grinned at him, vibrating with the thrill of discovery as well. Her energy and enthusiasm tugged at Nathan, urged him closer. Real moth to the flames situation, he thought in disgust.

"But why did sex re-evolved with the lines down here and not the other Shifters?" Glen asked. "If there's a dangerous parasite down here that can keep up with your shifting, then why doesn't it affect those above ground? I mean they're not exactly cut off from the outside environment here."

"If the majority of the Shifter population spent most of our lives here," Val said, "and attempt to reproduce here, we'd be vulnerable to the parasite too."

"Are you in danger, Val?" James asked, stepping closer to the Shifter.

A very protective gesture, Nathan noted.

"Not unless I move underground permanently." Val paused for a moment then said, "I may get sick if I stay below for more than a few days at a time. The parasite affects our nutrient absorption. It's taken in when we ingest nutrient molecules from the environment and damages our cells' ability to properly utilize our food. It feeds off of what we ingest, leaving us malnourished."

"You shouldn't stay here then. Not even for a day."

"Don't worry, James," Zim said in a soothing voice. "We would never allow a Keeper of the History to be damaged if we could prevent it. Infection to a level that would cause Val harm takes time. Brief exposure to the parasite can be compensated for by Val's immune system."

James nodded but didn't look convinced. Nathan wasn't sure he was either, but he kept his doubt out of his expression.

"Have you evolved any sort of competitive behaviors?" Ti'ann asked. "Are the sexes proportional or do you have more of one sex than the other?" Her face glowed with concentration and curiosity.

"Perhaps we should settle into our rooms now," Val suggested.

Ti'ann's cheeks reddened in the soothing light of the chamber. "Sorry. I didn't mean to get carried away with so many questions."

As if she and Krin hadn't been pummeling them with questions from the beginning. Nathan couldn't believe she was embarrassed about it now. He stared at her reddened cheeks and had to fight back a grin. She looked so cute and fluster, he felt an overwhelming need to pull her close.

Cute? His Ti'ann Jones looked cute? Sexy as hell, intriguing, irritating, maddening and irresistible, maybe. He'd considered her all those things before. But cute? It seemed so…intimate.

Damn.

"Don't worry, Ti'ann. We'll answer any questions you have later," Val assured her. "But there's still so much to tell and we have to prepare for the meeting with the Councilors."

"We should contact the group," James said. "Let them know we're staying the night."

"I'll send a message." Nathan didn't mention that he'd already sent several.

Ti'ann smiled at him, her eyes softening with emotions he didn't need to see.

One night. It had only been one night, and he was way in over his head. He should have paid more attention to the warning signs when Alex fell. At least he'd have known what to avoid. As he turned away from her, he knew he wouldn't have avoided the traps even if he had seen them coming. He'd lost this fight three years ago.

Sar returned then and directed them toward a group of doors at the far end of the cavern. He looked up at the other doors and couldn't help thinking of the place as a hive again. An empty hive. "Is there anyone else here?" he asked from his place at the rear of the group.

"Most of the family is out this evening," Sar said in a quiet voice.

Nathan realized it was the first time he'd heard Sar talk.

"A few of the older ones are in their…rooms?" She looked to Val for confirmation of the word before continuing. "Rooms this evening. Many will join in the meeting with the Councilors."

"Representatives from each of the lines will be there," Zim added.

"We didn't exactly come ready for a formal meeting," Ti'ann said with a slight tremor in her voice.

"They won't be expecting much from you. Just a simple conversation," Val assured.

A simple conversation, Nathan thought, with representatives from each line. That kind of attendance never meant a simple anything.

CHAPTER NINETEEN

Ti'ann felt an overwhelming desire to run as they stepped into an ornately decorated cavern later that evening. It was bad enough being surrounded by all the important representatives of this new city. But she had to face them looking like she'd spent the day digging in the dirt—which she had.

They'd been given water to bathe in but had been warned not to drink it as the underground river beneath the city was full of bacteria that could potentially be harmful to humans if ingested. Ti'ann had been so worried about accidentally swallowing some, she'd stuck to a simple sponge bath. The fragrant oil they'd been given was lovely, though, and she'd spent several minutes just sniffing the small, glass bottle before applying it. So she was sort of clean and she did smelled good. Unfortunately, she couldn't claim the same for her clothes.

The Shifters didn't wear much in the way of clothing, so maybe her dirty t-shirt and trousers wouldn't matter. They did wear layers of braided ropes and stones but used them more like accessories. A lot of those accessories were on display when they entered the meeting hall.

Yeah, I'm definitely underdressed.

She studied their new surroundings, hoping to calm her nerves. Galleries of seats with colorfully decorated balconies lined the walls. There seemed to be areas designated for members of the different lines, but it was a flexible separation with many Shifters moving between sections.

The atmosphere appeared relaxed and excited, though she couldn't say why since she couldn't read Shifter gestures or hear them speak. In fact, the hall was eerily quiet, just like the rest of the city. A single musician played from a gallery near the top of the hall, several levels above the topmost sitting gallery. The musician's wind song music was the only noise outside the shuffling of bodies. She turned in time to see a Shifter change into the shape of a blackbird before launching itself up to one of the upper galleries.

Blackbird? There'd been a lot of blackbirds around the site over the last week.

She sucked in a breath as she realized just how easy it had been for the Shifters to watch her group.

"You okay?" Krin whispered.

"No. You?"

"Terrified." He took her hand and squeezed. She squeezed back, embarrassed to realize how comforting it was to have Krin here with her.

"Don't let me say anything stupid," she murmured.

"Only if you keep me from opening my big mouth, too."

She grinned and nodded, then gave his hand a final squeeze and let go. Straightening her shoulders, she tried to follow Zim and Val with as much dignity as she could muster. Somewhere behind her, she knew Nathan followed, watching, on guard.

Knowing he had their backs was as reassuring as Krin's hand had been.

The Supreme Councilors sat at the far end of the hall on seven raised cushions. Each Councilor was adorned in braided lengths of rope and stones, the colors particular to the individual Councilor. She wondered if that was to do with their lines or with their individual positions in the community. They were all in their natural forms. Three of the seven had silver eyes.

Val and Zim went directly to the Councilors and exchanged what was probably a formal greeting. Ti'ann suspected a lot was said from the silence filling the hall. Val and Zim performed a series of hand gestures which Ti'ann couldn't follow but was sure were part of the greeting. Then Val stepped to one side and motioned them forward at the same time as a mouth formed in its golden face.

Ti'ann sucked in a deep breath and took her place before their hosts. She and Krin went first, followed by James and Glen with Nathan taking the rear guard as usual. Val made the introductions aloud, naming their group first before turning to introduce the Councilors.

James leaned forward and whispered, "Val is translating to them as she speaks to us."

"Can you understand them?" she asked, leaning back.

"Not really. I can kind of tell what's happening, but I don't have any idea what they're saying. No words."

They straightened again as Val said, with a touch of humor, "We have agreed on word names for the Councilors. They are pleased with the sounds." Val indicated the Councilor farthest to the left and moved right as each was introduced. "May I introduce Hyg, Bur, Deq, Maj, Ple, Sav and Xal."

Ti'ann nodded to each and received a polite nod in return. Okay, that at least was an acceptable gesture. She was hit once again with how little she knew about Shifters. What if she made some common human gesture that turned out to be rude and offensive? She kept her arms to her sides, her hands opened, and prayed Val would let them know if they did anything really stupid.

As she studied the city leaders, she noted four of them appeared to be female, the other three male. Two of the four females, Deq and Sav, and one male, Hyg, had silver eyes. Other than that, Ti'ann couldn't tell much else about them. In particular, she realized she had no idea how old any of them were. Val had told her and Krin at one stage that Shifter children were smaller and looked young. She'd seen a lot of what looked to be children since coming into the city. But once they reached the adult stage, they didn't seem to change much. Did they see a difference in each other?

"The Councilors give you greetings," Val said. "They wish me to convey their sincere thanks for keeping the location and nature of our city a secret. They know the inspectors were not friends to our kind but also that they don't represent all humanity."

Sav made a hand gesture and Val fell silent for a moment.

"Sav wishes me to tell you this city arose because of their distrust of humanity and its intentions here. They felt their concerns were justified after the destruction of our cities above ground. Now, after meeting you and James and talking with me, they see not all of humanity is to be shunned." Val was silent again, then said, "Bur says they're not prepared to reveal themselves to the majority of the population yet, but they are prepared to begin negotiations for forming an agreement with humans. They wish to await the final decision of the Senate before they commit themselves to exposure."

"Understandable," Krin said.

"But how will they keep this place a secret now?" Ti'ann asked. "I mean they've exposed themselves to our team. You and James and the others might be dedicated to keeping Shifter secrets, but my team isn't."

Val nodded and was silent.

"They're discussing your point," James said. "Don't understand it, but I get the impression they were aware they wouldn't be able to keep their secret long after introducing our people to the city."

"James is right. They realize they have a matter of weeks at most to prepare for this confrontation. They hope to persuade all of you to keep knowledge of the city quiet for as long as possible. With luck, the Senate will reach a decision soon. If not, then the nearer we are to the conclusion of the debates, the better their negotiating position will be. Without knowing what the majority of humans want in regards Shifters, it's difficult to plan a meeting."

"They're risking a lot here, Val," Krin murmured. "I'd like to say we could keep this quiet for a long time, but..." He spread his hands.

"There are too many of us and the inspectors will be back," Ti'ann listed off the problems Krin wouldn't utter. "Someone is going to want an accounting of what we're doing out here. I thought they'd decided to start talking with humans and that's why they approached us."

"They approached us because we would have uncovered their city anyway. You are too tenacious." Val grinned. "But they have not fully committed to an exchange with humans."

"They could have stopped us digging," Glen pointed out. "They could have killed us all."

"Shifters aren't violent," James told him. "They're incapable of killing."

Val didn't immediately support James' statement out loud. Instead, the Shifter turned away to glance at the Councilors again. Ti'ann frowned. Maybe Nathan was right. Maybe more had changed in these lines than just the evolution of sexual reproduction. They never did answer her questions about behavioral changes. Maybe these Shifters were capable of violence where Val's kind weren't.

"They didn't wish to bring harm to the group," Val said finally, confirming her fears. "They still want to conduct their re-introduction to the outer planet in peace. If the debates go against Shifters, they'll likely resume their isolationist policy, even cutting themselves off from other Shifters again."

"How?" Ti'ann's voice felt like it stuck in her throat. She swallowed and said more firmly, "How will they isolate themselves this time? Will they abandon this city?"

"No." Val didn't even look back at the others when answering. Its green/yellow eyes locked with hers.

"They'll form up a defense? They'll fight to stay isolated." She pressed her hands flat against her thighs to keep them from fisting or shaking at this realization. They were talking about war.

"They can. They will." Val sounded resigned and sad. "They are more advanced in this area than the Shifters above ground. It happened with the re-introduction of different sexes into the lines."

Reverting to sexual reproduction was one thing, becoming capable of violence, another.

James leaned forward again and put a hand on her shoulder. "It's not the first time this has happened to a line," he murmured. "We've been trying to keep it quiet, but some of the Shifters above ground have evolved the ability to inflict injury since the exterminations began. They aren't happy to have that particular trait in their lines, though. That's why Val is sad about it evolving here as well."

Ti'ann nodded. The idea that humans were driving the Shifters above ground to become violent when it wasn't in their natures made her stomach hurt. The lines here in the city, that was a different story. They'd evolved aggressive behavior along with the natural evolution of the sexes. In a way, it might make them easier to understand, their behaviors more what humans would expect. But she wasn't sure that was a good thing.

"Are they threatening us, Val?" Nathan asked. The question should have been blunt and offensive, but Nathan somehow managed to sound concerned and polite. She looked at him over her shoulder. As usual, she couldn't read much in his expression. But he didn't seem any tenser than at any other time since they'd entered the city.

"No. They won't hurt anyone here now. Even if the secret of the city gets out before they want it to. They'll only fight if they're attacked or one of their lines is hurt. And they'll defend themselves if the Senate launches an out and out assault."

"What if groups not sanctioned by the government threaten this city?" Glen asked. "There are a lot of anti-Shifter feelings among the populous. As many people still hate them as support them. And most people don't know Shifters are sentient, at least not for certain. It's still considered a rumor. This city is going to be a huge blow not just to the Senate, but to the entire human population. They'll have to face something a lot of them have been happy to remain ignorant of."

Val looked down at the platform before answering. After a long silence, "They won't declare war based on the actions of non-government based groups. They'll still defend themselves though. They won't allow any human group to destroy this place the way our cities above ground were destroyed."

"This could be a haven, Val," James said, stepping forward. "For the Shifters above ground." He turned to the Councilors. "Would that be possible? Is there room enough here to harbor other lines?"

"They would be welcome. But there would be a price," Zim said. The first thing he'd said aloud since they'd reached the meeting hall. "Any who live here for more than a few weeks would be exposed to the parasites that forced us to evolve."

"They might die," Val said. "They might get very sick. Or they might change, the way the Shifters here have changed."

"Some would take the risk for a safe haven," James said quietly, his gaze steady on Val's. "You know there's only so much we can do."

When Ti'ann looked at James, she saw the frustration and helplessness in his expression.

Val smiled and silence fell in the hall. After a moment, James nodded, a rueful smile lifting his lips. "You're right," he said aloud. "They'll choose as they always have. But at least it's an option."

"It is," Val said. "And they will be welcome in Lost City if they choose to come. At this point in the debates, I think most will prefer to continue the fight."

Silence fell again, and Val turned to Nathan. "They wanted me to convey their respects to your family, Nathan Longfeather."

"Is that why they're interested in me? Because of my family? Tell them I didn't have anything to do with that. My mother, her cousin, that was their fight. Not mine. Never was."

The venom in his voice surprised Ti'ann. There was something there, something in his past he didn't want to talk about. Her curiosity jumped forward, pushing her to ask questions. But now wasn't the time or place. And a part of her was afraid he wouldn't answer personal questions even if she asked. Why would he confide in her? They'd shared a couple of nights together, nights separated by more than three years. That didn't exactly scream intimacy. Her heart twisted just enough to hurt. She stomped down on the feeling.

Val smiled after a quiet moment. "They don't seem to mind. They like you. They see potential."

"Tell them whatever they're thinking, they can forget it. I'm a mercenary. I get paid to do what I do. I don't do freedom fighting. I made that clear sixteen years ago."

Val nodded, but the mouth in its face twisted into a knowing grin. From behind her, Ti'ann heard Nathan mumble something that didn't sound polite. It took a lot of effort not to laugh. It took even more effort not to turn and look at him.

The conversation moved on to more pleasant, less potentially volatile topics. The Councilors had a lot of questions about the world now and the way humans lived. They wanted to understand human art and music. Krin ended up in a long discussion with Maj, translated with some difficulty by Val, about the nature of Devin's art and did he find it difficult working in external mediums. There were so many questions from both groups that more cushions had to be brought forward for the humans.

In the galleries above, the Shifters began moving again and the musicians started playing. Sometime during the evening, the sealed food they'd carried into the city was brought out and served on flat squares of glass that worked elegantly as plates.

By the time they'd finished eating and the conversation started to slow down, Ti'ann felt her head drooping with fatigue. She was suddenly grateful for rooms and the softly padded bed cushions they'd been given for their overnight stay.

She couldn't have faced trying to walk out again and back to camp.

They bid their hosts goodnight and Zim and Val led them back to their lodgings. None of the other Shifters left the meeting hall.

"Will they stay up much longer?" she asked Val, glancing over her shoulder as they left through the huge, ornate doors.

"For a little while. They still have a lot to discuss. Our sleep schedules are different from humans, at any rate, so it's not as late to them as it is to you." Val grinned.

"I'm exhausted," Ti'ann confided. "You know, I didn't see Sar all night. I might have missed—her?—her in the galleries though."

"Sar was unable to attend. She's to give birth in another three days and has begun her period of transition."

"Sar's pregnant? How can you tell?"

"She told me." Val chuckled. "They've explained how it works, but it's a different form of reproduction so I'll be fascinated to see the birth. Apparently, a bubble is formed around the embryo and it is from this bubble that the infant is hatched. Not too dissimilar from our budding process, except that it takes a male and female to begin the process." Another grin.

"Are their young vulnerable in the beginning?"

"More vulnerable to disease and birth defects than our young. But if they survive the first couple of years, they can be stronger than our children."

"Will we be able to visit Sar and Zim's child when it's born?" Krin asked from behind them.

"It'll depend on its health."

When they reached the family home—which reminded Ti'ann a lot of a beehive turned inside out—they said their goodnights and retreated to the ground floor rooms they'd been given. They had to stay at the bottom level because there were no stairs to the upper tiers. Shifters merely changed into some form that could fly or scale walls. As tired as she was, Ti'ann was grateful she didn't have to trudge up stairs anyway.

A door of battered metal with a decoratively cut vent at the top separated her room from the central core. The room was a large, rounded cave of a space, with small cubbyholes carved into the wall and a stuffed mattress inside one large alcove. The walls and ceiling of the alcove were decorated with stones and dried plants.

The space was illuminated by a few of the "light bulbs" set into clear glass shapes resembling lamps. The lighting was lower now than it had been when she'd first been given the room to wash up in, low enough as to be almost dark. She had no idea how the lights turned on and off so she was glad someone had thought to dim them for her.

The cubbyholes in the walls were filled with pieces of sculpture and what looked like books. She'd pulled down one of the books earlier. The pages were filled with a flowing substance that looked like jelly or smoke caught inside the translucent pages. It swirled and shimmered, forming strange images and half scenes in three dimensions. She suspected there was some trick to reading one but was too tired to try.

As she stared at the bed alcove, she was suddenly grateful for her exhaustion. Otherwise the idea of sleeping cocooned by Shifter bodies might have kept her up all night. She shed her clothes, dropped them to the ground, and crawled into bed under the heavy velvet blanket the Shifters had provided. The city wasn't cold, as she might have suspected this far underground. In fact, it was comfortably warm. But sleeping naked without a cover made her feel vulnerable.

She snuggled into the soft material, sighing at the sensory

pleasure of velvet against her bare skin. Vaguely, she wondered where Shifters came up with velvet but couldn't manage enough energy to think about it for long, not when she felt so warm and cozy. So much for worrying about sleeping surrounded by corpses, she thought as she dozed off.

CHAPTER TWENTY

NATHAN LAY ON TOP OF THE VELVET BLANKET WITH HIS ARM over his eyes. The room was dark, now, the only light coming in through the door vent from the central core of the hive. It had been lit dimly by the things that looked like lamps when he'd first come in, but that limited light had faded after a short time, leaving the room dark enough to sleep in.

But he couldn't sleep comfortably for a couple of reasons, not the least of which was being in a strange city surrounded by aliens.

He fingered the tags hanging around his neck with his other hand, the metal cool against his skin. He'd removed the tags while the inspectors where in camp, keeping them secured in the safe aboard his ship, but he'd put them back on as soon as they'd left. He felt strangely insecure without them. When Val and the Councilors had brought up his family, he'd had to force himself not to reach for the tags. He tried not to call attention to them. The last thing he wanted was for someone to notice and consider them important. Wearing them into an alien city probably wasn't the brightest move he'd ever made. But they couldn't be easily deciphered. And he felt safer with them.

He listened to the hive, straining to hear movement or shuffling. All was silent. There could be an entire platoon outside his door, talking confidently to each other, and he'd never know. Though the Shifters did make noise when they moved, at the moment, he couldn't hear anything. He was trying so hard to listen, his ears rang.

Dropping his arm from his eyes, he rolled his head to stare at the door. No locks, nothing in the room big enough to form a barricade. No door to secure the entrance to the hive. The Shifters weren't big on internal security. Maybe they didn't have to contend with theft and crime. Probably not when they could read each other's minds. Could they lie? Did they ever physically fight?

Maybe it was perfectly safe here and he was letting his nerves get the best of him. BinRal had sent another "all's clear" message. Nothing seemed amiss on the surface.

The Councilors had been honest about their ability to defend themselves if they needed to, yet they'd been more than hospitable all evening. Alex would tell him he could afford to relax a little.

Nathan was pretty sure that wouldn't happen until he was out of the city.

Having Ti'ann in the next room didn't help. She was bracketed between him and Krin, a place where she'd be safe. Nathan had developed a real respect for Krin and his unwavering friendship and support for her. He knew the young scientist would defend her if the need arose. They hadn't even discussed taking the rooms surrounding her, just fallen into it as if it was natural.

Not that Ti'ann would be pleased to realize they were trying to protect her. Fortunately, he doubted she even noticed. She was caught up in the wonder of this place, her quick mind ticking over too many thoughts to notice something as mundane as her own safety. Maybe he should teach her how to use a weapon, for those times when he couldn't be around.

He closed his eyes and groaned. Shit. He wanted to protect her. And not because she was paying him to but because he needed to.

That wasn't good. Already he had trouble imagining not being with her. He needed to quit this job and leave. He should never have accepted it once he discovered Ti'ann was involved. But after three years, he'd forgotten how hard it had been to leave her the last time. All he'd remembered or thought about since arriving was how much he wanted to get her in bed again. He hadn't allowed himself to remember how difficult it had been to walk out the door of that hotel suite.

He'd gone out to the lobby to take a message from Alex. About a new job. He had to leave the next day to meet his partner on Ryan Station. After taking the call, he sat in the lobby for half an hour more, deciding if he dared stay the rest of the day and another night with Ti'ann. He wanted her again and he'd only been away from her for less than an hour. He knew it was a bad idea to stay, so he made up his mind to go. He'd return to the room, pack, and say goodbye. It was the smart thing to do.

When he walked into the suite, she was wandering around the living room wearing nothing but one of his shirts. She turned toward him, her eyes sleepy, her smile soft. "Where've you been?" she asked in a quiet, sultry voice. And he had to have her. Just one last time.

When he'd finally left the suite, his goodbye was abrupt and dismissive. But it was the only way he could leave. If he'd tried for a tender farewell, he would never have gotten out.

Taking this job was the stupidest thing he'd ever done.

He crawled out of the bed alcove and paced circles around the room. She was next door. Just a few meters away, probably snuggled under the blankets. She'd welcome him if he came to her. He wouldn't even knock, just go in and slip into her bed. If he wasn't going to get any sleep anyway, he might as well pass the time doing something he wanted to do.

He kept pacing.

Caught up in his thoughts, it took a moment for him to notice the shuffling noise just outside. When he did, his head snapped up and his nostrils flared. He grabbed the blaster from beneath his pillow and edged to the door. Listening. Everything was silent again. He slowly eased his door open, blaster ready and set to high stun.

As the beaten metal fully opened, he blinked in the dim light of the hive's central core. Not two meters from his door stood a man. A stranger, though something about him looked familiar. The man stared back, unblinking. He didn't move as Nathan raised his weapon.

"Can I help you with something?" he said quietly. This wasn't Zim or Sar. If it was another of the Shifters living in the city, why was it standing out here in human form?

The man tilted his head forward so he was looking up at Nathan from under his brows. He was average height, slim with a sharply angled face, pale blond hair and blue eyes. He wore multi-pocketed green/gold pants, a green t-shirt and boots. All of which blended so well with the city walls, it looked like camouflage. It was impossible to tell if he was carrying any weapons, but his hands were open and empty.

"You're Nathan Longfeather." The man's voice was quiet and scratchy, as if rarely used.

"Who are you?"

"E."

"Easy name to remember. What can I do for you, E?"

"You don't hunt them. But you carry a weapon. You defend her. You defend them all."

"I try." Nathan kept his voice neutral and his weapon raised.

"You can hunt them. Why don't you?"

"Who can I hunt?"

"Shifters."

"Why would I want to hunt them?"

"Because you can."

"I need more of a reason to hunt someone, E."

"Why?"

Nathan shrugged. "I'm just that kind of a guy."

"What reasons?"

"Why don't you tell me what you want here, then maybe we can relax and I'll answer all your questions."

"What reasons?"

Nathan raised an eyebrow. Single-minded. "Okay. I only hunt people who hurt those who can't defend themselves. I hunt when it's to defend and protect."

"Why?"

Nathan shrugged again. "I get paid to."

"That's not your only reason."

"What do you want?"

"To understand."

"What?"

"Why I'm different."

Nathan would have laughed if the man hadn't been so

solemn. E calling himself different was an understatement. He hitched his shoulders and leveled the gun at E's chest instead of his head. "I don't have any idea why you're different. I do know you're not supposed to be here. And I suspect you're a threat to the people I'm protecting."

"I am," E said with no emotion.

"Then I'm going to have to ask you to leave."

"No."

"You don't want me to shoot you, E."

"Your weapon is on stun."

Before Nathan's shocked eyes, E raised his hand and it changed, shifted to form a blaster the size of a laser cannon. "Fucking hell," he breathed, but he didn't lower his weapon.

"I'm not here to kill you, Nathan Longfeather. That's not in my orders. But I can."

"What the fuck are you? You're a Shifter?"

"No. I don't know what I am."

Nathan stared at the man with a cannon for a hand and had no idea what to do next. E could easily kill him. There was no question about that. But he didn't want to kill him. It wasn't in his orders. That E had orders was something to digest for later consideration. For now, it was more important to learn what they were. "What are your orders?"

E lifted his head and his mouth tilted up at the edges. It would have been a smile, but it fell short of displaying emotion. "Do you know, I can almost read their minds? And there's something about you. I can't read your mind, but…"

"Nice to know you can't read my mind."

E straightened his shoulders and the attempt at a smile turned to a definite frown. "I have to leave. We will talk again."

"You know I'm going to warn the city about you?"

"I know. It won't matter."

And suddenly the man was a small rodent, no evidence of clothes or the cannon or even the man remaining. Before Nathan could recover enough to stun the rodent, it had scurried away into a crack in the wall.

He slowly lowered his blaster. What the hell had just happened? He pulled out his comm-card and messaged BinRal. "I've just had a very strange conversation," he muttered into the link. "A guy who calls himself E and shifts like a Shifter but says he's not a Shifter just stopped by to ask me why he's different."

"Interesting. Is he still there?"

"No, but his hand shifted into a cannon you would have admired. I didn't think Shifters could change into things like machines and guns. He says he's not a Shifter, though. He could have killed me at any time. But he just wanted to talk."

"Sounds dangerous. You want to move your people out of there tonight? We could keep them better secured up here."

Nathan looked back at Ti'ann's closed door. She must be sleeping like a rock not to have heard anything. "I don't think he'll cause trouble tonight. He could have done something already. I don't mind telling you, though, he scared the shit out of me."

"That's not good, Nathan."

"I know. We'll leave first thing. I'm going to warn the Shifters here about E."

"Buzz if you need me."

"Thanks."

Nathan stared at Ti'ann's door for a long time after he disconnected with BinRal. He shouldn't go in. She was sleeping too deeply. But with something like E running around the city, he didn't want to leave her alone either. Would he be able to sleep beside her without making love to her? Probably not. Maybe just once and then he'd let her go back to sleep. He could protect her better if he stayed with her.

He didn't allow himself to think any more about his decision as he quietly opened her door.

CHAPTER TWENTY-ONE

Ti'ann jolted up in bed at the sound of noise just outside her room, forgetting the bed was inside an alcove. She bashed her head off the ceiling and collapsed back onto the mattress with a soundless curse, clutching her head. "Fuck, fuck, fuck," she hissed as spots swam in her vision. She swore by the fact that cursing helped ease pain—especially stubbed toes and bumped elbows, but it was good for heads too.

She fell silent when another sound from outside caught her attention. She froze with her hand still pressed hard against her head and strained to hear more. Voices? A conversation, aloud, between two men. They spoke so quiet she couldn't hear the words.

Sucking in a breath at the throb of the bump on her forehead, she eased out of bed and crept to the door. She stood on her toes to get closer to the vent. Nathan's voice was recognizable immediately, but the second male voice wasn't familiar. One of the Shifters? Not Zim. She knew the voice he used. It wasn't Val either. Sar, when she spoke, sounded too feminine.

She had an overwhelming itch to ease open her door and spy, but she froze mid-motion when the words of their conversation reached her.

"I'm not here to kill you, Nathan Longfeather. That's not in my orders. But I can."

"What the fuck are you? You're a Shifter?"

"No. I don't know what I am."

Ti'ann stopped breathing. Her lungs hurt, but she still couldn't manage to drag in a breath. Oh god. Oh my god! She couldn't think. Her brain froze. Nathan was facing a man that could kill him. She had to do something. But what? She didn't have any weapons, and she didn't have any training with weapons even if she had one. If she walked outside, would she make the situation worse, would she create another target, or would she give Nathan a chance to act?

The man said he didn't want to kill Nathan. That was good. Nathan was smart. He'd figure a way out of this. Oh god, what if he didn't? What if the man shot him while she stood inside too flustered to act?

She stood up on her toes again, pressing against the wall for balance as she tried to hear more of the conversation. Hearing Nathan's voice, strong and calm helped ease her panic enough to concentrate on what they were saying.

"Nice to know you can't read my mind, E."

"I have to leave. We'll talk again."

Hearing the man say he was leaving shot a jolt of relief through her system so strong it made her knees weak. Her heart hammered as she sank back to her feet. She listened a few minutes longer but didn't hear the stranger's voice again. When Nathan started talking on his comm-link, she eased away from the door. She could barely stand up as adrenaline left her system.

She wobbled across to the bed and eased herself back into the alcove, careful not to bump her head again as she sat on the edge of the mattress. Reaching up, she fingered the now growing lump and winced as her fingers came away sticky. She didn't have to see the red in the dark room to know her head was bleeding. Not much, though. Amazing for a cut on the head. But enough that it probably looked bad. Just what she needed on top of the adrenaline crash. A concussion.

She stood and felt around on the floor for her t-shirt. She'd have to go back to camp tomorrow one way or the other to get clean clothes, but there was nothing she could do. The room didn't exactly have a first aid kit on hand. She plucked up her shirt and dabbed it against the cut, sucked in a breath, held it until the sting subsided, then pressed the shirt harder to the wound.

She was sitting on the bed, the hem of her shirt pressed against her head, wearing nothing but her underwear, when the door eased open. She didn't even have time to make a noise when the tall, dark shape stepped into the room. The instant she saw the shadow of his hair, she knew it was Nathan and another surge of fear eased. "Sonofabitch. Nathan, you nearly scared me to death."

He went very still after closing the door, just stood, staring at her. Or at least she thought he was staring at her. She couldn't really see his eyes in the darkness. The lamps had gone out sometime while she slept and now the only light in the room came from the vent in the door.

She was about to ask what was wrong when she remembered she was practically nude. She dropped her t-shirt to cover her breasts. The logical part of her brain wondered why she felt self-conscious when he'd seen her naked breasts before.

"Are you okay?" she asked into the silence. "I heard that

man out there with you. What did he want? He didn't hurt you did he?"

"I'm fine. What happened to your head?" He stayed near the door.

"I bumped it on the ceiling in the alcove when I jolted awake." She shrugged. "It probably looks worse than it is."

"It's bleeding? You could have a concussion."

"I didn't hit my head that hard. I probably just cut it on one of the raised stones." She fell silent, tried to breathe normally and only succeeded in making her breathing more ragged. "Are you sure you're okay?"

"Yes. He…it…he didn't want to hurt me. He wanted to understand what he is. I couldn't help."

"He shape-changed, didn't he? You accused him of being a Shifter."

From across the room she caught the flash of white teeth against his dark skin. "You heard a lot."

She felt her face heat and was glad there wasn't enough light for him to see her blush. "Sorry. I didn't recognize the second voice. And then I heard him threaten you. I figured he wasn't a friend."

His soft chuckle teased her from across the room as he moved toward her. "He wasn't a friend. Was it our voices that caused you to sit up so quickly?"

She nodded. "I must be listening for noise, or conscious of its absence here. I suppose it must be very noisy if you have telepathy. Can you hear anything?"

"No." He stopped at her feet, staring down at her where she still perched at the edge of her bed.

She looked back up at him and couldn't think of anything to say. He was so tall and so perfectly male. His chest was bare and the urged to run her fingers over those hard muscles was overwhelming. She nearly forgot the lump on her head and the fact that she was virtually naked.

"Why are you here?" she finally asked.

"I want to be here." He touched her cheek, gently slid his fingers into her hair. With a gentle tug, he pulled her to her feet. The shirt she held in trembling fingers dropped to the floor between them. "I want you."

His mouth closed over hers, and she relaxed against his warm chest, happy to forget everything else but this.

He caressed her cheeks, her neck, her shoulders, his big hands tender. His touch was light enough to make her shiver. She pressed into him, wanting more. Where her hands rested against his chest, she felt his muscles flex, the tremble of restraint, the hammering of his heartbeat. His scent enveloped her, swamping her with the delicious essence of him.

She moved closer, wrapping her arms around his neck, her breasts flattening against his taught, warm skin. And still he held back, running his hands in barely felt caresses over her shoulders, down her back, along her waist. The movement, so close and yet not quite touching, was torturous and erotic all at once. His caress continued down to her lower back, over her butt. Her hips jerked closer, pressing against his erection, and still he held back.

He was driving her insane. She wanted more. She didn't want him to stop.

When she couldn't stand it any longer, she murmured, "Harder," against his mouth. "Touch me harder."

His groan shuddered up from deep in his chest. And his hands kneaded her flesh. She sighed with satisfaction and deepened their kiss. He eased her back into the alcove, careful of her head. His hands clasped hard on her ass, pressing her tightly against him. When they finally stretched out on the bed, she moaned in relief. She wasn't sure her legs could hold her much longer.

He pulled away and looked down at her for a long moment, his gaze caressing her face. Two metal tags, hanging around his neck from a leather thong, dropped into the valley between her breasts, warm from his body heat. The tickle of metal made her squirm. Nathan groaned and tossed the tags over his shoulder, getting them out of the way.

His fingers touched the skin near the lump on her head, brushing at the now dried blood at her hairline. "I'm sorry we woke you."

She grinned, squeezing his tightly muscled butt with both hands. "I'm not." God, he felt good.

He smiled back. "Okay, I'm not either. I was going to come in and wake you anyway, before our unexpected visitor stopped by."

"You were?" Her stomach danced.

He lowered his mouth to her cheek, kissing her gently. "I was," he whispered. "I was thinking about you." His mouth moved down her throat, lips brushing hotly over her skin. He inhaled deeply. "God, you smell good."

His exhale brushed hot air against her neck, making her shiver. "It's the oil they gave us." Her voice sounded strained in the quite room.

"No." His tongue flicked out, tasting. "It's you."

A low moan she couldn't control escaped her tight throat. Her fingers raked up his back. "I bet you're grateful…I have short fingernails." She was panting now. His tongue traveled over her throat and dipped delicately in the hollow.

"I wouldn't mind." He eased lower and touched her already peaked nipple with just the tip of his tongue.

She dug her fingers into his shoulders, squealing when he held back. "Nathan, if you don't start handling me harder, I'm going to die and leave you very unsatisfied."

He chuckled, then took her nipple in his mouth, sucking it hard. "Better," he murmured, his hot breath enveloping her breast.

"Yes. Oh, yes."

He sent her spiraling through her limits of sensuality, his touch alternating between teasing softness and hard urgency. Afraid to make too much noise in the silent city, she muffled her moans and whimpers in the velvet blanket. Every time she thought she couldn't take any more, he pushed her farther, eased her down and forced her up again. He kept her on an edge so sharp it hurt. She pleaded and begged for release, panted his name. When she got no mercy, she switched to returning the torture. She took advantage of the knowledge she'd gained the night before to touch him and tease him in ways designed to force compliance.

"You drive me crazy, Ti'ann," he breathed against her mouth.

Before she could argue or even utter a word, he slid into her. And she forgot what she wanted to say.

As soon as he was inside her, all semblance of gentleness left him. He moved fast and hard, catapulting her into an orgasm that ripped through her. He didn't give her time to recover. He drove her past all endurance, to a place where sensation was the only thing left. When she came again, it rolled over her in long waves.

"Nathan," she groaned, and finally pulled him over with her. The sound of his name echoed harshly in the alcove.

Later, when they could both stand, Nathan returned to his room for a flask of water and a bit of cloth from his pack. Then he helped her clean the worst of the dried blood from around her bump. Afterward, they crawled back into the relatively roomy alcove, deep enough to accommodate them both with Ti'ann curled up next to him.

She rested her cheek on his chest and fingered the metal tags hanging from his throat. "You didn't have these on last night. Are they a tracking devise or something?"

"Nothing so technical."

She heard the smile in his voice. When he didn't explain, she frowned. "Are you ignoring my question?"

"No. They're not a tracking devise. I answered your question."

She thumped him lightly on the chest. "You know what I mean. What are they?"

He chuckled, his breath brushing the top of her head. "They're a family heirloom."

"Strange heirloom. What do all these dots and numbers mean?"

"Secret code." There was still enough humor in his voice she knew he was joking.

"If you don't want to tell me, just say so," she huffed, which made him laugh. "What's so funny?" She propped herself up on her elbow to face him.

"You're funny. Your curiosity knows no bounds, Ti'ann."

"If that's supposed to be a polite way of saying I'm nosy, I already knew that. It's a side-effect of being a scientist."

"Side-effect or cause of?" He ran a hand down her temple, then cupped her cheek. "Being nosy suits you."

She frowned, despite the tingles emanating from his touch. "I can never tell if you're insulting me or not."

His smile was so tender it made her chest ache.

"Always not," he said very seriously, then pulled her down and kissed her until she relaxed against him again. He ran his lips along her jaw to the soft skin under her ear. "I think you're probably the most fascinating woman I've ever met, Ti'ann Jones." He tugged her up farther on the bed so he could kiss the juncture between her shoulder and neck. "I love your curiosity." He licked and sucked his way to the hollow of her throat. "Even if it gets you into trouble."

He ran his hand down her waist, so gently she shivered. Squirming against him, she tried to ease the excess of sensation. "When does my curiosity get me into trouble?" she whispered as he moved down to her breast. Her nipples were sensitive to the point of pain as he closed his lips around them.

At her hiss, he said, "Too tender?"

She nodded.

"I'll be gentle." And he was. So gentle that before long she was nearly screaming with the need for him to stop being gentle. Again!

"You never answered my question," she said. She tugged his head and arched against him, trying to force him to be rougher. He ignored her efforts and continued without hurry. "Nathan," she whimpered. "I'm not too tender anymore."

"I don't care." He kissed the underside of her breast.

"I can't take this again. You're driving me insane."

"Payback since you do the same thing to me."

"You haven't seen anything yet," she promised, gripping his wrists and shifting to straddle his hips. He pulled her farther forward so her torturous plans couldn't be carried out, and she groaned as he started kissing her stomach.

"You can pay me back later," he murmured.

"You've told me that before."

"We haven't gotten to later yet." He moved back up to her breasts then shifted until she lay under him.

"You didn't answer my question." If he wouldn't let her torture him physically, she would talk him to distraction.

"Which question?"

He dipped his tongue in her navel and she forgot for a minute what she was supposed to be badgering him about. Then, "When has my curiosity gotten me into trouble?"

"It's got you into trouble right now."

She couldn't argue with that. "This doesn't count. When else?"

"Nearly charging into a Shifter city without thinking about the dangers."

"But I didn't."

"Because I stopped you." His hand moved to caress the sensitive skin at the top of her inner thigh.

She tried wiggling to get his hand higher, but he resisted. "That was a once off. What else?" She ran her hands over his shoulders, into his hair, pushing and pulling because she couldn't decide where she needed him most.

"Bringing in members of a Shifter support team for your anomaly."

"I had to do that."

"Because you couldn't let the mystery go without finding answers."

"That's my job." She was losing the argument and was too caught up in what his hands and mouth were doing to care. If she could think, she'd be able to argue better, but thinking coherently wasn't something Nathan inspired in her.

"Exactly."

"What?"

"Your job. You've chosen a career that involves solving mysteries and puzzles."

"A lot of people are scientists." She could barely speak now. Her breathing was too sharp and shallow. "Nathan, you're killing me."

"You told me that earlier." He chuckled against her thigh. "I think you're exaggerating, Dr. Jones. I thought scientists stuck to the facts."

"This is a fact," she groaned. "I never exaggerate."

This earned a full–throated laugh. "Shall we put that to the test?"

"Oh, god." She couldn't talk again until some time later.

They napped, woke and made love again, then slept some more. When Ti'ann woke again, she shifted around, looking for a clock. It was impossible to tell the time in the dark room, and she'd left her wrist unit in her tent—as usual.

Nathan stirred beside her. "Not yet. I'm too tired."

She laughed quietly. "I'm just looking for a clock or something."

He leaned over the bed and pulled his comm-card out of his trouser pocket. "Another couple of hours before we need to show our faces," he said after touching a spot on the card.

She glanced at the glowing numbers as they faded away. "Good. I'm not sure I can walk yet."

He tugged her close to his side so her head rested against his shoulder. She snuggled into him and felt the cool touch of metal. She lifted her head enough to move the metal tags and stared at them for a moment before settling them on the center of his chest. Family heirloom. "Do you have a big family?" she asked. She'd always associated heirlooms with big families.

"Two younger brothers and an older sister. A few aunts and uncles with kids. Not too big."

"A lot bigger than mine. I was an only child and my mom and dad both only had one sibling."

"Why didn't your parents have any more children? Most Naravans have at least two."

He stroked her back in long lazy sweeps that made her sigh. "I was more than enough for them." She smiled when he chuckled. "Actually, there were some problems with my birth. My mom was fine, but she couldn't face having another baby after. So I got all their attention."

"You must have been spoiled rotten."

"A little. They pushed me, though. My dad's a scientist, too."

"Explains a lot. They must be proud of you."

She shrugged, fingering the metal tags again. "They're glad I'm doing something that requires I use my brains."

"Understandable when you've got such a good brain to work with."

"You think I have a good brain?"

"Of course. Imminent paleontologist running her own dig sites, top in your field if Krin's bragging is even partly true."

"He does exaggerate," she said, grinning inanely.

"Not that much."

"How about your family?" she asked to deflect further questions. She didn't want to talk about herself anymore. She didn't want Nathan to know how much it meant to her that he admired her intelligence. "What do your brothers and sister do?"

"All very respectable careers. Unlike me." There was definite affection in his voice.

"Are you close with your family?"

"Yes. For the most part. We have disagreements."

"About what?"

"The usual stuff."

"You're being evasive again."

"Habit. Do you argue with your parents?"

"Never. You'd have to meet my dad to understand. He somehow manages to defer or win any potential argument that might be had, so I just gave up trying."

"What's his field?"

"Sociology. Ethics and philosophies across interplanetary cultures."

"I can see why he wins arguments."

"You don't know the half." She moved her hand from the tags to his chest, drawing circles in his chest hair. "What exactly do your more respectable siblings do for a living?"

"My sister's a lawyer. My youngest brother is a test pilot for the Wyatt-Haines group. My middle brother owns a small business in Moorack. He married a rich woman so he mostly plays at his business now."

"Did he marry her for her money?" That didn't sound more respectable than Nathan's job.

Nathan chuckled. "No. He didn't even know she was rich until a week after the wedding. Almost caused them to split. But he gave in. He's crazy about her."

"Sounds nice. Romantic."

"I suppose."

Okay, he wasn't the romantic type, she thought, and moved on before they got into an uncomfortable conversation. "Have you always worked with BinRal?"

"We used to call in BinRal whenever we needed backup. He's the best I've ever worked with."

"We?"

"My ex-partner and I. I was working with Alex when you

and I met the first time. His name's Johan Alexander, but he hates his first name so he goes by Alex."

"Why's he an ex-partner?" She felt Nathan stiffen, his lazy stroking stilled for a telling moment. "Sorry," she said before he could say anything. "Too personal?"

"No. He got married."

"He stopped working because he got married?"

"He stopped doing the freelance work we did as partners when he got married. He confined his work to a single company so he could stay near his wife."

"Oh." She fell silent and was relieved when his hand started stroking her back again. Then she straightened, looking down at him. "Mr. Alexander? Is this the same Mr. Alexander you claimed was on the museum board?"

He brought a hand up to play with a long length of her hair where if fell onto his chest. "The very one," he said, distracted, his full attention on the lock of hair.

"Is he really on the board?"

He smiled, still looking more interested in her hair than the conversation. "He is. Now. His father-in-law has some influence."

"He married rich, too?"

"I guess you could say that. But Alex already had plenty of money. He's good with his finances."

"How 'bout you?"

"I'm good too." The lazy-eyed look he gave her had nothing to do with money.

Her heart started pumping faster as a slow, liquid heat seeped into her limps. "I thought you were too tired," she murmured.

"I'm not anymore." To prove his point, he pulled her head down to his and kissed her.

E SAT BACK after sending his coded message to the senator and Dr. Ripley, wondering at the odd feeling in his gut. It was his task to report his findings. And the city was definitely a finding. They would want to know. They would come here to destroy the city. They'd want him to help.

He looked at the huge statue across the corridor from him. It was beautiful. He could almost feel the emotions churning from it. It had once been a Shifter.

He walked among them, taking the shape of their natural form. He even gave himself silver eyes so he could blend in better. They talked a lot. They greeted him, even though they didn't know him. He heard them clearly now. Heard what they thought, felt, talked about—though talking was too small a term for the way they communicated. It felt right, he realized. Their way of communicating felt right to him. Natural. Easier than words. Yet he knew words and these did not. None of them used words except those dealing most closely with Val, Ti'ann Jones and Nathan Longfeather.

He wasn't like them. This shape he took wasn't his natural state. It took energy to maintain, as any shifted form took energy. But he was male the way some of these were male. Val wasn't male or female. Val was like most Shifters. But there were males and females here in the city.

Dr. Ripley didn't know Shifters could be male and female. It was new and important information.

And he hadn't told them about it in his message. He wasn't exactly sure why, except that he didn't want them to know. He was defying his orders. Surprising. But he didn't regret it.

He'd almost kept the information about the city to himself as well. Almost. After talking to Nathan Longfeather, he had considered lying in his report. That was a new idea. He hadn't considered lying to Dr. Ripley before. Following orders was his entire purpose for being. Dr. Ripley had drilled that into him. But traveling among the Shifters of this city, E was no longer sure if his only purpose was following orders.

Perhaps he had another purpose.

CHAPTER TWENTY-TWO

Ti'ann and Nathan managed another hour of sleep before reluctantly climbing out of bed. Ti'ann's body felt sore but sated. She was exhausted but in a nice way. Though if she kept this up, she'd never sleep a full night again.

Nathan slipped back to his own room while she dressed. She pulled on her blood stained shirt and thought longingly of clean clothes and a bath. Using the washing water from the day before, she cleaned up a little, but she was heading for the showers as soon as she got back to camp. She fingered the lump on her forehead. Still sore, probably pretty ugly by now. But at least she didn't have a headache and she wasn't seeing spots. The bump would get a thorough cleaning too as soon as she got above ground.

She sat on the edge of the bed to put on her pants. Without Nathan in the room, she finally had some time to think. She still didn't know exactly why he'd come to her last night but she would never have turned him away, no matter the reason. And the night had been everything she could have wanted, living up to her memories of the last time they'd been together. Only two nights that first time. Would they have more now? Or was this it? She didn't want to face the possibility yet.

When they were in bed, Nathan was so tender and open. She felt warm and cosseted and safe. And comfortable. She'd never felt like this with a man before, not a heterosexual man anyway, and definitely not one she was having sex with. She could hardly believe she was comfortable around a man as gorgeous as Nathan. He also made her feel free and relaxed. She could be herself. He even admired her intellect and curiosity.

She knew she was in trouble when she started asking about his family, and he answered. Worse trouble than she'd thought. She'd moved beyond lust into emotions she had no business feeling for a man like Nathan Longfeather. He might be happy to come to her bed for now. But like last time, sooner or later, he'd leave. He didn't even pay much attention to her when they weren't in bed. Not personal attention. He avoided touching her for Pete's sake. He gave her no reason to hope for more from him.

But she did want more from him. And she hated that she did. The hurt Brad had inflicted would be nothing compared to having her heart broken by Nathan. With a sharp pain, she realized he'd already broken her heart once. She hadn't recognized it before. One didn't fall in love with someone after only two nights and three days of lust-filled sex. Especially not after just being dumped by someone else. It wasn't logical, and logic was the only thing in her life she trusted.

Except her very first lover, a professor, had been a logical choice, and he'd left her too.

She groaned and leaned down to put on her boots. Logic didn't seem to work in her romantic life, so why not just admit the ridiculous truth. She'd been in love with Nathan for three years. She stared across the room at the beaten metal door.

This was going to hurt—a lot.

There was no way around it. He'd leave and she'd be devastated and there wasn't a damn thing she could do about it because she was already in love with him. She couldn't take it back now. It had been festering without her knowledge for years.

Krin was going to kill her for getting into this mess.

NATHAN QUICKLY CLEANED up and dressed then went in search of Zim. He didn't know who E was, but the Shifters here had to be told about him. If they didn't already know. If they did, Nathan wanted information and he wanted it now.

Anything to keep his mind off Ti'ann Jones and the trouble he was in.

It didn't take long to find Zim. The Shifter was sitting just outside the family hive in a small, private garden. The overhead lighting was bright enough to give the illusion of a sunny spring morning.

He greeted Zim with a nod and, at a gesture from the Shifter, sat down next to him on the bench. "Can we communicate without Val?"

"Yes."

"I had an encounter last night with a…creature. He looked like a human male. He claimed he wasn't a Shifter but he could shape-shift. He called himself E. Do you know who this is? He's a killer. I'm sure of it. He talked about hunting Shifters."

Zim went very still, the mouth formed in his Shifter face wavered and faded. He turned to stare off at the wall opposite their bench. It was covered in florescent plants and ivy-like greenery. Then his mouth formed again and said, "I do not know this E. No one in my family has heard of him either." He turned to face Nathan again. "You are sure he can shift?"

"I watched him."

"I have sent word to the Councilors and the heads of each line. If there is any information, we will receive it soon. Thank you for telling me. You think he is a threat to us?"

"Definitely. I think he's a threat to anyone he comes into contact with. The ability to shift combined with the skills and ability to kill makes for a very dangerous combination."

Zim nodded. "I know. It is one of the reasons your people feared us, even though we weren't dangerous to them during those early years. With the ability to shift, if we could kill, we would be difficult to defend against."

"Can you blame us?"

"Not for the fear. But for your reaction to it. Humans did not take the time to learn that we could not kill before declaring war on our species. We can blame you for that."

Nathan didn't know what to say to Zim's comment. If an alien species invaded his home planet and started systematically exterminating his people, he'd probably feel the same way. His reaction would be more violent than the Shifters, though.

He rose to leave. "I'll take my people out of the city as soon as they're all awake. Let us know when you're ready for the rest of the groups to start coming down."

Nathan headed back into the hive to find nearly everyone awake and hovering around Val. He felt the ripples of excitement emanating from the group before he reached them.

"What's going on?"

Val spun to face him with a smile so huge it could have lit

the room. "Sar is giving birth. She's early, but all seems to be going well."

"Why isn't Zim with her?" Nathan asked, glancing back toward the door to the garden.

"The male isn't present when the female gives birth," Val answered tartly.

If Nathan didn't know better, he'd swear Val was actually female.

James laughed and said, "Zim is still with her. Telepathically. But it's better for her to be alone with the…midwife I suppose we'd call him. He's a cross between a healer, a doctor, a midwife and a therapist. He's a non-reproducing member of the line that helps with the births of the females in his line."

"I take it we're not leaving yet then." He didn't have to ask. One glance at Ti'ann's face and he knew he wouldn't get her out of the city until after Sar had her baby. "How long does this usually take?"

Val burst out in a sudden shout and Zim came flying into the central core of the hive. He had shifted into a huge winged creature that reminded Nathan of the griffins from Earth mythology.

"She's succeeded," Val told them as Zim alighted on one of the upper layers of the hive. "A healthy female. Oh, good. They were hoping for a female."

"Tell them both we send our congratulations," Krin said, grinning at Ti'ann's own smiling face.

Nathan looked away. "Where's Glen?" he asked.

"He hasn't come out yet," James said, his grin as big as Ti'ann and Krin's. "I'll get him. I'm sure he'd want to hear the news."

James disappeared into Glen's room and reappeared a minute later with a puzzled frown. "He's not there. Maybe he left earlier this morning."

"Anyone know where he's gone?" Nathan turned to Val. "Can you find out where he is? He shouldn't be alone in the city." He kept the edge of panic out of his voice. Whether his panic was caused by fear for Glen or fear of what he might do, Nathan wasn't sure.

He'd stopped suspecting Glen's motives over the last day. And after meeting E, he had a new suspect for the sabotage on James' ship. Probably a better suspect than Samuels.

A brief moment of annoyance tugged at him, not for the first time. He hadn't searched Samuels' ship. He'd been too busy in bed with Ti'ann to think about it. He'd lost the chance to collect some potentially valuable information, even if Samuels wasn't responsible for the sabotage.

He pushed the guilt aside. He had other things to worry about now. Like the fact Glen was missing.

And with E running around the city, none of them were safe. But he couldn't quiet the nagging worry Glen's disappearance had nothing to do with E. He still didn't know which side of the Shifter issue Glen supported.

Nathan should have tagged the group so he could keep track of them. Again, something he'd forgotten to do because he'd been too preoccupied thinking about Ti'ann. He had to leave this job. He wasn't doing these people any good like this.

"Glen is in the next cavern, watching some of the artists perform," Val said. "One of the family is going to find him, to tell him about Sar's baby."

Val met his gaze and he knew the Shifter had asked that Glen be brought back to the group as well. At least someone was thinking straight.

A small group of Shifters suddenly descended on them, all clustering around Val. It reminded Nathan of a flock of ocean gulls around a scrap of food, but less noisy. From the eye color, he guessed they were members of Zim and Sar's line. The only evidence they were having a conversation with Val was in the animated hand and head gestures. Val grinned, the mouth used to talk still in place. It must be nearly habit at this point, he thought, wondering if it was hard to communicate in a way so different from what you're used to?

After a few moments of the silent conversation, Val turned to Ti'ann and, if anything, grinned more. "They came to talk about Sar, but they really came to find out more about the visiting humans. They'd like to know if you're pregnant, since you have so many males, and if you have many children."

Ti'ann blanched. "I don't have any children, and I don't have so many males, Val."

"I know." There was sympathy in Val's voice if not in Val's grin. "They don't understand. Since you're the only female in your group here, they assume the men belong to you."

"The men belong to themselves," Ti'ann said, her face bright red and her eyes focused on the ground. "And I'm not pregnant."

He tried to feel offended when she didn't admit to their affair, but he couldn't. Her embarrassment was too charming and too in character for his Dr. Jones. He glanced at Krin and James. James was trying not to smirk, but Krin had no such restraint and chuckled quietly behind his hand. Ti'ann elbowed him in the ribs, but he didn't stop.

Nathan tried to catch Ti'ann's attention, but she wouldn't look at him. In fact, she seemed to be doing a damned fine job of avoiding his gaze. He knew she'd be too embarrassed to say anything blatant about their relationship. She wasn't the type to gossip about her affairs. In a way, he was grateful. The last thing he needed from Krin was a grilling on his intentions. He'd have to know what his intentions were first.

"They don't understand how you aren't pregnant with so many fertile men."

At that, Krin laughed out loud, not bothering to cover his mouth. Nathan coughed to cover his own amusement.

"Val, you have to know about birth control. Explain it to them."

"I tried," Val said emphatically. "They don't understand why your species would go to the trouble of taking a shot that makes both men and women essentially sterile, even if it can be reversed."

"It's not sterility," Ti'ann mumbled.

"Tell them we prefer to plan when we have children and with whom instead of having them spontaneously," James said, humor evident in his voice.

"I'll try. They don't understand it. They seem to understand sex for fun, but they don't know why you purposely prevent pregnancy."

"Cultural differences," Krin said, still chuckling. He dropped an arm around Ti'ann's shoulders. "Except for the part about sex for fun. We can all understand that."

Ti'ann's face flamed redder and Krin got the dangerous end of a glare that Nathan was glad he didn't have to face.

She was saved from further embarrassment by the reappearance of Glen, followed by two male Shifters. "Hey. What's going on?" He didn't seem bothered by the escort.

"Sar had her baby, so we won't be leaving as soon as we thought," James told him. "If all's well with the baby, we'll stay long enough to pay our respects in person."

Glen shrugged. "Great. This place is so full of stuff to see, you could spend a lifetime here and not get bored. Shame I can't really talk to them." He glanced at the two Shifters still flanking him.

"There are members of each line trying to learn how to use words now," Val said. "I imagine you'll be able to talk with a number of them before too long."

"Yeah, Zim picked up the language pretty fast," Nathan said.

"It helps having me to translate. I'm not sure how the first Shifters managed. I forgot how difficult it was to confine our language down into words for someone who doesn't have an understanding of words."

"Why are only a few members from each line learning our way of communication, Val? For that matter, why are any of them learning in the first place?" Krin asked. He dropped his arm from around Ti'ann's shoulder and pushed a heavy fall of hair off his forehead.

"They've accepted that they'll have to negotiate with humans. Their city can't remain hidden much longer. But if they can't speak with humans, if they have to work through a translator, even another Shifter translator, they're at a disadvantage. I'd guess most of them will learn to communicate with words eventually."

As they fell into quiet conversation, Nathan moved off to contact BinRal. If he had to be honest, he was looking forward to seeing Sar's baby, too. His mother would kill him if he didn't bring back an eyewitness report.

It took BinRal nearly a minute to respond to his hales. Just when Nathan was starting to worry, the Binnean answered. "Problems?" Nathan said without preamble.

"I've picked something up on the wide-range scanners and a coded message being relayed along a secured channel. We're getting company."

"Fuck. Who? When? Where are they now?"

"At a guess, the who is a government ops group, probably

military instead of Guard. The code they're using and the channel it's on are standard military secret ops. Unusual for a Guard company to use them."

"If they're standard enough that you know about them, why are they using them?"

"Probably because they assume no one's cracked them yet." There was a mixture of pride and humor in BinRal's voice.

"Okay, what about the when and where?"

"The where is roughly fifteen kilometers west of the site. They avoided Gremblewreath. They're coming in quiet, on foot. I don't know exactly how many, but there's at least thirty of them."

"How'd you pick them up?"

"I set some long range sensors after I arrived. Just in case. They tripped one just before dawn."

Nathan frowned and glanced across at the group of humans and Shifters who were in animated conversation. Ti'ann was right in the middle, probably full of questions. Just before dawn he'd been inside her, too caught up in her to think beyond the moment. "You think they'll attack?"

"Yes."

"When?"

"Soon. They went to communications blackout just as you called."

"Get the camp evacuated—"

"Almost done," BinRal interrupted.

Nathan said a quiet thanks for the Binnean's efficiency.

"Only people left are Clare, Juanita, Mike, two of the collectors and that young volunteer, Micca. Clare, Juanita and Mike are refusing to leave. There wasn't enough room on the single transport we sent out for all of Dr. Jones' team. We used one of the team's lift-trucks, but it was overloaded as it was. I didn't want to send all the ships and give away the fact that we know they're coming."

"Good plan. Why didn't you contact me earlier?"

"I wanted most of the team evacuated before I tipped our hand by opening a comm-link."

"You think they've picked us up?"

"Probably. But I've set a few traps so they won't be able to decipher this for another hour or so. That's the other reason I didn't contact you earlier. Making sure the traps were in place first."

"Did I jump the gun?" Nathan started back toward the group.

"No. We should be okay. You bringing them out?"

Nathan thought about that for a minute. Where would everyone be safest? Where would Ti'ann be safest? "This team is coming for the city?"

"That'd be my assumption. There wasn't enough here while Samuels was around to bring down this kind of action. I'd bet that thing you met last night tipped them off."

"E. He talked about his orders. I was hoping he was free-lance since I don't know how to track him or fight him."

"Given the team heading this way, he's got some govern-ment connections."

"They're coming in on foot, right? Okay. We can defend from the city," he said when he was near enough for the others to overhear. Everyone swung around to face him. "You want to bring the others down here, or find a defensive position up there?"

"They're gonna hit that place hard, Nate. From what you've said about the past actions against Shifter cities, they're likely going for total destruction. You want to be under all that rock when they strike?"

"No. So we're gonna make them come down into the city after us. You think you can arrange something?"

BinRal's chuckle sounded eerie over the comm-link. "I can. I'll send the rest of the group to you now. Have someone meet them at the entrance."

"I will. Out." He cut the transmission then faced the group of wide-eyed humans and silent Shifters. "BinRal's picked up a military group heading this way. They're not friendly visitors. We don't know about numbers yet, but there're at least thirty of them. We can assume they're heavily armed. Val, you'd better warn the Councilors. We need to set up some traps around the city. They'll have detectors on them so we won't be able to take advantage of your ability to shift, but we'll see what we can do. I know you can't actually kill or hurt them. I'll take care of that. But I will need help distracting and corralling them."

"What about the team above? Are they coming down into the city?" Ti'ann said, her voice sharp and urgent.

"BinRal's evacuated most of them. The rest are coming down. James, your people are still here. They refused to leave. Ti'ann and Krin, you've only got three left. BinRal didn't want to send too many ships away and tip off the gnats approaching that we're aware of them."

"I'll go to the entrance to meet our people," James said. "What's your plan?"

"We're going to try to take them out as quietly as we can, in whatever way we have to. Then we're going public as loudly as possible, as soon as possible. These guys are here to destroy this city and, if they follow the past patterns, to keep news of it from getting out. We're gonna make sure they fail at both."

CHAPTER TWENTY-THREE

Ti'ann watched the preparations with only a vague idea of what was going on. She'd never played war games or games of strategy. She didn't even play chess. The efforts were mesmerizing. Nathan commanded like a general, using Val and Zim as translators to deploy Shifters from each line around the city to set traps. The Shifters not involved in the defense were evacuated to an area nearly twenty kilometers from the main part of the city—hopefully at a safe distance if anything went wrong.

And according to Nathan, so much *could* go wrong. He had less than two hours to organize everything, and only that much time because BinRal was still above ground distracting the soldiers, keeping them away from Ti'ann's campsite and the city simultaneously. Yet, Nathan managed to come up with a decent plan. At least Ti'ann thought the plan was good—they'd corral the soldiers in an isolated spot and hold them prisoner until negotiations with the government could start and knowledge of the city was made public. But then, she was way out of her depth with all this.

To her surprise, when Nathan started handing out the weapons BinRal had sent down for the humans, a large number of the city Shifters took them up as well, even making Nathan explained the higher, lethal settings above stun. She wasn't entirely sure she wanted to know how to shoot anything worse than a stun shot. But the Shifters didn't flinch.

James' people flowed into a defensive, military-like precision. They'd probably had to face similar situations before, but their efficiency still impressed her. Each carried a number of weapons and followed orders without question with James acting as Nathan's second.

When Nathan mentioned making the Shifter city public, Clare jumped at the information. "I know the perfect person to help with that," she said. "Name's Riley." Looking around the extravagantly decorated meeting hall, which had become their central command, she put her hands on her curvy hips and laughed. "Riley will love giving this story to the planet."

After they'd done as much as they could to prepare, and the evacuation of most of the Shifters—including Sar and her baby—was underway, Nathan sent the humans off to their stations around the city, charged with making sure the soldiers went where they were supposed to go.

Before sending her off with Krin, he handed her a blaster, somehow managing to pass her the weapon without touching her. Back to not touching again. She sighed. How could he do that? Move from affectionate one moment to all-business-like and impersonal the next. She handled the blaster gently and studied the settings to hide her hurt feelings. She hated this distance he put up between them during the day. Hated more that he wouldn't even touch her. But she wasn't sure she had any right to that response. He'd never promised her anything.

"You're not afraid to use that?" he asked, his tone hard and steady.

She stared at the weapon in her open palm. "Not afraid to." Well, maybe a little, but she wasn't going to admit it to him. "I just hope I don't hit the wrong button and shoot off my foot or something."

"Keep it pointed away from your body," he said in all seriousness.

She grinned, or at least tried to. When she looked at his stern expression, the grin slipped away. "I'll be careful," she assured him. "Besides, Krin will be with me. He knows how to use these things."

Nathan grunted and turned away. She watched his back for a minute. Not so much as a "see you soon" or "don't get killed" from him. She supposed the last comment was as close as she'd get to concern for her health. With another sigh, she trotted after Krin.

What did she expect? Nathan was trying to organize a combination defensive/offensive action against a group of highly trained soldiers who outnumbered them.

Unless they counted the Shifters. She glanced at the two accompanying her and Krin, there to help even though they couldn't use words very well yet. Though the city Shifters hadn't said they *would* kill, they were obviously open to the possibility. The two with them both had blasters. Left to their own devices, Ti'ann wasn't sure they'd leave any of the soldiers alive. While that might save the city now, it would only bring down more military action and spark more human fear. She really hoped they'd be able to keep the soldiers alive. Living, they were more dangerous but also more valuable. Would the city Shifters realize this?

She shivered as she and Krin took up opposite sides of the tunnel where they were stationed. As she pulled out the comm-card Nathan had given her team to check in, she realized, really *knew*, for the first time that they stood on the brink of war.

NATHAN WATCHED the main entrance into the city. They hadn't made it too easy on the soldiers. Wouldn't want to give away the game and make them suspicious. So they'd closed the gate and set traps just inside the first tunnel—a distraction from the bigger traps ahead. BinRal made sure the soldiers got into the city at the right entry point, then join Nathan's group through an alternate entrance.

That was nearly half an hour ago. Either these soldiers were dumber than he thought, or they were a lot more cautious. He was sure they'd scanned the gate, or tried scanning through it and found it nearly impossible to breach. Thanks to the use of ground elements from the area with the Shifter bodies to build the outer walls, standard scanning equipment had trouble pene-trating very far. That was one of the few advantages Nathan had. Their hand scanners would even have a limited range once inside.

He stared at the gate, his impatience carefully controlled. He wanted this done, he wanted Ti'ann and the rest of them safe. But he knew it wouldn't be easy. Or quick.

As he watched, the gate began to shudder under a weapons assault. Finally. He raised his blaster, intending to wait until they got through before falling back. His job was to lead them in the right direction, leaving a tantalizing trail. A shaky plan at best, he knew. A lot relied on luck and the Shifters' preparations. They'd moved fast when he set them a task. He admired their efficiency. But they'd never had to fight before. Not like this.

The gate vaporized under the laser cannon fire. They'd brought out the heavy equipment early in the game. Nathan sighed. He knew this was going to be a tough fight, especially as they were outnumbered in weapons and experienced manpower. The soldiers came in crouched, weapons raised, moving in cover formation. Forty, forty-one, forty-two. Forty-two of them. Could have been worse. He couldn't make out faces behind their helmets and vision goggles, but he didn't need to know what they looked like. A swift inventory of the weapons they carried was enough to let him know what he was up against.

He moved back, taking care not to make noise until he was safely out of weapons range. Then he let a pebble roll. He heard the click of weapons and the hush of orders. With a feral grin, he trotted silently to his next position.

Their hand scanners would track his movements, but the sensors wouldn't show how many individuals they were tracking thanks to a pin-sized disrupter clipped to his shirt. The disrupter was one of BinRal's brother's inventions not yet on the market. Handy, given the high-grade of the soldiers' equipment. Unfortunately, BinRal only had two with him. That meant the other humans in the city were going to be relatively easy to track once the soldiers were within range. He only hoped by then the soldiers would be so confused and disoriented they wouldn't notice the difference.

He settled on his haunches at his next station and listened. Silence. He pulled out his hand scanner and called up a mini-holo image of the position of the soldiers. Each looked like a blue ghost moving across the three-dimensional, topographical location grid. They were indistinguishable from each other but their numbers and movements were clear.

The soldiers were forced to follow the main corridor through a series of tunnels where no alternative routes were available. At the first place where the tunnels diverged, one of the Shifters formed a psuedo-wall to cover one direction. If the soldiers had detectors, and used them, they'd discover the Shifter immediately. But since up to that point the tunnels hadn't split, Nathan hoped they wouldn't use their detectors yet.

Unfortunately, in the scratchy, distorted image of the mini-holo, it looked like every other one held a detector out, scanning in a wide arch. Damn.

He started to signal the Shifter covering the tunnel, using a code of flashes and flickers from a penlight, when he noticed something strange about the miniature soldiers on his scanner. First one, then another, shook the long rectangular box that was the detector. Though it was hard to tell on the image, it looked as if several others slapped them on their hands or thighs and shook them more before continuing to scan.

He frowned and tried adjusting the image to clear up some of the interference. The holo was still too fuzzy. He switched to screen imaging. The picture remained distorted but was now in flat, two dimensions. He couldn't monitor their movements as well, but he could focus in on one individual blue ghost better. That one shook his detector like it was a snake. He held it up in front of his face then tossed it aside.

Nathan sat back and let out a long, slow breath. Their detectors weren't working. He looked at the walls, all those Shifter bodies. The detectors probably hadn't been designed to filter out dead Shifters from live. And who would guess they'd built an entire city out of dead Shifters. He looked up, grinning. They couldn't tell what was and wasn't a Shifter.

He almost laughed out loud. He coded a message to BinRal then sent a secured update to all the comm-links he'd distributed to the various groups throughout the city. The soldiers would break that communications code soon. But for another hour, they could send messages without being overheard. After that, they'd switch codes. The message was simple. "Gnats in the city. Detectors don't work."

Fucking hell, they could take the soldiers at any time now. The Shifters could converge on them at will without having to worry about getting shot before they got near. But would the Shifters kill them outright if they were turned loose? Before he would have said no. Now, he wasn't so sure.

He flicked on the holo-image again and started moving. They'd have picked him up by now. The detector chips in their scanners may still work, so they probably knew he was human, or at least the group of people he represented on their scanners was made up of humans. He moved off to his next station at a trot. The holo-image flickered and went flat when he moved out of range. They wouldn't be able to see him now either. Time to meet up with BinRal and discuss their next step.

TI'ANN NEARLY COLLAPSED when the first message came through. The soldiers were inside the city, but the good news was that their detectors weren't working. Just that fast the soldiers were at a disadvantage. Even with all their weaponry. They couldn't shoot everything just because they didn't know what to shoot. At the very least, they wouldn't want to run down the power cells in their weapons.

She left her post at one end of the tunnel she was stationed in to relay Nathan's message to Krin at his position at the opposite end of the tunnel. She nodded to the two Shifters as she passed. Hopefully, Val was spreading word through their ranks about the detectors because Ti'ann didn't think they'd understand her if she tried to explain. She did say, "Soldiers in the city" as she passed. They stared at her for a moment then the copper-eyed one formed a mouth and said, "Thank you."

When she told Krin the news, his eyes widened. He looked around at the walls and smiled. "Probably didn't expect to be surrounded by Shifters. Any other news?"

"Not yet. You think they'll change the plan?"

His smooth forehead wrinkled in thought. "They could pretty much give the Shifters free rein now. But more of them might get killed that way than following Nathan's original plan. And they may kill the soldiers."

"You thought of that too? You think they would?"

"I don't know. They're more capable of violence than Shifters like Val. But I don't know if they'd kill easily. They might to protect the city."

"They'll bring on a war if they do. If they avoid killing, they're in a better position to negotiate with humans."

"Maybe. Shifters able to kill would definitely terrify some people."

"But...?" Ti'ann asked.

"But it might also provoke the government into real negotiations. If they can't just simply destroy Shifters anymore, they'll have to find a way to make peace."

"Or there'll be a resurgence of support for the exterminations. It's a pretty terrifying thing to know Shifters can be anywhere, anytime, and are capable of killing you."

"A lot of people already think that." Krin's voice was quiet, but his words were heavy.

"Which is why the exterminations are still legal, despite the debates and the efforts of the Shifter support groups. This might confirm fears that were just starting to be alleviated."

"You think we're facing war?"

She shrugged and glanced back at the Shifters still crouched in the center of the tunnel. Their heads were tilted close together, their hand gestures hinting at an intense conversation.

"I sure as hell hope not," she murmured. "If it's war, there's a very good chance we'll lose."

"THEY'RE GOING where we want them to." Nathan watched BinRal study the fuzzy figures of the soldiers moving through yet another tunnel. So far, they'd triggered one trap, released a series of blaster shots at nothing, and moved on. "Looks like they've completely abandoned the detectors, too." BinRal shook the scanner in a rough attempt to clear up the picture. "Good for our decoys. They've got to be wondering about the handful of Binneans running around with you now." He grinned.

"At this rate, we'll have them in the cage within a couple hours," Nathan said.

"We should plant some eavesdropping monitors along the route. See what they have to say. Too bad the Shifters can't understand them."

"Yeah." Though Nathan wasn't so sure that really was a bad thing. "You have eavesdroppers with you?"

"I do."

"Great. Around the next cavern we should be able to set

them up. We probably won't get much. They're moving pretty fast."

"I'm surprised they're not destroying as they go."

"We haven't given them an alternate escape route. They don't want to cave in their only way out."

"You think they'll take the chance we're giving them to split up?"

"Definitely. Have you cracked their intra-group comm-links yet?"

"No. They're as good as we are at jamming up the links and coding messages. And they're not using them much yet since they're still in one group. Doesn't give me much to work with."

Nathan sighed. That was one of the few benefits of letting the group split up, but as soon as they did, he'd have a more difficult time tracking them. That was why his people and the Shifters had to be deployed around the city. But it couldn't be avoided. They'd get suspicious if they never came across an alternate route. The last thing he wanted was this group pulling out all guns blazing, moving in full retreat.

"You know, this would have been easier on them if they just blasted the mountain all to hell and back from the air," he thought aloud, not for the first time. "Why come in on foot?"

"Would have made a lot of noise and drawn a lot of attention to destroy it from the air. They can't just blow up an entire city these days without someone knowing about it. And you're pretty sure they don't want the public to know this place exists. That kind of cover up would have been a lot easier in the frontier days of settlement. So they've chosen a riskier but quieter destruction."

"But humans were on this planet for a generation before we knew about Shifters. The press would have been up and running by then. Why didn't they pick up on the other cities getting destroyed?"

"You humans have expanded a lot more in the last seventy years. The first fifty were still settling years."

Nathan grunted at BinRal's assessment. How the secret was kept wasn't a mystery he needed to solve. He didn't really care. He did care about making sure everyone—including as many of the soldiers as possible—survived this encounter.

They were a ten-minute jog from their next station, and they need time to set up the eavesdroppers. "Let's get moving," Nathan said, watching the soldiers inch closer.

E MONITORED the movements of the soldiers and the way Nathan Longfeather directed them. As Nathan Longfeather had a lot less weaponry, his tactics were sound. He could slaughter them all in the single spot he was sending them to without risking many of the others. This technique he was using appealed to E.

E smiled. He liked Nathan Longfeather. He was a good opponent. Tricky and smart.

Nathan Longfeather had said something... He only hunted to defend. He was hunting now. So he was defending. The city? The humans maybe. Or Ti'ann Jones. He'd watched Nathan Longfeather around Ti'ann Jones. He would hunt to defend her.

E thought about that a moment. Dr. Ripley said E was supposed to hunt Shifters to protect humans from them. He hunted to defend too. To defend humans. But these humans defended Shifters. That didn't make sense. Why would he be sent to hunt Shifters to defend humans who were defending

Shifters? Nathan Longfeather wouldn't defend Ti'ann Jones by sending someone to hunt her.

So did he really defend humans by hunting Shifters?

He watched the soldiers pass beneath him, each with blaster raised, unaware of him hanging just above their heads in the luminescent plants lining the tunnel. They didn't speak much. They were jumpy and turned to point their weapons at any sound. But they didn't know he was here. He could hunt them as easily as he could hunt Shifters. Yet Dr. Ripley and the senator sent these inferior fighters to destroy the city. Poor tactics.

They'd sent E a message to avoid the soldiers and stay out of the way. They didn't think he could help? Dr. Ripley said it was for his own safety, because he was so new and superior. But that wasn't the reason. He wasn't in danger from the soldiers. They didn't want the soldiers to know he existed. Why? If he were superior, wouldn't they appreciate his help destroying the city? Perhaps they thought him flawed? But Dr. Ripley told him he was advanced. Perfect.

Dr. Ripley lied to him.

Nathan Longfeather hadn't lied. He had been afraid—he recognized E's superiority. But he hadn't lied.

E studied the last soldier passing beneath his hiding spot. The soldier was walking backward, keeping an eye on their rear. E allowed himself to flutter to the ground near the wall, a loose bit of plant life. The soldier turned his blaster on the movement, cursed and lifted the weapon. "Getting fucking jumpy in this place," he muttered. Then turned to walk faster, catching up with the others.

E waited to shift until they were around the corner. Then he followed.

Time to hunt.

CHAPTER TWENTY-FOUR

"That's it," Nathan muttered. "They're splitting up." He looked at BinRal. "Time to divide our efforts."

BinRal nodded and headed off to the right. The Shifter waiting for them to separate immediately covered the entrance to the tunnel BinRal took, blending seamlessly with the main wall.

Nathan grinned. He pulled out his comm-link and messaged James. "Monroe, you'll have company in another fifteen. No heroics. Just track their movements. Make sure they go where we want them to." He got a single beep in acknowledgement.

With the soldiers split, he was now dependant on the web he'd spread around the city to keep track of them. He'd still be able to use his scanner on the group following him, but soon they'd be down to only two or three men. The others would have to track the remaining soldiers as best they could. He watched the group following him a moment, then moved out, teasing them with his presence.

If Ti'ann hadn't been in the city, he'd really be enjoying this game.

"WHAT THE FUCK WAS THAT?" Jackson spun in a circle, swinging his weapon at the empty air.

"Calm down. You start blasting everything that flutters in the breeze and you'll be out of power before we find anything living to shoot." Lieutenant Wgreal's voice was calm and at ease, as if this were just another training exercise and not an incursion into enemy territory.

Jackson snorted. "They could be anywhere, lieutenant. How can you be so calm?"

"They aren't dangerous, you idiot," Wgreal said, his tone full of disgust. "They won't fight or attack. They'll just try to hide."

"You're acting like a pussy, Jackson," Hanlon snorted. "Forget everything you learned in training?"

"Fuck off, Hanlon. When was the last time you went into a Shifter city?"

"Shut up, both of you," the lieutenant snapped. "They hide, all right, Jackson. They don't attack."

"How do we know for sure though, lieutenant? What if these Shifters are different?"

"Have you seen one yet? Have we been attacked yet?"

"No, but…"

"But nothing. The only thing down here we have to worry about are the humans and Binneans. I don't know what the fuck they're doing here, but they're the only ones in this city besides us that will—"

Jackson, focusing on the empty darkness behind them, spun around when Wgreal fell silent. "Lieutenant?"

The lieutenant was standing perfectly still, his blaster relaxed at his side. Hanlon moved closer to him, weapon up, searching the dark tunnel in front of them. He pushed a button on his night goggles and Jackson followed suit. The rest of the company did the same, scanning the tunnel with heightened vision.

"What is it?" Jackson hissed, searching behind them as he moved in closer to the rest of the team.

"Lieutenant?" Hanlon said. He reached out and touched the man's shoulder, nudging him around. Jackson turned in time to see the gaping holes that had once been Wgreal's chest and neck.

"Fuck," Hanlon shouted. "Jesus fucking Christ." He started firing into the dark tunnel ahead of them. "Mother fuckers! Come out and face us, you chicken shit cock suckers!"

"Hanlon," Dobavich, the med-tech and second-in-command, shouted. "Hanlon, goddamn it, hold your fire!"

The big man yelled one last curse, fired one last time and stopped.

"You're wasting power," Jackson hissed. "Like the lieutenant said."

"Anyone see anything?" Dobavich asked. "Anything showing up on the scanners?"

"I got a blip," Veunre said. "Two hundred meters ahead."

"Human or Binnean?" Hanlon's voice was calm again, deadly calm.

"Neither."

"What is it then? Shifter?"

"No, not Shifter. The detector in this thing still isn't working right. We've got thousands of Shifters all around us according to it."

"Then what the hell is it, Veunre?" Hanlon stepped away from the lieutenant's body as it fell against the wall and slid to the floor.

"Don't know. But it's not Binnean or human."

"You telling us there's something else down here?" Sweat trickled down Jackson's back and his hands started to tremble. "What the hell could do that?" He motioned with his blaster toward the lieutenant. Dobavich was leaning down next to him, running a med-scan over the wounds.

"Got me," she said, standing up again. "Whatever it was, ripped those holes out in two strikes, throat first then chest. His heart and lungs aren't there anymore. Whatever it is, it's strong as hell and moves faster than anything I've heard of. The lieutenant never had a chance."

"Hey," Veunre said, "the blip is gone."

"What? Where?"

"It disappeared. Just now. Like it wasn't there."

"Fuck." Jackson's gut clenched. He scanned the tunnel, including over head, leading with his blaster. "Now what?"

"We go on. Our mission is to destroy this city and everything in it," Hanlon said. "If we do that, we destroy whatever the fuck that thing is."

The big man's rage was now carefully controlled but it still tainted his voice. Jackson could appreciate the rage, but his own was layered with fear.

"Stick closer, stay in formation," Dobavich said, taking up command. "Xavier, message the others that the lieutenant's down and we're going on. Keep your eyes open."

Jackson fell back into position at the rear, sucking in a curse as he passed the lieutenant's body. "We coming back for him?" he shouted up to Dobavich.

"If we can."

Jackson watched the tunnel with his heart pounding in his throat. "If we can," he murmured. "If we survive."

"I DON'T KNOW WHAT HAPPENED," BinRal said to Nathan over the comm-link. "But his throat and chest are ripped out. He was dead before he knew what hit him."

Nathan cursed quietly, keeping a close eye on the figures on his scanner while he digested BinRal's news. "You thinking E?"

"I'm thinking no one else in the city is capable of this," BinRal said. "And if E is capable of this, I'm just glad he's attacked the soldiers and not us."

"Doesn't mean he'll stick to the soldiers." Shit.

The group Nathan was keeping track of had split and split again. Monroe was trailing one, Juanita another and Glen another. No one else had reported finding a body. "Warn the others to look out for E," he told BinRal. "I'll send Val a message to spread to the Shifters. In the meantime, if all he does is concentrate on the enemy, leave him to it. I'm not gonna object to him making our job easier."

"I just hope he sticks to the soldiers."

Nathan couldn't agree more.

"TI'ANN," James' voice came over the comm-link. "You've got a group headed your way now. They should flank you and Krin.

Val is relaying a message to the Shifters with you to cover the tunnel until the groups pass. If they continue to split up the way they have, you should each only have three to follow."

"Thanks," Ti'ann answered and took a deep breath. Finally. Almost over. She hated all this waiting. But then she'd always sucked at hide-and-seek as a kid. And that had never been life or death like this.

She trotted down to relay the message to Krin. He took out his short-range comm-link and keyed it up. It wasn't a secured link, but he could send out a code of beeps and trills to communicate with anyone near enough. He could also monitor any other links within its limited range, which would include hers, James' and Claire's.

"You ready for this?" he asked, settling a hand on her shoulder.

"No," she said. "I was ready a couple of hours ago. Now I'm scared."

He smiled. "Me, too. Be careful. Remember, no heroics."

"Don't worry. I'm a scientist, not a mercenary."

Krin nodded and squeezed her shoulder.

The Shifters were already moving in opposite directions to the tunnel entrances when she returned to her position. "Will I be able to see them pass?" she asked the Shifter at her side of the tunnel.

She stared at Ti'ann a minute, her copper eyes whirling like melted metal. For a moment, Ti'ann didn't think she understood.

Then a mouth formed in the Shifter's face. "No," she said with obvious difficulty. "I will dissolve—reform?—when they have passed."

"Thank you."

She held her breath as the Shifter formed a barrier filling in the tunnel entrance. If she didn't know better, Ti'ann would swear she was staring at a dead end. The light from outside cut off abruptly when Krin's end was sealed up too. She felt panic rising and knocked on her penlight to give her the allusion of light. It was so pitch dark she couldn't see a thing beyond the tiny beam. At the opposite end of the tunnel, a second beam of light was visible, but it didn't cut any of the blackness in between.

She sucked in a breath, then another, and still couldn't get enough air. She started to pant, taking in shallower breaths, and closed her eyes. Spots danced against her eyelids.

You're going to hyperventilate, she told herself. *Calm down. It's just darkness. Nothing in here but you and Krin.* In fact, she was probably safer now than she'd been a minute ago since the soldiers wouldn't be able to see through the Shifters' camouflage.

She concentrated on inhaling one deep, full breath at a time before letting it out slowly. There was plenty of oxygen here. More than enough. Her breathing slowed, along with her heartbeat.

In the moments that followed her near panic, she noticed the utter silence. She didn't dare call out to Krin because the sound would probably carry through the wall formed by the Shifter. But she had an overwhelming urge to shout into the darkness just to make noise. She listened to the silence until her ears hurt. Would she be able to hear the soldiers pass?

She hesitated then pressed an ear against the wall of living Shifter. It felt just like the other walls. For some reason, she'd expected it to be warmer, or colder, or different from the surfaces made of dead Shifter bodies. The fact that it wasn't different disturbed her. How would she know if this Shifter died? Would she and Krin be trapped if the two Shifters were hit with blaster fire and killed while they still blocked the tunnel? The thought made her shudder.

To her surprise, a place on the wall against her cheek warmed, warmed until it felt like the soothing kiss of hot water in the shower. She pulled back and stared at the spot, focusing her penlight on the area. It still looked normal.

Then a small mouth formed in the circle of light. "You will not be trapped," the mouth whispered and was gone.

Ti'ann stepped back and stared. After several quiet seconds ticked by, her muscles relaxed and her shoulders slumped. It was weird, talking to a mouth in the wall, weirder yet that the wall seemed to understand her fear. But knowing the wall wouldn't trap her was an immense relief.

She pressed a hand to the Shifter, hoping she understood her gesture of gratitude, before leaning against the side wall to wait.

Fortunately for her nerves, she didn't have to wait long. Just as she settled into the dark, her eyes adjusting enough so she no longer strained to see beyond her penlight, the wall dropped away. Blinking in the sudden brightness, Ti'ann smiled at the Shifter standing where the wall had been. She smiled back. Without trying to talk, she gestured down the tunnel taken by the soldiers and indicated three of them with her fingers.

Ti'ann placed a hand on the Shifter's shoulder and mouthed, "Thank you." She glanced back into their hiding spot to see Krin disappear down another corridor, following his assigned group, and then she moved off after her quarry.

She didn't have a scanner but her eyes and ears helped her keep track of the soldiers. The only thing she had going for her was the confusion Nathan and BinRal had created and the Shifters hiding along the tunnel ahead of her. The soldiers should be picking her up on their scanners, but hopefully, they'd think she was a shadow.

So far, according to the messages being relayed, only Juanita had been fired on. She did as instructed. As the soldiers tracked back to find her, she retreated behind a wall and was hidden by a Shifter already stationed in the corridor. When they came against a solid wall registering as a human, they moved on. Juanita had giggled over the comm-link when recounting their curses. It was the first time Ti'ann could remember hearing Juanita giggle.

Clare and Glen both reported similar experiences without blaster fire. From what she could tell, the soldiers were confused as hell and jumpy. There was also the issue of E and the way he seemed to be hunting and killing the soldiers, a number of the soldiers so far, but she didn't want to think about that too closely. So long as he wasn't hunting any of her people or the Shifters, he could do as he pleased.

Ti'ann had heard Nathan's voice a couple of times, relieved beyond reason just to know he wasn't hurt. He never addressed her directly in communications. Given the circumstances, he didn't have to, so long as she knew he was okay. After the report of the first dead soldier, she'd had to force herself to stop thinking about Nathan or terror would get the best of her. If E didn't distinguish between the soldiers and Nathan…

Even now, she had to block those thoughts. So far, only soldiers had been killed. They didn't know how many exactly, but they'd found five bodies. This was probably the only time in her life when her curiosity didn't demand details.

She trailed far enough behind the soldiers so she could just hear the sounds of their boots on the stone floors and the occasional hissed comment from one to the other. Were they scared now, too? They'd lost at least five of their companions to something they couldn't track or understand. They must be terrified. She felt a twinge of sympathy for them. They might not even know why they were here beyond destroying the city. Maybe they didn't know Shifters were harmless and peaceful—at least most of them. They were probably subjected to the same propaganda as the rest of the planet. Maybe worse. They probably thought they were protecting humans.

She edged closer, careful to stay in shadows and around corners, but she wanted to hear what they were saying.

At one cavern, they paused and she was able to hide in the tunnel and actually watch them. Their voices carried loudly in the small chamber, despite their attempts to keep quiet.

"This is stupid," one hissed. "We're letting ourselves get picked off one at a time. I say we get the fuck out of here and blow the place from the air."

"You know we can't do that, Jackson. Now shut the hell up already."

"Listen, Hanlon, I don't want to end up like Wgreal. This mission has gone nova. We need to leave. Now."

"We've got our orders," the third solider said. She was watching the tunnel they'd just come down, the one Ti'ann was hiding in. Her night vision goggles were pushed up into her short-cropped hair, useless in the bright lights of the cavern. The green camouflage paint covering her face made it difficult to see what she really looked like. "We do what it takes to destroy this place quietly. Pretty useless blowing the thing so loud it registers on every satellite and monitor on the planet."

"Yeah, Jackson, you dumb shit. We're here to keep this quiet, not announce it to everyone and their dog."

"Why the fuck do I care anymore, Hanlon, huh? These fucking Shifters are supposed to be harmless. They're not supposed to fight back." Jackson's voice dripped with sarcasm. "They only hide." He sounded as if he were mimicking someone else. "Fuck that. We've got seven down. Peaceful my ass."

The other two shifted from foot to foot. No one made eye contact.

"So what do you want us to do?" the woman asked.

"Get the fuck out of here, that's what."

"You're a coward," Hanlon said. "You'd abandon your duty just like that?"

"Fuck you, Hanlon. I will not end up like the others."

Hanlon snarled at him, stepping close to the smaller man. "You'll do your duty, Jackson. You'll follow your orders. Even if I have to break every bone in your body to make you."

A sudden beeping broke the tense stand-off. The woman reached into a vest pocket and pulled out a comm-link. "Dobavich."

The sound was too quiet for Ti'ann to hear, but the look on Dobavich's face changed from concentration to surprise to anger. "Goddamn it." She disconnected and pointed her blaster toward the tunnel where Ti'ann stood. "You're not gonna believe this," she said to the two men. "It's a trap."

CHAPTER TWENTY-FIVE

Ti'ann froze. She didn't dare even breathe.

"What?" Hanlon and Jackson both turned to point their blasters at the tunnel.

"Come on out," Dobavich called. "We know you're really there. Word's gone out. We're not moving forward anymore."

"What the hell's going on?" Jackson hissed. Hanlon didn't even flinch.

"They've been herding us toward a cavern. They were going to trap us and hold us until they could leak the story of the city to the press."

"Shit," Hanlon cursed. "How'd we find out?"

Dobavich raised her voice. "One of their own. Came forward and told us everything."

Ti'ann felt her stomach hollow out. One of their own? Who? Who would betray them? She eased her comm-link out of a pocket in her pants and hit the emergency code that warned the others something had gone wrong. Once done, they'd stop using this channel and switch to a less secure backup.

"You might as well come out," Dobavich called again. "We know you're not a shadow on the scanner. We also know you don't mean to kill us."

"Stupid," Hanlon hissed.

"Come out and we won't hurt you," Dobavich said reasonably. When Ti'ann didn't move, her voice got edgy with impatience. "We're coming back through there anyway. You won't be able to run fast enough to avoid blaster fire. Come out. We don't want to kill a human. We're here for the Shifters. That's all."

Ti'ann knew there were Shifters in the tunnel around her. They might be able to help her, but it would give their presence away and they'd be killed. She closed her eyes, took a deep breath and stepped out into the cavern. She raised her hands. The blaster was still in her belt. "I never was very good at hide-and-seek," she said.

"Disarm her," Hanlon said to Jackson. The man edged up carefully, keeping his blaster trained on her. She didn't move as he took her weapon and patted her down with impersonal efficiency, taking her comm-link as well. When he was satisfied, he stepped back to the others.

She looked over her captors, noting a distinct lack of feeling in their expressions now. "I don't suppose you'll tell me who gave us away?" she asked without much hope.

"Why would we do that?" Hanlon said.

She shrugged. "I'm excessively curious is all. I didn't really think you'd tell me."

"Doesn't matter," Dobavich said. "She's dead."

She? "What?" Ti'ann felt the air rush out of her, and she wobbled a step backward.

"She could have been a Shifter, part of a trap. We couldn't afford to take the chance. Turns out her story was true."

Dobavich shrugged. "You should thank us for taking out the traitor in your group." She motioned with her blaster for Ti'ann to move to one side of the tunnel.

They approached carefully, checking their scanner for more people. "You're alone? Not very good tactics."

Ti'ann didn't comment. Jackson moved behind her and motioned her forward, sending her into the tunnel first. She was so terrified she couldn't think. The blaster poked her in the back once when she faltered, reminding her she was probably going to die. If they killed whoever the traitor was just because they thought she might be a Shifter, there was no reason for them to keep her alive.

Her heart hammered so fast she thought she might pass out for real this time. The traitor was a she? She who? She doubted it would be Juanita. That left Clare, Micca, or the collector Gillian. Micca seemed unlikely. She was so quiet. And since they'd started mentioning a Shifter graveyard, Gillian had been very outspoken in her support of the Shifters. That left Clare. Could she be a traitor after being part of a Shifter support group? Maybe that's why she joined the group.

Ti'ann had an overwhelming urge to rub her temples but didn't think Jackson and his blaster would understand. She suddenly realized the rest of her group could be in the same position she was in right now. Krin. Nathan. Oh god, what if they tried to fight back? What if they were dead now, too? Her brain tumbled with fear as panic set in. They might not have gotten her signal in time. They could all be dead now. She might be the only one left.

They came to the next cavern and the soldiers froze. Silence, and then they erupted into creative strings of curses.

"They've been disguising the tunnels. Mother fucker," Jackson spit. He shoved her forward with the blaster point.

"You're working with the Shifters, huh? Trying to herd us like fucking rats in a maze."

That was the plan you just uncovered, Ti'ann thought, but refrained from mentioning it. She was too terrified. The blaster nuzzle punched into her back again. She winced but stayed quiet.

"Which tunnel do we take to get out of here?" Jackson asked in her ear.

She stared at the five corridors branching off from the cavern. She didn't have any idea which direction led out. She didn't know the city well enough. Immediately, she discarded the idea of trying to lie. Even in the best of circumstances, she was a terrible liar. And this was definitely not the best of circumstances.

"I don't know," she said.

"Like fuck you don't. Which one?" Jackson grabbed her braid and jerked her head back painfully, forcing a shout of protest from her.

"Listen, I suck at lying all right. I honestly don't know the city well enough. I only know the direction you came from and where you were going."

"Heading into a massacre probably."

"No." She tried to placate him, but it was difficult with her neck wrenched back. "We really were just intending to hold you captive till the news of the city leaked to the public. No one was supposed to get hurt."

"Yeah?" Jackson hissed against her cheek. "Well seven of our company were slaughtered in this city of yours, so why do you think I'm going to believe a word you say?"

"Then why did you ask me which tunnel?" Her braid was jerked again, nearly pulling her off her feet. She reached back to grab the base, trying to relieve the pressure on her head. "I wasn't being smart," she said, her voice straining.

"Shut up," Dobavich said. "Both of you." She studied the three new tunnels, studied a small gage on her wrist unit and finally pointed at one. "We'll take that one. It's heading back east."

Jackson pushed Ti'ann forward, knocking her into Hanlon's large back. "Sorry," she mumbled, but he didn't even acknowledge her.

With Hanlon leading the way and Dobavich taking up the rear, they headed down the tunnel. This one was wreathed in glowing plants, the only source of light. They emanated a florescent blue glow that cast long shadows. Nathan had had the Shifters leave some of the city brightly lit while other parts had been dimmed, to make the use of the soldier's vision goggles more difficult. This tunnel didn't have any of the extra lighting to give it more than a soft glow from the plants. Too bright for the vision goggles but too dark to see well.

Hanlon and Dobavich scanned the walls and the covering plants with their blasters raised and ready. Jackson kept his at her back, poking her with it every time she slowed down. A breeze rippled through the tunnel, moving the plants in a gentle sway. The soldiers froze. Jackson jerked her to a halt by pulling her braid.

"Ouch," she hissed, grabbing the base of the braid again. Between his random jerks on her hair and the blaster in her back, Ti'ann's already stressed body was starting to ache.

"Quiet," Hanlon said.

The soldiers stood back to back with her in the center, their blasters steadily moving in a wide arch, the three of them covering the tunnel. She glanced around as the plants settled.

"It's just a breeze," she said, still looking at the plants. "There are a lot of air currents down here."

"Shut up," Hanlon said, his voice eerily calm despite the harsh words.

They stood frozen for another minute or two before cautiously moving on. Ti'ann watched the walls as they passed, reminded of E and the dead bodies found. Maybe the soldiers weren't overreacting. Her heart hammered even harder with fear.

They came to one of the giant caverns filled with shops, tall buildings on both the ground and the ceiling, and narrow streets. The cavern itself was so large they couldn't see the opposite side from where they stood. The lights that usually lit the area like a Yule tree were nearly all extinguished, plunging the space into twilight. It was just dark enough to make it difficult to see, but too light for the night vision goggles to work well. The soldiers fell back against the wall at either side of the rounded tunnel entrance into the cavern.

"Now what?" Hanlon asked.

"Christ, this place is big," Jackson said. "What the hell are all those? Buildings?"

"It is a city," Ti'ann said, quite reasonably she thought.

Apparently, Jackson didn't think so. "You need to stop talking, lady, or I'm gonna kill you now and leave you for the worms."

She swallowed hard and resisted the urge to ask why they were waiting to kill her. Knowing they were going to no matter what made her legs wobble.

"We keep to the outside," Dobavich said into the silence. "Circle until we come to a tunnel heading east."

Keeping their backs to the wall, they started around. A beeping sound broke the quiet and Dobavich reached into her vest for her link. She dropped her gaze to the visual message for an instant before looking up again to scan the buildings. "Two more down. We rendezvous at the ships."

Two more down, Ti'ann thought. Had to be more soldiers. Were all of her people dead now? She stumbled over a rough patch of ground and fell against the wall, scrapping her wrist. With a silent curse she lifted her arm to inspect the damage. A little blood trickled down her hand. She pulled up the hem of her shirt and pressed it against the wound. What was a little more blood to her already ruined shirt? Remembering her longing for a hot shower and clean clothes that morning nearly brought her to tears. It seemed like a lifetime ago. She stumbled again but righted herself without damaging anything this time.

She looked out at the dark shadows of the great cavern, cast furtive glances at her captors. She had to get away from them. She had to warn…somebody. They were going to blow the city now. She was sure of it. No more quiet infiltration. They'd hit the city with heavy fire until it collapsed then probably come up with some convenient story to explain the noise and destruction. The city would be demolished and a huge number of Shifters killed and no one would ever know the truth. Some other scientist would find the remains years from now. Someone else would get to tell the tale of the lost Shifter city.

Not if she could help it.

She didn't have any weapons, she didn't have any way to contact the others if they were still alive, and she didn't have any training. So what could she do? If she tried to escape in the city would she be able to reach help before the city came under fire? She wasn't completely lost yet. If she got away soon, she'd be able to find her way back to the meeting hall. But how could she get away from their scanner? They knew she wasn't a shadow now. They'd be able to track her through the city.

Would they risk it, or would they just let her go? As far as they were concerned, they were evacuating to blow the city, so would they care if she were running loose?

Maybe, since she was planning on warning everyone to get out.

Shit. She didn't know the city well enough to duck and hide from them. Were any of the Shifters around to help her? Maybe all she needed to do was gain a little distance, enough that the Shifters could cover her. But she didn't even know where they were. They weren't supposed to have come into this part of the city.

She didn't hold out much hope, but she scanned the shadows anyway, hunting for some corner or convenient building she could duck into. Unfortunately, a broad avenue circled the outer edge of the cavern so that the closest buildings were several meters away. Too far to avoid blaster fire unless the soldiers were incompetent. And she didn't think they were.

They reached another tunnel branching out of the cavern. Dobavich scanned it, shook her head and they continued with Hanlon pointing a blaster down the tunnel until the others were past the open space. Dobavich took up the lead, leaving Hanlon to follow. Ti'ann looked longingly down the pitch-black tunnel, but Jackson didn't give her an inch of space to escape.

As they started creeping along again, she wondered vaguely if the soldiers had first names. The idea nagged at her enough she asked aloud, "What's your first name, Jackson?"

"What?"

"You have one right? A first name?"

"Of course. What the fuck do you care?"

She sighed, knowing she shouldn't have expected an answer. "Just curious. Sorry. Can't help it. It's my training."

"Training?" The blaster edged against her spine.

"Science. I'm a paleontologist."

"What the hell are you doing down here?"

"We found this place. On accident." She sighed. "It was the greatest discovery of my life."

"It's gonna cost you your life, you know." There wasn't any emotion in his voice when he said it.

"I know." She glanced around the spires of buildings, the richly decorated facades against the green/gold stone of Shifter bodies. No human had ever seen anything like this before. She smiled slightly. "It was worth it," she murmured, not expecting him to understand.

"Brett."

His quiet word took a minute to sink in. "Brett Jackson?"

"Yeah."

She looked over her shoulder and smiled at him. "Ti'ann Jones."

"Keep moving, Ti'ann Jones."

She did. She glanced back again, but he poked her with the blaster so she kept her gaze forward. In the dark, she couldn't really tell what he looked like. He was broad but not very tall. His face looked pale beneath the green paint covering it. His eyes were dark and darting, only falling on her for fleeting moments. She wondered if he believed in what he was doing. He knew Shifters weren't dangerous. Did he still think he was doing some good by killing them? Or did he hate Shifters just because of what they were, hate them so much that annihilating them seemed reasonable?

"You been a Shifter supporter long?"

Jackson's question startled her. "I didn't believe in the exterminations. But I didn't really side with anyone until I met them."

"Them?"

"The Shifters. After a few conversations, I was a supporter."

"You talked to them?"

"Yes. They're amazing."

Jackson fell silent. Ti'ann didn't dare say more. If she could get even a little sympathy from him, maybe they wouldn't kill her. Maybe they'd just stun her and leave her somewhere.

But they'd still destroy the city. And Nathan and Krin might already be dead. Her heart hurt so much she could barely stand it. The idea struck her sharply. What would she do if she lost them both? Her best friend and the man she'd been in love with for three years. She swallowed hard and opened her eyes wide to keep from crying. She wasn't going to cry now. It wouldn't help. She didn't even know if they were dead. She needed to concentrate on staying alive, just in case.

They reached another tunnel, this one so brightly lit not a single shadow hid against the walls. The light actually glowed out into the darker chamber they were circling. Dobavich checked the gages on her wrist unit again then angled the scanner down the tunnel. "This way."

They walked for another fifteen minutes, checking tunnels, skirting caverns, blasters always raised and ready, until they finally came to a tunnel leading out of the city. The scent of fresh air, dirt and leaves carried down on a breeze.

"'Bout fucking time," Hanlon muttered as they headed up the last few hundred meters to the outside.

Ti'ann expected to be blinded by sunlight, but to her surprise the sun was low on the horizon. "So late already?" So much of the day gone to hiding in dark corridors and futilely trying to save a city these guys were about to blow up.

Once out in the open, Dobavich scanned the immediate area then put the scanner into her belt. "Let's move. We've got rendezvous in twenty."

They started to trot, blasters still in hand. Ti'ann tried to keep up but she was exhausted, physically and emotionally, hungry, soar and scraped. Her head was aching around the small lump and the base of her braid from all Jackson's earlier pulling. Her body shook with the need to rest. They hadn't gone a hundred meters when her legs gave out and she sank to the ground.

"Get up," Jackson ordered. "Move it."

She shook her head, sucking in air. "Can't. If you're gonna shoot me, you're gonna have to do it here. My legs won't hold me anymore." She looked up at him, her shoulders slumped. They would either kill her now or let her go. She hadn't even fallen on a rock to use as a weapon. Though what good a rock would do her against three blasters, she wasn't sure. That sort of thing only worked in movies.

Jackson leveled the weapon on her. "If I stun you, you'll die when the city is incinerated anyway. Blaster fire is quick."

"It'll hurt though, won't it?"

"You ask a lot of questions, Ti'ann Jones."

"Yeah. I know."

He clicked the blaster to kill.

She raised an eyebrow. "On stun all this time?"

He didn't reply. He met her gaze with serious, emotionless eyes. Hanlon and Dobavich were already a hundred meters away and moving fast. So much for sympathy. She thought of Nathan, and the fact that she hadn't had time to tell him she loved him. Even if he'd left her in the end, at least he would have known.

She met Jackson's emotionless gaze again. "Thanks for making it quick," she said and closed her eyes.

CHAPTER TWENTY-SIX

Ti'ann heard two blaster shots and winced, expecting to feel pain. She didn't. In fact, she didn't feel anything. Maybe that was it and she was dead. But she didn't feel dead. She still felt exhausted and sore. She opened her eyes. Brett Jackson lay sprawled on his side a few meters away, eyes vacant. She blinked. She couldn't see what had knocked him down. He didn't look wounded anywhere. Then she looked closer at his face and saw the blood trickling over his forehead and down his cheek.

She hadn't thought she could move, but with renewed energy she scrambled backward from the body. A hand dropped on her shoulder and she jerked around to see Clare O'Malley standing over her, frowning.

"You okay, Ti'ann?"

"Clare? Where'd you come from?" She glanced back at the body. "You did that?"

"My mom thought it'd be a useful skill," she said with a hint of irony in her voice. "Did they hurt you? Can you walk?"

"I'm fine. I'm not sure I can walk, but that's because I'm too shaky." She grabbed Clare's proffered hand and struggled to her feet. She looked one last time at the body then turned her back on it. "Thanks. You saved my life."

Clare grinned, her pretty face all the prettier for the expression. "You're welcome."

There was a glint in her eyes that would have made Ti'ann nervous if she wasn't already so emotionally worn out. "The other soldiers?"

"Must have thought the shots were that guys." Clare nodded at the body. "Or they'd be here already. I saw them disappear into the trees, but I'm not sure how far ahead of us they are."

They both looked toward the woods.

"Doesn't sound like they're coming back," Ti'ann said. "Yet. What's happening? Are the others…?"

"Most everyone is all right. You signaled in time for the rest of us to get away from the soldiers we were trailing."

"Krin? Nathan?"

"Both fine."

Ti'ann felt the tension drain out of her. She reached out a hand to the nearest tree to steady herself. She couldn't even smile, she was so relieved.

"The soldiers are almost out of the city now. The Shifters are tracking their movements for us so we know where they are." She grinned. "That's how I got here. They relayed your location to Val and Val relayed it to me over another channel. I was the closest to your position. They had to help me avoid the scanners. That's the reason I didn't get to you sooner. Fortunately for us all, they stopped scanning after they got out of the city. Stupid of them, but fortunate. You know, you about gave us all heart attacks getting captured like that."

Clare's cocky grin fell away when she said, "Micca gave us

away to the soldiers. We found her body while we were tracking their retreat."

"Micca!" Ti'ann gaped at Clare, too shocked to comment more.

"'Fraid so. She was very anti-Shifter. Apparently hated them, though I can't imagine why. Wouldn't have expected it, would you?"

"No," Ti'ann murmured. No, she hadn't suspected Micca at all. She was ashamed of her earlier distrust of Clare but grateful she'd been wrong. She wasn't sure Micca would have been up to the challenge of rescuing her.

"We'd better get out of here," she said, though she didn't release her hold on the tree which was keeping her upright yet, "before the other two soldiers come back for Jackson."

She frowned, looking around the surrounding forest. They were farther west than she'd expected since the soldiers had been moving east. They weren't too far away from the camp's landing pad.

"What's wrong? Outside of this entire situation," Clare said.

"They're going to their ships. They intend to annihilate the city." She met Clare's gaze. "We have to stop them."

"We? We have one blaster between us and are on the opposite side of the city from any backup. How are we going to stop a regiment of soldiers?"

"I don't know. Come on."

"Wait." Clare moved around her to Jackson's body and took the blaster out of his hand, then took the one he'd taken off Ti'ann from his belt. She handed Ti'ann one weapon and hefted Jackson's herself, getting a feel for it. "At least we'll have something to use."

From somewhere, Ti'ann pulled a reserve of strength, pushed away from the supporting tree and set off at a shuffling run in the direction Hanlon and Dobavich had gone. She expected to meet them at any moment on their way back to find Jackson, but they never appeared. They obviously weren't concerned with covering their tracks either because she was able to follow their path easily.

"Ti'ann," Clare said, trotting alongside her with a great deal more ease. "We really need a plan here. These are trained soldiers. You and I are not their match."

"I know. Can you signal Nathan and BinRal? Maybe they'll have some ideas."

Clare shook her head but took out her comm-link. "They're not going to be able to say much on this channel. It'll be compromised soon. It's not as secure as the one we were using before."

"I'll take anything they can give us," she panted. She shook off the sweat beading into her eyes and pushed herself further. She was concentrating so hard on moving she nearly stepped out into the clearing where the soldiers' air-transports sat under camouflage shields. She and Clare twisted behind a couple of trees, backs to the landing area. When Ti'ann caught her breath, she peaked around the tree.

There were three ships altogether, one large transport and two smaller jets. From the air, an observer would never see them beneath the camouflage shield. From the ground, they were difficult to spot but not impossible. She suspected they'd be hard to detect with scanning equipment as well. That reminded her. She and Clare were probably being picked up by the ship's scanners already. Now what?

"Nathan come back with any ideas?" she whispered as she watched the handful of soldiers moving on the ground beneath the large transport.

"Yeah. He said to get the hell out of here. Get to the nearest ship and leave the area before the shooting starts."

"And since we're not going to do that?"

Clare shrugged. "Your guess is as good as mine." She poked around the tree. "You know, even if they're scanning, they're still expecting some of their own people back. They may not realize we're not part of the team yet. Except that we're hiding behind trees." She grinned. "Too bad we didn't think about taking some of the uniforms, even Jackson's would have been useful. One of us could have gone in undercover." The grinned widened as she studied the ships.

"We weren't thinking far enough ahead," Ti'ann agreed. She glanced down at her torn and stained t-shirt and baggy pants, then at Clare's tight pants and cropped shirt, and didn't have much hope they'd be able to fool the soldiers at a glance. At least Clare had the forethought to get them two more blasters. "Any other ideas?"

"We could just run in shooting and hope for the best."

"I like that idea less than running away. We'd better move soon. They're starting to load up." As she said it, two soldiers moved to the two smaller ships. The camouflage shields went down revealing two sleek fighter jets with what looked like enough guns and laser cannons to destroy a small moon. "Uh-oh."

"That is no little uh-oh," Clare breathed. "That's one big load of trouble." She looked at Ti'ann. "Our little blasters are not going to do much against those."

"How good a shot are you? Can you take the soldiers out before they get in the ships?"

Clare stared back, dubious. "I'm an ace shot," she said without a hint of boasting, "but as soon as I hit one, someone else is going to fire on us and make it tough to hit the other guy.

Plus they're probably not the only ones who can fly those things. I can't shoot them all one by one. I'm not that good, and we don't have that kind of time."

"Oh," Ti'ann said with sudden inspiration. "What if I run around as a distraction, draw their fire, while you blast them? I can't hit the side of a mountain, but I can fire back to keep them busy."

"Bad idea. Ti'ann, that's a very *very* bad idea."

"Best we've got. Start firing. I'll make a visible target so you can move to a new place and shoot again."

"No."

"Clare, it's all we've got. We can't let those ships get into the air."

"Then let me do the running out into view as a distraction. You're exhausted and bleeding." She nodded to her wrist.

"But I can't shoot as well as you can. And you're still gonna have to move because they'll turn their fire back on you as soon as you hit something."

"They'll just send people out to pick us up. If they don't kill us first."

"Well then we run away. And sneak back while they're searching the forest for us."

"This is such a bad idea, Ti'ann. This is gonna get us both shot. If we're lucky." Clare stared at her for a heartbeat and then chuckled. "You're insane." She twisted around the tree, took aim and fired, hitting one of the soldiers square in the head, dropping him to the ground. She managed a second shot, winging one of the surprised soldiers and then took off in one direction.

Ti'ann started running in the opposite direction, weaving in and out of the treeline so they'd see her but couldn't get a shot at her too easily. A tree behind her splintered and crunched. She hunched her shoulders and moved faster, terrified the tree would fall on her. She heard the crash and would have turned to see where the tree landed if another shot hadn't sizzles past her head.

"Shit," she squealed and moved farther into the forest.

Just then Clare took another shot. Ti'ann stopped behind a tree long enough to see a soldier fall. She started firing herself, the blasts going wild and hitting more dirt than anything of significance. But it still made the soldiers duck. Screams and shouts rebounded around the clearing, a mixed chaos of orders and demands. Clare shot again and Ti'ann heard very clearly one soldier shout and point toward Clare, so she went charging into view again, running in the direction she'd just come from. She hoped Clare wasn't running the same way.

She jumped behind a tree just before a shot ripped the ground at her heals. She pushed a screech through her teeth, not quite a scream, and dodged to the next tree, firing as she moved. Clare got off two more shots, but Ti'ann was too busy ducking to see the result.

Her breath came in gasps. Unable to move very fast, she made due with lurching from cover to cover, firing when she got the chance, moving back and forth and trying not to move in the same direction too often. Her arms were heavy, her eyes blurring with sweat.

A deep rumbling filled the clearing. Ti'ann ducked behind a tree and watched in horror as one of the small ships lifted off. She started firing her blaster, aware of Clare firing somewhere off to her left. They managed to hold the other soldiers down, and Clare hit one trying to get to the second fighter. But the damage was done. The first had lifted off.

She hoped they'd given Nathan enough time to finish evacuating the city. Too late to do anything about it now. She cursed, shouted against the noise of the retreating ship, and pushed off to another tree.

She continued to fire, continued to move, until her limbs felt numb and heavy. Keep going, she thought. Next tree. Fire. Two more trees. Fire. She was running low on power. Her blaster wouldn't hold out much longer and then she'd just be a running target. She kept moving. Another tree. Another shot, and duck for cover. She was just a step too slow on one lurch and a blaster shot glanced off her hip. She screamed and lurched behind a tree, pressing her back against it to keep upright.

"Shit," she shouted, knowing they couldn't hear her over the noise. She cursed a steady stream as she looked down at the wound. The cursing helped a little against the pain, until she pealed back a section of her trousers and saw the scorched skin and blood. Her stomach lurched, and bile rose in her throat. She closed her eyes, focusing all her energy on not throwing up. There was more blaster fire, several shots arching into the ground around her, but she couldn't move anymore. When she tried to push off the tree, her hip screamed and her vision blurred.

She leaned back, squeezed her eyes shut, alternately panting and clenching her teeth against the pain. She hoped Clare was still okay. She tried raising her blaster to fire over her shoulder, just to give Clare more cover. But she couldn't manage without another roll of nausea.

Numbness settled into her wound, the pain cut back by shock. The nausea subsided. She tried lifting her blaster, and when she didn't throw up, she opened her eyes and gathered her strength to look around.

A shadow passed over the clearing, cutting out the weak evening light and plunging her into momentary darkness. She froze, her back still against the tree with its rough bark scrapping against the bruised spot where Jackson had kept poking her with his blaster. The clearing fell quiet. And then an ear splitting screech shattered the silence. Ti'ann clamped her hands over her ears. The shrill cry went on and on for what seemed like forever, but was really no more than a handful of minutes. And then silence.

She dropped her hands and looked up in time to see a line of fire burst into the clearing. A ball of flames exploded, engulfing the larger transport ship. Soldiers ran screaming for cover as another fireball slammed to the ground. She stumbled back from her shelter, an arm raised to shield her face from the heat. She looked up, trying to see where the fire was coming from. All she saw was a lot of metallic blue scales and sharp claws. For almost a minute, she stared at the thing overhead before she realized she was looking at something from a myth.

It had a wingspan at least two hundred meters wide and was covered by glittering scales. Front and back legs were tipped with razor claws and its thick tale had a ball of spikes the size of long swords on the end. A mane of spines lying flat against its neck circled a head as large as the smaller ship in the clearing. Its black eyes were like obsidian stones, solid and unblinking. Balls of fire spewed from a huge mouth lined with rows of sharp teeth.

"A dragon." Ti'ann gasped. But the screeches and screams of both soldiers and dragon were so loud she couldn't hear her own voice. She watched the dragon circle, watched it dip its wings. Her eyes widened.

Ah, hell, it was going to land.

CHAPTER TWENTY-SEVEN

Ti'ann stumbled backward, her hip burning but she still struggled to get as far from the clearing as she could. Despite her efforts, the rush of wind from the dragon's wings knocked her down as it dropped into the center of chaos. She rolled to face the ground, covering her head as dirt and debris washed over her.

Coughing, spitting and blinking as the dust settled, she looked back over her shoulder at the clearing. The fires were out. The two remaining ships were lumps of twisted, scorched metal, and what looked like burned bodies littered the ground. She didn't look too closely at the bodies, but the stench carried, making her throat close against a punch of rising bile.

The dragon stood in the middle of the wreckage on its hind legs, sniffing and looking over the damage. It roared again, the sound vibrating through the soil. Ti'ann tried to scramble to her feet but pain laced through her hip and stole her breath. She groaned and fell onto her back in the dirt.

Not a good time to be incapacitated. There's a murderous

dragon within sight of you and you're resting on your back, Dr. Jones. Get up and move or you're a dragon appetizer.

She lurched upward again. Stopped. Blinked. Rubbed dust from her eyes. Blinked again.

In the center of the clearing, amidst the wreckage, stood a slender blond man in fatigue pants and a green t-shirt. He looked at the destruction completely unconcerned, not a hint of dirt on his clothing or smudging his face. Ti'ann looked frantically around, up and then through the woods around her. But she hadn't felt the dragon take off, and if she'd felt it land, she certainly would have felt it lift off.

She gaped at the man.

E?

It had to be.

From the opposite side of the clearing, Clare moved out of the trees, blaster pointed at E. She was covered in purple dust and blood dripped down her left arm, but she held her weapon steady.

Ti'ann tried to lurch to her feet again, sucking up another scream as her hip exploded with pain. With the help of the nearest tree, she pulled herself up, but she had to brace against the trunk or risk falling again.

She glanced down. Blood still seeped slowly out of her wound, soaking into the leg of her pants. It looked messy. She needed a med-kit. Even their crappy camp med-kit would help.

She heaved off the tree and limped out to the clearing. E didn't move. Not in reaction to Clare's blaster or Ti'ann's own limping entrance. He stared at her with unblinking blue eyes as she approached. She sucked in shallow breaths through her mouth so she wouldn't have to smell the burnt flesh and melted metal around her, but she was only partially successful. Her nostrils flared as she tried to narrow them against the stench.

She stopped about twenty meters from E, at an angle that wouldn't put her in Clare's line of fire if he lurched to the side. He watched her with such close scrutiny, she wanted to squirm, but she was way too exhausted to put in the effort.

"You're E."

"You are not a very good tactician, Ti'ann Jones." His voice was soft and sounded unused.

"I know," she said. "That's why I'm a scientist and not a soldier."

His lips twitched. It wasn't a smile. It wasn't really any kind of expression. It was just a change in the lack of expression. "Nathan Longfeather will not be pleased that you endangered yourself."

"Probably true. It's part of his job to make sure I'm safe." She shifted feet, winced, and shifted back. "What just happened here?"

"You are wounded."

"I noticed that. What happened here?"

"They were attacking you. Nathan Longfeather thinks defending you is very important. I was aiding him."

"That was nice of you. Why were you helping him? You threatened to kill him last night." She listed to one side and stumbled to catch her balance.

"Ti'ann," Clare shouted.

She raised her hand as she regained her equilibrium. "I'm okay." For now. "So what was all this about, E? You didn't just defend us, you destroyed these people." She gestured at the carnage around her without looking at it.

"It was the correct tactic. They would have destroyed the Shifter city and all of you with it."

"You did this to save the city?"

He looked away, his head tilted down. "I did."

"Why?"

He didn't answer. In the fading sunlight, he looked very human and normal except for the lack of anything human in his blue eyes. She risked a look at Clare. The other woman was still holding her blaster on E. Clare caught her gaze and flicked a look down to the wound on her hip. Ti'ann nodded. She needed to get it taken care of. E wasn't very forthcoming with answers. But at least he wasn't trying to kill them. That was something. And he'd saved the city. For a little while anyway. What to do about E and why he did what he did would have to wait.

"I have to get to our camp," she told him, gesturing to her hip. "I need the med-kit."

His blue eyes focused in on her, then on her wound. Before she had time to react, he closed the distance between them and lifted her off the ground, cradling her gently in his arms. He spun to face Clare before she had a chance to get off a shot.

"I will not hurt Ti'ann Jones," he said to the now trembling Clare.

Ti'ann looked at the woman and shook her head. She wasn't sure blaster fire would do much damage to E anyway, and she sure as hell didn't want to aggravate him. "I'm okay, Clare. I'll be okay."

"I will get her to medical help. Find the others. Tell them what has happened. Tell Nathan Longfeather he can meet us at his ship."

And with a lurch that had her stomach fall away and her throat closing, E launched into the air. This time he only formed a pair of wings, leaving the rest of his body human. It would have made him look like an angle if his face wasn't so scarily emotionless. She risked a glance at the ground, but nearly threw up, so she closed her eyes. His wings snapped, catching a thermal current and pain shot through her, so strong this time, her vision went totally black and she stopped feeling anything.

PANIC CREPT along Nathan's nerves until he couldn't think. With every report of Ti'ann and the soldiers' movements through the city, Nathan suffered an agony of fear. When Clare finally reported that Ti'ann was safe, he nearly fell to his knees with relief. BinRal was quick to put a chair under him so he didn't embarrass himself.

But just when he thought he could relax, Clare sent another message making his blood run cold. He cursed and snatched up the comm-link. "Get the hell out of there, Clare. Get to the nearest ship and leave the area before the shooting starts. Do not go after the soldiers yourselves."

He got no reply. Nothing. For nearly two minutes he waited. Nothing.

"Fuck!" He was up and moving before anyone else in the room could react. "Evacuate the rest of the city," he shouted over his shoulder and took off at a run.

He was down a side tunnel when he noticed BinRal keeping pace with him. They didn't waste words, just ran flat out for the exit that would bring them closest to their ships. Nathan glanced down at the tracker on his wrist, following the path Val had laid out for him earlier that day. Panic distorted time and it felt like hours before they were out in the pale evening light and warm forest air.

A quake trembled through the ground, nearly knocking him off his feet. He stopped his head long run to look around. The ground shook again, jumping beneath them. He turned to

BinRal who looked grim. "One of their ships got into the air," he said.

Terror like he'd never felt beat at him.

He pushed off, running harder this time, wishing for BinRal's speed as they darted through trees. "Go on," he shouted to the Binnean. "You can get to her quicker."

He nodded in response, stretched his stride and outpaced Nathan with ease, disappearing into the woods ahead. Nathan kept running, alternating between silent curses and prayers that they reached Ti'ann in time. He was going to ring her neck when he found her.

He was heaving in air, his lungs stinging, by the time he reached the landing pad. Without looking around, he ran to his ship, pushing his endurance to the limit. He rounded the ship, already hitting the code on his comm-card to lower the ramp, when he plowed into the back of BinRal. He opened his mouth to ask what was wrong, but the words froze in his throat.

At the base of the lowering ramp stood E holding an unconscious Ti'ann in his arms. Her side and leg were covered in blood, her clothes battered and thick with purple dust. Her long braid hung over E's arm. She was so limp and pale, she looked dead.

"For the love of all that's holy, E, don't hurt her. Please."

E's head tilted down. "I have defended her. She is not a good tactician, Nathan Longfeather. But she is brave. The attackers have been destroyed. She needs medical attention."

Nathan decided an explanation could wait. He led the way up the ramp and into his ship, directing E toward the bunk in his small cabin as he snatched down his medical kit from an overhead locker. When Ti'ann had been laid on his bed, he tried pulling her torn pants away from the wound gently, but his hands shook too hard. He squeezed his eyes closed, jerking his hands away.

BinRal laid a calming touch on Nathan's shoulder. "I'll tend the wound, Nate."

Grateful, he rose to his feet and left the small room so BinRal could work. He and E stood in the corridor outside and waited. He leaned against the doorframe, watching BinRal as he ran the med-scan over her wound.

"She's lost some blood. I've started the replacement sequence. She was lucky. Nothing vital was hit. She'll be sore for a week or so and in need of physical rehab." He set the med-scan aside and picked an epidermal skimmer out of the med-kit.

"But she'll heal?"

"Of course. There'll be a scar if she can't afford a skin graft."

"I'll get her one."

BinRal didn't look up from his work when Nathan made the bold statement. "This will take some time. I've put her under with a mild anesthetic. I'll wake her when I'm finished." When Nathan didn't move, BinRal said, "You should go check on the others. See if the city is still there. Make sure everyone is safe."

Nathan knew he was right. Ti'ann was in capable hands. BinRal would treat her properly. But the idea of leaving was like agreeing to have one of his limbs removed. "She'll be okay? You'll make sure she's okay?"

"She'll be fine, Nate." BinRal did turn to look at him then. "I'll make sure."

Nathan nodded and pushed off from the wall. "Call me when she wakes up."

He walked away from the room, motioning E to follow him. When they were in the communications room, he said, "I don't know why you helped her, E, but thank you."

"You wanted her defended."

"Yes. But you weren't here to defend her. You were here to hunt Shifters and report information, weren't you?"

"Yes."

"You were working with the soldiers?"

"No."

"But they were sent by the person you report to?"

"Yes."

"Yet you killed them? Why?"

"I don't like being lied to."

Nathan stared at the…Shifter…man…before him. He wasn't sure what to make of him. He wanted to ask why E saved Ti'ann, but he wasn't sure he'd get much more of an answer than he'd already gotten. He wanted to ask who had lied to him to make him turn on the soldiers, but he was afraid the answer would open a deluge he wasn't ready to deal with. Instead, he asked, "Have you found out why you're so different?"

"No. I'm still searching."

"As far as I'm concerned, you're doing good so far. But I'm not too sure your employers are going to agree."

"I'm not employed."

His gaze narrowed. "But you had orders? You're working for someone?"

"I had orders. Employment is a paid occupation. I'm not employed."

Nathan put his hands up. "Okay, okay. We'll deal with that later. I do have a lot more questions I want to ask you, E. Will you be willing to answer them?"

E blinked slowly. It was one of the few times Nathan had seen him blink. "Perhaps. If I can."

"I'll take what I can get. In the meantime, is the city safe?"

"Yes. For now."

"The ship that got off the ground?"

"Destroyed in the air."

Nathan nodded then settled into the seat at the communications board. He sent out a message to James for an update on the situation. With the soldiers all dead, they were safe for the moment, but he didn't believe whoever sent the soldiers would stop trying to destroy the city.

James answered his hail immediately and confirmed everyone had survived. Only an unoccupied part of the city had been hit when the single ship got off the ground. Nathan filled James in on his side of things, with some help from E.

"See you in a few," Nathan said to James after confirming he was on his way.

Nathan closed the channel and turned in his seat. At the entrance to the communications room, Val stood staring at E. In Shifter form, without a mouth to convey any expression, it was hard to tell what Val was thinking. The focus between the Shifter and E was so intent Nathan realized they were probably talking.

Behind Val, two other Shifters filled the corridor. One was Zim. The other was a copper-eyed female.

He watched for a few minutes, curious about the information being passed. Val was probably getting more from E than Nathan would be able to in twice the time.

But his worry for Ti'ann distracted him from the potential in Val's conversation with E, and he moved passed them to check on her. He met BinRal coming down the corridor.

"Ti'ann?" he asked, trying not to reveal his panic.

"Fine. Resting."

"She's awake?"

"She will be in a few minutes. Give her about ten to be fully conscious again."

Nathan nodded. He debated going in to wait by her bed. There was nothing he could do for her until she woke, but still…

"We should go find Clare," BinRal said.

"I don't want to leave her." Nathan nodded to his room and the sleeping Ti'ann.

"She'll be fine, Nate. I promise."

Nathan debated for a few minutes more. Leaving her right now was harder than he could possibly have imagined. She was safe. BinRal had taken care of her injury. And still Nathan hurt at the idea of leaving her side. He'd never been so terrified in his life as when he'd seen E holding her. He wasn't sure he'd recover from the bone-deep fear any time soon.

He was in a lot more trouble with Ti'ann than he'd allowed himself to admit. And he wasn't sure he could live this way.

Finally, he forced himself to leave, if only to help clear his head in the minutes before Ti'ann regained consciousness. He followed BinRal from the ship, passing the Shifter conference on the way out.

"Have any idea what they're talking about?" the Binnean asked.

"Nope. Not sure I want to know all of it."

"He doesn't look dangerous on first glance. Until you look into his eyes."

"You noticed that too? Got any idea what he is?"

"Advanced."

"That helps, BinRal. Thank you."

He shrugged. "It's true. Whatever he is, he's more than Shifter, and more than human. He's advanced. Probably engineered by someone with a sick sense of humor."

"Why any sense of humor?"

"Don't you recognize him? You're Naravan. Don't you pay attention to the news?"

"No. Explain."

BinRal nodded toward the woods, and Nathan was distracted enough to wait on the explanation. Clare came trotting out of the trees, covered head to foot in purple dust. Blood trickled down her left arm. "Is she okay?" she shouted, as she got closer to them. "Did he bring her back here?"

"He did," Nathan said. "Ti'ann's fine. Didn't James signal you?"

Clare's shoulders dropped and she heaved a sigh. "My comm-link was damaged during the fire fight. I haven't been able to get in touch with anyone. How's the city?"

"Part of it collapsed when the single ship got in a few shots. E destroyed it in the air, though what that means—"

"He was a dragon," Clare said, her voice full of awe. "I thought I'd seen a lot, but a dragon... He destroyed them. Completely." She shuddered. "Not pretty."

"And no evidence." Nathan sighed.

"I wouldn't count on any, no. There's not much left."

"Your arm is injured. You need that taken care of," BinRal said.

She glanced down. "Yeah. Someone got a lucky shot."

"What did you two end up doing?" Nathan wasn't sure he wanted to know.

Clare grinned. "Your girlfriend is insane, Longfeather. I take none of the blame. It was all her idea."

"What?"

"I fired, she ran. She made herself an obvious target so I could move around and try to take the soldiers out one at a time.

She fired, but she's not a great shot. Mostly, she was a distraction."

Nathan closed his eyes. "And why did you let her do that?"

"I didn't have a lot of say in the matter. Have you ever tried to talk her out of something before?"

"Yes. You're right. I can't blame you." He heaved a sigh and opened his eyes. "Come on, we'll get you fixed up and then we need to contact your reporter friend. This story has to break as soon as possible if we want to avoid another attack."

Clare's grin fairly glowed. "I'm sure that can be arranged."

CHAPTER TWENTY-EIGHT

Ti'ann woke to a reunion of people crowding onto Nathan's ship to check on her. When she managed to stand, Krin hugged her so tight he practically pulled her off her feet. She was grateful beyond words that everyone was okay, but she found herself hunting for Nathan in the crowd, the first person she wanted to see after waking up.

He stood a little to the rear, as distant as he could get from all the people, not smiling. He glanced at her, but his expression didn't change from his "security specialist" mask. The lack of emotion in his eyes made her heart hurt in a way the painkillers BinRal had given her couldn't ease. She wanted to talk to him, but with all the people clustered around, she couldn't even navigate the corridor to reach him.

She was pulled from her thoughts when Clare asked after Val.

"They were forward in the communications room earlier," Nathan said. "I assumed they were talking."

"I passed there on the way in and it's empty," James said. "They must have gone outside."

"Don't blame them," Krin said, still holding Ti'ann. "Bit crowded in here now."

"So get out," Nathan said.

"Good idea," James said, giving Nathan a narrow-eyed look.

They filed out, Krin supporting Ti'ann as she limped along. When they were all standing on the landing pad, Ti'ann realized Nathan hadn't followed. Tears stung her eyes, but she wrote them off to exhaustion. Things would be better after she rested, and she had a chance to talk to him.

When Nathan did join them a few minutes later, his brooding presence distracted Ti'ann from the relief of seeing most of her people well.

She limped away from Krin, stopping close enough to Nathan to touch. His face looked grim and serious. She reached out and laid a hand on his arm. When he looked down, she asked, "Is everything okay? You weren't hurt were you?"

"No."

"I'm glad."

He nodded, his dark gaze finally softening a bit. Then he moved a few steps away, forcing her to drop her hand from his arm. Her bottom lip trembled. She looked away, blinked repeatedly to hold her tears off, and turned back to face the group. She felt like her heart was squeezing tightly in her chest. She was too emotionally raw from her day to deal with this right now. Good thing it's dark, she thought as she tried to sniff quietly. She sucked in her bottom lip to stop it trembling.

Light from Nathan and James' ships gently illuminated the landing area. In the gathering dark, they looked a small and ragged group. She could hardly believe only a day had passed since they'd been introduced to the Lost City leaders.

"Clare," Nathan spoke up when she'd finished talking. "We need to get this story to your reporter friend. Now."

Clare nodded. "I'll go send the message this minute."

"Do you need anything from us?" James asked.

"Maybe an anonymous witness comment or two for the networks." Clare gestured to the members of the Shifter support group. "We won't want to go public just yet. Ti'ann and Krin, the networks will probably want to interview you. But all that will be arranged later. They're gonna want to break the news first, then start the interviewing." She laughed, a light and happy sound. "This is gonna be great."

Clare started toward James' ship but stopped when Val, E and more than a dozen Shifters surrounded them.

"Everything all right, Val?" James asked, his attention focused on E.

There was a straightening of shoulders, an adjustment of stance by all the humans. Even BinRal seemed to brace and make himself look bigger—not a feat Ti'ann would have thought possible. She straightened, too, being face to face with E again. He'd saved her life. He'd brought her back here to get medical help. And she still wasn't sure how she felt about him. Was she now in his debt? Did he consider what he'd done a favor?

"Yes," Val answered James. "Maybe." Turning to Clare, the Shifter said, "Stay, please. There's more to this story. We're undecided as to whether it should be revealed. And we don't have time for a typical Shifter debate."

That got their attention. They all moved a few steps closer to Val and E. In the dark, the Shifters' golden skin held a slight luminescence. Not enough to cast light, not really a glow. It was just visible despite the dark. Strange, Ti'ann thought, given the species was all about camouflage. She hadn't noticed the effect in the city either.

Val looked for a long, quiet moment at E. Then said loud enough for the entire group to hear, "I see this face in your mind. You don't think you know her. You don't. But we do."

Val shifted and there stood a young woman, golden hair with streaks of red and the most amazing shade of gold eyes. Her eyes nearly matched her hair color. Something about her eye color looked familiar.

Beside her Nathan sucked in a breath. "Kira Farseaker."

Ti'ann startled, then looked closer at the woman Val was now. Kira Farseaker's face had been all over the network news reports a year ago. No wonder she looked familiar. Ti'ann caught a gesture from the corner of her eye and turned to see Nathan fingering the metal tags visible on his chest through the open top of his shirt. She frowned at him.

He didn't give anything away, but he mouthed the word, "Later."

"Holy shit," James said. He turned to E and his eyes widened. "Sonofabitch, I thought you looked familiar. You're Ennoren."

Ti'ann didn't think anything else could shock her after the last two days. She was wrong.

"You're supposed to be dead," Juanita hissed.

"What the hell's going on?" Mike said.

Glen let out a soft curse. "I'm glad Micca didn't know about him."

"I'm not Ennoren," E said into the rumble of comment, silencing everyone. "Commander Ennoren is dead." He didn't sound certain though.

"Then how can you know Kira Farseaker?" James asked.

"I don't. Her face is in my mind. I have no association for it. I don't know why it's there."

"He doesn't feel anything toward the image except confusion. He doesn't know her. He hasn't been conditioned for a response to her. At least not one that we can find."

"You were worried he was an assassin?" Clare said, her gaze sharp.

Ti'ann gaped. She hadn't made that connection.

"When I recognized in him the face of Commander Ennoren, and when I saw the image of Kira in his mind, we thought he'd been sent to find her. To kill her. She still has a lot of enemies here."

"We don't know where she is," James said.

Ti'ann thought that made sense. They couldn't be coerced into giving her away if they didn't know.

"It doesn't matter. He's not here for that. Not yet. They haven't triggered an innate reaction in him to her. If they had, I wouldn't have shifted to her shape." Val grinned with Kira's face and shifted back to natural form but for a mouth. "But the image is there. It's hard to tell if it's been implanted or not."

"If he doesn't know Kira, how could her image be in his mind if it wasn't implanted?" Krin asked.

"Why does he look like Commander Ennoren?" Juanita asked at nearly the same time. She stared at E in horror.

"The answer to both questions has to do with his nature, how he came to be." Val paused and seemed to consider how to explain. "I'm not sure I understand what was done to him. E doesn't know, so we can only guess. But this is his natural state."

"I was part of a greater experiment," E said, for the first time adding to his story. "There were four others before me, but they all failed. I'm the only successful result. Dr. Ripley told me

I was different from the others. I thought he meant I was successful where the others had failed. I'm not sure of that now."

Dr. Ripley? "What kind of experiments were these?" Ti'ann asked, a sudden wary suspicion overcoming both her sore hip and her sore heart.

"Genetic."

"Dr. Ripley is the same scientist from Shifter Research Center, the one who co-authored the paper on Shifter remains? Oh, my god, he's mixing Shifter and human DNA, isn't he?" The realization hit her and she knew. This was the same Dr. Ripley and he'd gone beyond just working with Shifter DNA.

"We aren't sure. Only guessing."

"But," Ti'ann hesitated. She faced Krin. "I know he was doing some innovative work fifteen years ago, but do you think he could possibly blend two completely different types of DNA? They don't even have the same base pairs. Could it work?"

Krin shrugged and shook his head. "It would take special enzymes that recognized all eight base pairs. Or maybe he manipulated the purines of one type of DNA in such a way that they could form hydrogen bonds with the pyrimidines of the other strand. Or some combination to bring the total number of base pairs back down to four."

He frowned, then said, "That would probably be the easiest way to mix the two types. It would more than likely render the resultant embryo sterile. And it would be damned difficult to predict the results of the genetic combinations. You'd end up with mush as often as a viable…anything, I would think. How would you even maintain the ability to shift in the context of the human genetic code?"

His narrowed eyes widened as the full impact hit him.

"Jesus, Ti'ann, it would take some technological advances I haven't heard of before. And it'd still take an embryo years to develop to maturity. He'd had to have started E more than ten years ago, even with advanced clone aging techniques."

"I was fully functional two months ago," E said. "I was started thirteen months ago."

"You were started only thirteen months ago?" Krin asked, incredulous.

"That was around the same time Ennoren died, wasn't it?" Ti'ann looked hard at Krin. "They didn't. They couldn't."

Krin grimaced. "They might have."

"What do you think they've done?" James asked, clearly confused.

"I don't know for sure," she said. She hitched to her good leg, even though she couldn't feel pain in her hip through the painkillers. "I could be wrong. But for E to be fully developed in only eleven months, it's entirely possible they used Ennoren's fresh corpse for this experiment."

"Why?" Glen asked, snarling in disgust.

Ti'ann glanced around the group. Most of the humans looked repulsed by the idea. Clare looked horrified but intent. There was no discernible expression on any of the Shifters' faces or E. But that was pretty typical for E.

"It's faster to repair than to grow from conception," she started, looking to Krin for support. She was trying to explain something she didn't fully understand herself. "If they got to him quick enough," she said slowly, "they could fix the cellular damage to the body using epidermal and endodermal skimmers, and DNA recombined from the original host with DNA from a different source to…'refresh' the vital organs. After repairing the damage, the body would be placed in a microbial bath, giving it time to allow the recombined DNA to…infect the rest of the body. The cells made from recombined DNA would replace all the original cells in the body and a new life form develops using the corpse as a template."

"In theory," Krin said. "Using DNA from the dead body alone doesn't jump-start the process of cell regeneration. The old DNA has to be recombined with new. The recombination process is similar to the results you get using sex. You start a new life. So you aren't getting an exact copy, like a clone, or bringing the person back to life. The process is illegal, though—too similar in idea to the old Frankenstein's monster story of reanimating a corpse. So no one has actually done it successfully."

"That we know of," Ti'ann said grimly. "But at least what we're talking about is scientifically conceivable with modern technology. Recombining Naravan DNA with Terran DNA is… beyond anything we've ever done before."

"Obviously not." E's reply would have been droll if he could express a sense of humor.

"So you're saying that they used Ennoren's body as a template, blending his DNA with a Shifter's DNA and created E?" Clare's mouth was turned down, her brows lowered in concentration.

"In a nutshell," Krin said.

"We're just guessing," Ti'ann added. "We don't know if any of this is true."

"But if it is," Krin said, "it is such advanced science I'm afraid what it might mean."

"This is why we're uncertain whether to reveal E or not," Val said. "It's important humans and Shifters know this type of experimentation is being done. No matter how they've manipulated the creation of E, work is being done to alter Shifter DNA and natures. Both species should know. But it may spark more fear than ever." Facing the other Shifters in turn, Val said, "The news will spread among our own. We won't be able to stop it." A brief grin flashed. "Our gossip channels are more pervasive than your press. We bring to you the decision as to whether humans should know or not."

"Humans do know," Nathan said. "The ones performing the experiments know. There's too much pride and arrogance involved in this kind of work for them to keep it silent forever. They'll want credit, recognition. Eventually."

"But is eventually better than now?" James said. "There's going to be enough fear when the news of a Shifter city breaks. Do we really want to add fuel to what's already going to be a volatile situation?"

"It may bring sympathy," Glen said quietly. "Humans may start feeling some affinity for Shifters, knowing both species were manipulated this way."

"Or they'll just fear them more, thinking their dead corpses could be used to make super-Shifters," Petrov, one of the collectors, said. It was the first time he'd spoken since the Shifters arrived. "I don't mind telling you, the idea of my corpse being used this way creeps me out."

Ti'ann knew how he felt.

"I'm sure Ennoren would have been disgusted, too," Mike said. "He detested Shifters. To know his body was used to make E would infuriate him."

E tilted his head down, a gesture Ti'ann was coming to recognize as his thinking pose.

"So, if he's not really Ennoren," Krin said, his mind obviously running a different track from the conversation, "if we consider Ennoren was more like his father, then why would he have a memory of Kira Farseaker unless it was implanted?"

"You're stuck on that idea," Juanita said. "What's bothering you?"

"The fact that he shouldn't have Ennoren's memories. He's not Ennoren. Ennoren is dead. But he's carrying a distinct image of Kira Farseaker around with him. I'd be willing to bet if you looked, you'd find David Cario and a number of other people prominent to Ennoren's downfall and the beginning of the Senate debates." Krin looked at E. "It's still possible you were originally designed to be an assassin. Maybe this time was just a test. Maybe they're waiting to see if you succeed before they invest more time in you."

An actual expression crossed E's face. Surprise. "How would I not know that I was designed to be an assassin? Dr. Ripley has been telling me of my purpose since I could understand his words. Perhaps even before that. Why wouldn't he tell me my real purpose?"

"He probably didn't want you to give away your true purpose if you failed," Ti'ann said quietly.

E stared at her with his emotionless blue eyes. It was impossible to guess what he was thinking. She wondered if Val could tell.

"So are we telling the public or not?" Clare said into the silence. "This is a brilliant story. The networks would kill to get it."

"I think we're better off keeping it quiet for the moment," James said. "It may be useful later in the debates."

"Dr. Ripley should be arrested for this," Krin said. "He's performing illegal and unethical experiments."

"But he's been doing that for years at SRC," Ti'ann said. She could already see Krin getting his teeth into the ethical debate this created. "He's going to have some very high up support to keep him and his experiments out of court."

"Or maybe he'll turn on the ones running and funding SRC? Maybe if they arrest him, it will put an end to a lot of the criminal activity," Krin said.

"Or maybe it won't." Ti'ann sighed. "Maybe it would just get Ripley killed to shut the scandal up."

"And maybe that wouldn't be such a bad thing," Krin retorted.

She shook her head and gave up. She was too tired to debate ethics with Krin. In fact, the whole conversation left her exhausted, not that she wasn't already. She was a scientist. She'd never had any intention of getting involved in planetary politics. With grim acceptance, she realized she no longer had a choice. As soon as she started doing interviews for the press, she'd be in the middle of the issue. Her opinions would be asked, scrutinized, criticized and distorted. All she wanted to do was solve a mystery. Now her life would never be the same.

"I'm with James," Mike said, straightening his glasses. "I think we should keep knowledge of E quiet for the moment. But only for now. There will come a time when it's important for the public to know about him."

"A vote?" James asked.

In the end, the vote was seven to three against telling the public. BinRal abstained on the grounds that he wasn't Naravan. Clare, Krin and Glen voted for telling the public. Clare looked like she wanted to argue with the vote, but in the end, she accepted it. Ti'ann hoped she could keep the secret from her friend in the press.

"I'd better get this story to my contact," Clare said. "How am I going to explain the deaths of the soldiers if I'm not allowed to mention E yet?"

"Tell them it was a dragon," Ti'ann said with a grin, not really meaning for Clare to take her seriously.

"You could, actually," Val said, in all seriousness.

"What?" Krin and Ti'ann said at the same time.

"What you call a dragon," Val said, "is very similar to one of the predators that drove our evolution. They're thought to have gone extinct when we evolved shifting. We weren't their only food source, but they used to eat many of our other large predators. As those predators died out, the dragons ran out of food."

"You mean we could find a dragon skeleton?" Ti'ann was nearly bouncing, despite her hip. She and Krin exchanged excited grins. "Would you be able to tell us a likely place to hunt for dragon bones?" she asked a now grinning Val.

"I think we can arrange something."

"But if they're extinct," Clare said, already edging toward James' ship, "how could one have saved us?"

"Maybe there are one or two left," Val said.

They all stopped to stare at the Shifter, whose expression gave nothing away.

"Are there?" Ti'ann asked in a hushed voice.

Val just smiled.

Clare laughed. "This is gonna be great." She hooted and charged off toward the ship.

CHAPTER TWENTY-NINE

Krin walked Ti'ann back to camp. All their tents and equipment were right where they left them. Nothing had changed except the people were gone. They'd have to contact the team, arrange for them to return in the next couple of days so they could get back to work on the dig. Ti'ann couldn't think about it tonight, though. Krin didn't seem in any hurry either.

He helped her into her tent and hugged her. "I'm so glad you're okay."

"I'm glad you're okay, too," she said into his hair. And then she started to cry.

"Ti'ann!" Krin pulled back, looking alarmed. She didn't cry often. "What's wrong? Are you in pain? Did I hurt you? Let me go get some more painkillers from BinRal."

"No, no," she sniffed. "I'm just… It's been a long day." She gave him a crooked, watery smile. "I just need to cry a little."

"Okay." Krin looked nervous, but he pulled her back into a hug and patted her back while she let the tears flow.

She felt both better and worse when she finished. Better because the tension was gone, worse because she was even more exhausted than before. And she still didn't know what was happening with Nathan. He hadn't even volunteered to come back to the camp. He'd asked Krin to make sure she got here and said he had some security checks to take care of. He'd wished them both a gentle but neutral goodnight and went back to his own ship.

She rested on her cot after Krin left, staring up at the top of the tent, and felt very alone. She was so tired. Too much had happened today. She'd nearly died. Twice. She was grateful to be alive, but she ached for Nathan so much she couldn't feel good.

She rolled onto her good hip, careful so the sheet she'd tossed over herself didn't rub against the bandage. Her hip was still numb, but BinRal had warned her the painkillers would ware off by morning. She closed her eyes. Despite her aching heart, or maybe because of it, she drifted off into a deep, black, dreamless sleep.

When she woke, she knew he was in her tent. She didn't even have to open her eyes to know it was Nathan. His scent, his presence filled the air.

"Does your hip hurt?" he asked quietly.

She opened her eyes. "How did you know I was awake?"

"Your breathing changed."

She moved, testing her injury. "It's a little sore now. Not too bad."

"BinRal sent another hypo of painkiller for you to take when the pain returns."

"Thanks."

Silence settled into the pre-dawn dark. He held her gaze, his hazel eyes unwavering. "Your eyes," she murmured, startled by the realization. "They look a little like Kira Farseaker's. Not quite as gold, but almost."

"Probably because she's my cousin."

"What?" She sat up in bed, letting the sheet fall into her lap. She winced a little and adjusted her hip to a more comfortable position. "Kira Farseaker is your cousin?"

"Second cousin. Her grandfather and my grandfather were brothers. Nathaniel and Bridget Farseaker's two sons."

"You're related to Nathaniel and Bridget Farseaker? The Nathaniel and Bridget who discovered Narava and dozens of other habitable planets?"

"They're the ones."

"Wow. What a pedigree."

He smiled. The first smile she'd seen from him since waking up on his ship with a bandage on her hip.

"The brothers were estranged," he said. "Kira's father and my mother were the ones to heal the rift." He fingered the metal tags on his chest. "That's how I got these."

"I see." Except that she didn't.

"They're part of a legacy that Nathaniel and Bridget gave to their family. The brothers fought over what to do with the legacy. My grandfather wanted to use it to make money. Kira's grandfather wanted to hold it safe for the family alone, the way his parents had intended. My grandfather was quite the mercenary. He lost his access to the legacy when he tried to go around his brother and sell it. Nathaniel and Bridget came out of retirement to end the fight. They took the legacy away from my grandfather. It wasn't until Kira's father approached my mother to make peace that it came back to us."

"Sounds like an important legacy."

"It is."

She fell silent and waited. She was nearly bursting with the need to ask him exactly what the legacy *was*, but if he didn't volunteer the information, it was probably because he didn't want to. He was here for a reason. She'd only delay him getting to the point of his visit if she tried to satisfy her curiosity about the tags.

He didn't say anything for a long time. Just watched her. She watched back and waited.

Finally, he said, "I'm going to leave the rest of your security to BinRal. He'll be able to handle this from now on."

Ti'ann swallowed as her stomach dropped and her world started to break into pieces. He was leaving her. Again. She knew he would, knew this time would come. And she still wasn't prepared. "This place will be crawling with reporters in a week. Are you sure it's a one person job?"

"If he needs help, he'll call some in. He's good. Your site will be safe."

She nodded and looked down at her hands where they bunched in her lap. Her knuckles were white. She flattened them against her leg. Her throat was closing up on her, making it hard to breath. The ache in her chest didn't help. "Okay." Pushing the single word out was almost impossible.

Her mind screamed at her to tell him she loved him before he left. She needed him to know. But she couldn't. He was going. Nothing she could say would stop him. He'd only think her pathetic if she tried to make him stay now. She took a deep breath and looked up at the wall of her tent. She couldn't face him. She darted a glance in his direction and had to look back at the tent.

"Thank you for helping us," she muttered.

"Nothing to thank."

She felt him staring at the side of her face. Was he waiting for her to do something? Did he expect her to say something more? Maybe he wanted his payment. But Krin was dealing with that. She couldn't think about it right now. It was taking too much of her concentration not to fall apart in front of him. Only two nights. That's all it was again. Two nights.

He stood so suddenly he drew her gaze away from the safety of the tent. Without thinking, she scooted out of bed and got to her feet. He stepped closer to her, scowling, ready to catch her if she fell. She kept her balance. But she didn't know what to do now that she was standing. She just knew she couldn't let him leave this way. Not again.

She limped close to him, put her hands on his shoulders for balance and rose onto her toes, most of her weight on her good leg. "Thank you for everything, Nathan." She leaned in and kissed him gently on the lips. He remained perfectly still, not returning her kiss, not touching her. After a moment, when he didn't respond, she stepped back. She pressed her lips together and looked away.

"You're leaving this morning?" she asked to fill the awkward silence between them.

"Yes."

"Okay," she muttered, turning back to the bed. She couldn't watch him leave.

"That's it? 'Okay.'"

She shrugged. "Have a safe trip?" What did he expect her to say? He was ripping out her heart. She could barely talk around the lump in her throat.

He didn't move or speak for what felt like an eternity. Now that the time had come, she just wanted him to go away so she could fall apart in private. When he did finally move toward the tent flap, she sucked in a breath to keep the tears back a few minutes longer. He paused again. Damn it, if he didn't leave she was going to start crying in front of him.

"Give me a reason to stay," he said, his voice quiet and intense.

Her head snapped up, but she didn't turn to face him. "What?"

"Give me a reason to stay. I need a reason."

She turned very slowly, careful to keep weight on her good leg. He looked bleary through the tears filling her eyes. "Is the fact that I'm in love with you reason enough, or do you need something else?"

He shook his head. "Damn it, Ti'ann." He crossed to her and took her in his arms. "You ask too many questions." And he kissed her, deep and slow, for a long time.

When he finally lifted his head, she was breathing hard. "I don't understand," she said.

"What don't you understand?"

"Anything. This. Why were you going to leave? Why wouldn't you kiss me when I kissed you? Why were you ripping my heart out like that, damn it?"

He reached up to run a hand over her hair. "I've never been so terrified in my life as when you were taken captive. And then when you went and took on a platoon of soldiers with nothing more than a blaster, I thought you'd killed me. You'd get yourself killed, and then I'd have nothing left in life. You've ruined me. That's a hard thing for a man to accept."

"I didn't ruin you. How could I do that?"

"Without much effort, obviously. I've been hoping this whole time what was between us was just sex. That I'd be able to get over it. I didn't want to be in love with you, Ti'ann Jones. But I am. I have been for three years. I hated leaving you the first time. Now I've recognized how much trouble I'm in, I knew I either had to settle things with you or get out. When I saw you with E, when I thought you were dead or dying, a part of me died. There was no way I was going through that again if you didn't feel the same way about me as I feel about you."

"So you thought you'd batter me a little to find out if I loved you?"

"No." He scowled. "I wasn't trying to batter you. I figured if you did love me, you wouldn't let me leave. You'd say something. And then you didn't. You just said okay."

"I kissed you! You wouldn't even hold me or kiss me back."

"You just kissed me as a thank you."

It was her turn to scowl. "That was not the only reason. And you're one to talk. You've never given me any hint you'd stick around when you were finished here. As far as I knew, you intended to leave from the beginning. And then you come in and tell me you're leaving. And I kiss you and you won't even touch me. How was I supposed to know you were fishing for reassurance?"

"How could you think I'd leave so easily?"

"Because you did it last time! Because you've never said otherwise. Because when we aren't in bed, you barely pay any attention to me. You refuse to even touch me."

He squeezed her closer, startling her with the fact that he had an erection. "I can't touch you without wanting you. Do you know how debilitating that is? I get near you and my skin sizzles. I touch you and I can't think straight anymore. For my own sanity, I have to avoid touching you in public. That only got worse after we made love again. I thought I'd be able to work you out of my system, but you're like a drug. The more I take, the more I want."

"Really?" Her breathing had sped up again. She was in no shape for sex. With her hip injured, making love would probably hurt, if not be impossible. Her common sense told her they'd have to wait until her wound had healed some more. But his intense gaze, his strong body, his heady words were making her forget common sense.

"Really."

One of his hands dropped to her bottom, the side opposite her injured hip. He squeezed her gently. She felt restraint in his touch.

"I know I can't make love to you right now," he said. "You're in no condition. I need to let you recover first. But as soon as I touched you, I found it hard to remember that." He moved his hand up her back. "Do you know what it's like to want to protect you from myself?"

"So stop protecting me."

"Don't tempt me. I want to take care of you, too. I want more with you than just lust. But how am I supposed to care for you when all I can think about when I touch you is touching you more? I hate that I can't control myself with you."

"I don't." She swallowed hard and leaned her head against his shoulder. She couldn't admit this to him and still look at him. "I like it. In the past, men haven't really found me very sexy. I love sex. But… I don't know. I've never felt free to fully enjoy it before. I was embarrassed by my wants. And then it seemed like with the others, they got bored with me. After a couple of months, a few weeks, they just weren't interested in sex with me anymore. I got tired of asking for it. That was humiliating. Despite my best efforts, I couldn't be what they wanted in bed, not enough to keep them interested in me. So I just accepted the fact that I wasn't what men wanted in a lover and tried to move on."

"Idiots."

"What?"

"Whoever these other men were, they were idiots. With very low sex drives."

She pulled back to stare up at him. "They both left me for other women. If they had low sex drives, why…?"

"Probably because they found women with even lower sex drives than they had. Then they could feel like men. They were probably embarrassed they didn't want sex as often as you did." His hands on her back tightened, and he rested his cheek against her temple. "I'm glad they never figured out what they had."

"Why?"

"Because then I might not have found you."

She sighed. "So you don't think you'll get bored with me?"

"Not if we have four lifetimes together. I don't think it's possible for me to get bored with you."

"You say that now…"

He squeezed her waist, cutting off her protest. "I mean that always."

"So now what?"

"Now, I go take a cold shower while you get more sleep."

"You don't have to." She didn't know how they'd manage it, but she was willing to accept a little pain if that's what it took to make love to him that minute.

He pushed her away from him and glared down at her. "No. I'm going to make sure you heal as quickly as possible. I'm not going to risk delaying your recovering because I can't control my dick."

She couldn't help it, she started to giggle. All the tension and pain and heartache eased out of her. "I love you, Nathan Longfeather." She grinned.

"I love you, Ti'ann Jones."

"Enough to tell me what the family legacy is?" she teased, not really expecting him to.

"Of course. You're about to be part of the family."

She went very still and had to remind herself to breathe. "I am."

"You are."

"Then what is it?"

He grinned, and her heart started dancing.

"You ask a lot of questions, Dr. Jones." He pulled her close and leaned his face near to hers so that their foreheads touched. "The legacy is a secret planet. A place not on any charts, a place no one but my family knows about. A haven for my family and those they love. It was a present from Bridget and Nathaniel. It's called Kierna'Rhoan."

EPILOGUE

Terrance Samuels stared at the vid-screens lining the wall of his den. On one channel, Barbury was being walked into Guard Head Quarters, escorted by a phalanx of Guards. The reporter's voiceover was condemning him as a violent terrorist who'd used his association with Senator Johnson to order a military assault on a scientific research station that had just made the amazing discovery of a Shifter city. Senator Johnson's press secretary gave an eloquent speech on the senator's behalf condemning the actions of the senator's aide, claiming, "Everything necessary will be done to make sure this type of thing never happens again."

In other words, the senator was going to be more careful next time so nothing leaked to the press.

On another channel, the "exclusive" story of the discovery of the city was being reported. This was the same channel to break the news. They were taking advantage of their status, securing exclusive interviews with Dr. Ti'ann Jones, Dr. Krin Freemont, and a handful of the other people working the original site. Doctors Jones and Freemont were moderate in their retellings, sticking to a few facts and focusing on the fascination and thrill of the discovery instead of the more sensational events of the attack on the city.

Another channel devoted to gossip was announcing the impending wedding of Ti'ann Jones to Nathan Longfeather. "The couple who saved the Shifter city from destruction."

Samuels snorted in disgust. He had no doubt the Shifters had something to do with saving their own city. He didn't believe the story of a dragon for a minute. And if it was a dragon, it was a Shifter in dragon form. Which meant these new Shifters could kill. That was an interesting bit of information. He'd have to see how this could benefit him.

He still couldn't believe he'd been standing on top of a Shifter city and hadn't known. If he hadn't thought the incursion premature, he would have gone in with the military team himself. Just to see the city. In hindsight, he was glad he'd thought better of it. And despite the blundering, the city was still there to see. One day maybe.

But what really bothered Samuels was the inside "source" who had given the senator the information about the city. Was it one of Ti'ann and Krin's team? That seemed unlikely after the extensive interviews he'd done while posing as an inspector. None of them, even the Shifter-hating Micca—apparently killed during the military strike—had high enough connections to get the information to the senator so fast.

So who was it? He didn't like when information was withheld from him. Whoever it was had managed something he couldn't. He didn't like that either.

Samuels lifted his snifter of Binnean brandy and watched the drama play out for the public. He'd have to find this inside source of the senator's. It might prove a very useful bit of information.

Thank you for reading SECRET
(The Naravan Chronicles 3).
If you've enjoyed this book, please continue reading for
sneak peek from the next story, PARADISE.

EXCERPT: PARADISE

THE NARAVAN CHRONICLES 4

CHAPTER ONE

The minute Lieutenant Brand stepped into her office, Security Chief Meiling Trudeau knew she was about to receive news she didn't want to hear.

She sighed and leaned back in her chair. "Please tell me it's not the Binneans?"

They had two clans on FarMore Station at the same time, which was a recipe for disaster. Different clan members couldn't be anywhere near each other without trying to tear each other—and any poor bastard in the vicinity—to pieces. It was biology. It was also incredibly dangerous on a space station.

But since FarMore was an "open and neutral" station, mecca to both pleasure seekers and business people alike, Meiling was forced to contend with all kinds of potentially disastrous combinations of occupants on a regular basis. She worked hard to foresee the disasters and head them off.

She was successful more often than not.

"The Binneans are staying in their respective quadrants." Lieutenant Brand shifted from one foot to the other, not quite meeting Meiling's eyes.

That was so unusual it only deepened the level of dread tightening her stomach. "I know for a fact the Leeches aren't causing trouble." She hated having the mutants on station. She'd rather the entire Binnean populous descended on FarMore and held their impending war here than have to deal with Leeches. So she ensured they were watched closely.

"Correct, Chief."

Meiling waited a beat. When her lieutenant still didn't explain her presence, she said, "Brand, you need to spit it out, or I'm going to get very annoyed."

The lieutenant made a face, half cringe, half resignation. She held her hands out at her sides and said, "It's McClane."

Meiling scrubbed her hands over her face and tried hard not to groan. She'd warned Captain Varty not to let Duncan McClane back on station. He was a crook and a conman who couldn't resist pushing his luck and station law. As a result, he was one of the few people ever banned from FarMore. It didn't matter how rich he was now, how often he swore he'd gone straight, con-artists didn't change.

Meiling should know. She'd grown up surrounded by them.

She dropped her hands and stared at Brand. The recycled station air swirled around her, pleasantly scented and cool. It did nothing to stave off the heat of anxiety clawing at her muscles. "What's he done?"

"Cheated at the casino tables. Again. Not subtly this time, either."

Which meant he wanted Meiling to know. She'd been avoiding him since he'd returned to FarMore. The sonofabitch knew this would force her hand.

"Which casino?" *Please not Paradise. Please not Paradise.*

"Paradise."

"Of course." She pressed her fingers into her temples to stave off a building headache.

Paradise was only the largest resort, with the most powerful owner, on FarMore. Ky Greven was the man responsible for having Duncan banned two years ago. The fact that Duncan was cheating him again could only mean impending disaster.

"Greven sent word that if you don't take care of McClane, he's gonna have his legs broken," Brand said.

Meiling was a little too tempted to let that happen. It went against everything she was supposed to be doing on this station, everything she'd made of her life here, but it would serve Duncan right for forcing her into this meeting.

"That's very restrained for Greven," she said. "Last time he nearly threw Duncan out an airlock."

Brand shrugged. "McClane's rich now and can actually repay debts. Greven can't get his money back from a corpse."

"True." Still…

How the hell was she going to face Duncan after all this time? She'd barely been able to resist him last time he was on station. Despite her best efforts, she had a weakness for sexy, clever conmen. Even after he'd betrayed her trust, Meiling had had trouble watching him leave, knowing he wouldn't be allowed back.

When he'd boarded the station two standard weeks ago, now one of the richest men in the galaxy, one look had been all it took to confirm she was still vulnerable to him. Which was why she'd assigned other people to deal with him. Why she'd been refusing his requests to meet.

Cowardly, but she saw it as self-preservation. Now Duncan

had pushed the issue, and the only outcome would be more heartbreak.

She settled her hands on her desk and pushed to her feet, slowly, like a much older woman, body aching from the effort. She didn't want to do this. She didn't trust herself around him.

Though whether she was more afraid she'd take him to bed or kill him was a tossup.

"Come on, Lieutenant." She motioned to Brand. "I might need you to hold my blaster."

She ignored Brand's slight smirk as they left the office, heading down to Paradise—and Meiling's version of hell.

**Don't miss the next romantic science fiction adventure in
The Naravan Chronicles Series
PARADISE (The Naravan Chronicles 4)**

ACKNOWLEDGMENTS

First, I have to thank Kem and Peter immensely for not only helping me name Narava (I'm looking at you Peter—I blame you for why I can't spell the name half the time!) but for traveling with me on the journey of this book and then helping me bring it to readers. Thanks very much for all your help.

I'd also like to thank a few of my writer friends for keeping me moving forward and reminding me regularly that I really need to finish some of the series I start. Thanks Leanna, Stacey A, Stacey K, Linnea, and Kem for everything.

Much love and thanks to my family for the years of support and faith. You all are the best! I couldn't do this without you.

And finally, a very big thank you to my wonderful husband, because he tells me I'm good at my job when I don't feel like I am, and proudly tells people I'm a writer. I couldn't ask for better support. Thanks, my love.

ABOUT THE AUTHOR

Isabo Kelly is the award-winning author of numerous science fiction, fantasy, and paranormal romances. She also writes best-selling paranormal romance under the name Kat Simons. Her life has taken her from Las Vegas to Hawaii, where she got her BA in Zoology, back to Vegas where she looked after sharks, then on to Germany and Ireland where she got her Ph.D. in Animal Behavior. Now Isabo focuses on writing. She lives in New York with her Irish husband and two beautiful boys, working as a full time writer and stay-at-home mom.

Don't miss out on new releases from Isabo! Sign up for her Newsletter here: http://eepurl.com/caxHa9

For more on Isabo and her books:
Website: http://www.isabokelly.com
Facebook: http://www.facebook.com/IsaboKelly
Twitter: https://www.twitter.com/IsaboKelly

BOOKS BY ISABO KELLY

The Naravan Chronicles

Promise

Interface

Secret

Paradise

Flight

New York Empires Anthologies

Going All In

Icing The Puck

Fire and Tears Series

Brightarrow Burning

Darkness Singed

Dawn Ignited

Fate's Hand Series

Thief's Desire

Destiny's Seduction

Kellyn's Sacrifice

The Last Guardian

Bonfire Night